Done

WHEN THE WOLF COMES KNOCKING

KEN PRATT

D1248340

When the Wolf Comes Knocking
Paperback Edition
Copyright © 2022 (as revised) Ken Pratt

All rights reserved. No part of this book may be reproduced
by any means without the prior written consent of the
publisher, other than brief quotes for reviews.

This book is a work of fiction. Any references to historical
events, real people or real places are used fictitiously. Other
names, characters, places and events are products of the
author's imagination, and any resemblance to actual events,
places or persons, living or dead, is entirely coincidental.

Published in the United States by Wolfpack Publishing, Las Vegas

CKN Christian Publishing
An Imprint of Wolfpack Publishing
5130 S. Fort Apache Road 215-380
Las Vegas, NV 89148

CKNchristianpublishing.com

Paperback ISBN - 978-1-63977-294-0

WHEN THE WOLF COMES KNOCKING

PROLOGUE

NEW YEAR'S EVE

MIDDLETON, OREGON, WASN'T THE KIND OF TOWN YOU'D miss along the highway if you blinked; it was more of a town you had to go out of your way to find. It was the kind of town where one might have to wait in line at the store for a bit, while a neighbor talked about his newborn calf. The pace was slow and unhurried. O'Leary's Market was a second-generation family-owned country store in one of the old two-story brick buildings that made up the heart of Middleton's historic business district. It was a simple city block that supplied two taverns, one restaurant, a small post office, O'Leary's Market, and a Hispanic store, catering specifically to the Spanish culture in the Middleton community. Spread out along the length of the sidewalk, every forty feet or so, were five maple trees. Across the street from the downtown businesses was a city park constantly shaded by large Douglas Fir and native Oak trees.

O'Leary's was a unique kind of store that only small country towns seem to have. It had original old plank floors, and the walls were decorated with the same decorations from two generations before. There were photographs of the store from the 1940s and colorful ads for motor oil, various seeds, and a collection of old bottles of different shapes and sizes. A large wolfskin stretched across one wall next to a line of mounted ducks. Not far away, a buck with sizeable antlers had been hung up proudly many years before. One of the more unique attributes to O'Leary's was the fact that they still served their customers. In most places, the days of in-store credit were gone, but O'Leary's still allowed their customers to charge their groceries until payday if they needed to. O'Leary's was community-oriented, with a decent-sized grocery section and a co-op for the local farming community.

There was also a selection of Middleton High School athletic wear. Hats, shirts, and sweatshirts that represented football, volleyball, and the other sports, were for sale. They were always a sellable item in a town that loved its local athletes. During the fall, Friday nights in Middleton were a social must at the football field. In recent years, the Middleton football team had won two consecutive state championships. Greg Slater happened to play on that championship team as the offensive right guard and an outstanding defensive linebacker. Greg was one of those high school athletes that were exceptional in multiple areas. He was an honor roll student that had won two state wrestling championships at 177 pounds. He was a well-rounded young man, and it came as no surprise when he received a football scholarship to Boise State. Greg had become a local hero, in a manner of speaking; he was now the starting linebacker for the Boise State Broncos football team. He was the first local boy to make it big, as it was. He was now a junior at Boise State and had just finished a strong season. Greg had a great future ahead of him as a potential NFL candidate and if not, he'd make a fine teacher and coach. Some people rumored that Middleton's future football and wrestling programs were waiting for Greg to graduate and return to take over the reins.

Dan O'Leary smiled with surprise when he saw Greg

come into the store with his younger sister, Candice. "Welcome home, Mister Slater. I see you're doing us proud over there in Idaho."

Greg Slater was five foot eleven and was about as muscular as one would expect a college linebacker and NFL hopeful to be. He wore Levi's and a blue Boise State sweatshirt that outlined his broad shoulders and upper body. Greg's brown hair was cut short and parted to one side respectfully. His square-shaped face and jawline were covered with stubble from not shaving for a few days. Greg's brown eyes shined as he smiled at Dan's greeting. "I'm trying. How are you, Mister O'Leary?"

Greg reached into an old wooden wine barrel filled with peanuts in the middle of the entry. Peanut shells covered the floor. It was a yearly event from December 1st to the 1st of January that customers could eat free peanuts and throw the shells onto the floor carelessly. The floors were not cleaned until New Year's Day. It was one of the unique hometown rituals that Greg loved; he broke a peanut open and dropped the shell.

"I'm good," Dan O'Leary responded. "Your dad was telling me that you graduate next year already. How long after that do you think until you come back here and take over the reins of Coach Wilson's football team?"

Greg laughed. "Coach might not let me take over. He's got a while to coach still."

Dan chuckled. "Yeah, he does. Did you have a good Christmas, Candice?"

"Yes," Candice Slater replied. She was fifteen years old and a sophomore at the high school. She had shoulder-length thick brown hair with a natural curl and had a cheerful youthful face with a pretty smile, even with her braces with the pink rubber band that stretched across them. Like her brother, Candice was becoming one of the better female athletes and consistently on the Honor Roll. She had missed her older brother greatly over the past three years that he'd been at Boise State. Greg worked the summers for the Idaho

Forest Service, so he had seldom been home for any length of time since he left Middleton. Candice stayed close to her brother as if she was afraid to let him out of her sight.

After getting a handful of peanuts, two 2 liters of soda, and a couple of bags of chips, they returned to the counter, where Greg grabbed another handful of peanuts.

"So, do you have any big New Year Eve plans tonight?" Dan asked as he rang up the till.

"We're just staying home and watching movies. I'm going back to Boise on Tuesday, so I want to spend time with the family."

"Good boy," Dan replied. "Don't most college kids want to party, though?"

"Some do, but I have better things to do." He looked at his little sister fondly and gave her an affectionate nudge with his shoulder. She grinned brightly.

Dan took Greg's cash and refunded the change. "It's good to see you again, Greg. Take care of yourself, young man."

"I'll see you later, Mister O'Leary. Happy New Year."

"Yes, happy New Year to you and your family."

Greg held the bag and opened the door for Candice to walk out. She stopped after walking four or five steps to the left of the door. In front of her stood a young man with neck-length black hair and a few days' of growth on his face, giving him a rough appearance. His name was Rene Dibari. He was Greg's best friend all through high school, but Candice had grown weary of him and the coldness that had filled his eyes in recent years. Rene wore a heavy metal band's T-shirt underneath a black leather coat.

Rene smirked slightly. "Hey, what's going on, Greg? It's been a long-time, man." His voice was low and guarded with little enthusiasm to see his old friend. Beside him stood Rene's young wife, Tina. She carried their young daughter in her arms. Tina seemed to be hiding her face shamefully behind their little girl. Tina's shoulder-length straight brown hair appeared lifeless and dirty. She wore dingy, faded blue jeans with a rip in the upper thigh and a white coat that needed to be washed.

Greg smiled pleasantly. "I'm home for Christmas break. So how are you two doing? My, she's getting big. How old is she?" He nodded at their baby girl in Tina's arms.

Rene answered, "She's two."

"Time goes fast, doesn't it? So how is married life treating you two?" he asked, feeling strangely awkward.

"Good," Rene answered without any enthusiasm in his voice. "It's going good."

"Great," Greg said and turned his attention to Tina Dibari. Her once beautiful blue eyes appeared lifeless and dull. "How are you, Tina? Are you in school this term?"

Tina shook her head. "No, I'm...just a mother," she responded dryly with a slight shrug.

"Well," Greg stated awkwardly, "she's a beautiful girl, just like her mother. What's your name?" Greg asked the little girl who hid her face in her mother's coat.

Rene appeared to be in a hurry to end the meeting of old friends. "Her name's Karen. So, we're having a party tonight if you want to come by. It would be great to see you. We'll catch up later, man," Rene said without interest and took a departing step towards the store's door.

Greg was slightly taken by surprise by his old friend's apparent attempt to end the conversation. "Where are you living at?" Greg asked without thinking about it.

Rene paused by the door. "Remember where Loraine used to live on Sixth Street?"

"Yeah."

"There. Come on by if you want. We have to buy some stuff. Come on, Tina. Good to see you," Rene said again with the sound of annoyance.

"Well, perhaps I'll see you later," Greg said with a touch of sadness. "It was nice to see you again."

Her nervous tight smile appeared restrained. "You, too.

You should come by tonight if you can." Her eyes flickered with an anxious glance towards Rene.

"I won't promise. I don't party much."

Rene spoke from six feet away by the door. "I do. See you later, man. Tina."

"Bye," Tina said with a touch of remorse. She grinned with a slight snicker as a large drop of rain fell from the branches of the maple tree they were under fell onto Karen's forehead. "Oops," she said as Karen grumbled. Tina wiped it off and peered longingly at Greg, losing her grin. "Maybe I'll see you later." Her eyes lingered momentarily into Greg's.

"Let's go!" Rene called impatiently.

"Bye," Tina said quickly and followed Rene into the store. She turned her head back to look at Greg one last time before she stepped through the door.

"You're not going tonight, are you?" Candice asked, sounding disappointed.

"No, I don't think so. I might stop by there, though. It could be fun."

"Rene's a drug dealer now, Greg. You better not go there, or you might be arrested for just being there if their house is raided," Candice warned.

"No, he's not," Greg questioned more than stated.

"Yes, he is. Ask anyone. Everyone in town knows that." Candice walked towards Greg's car. "They're druggies now; even your old girlfriend is. You better not go over there, or I'll tell dad."

Greg grimaced at her words. "I don't believe that. Tina wouldn't involve herself with drugs, at least not when I knew her."

"People change," Candice said as she got into Greg's car. "I can't believe you won't let me drive your car. I have my driver's permit, you know."

Greg hesitated by his door. "Okay, you can drive, but you better listen to what I say and not think you know it all."

"I know."

"See? You already think you know everything!"

Candice laughed.

The Dibari's rented home was a small two-bedroom, near dilapidated house, set back off Sixth Street just enough to be unnoticed if one wasn't looking for it. The house was painted white and in serious need of some touch-up. The interior was not much nicer than the exterior. The carpeting throughout the house was old orange shag, and the vinyl in the kitchen had cracks and large holes. The home was owned by Gene Owens, a well-known slum lord with a reputation for cheap affordable housing, but the renter got what they paid for.

It was New Year's Eve, and Rene had his stereo playing hard rock music at a low volume so he could talk with his friends. Manny Rodriguez was Hispanic and kept his hair cut short, neatly combed, and a clean-shaven face, except for a short goatee. Manny was of medium build and well dressed as he sat in an old blue recliner holding a cigarette and a beer.

On the orange-flower patterned sofa from the 1970s sat Manny's girlfriend, Stacy Green. Stacy was heavyset with shoulder-length brown hair and a round face with large brown eyes heavily traced with eye liner. She wore tight blue jeans and a heavy red sweater that caused her to sweat in the warm house. On the other end of the couch sat Jessie Hupp. Jessie was tall and thin with shoulder-length brown hair. He was dressed in blue jeans and a black T-shirt with his favorite heavy metal band's logo on the front. He also held a cigarette in his hand. He was bored and anxious to do something else; his knee bounced quickly with the anticipation of leaving to find something more exciting to do than sitting in his friend's living room. "Let's go to the bar. It's going to be full of girls tonight."

"Trust me," Rene said from his standing position in front

of the TV, with a beer can in his hand. "You don't want to meet any girls. You might get trapped into marrying one like me. You don't want that, man." He scowled at Tina, who stood in the wide entrance into the kitchen.

"You weren't trapped," Tina replied without emotion.

"I wasn't?" he questioned as his eyes grew darker. "You're the one who didn't get on birth control. You're the one that came crying to me when you were pregnant. What was I supposed to do, let someone else raise my daughter? I don't want Karen to grow up to be like you!"

Tina's lips tightened with anger. "No, you wanted me to abort her. I could've raised her on my own. I still can."

Rene quickly tossed his can of beer at her; it hit her in the chest, splashing her white blouse with beer before falling to the floor. "Shut the hell up and go change your clothes. We're going to the bar, so try not to dress like a whore!"

Tina held her wet blouse away from her skin and scowled at Rene with a slight tearing of her eyes. "You're a bastard!" she yelled and stepped in through the kitchen to go toward her bedroom.

Rene addressed his friends, "The problem with taking my wife to the bar is the police might think I'm her pimp!"

"No, man, she's a cool girl," Jessie said uncomfortably.

Rene's expression grew scornful. "Don't compliment my wife. I know what you want from her, Jessie. Like I told you before, don't act like a snake slithering around my wife! Snakes get their heads stomped, especially by me. Don't make me tell you again."

"I'm not!" Jessie exclaimed. "Come on, man, we're friends. I would never cross that line."

"That's not what you told me," Manny Rodriguez stated with a hidden smile.

"What?" Jessie's eyes widened in alarm. Rene was his friend, but he had a temper and wasn't anyone to mess with. "I've never said anything like that!"

"Yeah, you did! You said when Rene makes runs to Cali,

you come over here for a good time," Manny accused with mock seriousness. Stacy nodded her head in agreement.

Rene's eyes went back and forth between Manny and Jessie and grew increasingly enraged.

Jessie chortled nervously. "They're lying, Rene. That's not true."

Rene glared at Manny intensely. "You better be lying to me!"

Manny laughed. "I'm kidding! He's never said anything like that."

Jessie sighed.

Rene gazed at Jessie dangerously. "You probably do, though. Does she invite you over? Come on, Jessie, does Tina call you when I'm not here? I'm sure she probably does. That little tramp is only good for one thing and now that's probably going to you and everyone else when I'm not around. She calls you, doesn't she?"

"No, man! She's never called me. I don't know what you're talking about. Manny was talking crap!"

"We'll find that out soon enough," Rene said quietly more to himself.

When Tina came back into the living room, she was wearing a more revealing gold-colored blouse and a pair of tight black jeans. "Thanks for ruining my other shirt. This is the only clean, nice one I have left to wear."

"So, do you and Jessie have something going on?" Rene asked accusingly.

"Excuse me?" The question repulsed her. She could see the rage building behind his eyes, but she no longer cared. He could hit her, and he probably would, but she despised the man who stood in front of her.

Manny spoke uncomfortably, "Dude, I told you I was just kidding."

"No, she can answer the question," Rene replied with a glance to his friend. He spoke venomously to Tina. "Are you screwing around on me when I'm not here?" His breathing grew shallow and quick as his rage grew.

Tina shook her head and put her hands up in surrender. "You...I know where this is going. I don't even want to go to the bar with you. You're going to want to fight and blame me for it. I already know, so please go without me. I do not want to be around you!" Incensed, she walked back toward her bedroom.

Rene stared down at the floor. "Go out to the car, guys; I'll be there in a minute." He waited for his friends to leave before following Tina. She was waiting beside the bed with her arms folded and an angry expression on her face. Rene watched her for a moment before saying with disgust, "It's better that you're not going. You're getting so fat you'd embarrass yourself and me. I don't know what happened to you, but you're not the same girl anymore. You're fat, ugly and you let yourself go to hell. You're trash, Tina, just another trashy whore." He took a deep breath and added, "Don't wait up." He turned to leave.

"I'm leaving," Tina said.

"What?" Rene turned slowly back towards her.

"I'm leaving you. I'm moving back in with my parents and I'm getting a divorce. I won't be here when you get back."

"You're not leaving! No way in hell will I let you leave. Do you understand me?" He quickly grabbed her by the throat and slammed her against the wall. His eyes burned with ferocity. His hand tightened around her throat, interrupting her airflow. "You're not going anywhere, Tina! You will be here when I get home. Do you understand me? I will kill you if you leave me. Do you understand me now?" he hissed with a cruel snarl. His hand squeezed her throat harder, yanked her forward, and then slammed her head into the wall while she tried to pry his hand from her throat. "You better be here when I get home. I won't warn you again!" He slammed her against the wall one last time and let her go.

Tina slid down the wall, catching her breath while choking over her terrified sobs as she reached the floor.

Rene watched her catch her breath. "If you're not here, I'll come to get you! And trust me, your daddy won't stop me! You won't live without me, Tina, I promise you that!" He walked out of the bedroom just as Stacey honked the horn.

Tina put on a pair of gray sweatpants and a T-shirt. She turned on the TV and watched the New Year's Eve countdown from New York City. Tina was twenty-one years old, and her life was already in the gutter of society. She was married with a child, on welfare, and had no plans of a better future. She didn't have a job, nor would Rene permit her to get one. She hoped to go back to school and get an associate social services degree after Karen was born, but Rene never allowed it. She was simply a young mother on welfare. Tina was once an honor roll student with a 4.0 GPA and had an academic scholarship to the University of Oregon, where her future dreams of attaining a law degree were not out of the realm of possibility. She was once a bright and cheerful young lady who had every hope of a bright future as a prosecutor with the District Attorney's Office. Now three years later, she would be lucky to be hired at a fast-food restaurant, let alone ever get to attend college.

It wasn't supposed to be like this, she reflected as she looked around the room. Tina was raised in a middle-class conservative Christian home and held to her moral values. She had many friends in the small school, but she wasn't necessarily one of the more popular female students. Greg Slater was the most popular guy in school and there were many girls far more popular than Tina interested in him, but he was only interested in one girl, and for reasons she didn't understand, it was her. They began dating the first week of their junior year and were together constantly from then on. They were the most popular couple in the school and the longest lasting. It came as a surprise to many when their relationship ended the day after graduation. It wasn't a mutual decision; Tina decided to break up with Greg because she was moving to Eugene to attend the University of Oregon in the fall and Greg was moving to Boise, Idaho. The deciding factor for Tina was when Greg accepted the opportunity to work for the Idaho Forest Service over the summer, rather than spending the summer with her.

Greg left for Idaho soon after graduation. He left Middleton for good, and he left her. Tina found herself soaking in her sorrow and found an outlet to escape the pain of her broken heart, which offered a source of laughter with some of her more distant friends. Though Tina had never been one to partake in the drinking and partying, that summer, she discovered how fun some in that crowd could be. The laughter produced by alcohol buried the pain of her broken heart. It wasn't long after graduation that she saw Rene at a party and their relationship grew from there. They were both left behind by Greg and took comfort in each other. She had dated Greg for two years and graduated with her innocence intact, but with the impaired judgment that comes with drinking alcohol, it wasn't long until she gave her virginity away to Rene. Though she was guilt-ridden the day after and ashamed of the suddenness of it, it would become a familiar position she found herself in. Consequently, before August was over, Tina discovered she was pregnant. Her scholarship and everything she had worked so hard for were gone.

Though her parents disapproved of Rene intensely, she decided to marry the father of her baby. It was a decision that seemed right at the time, but she regretted it now. They were going on three years of marriage, and she hated him. Rene worked part-time at a gas station in Ridgefield, but he had no interest in working full time at any job. Rene supplemented his income by selling marijuana and meth for his supplier. He had somehow earned the trust of his dealer and twice a month he made runs out of state to bring in contraband. It was dangerous work, but it assured him a more lucrative future with his dealer. Selling drugs was the only profession that Rene was striving to excel in and better himself at. It didn't leave Tina much hope of a brighter future, except that hopefully someday, Rene would be locked up long enough for her to escape from her marriage. Rene had always played guitar and dreamed of becoming a famous rock star. He had picked out his stage name in High School; Johnny Gibson. Rene had once answered a want ad for a Portland band looking for a guitarist. He used his alias thinking it might help his musical career, but he was humiliated by his lack of skill and musical knowledge. He never tried out for another band. People frequently called their home and asked for Johnny Gibson, but it was never a band needing a guitarist; it was always a buyer or his dealer calling. Usually, Rene earned just enough money to use and spend on himself. When it came to feeding his family, he was dependent upon welfare.

Tina lit a cigarette and set her lighter back down on the living room coffee table. She sat on the couch with a blanket and tucked her feet up close to her to be comfortable and watched the New Year's Eve countdown show. While the world enjoyed their New Year's Eve with family or friends, she sat alone in a crappy home, without a hope that it might ever get better than it was.

A knock on the door startled her. She set her cigarette down in a full ashtray and stepped over to the door. "Who is it?" she asked. She glanced at the clock again. It was nearly eleven.

"Greg."

Tina frowned and opened the door partway to peek out.

"Hi." He was wearing a blue Boise State Bronco sweatshirt while standing in the light rain. He had walked over from his parents' house across town. "I thought I'd stop by," he added after an uncomfortable silence.

"Come in," she said hesitantly. "Rene went to the bar with his friends. Have a seat." She motioned towards the couch.

Greg sat on one end of the sofa. He noticed the burning cigarette in the ashtray and the empty beer cans spread throughout the home. She sat on the other end of the couch and tucked her bare feet underneath the blanket facing him. She reached for her cigarette to take in a long breath. She exhaled away from Greg. "So, how are you?" she asked.

Greg nodded uncomfortably. "Good. I'm doing well. How about you?"

Tina shrugged. "I'm fine." She seemed to be far from it. She avoided looking into his eyes.

Greg nodded at the cigarette in her fingers. "When did you start smoking?"

Tina frowned. "How's school?" she asked, ignoring the question.

"Good. I'll graduate next year. So, did you watch us play Oregon this year?"

Tina shook her head. "No, but I know it was big news here in town. Everyone watched it except us. My dad said you played a great game." Her blue eyes looked into his with an affectionate gaze, covered over by a thin layer of regret. "He was very proud of you."

The praise of her father humbled Greg. "That's nice to know. So how come you didn't watch it? From what I remember, you're a football fan. I remember watching football after church with your family every Sunday. Are you still a Forty Niner's fan?"

Tina smiled for the first time. "Yes, I am. No, I wanted to watch you play, but Rene, well, he wasn't interested."

"That's alright; we'll do better next year and get into a bowl game, hopefully. You can watch it with your dad. He's fun to watch games with."

Tina frowned. "Yeah, he is. I haven't watched football with him since you'd come over and watch it with us."

"Really?" Greg asked, surprised. "Well, tomorrow's New Year's Day. You should go watch some bowl games with him."

"Maybe," she said reluctantly. "Rene will be hungover all

day, so I might stay there when I go pick up Karen. She's with my parents. Surprisingly, they agreed to watch her tonight."

"How do you like being a mom?" he asked caringly.

Tina breathed in the smoke from her cigarette. "Karen is my life. She's my daughter," Tina answered with a prideful smile. "I couldn't imagine being without her."

"How's married life treating you?"

Tina hesitated to answer. "Good. You know we have our arguments, but what marriage doesn't?" she spoke slowly as if negotiating whether she should confide in her old friend or not. She changed the subject, speaking in a more cheerful tone, "So, what about you? I bet you have a beautiful girl-friend over in Idaho?"

Greg shook his head. "No, I don't. I've had a few dates here and there, but nothing came from them. I hold to the philosophy that what's in the heart comes out of the mouth. You told me that once, remember? We were sitting on the school steps one night after the back-to-school dance."

Tina turned her head to conceal the slight mist filling her eyes. "I remember. It was so much easier back then, wasn't it? There was nothing to fear and life was just simple and fun." She turned her head away and spoke sorrowfully, "Man, I'd give anything to do it all over again. I wouldn't make the same mistake, that's for sure."

"Well, we've all made mistakes."

Tina shot a skeptical glance at him. "What mistakes have you made, Greg? You're a year away from graduating college. According to my dad, you could go to the NFL when you graduate. You don't party and you haven't gotten any girls pregnant. The life you're living is the pride of this town. You haven't made any mistakes, Greg. I have."

"Like what?" he asked.

Tina sighed and lifted her hands while her eyes filled with tears. "Look at my life, Greg. Look at where I am. I was the class valedictorian at graduation with an academic scholarship to the University of Oregon. I could've had a future like you, but I threw it all away!" She closed her eyes and continued, "I mean, look at me. I've become the shame of this town. The good girl gone bad." She wiped the slight tears from her eyes.

Greg frowned and turned towards her on the other end of the couch. "Tina, whatever decisions you made, and for whatever reason you made them are now in the past. You are much too intelligent and resourceful just to sit here and waste away. You're twenty-one years old, much too young to be thinking about the glory days of just a few years ago. Go back to school. Get the law degree you always wanted to get. Nothing is stopping you from making your life better except you. There are no red lights for you, Tina, none."

"There's one big red light, Greg, and that's Rene. You have no idea who he is anymore. I can't do anything or go anywhere without him getting mad. He would never let me go back to school. Plus, I have a baby to take care of. This is my life," she spoke with disgust in her voice.

"Everyone struggles when they're first starting out. But that doesn't mean you can't go back to school. Maybe it's tough right now, but things can get better."

Hopeless, she answered, "No, they won't."

Greg tapped her leg. "Whatever happened to the always optimistic Tina that I once knew? Where's your faith?" he finished with a comforting smile.

The agony of her high-pitched voice revealed more than her words, "I never should've started dating Rene." She wiped the tears that slowly slipped from her eyes.

"Why did you?" he asked.

"Because you left me," she said through her soft tears.

"You broke up with me," Greg reminded her.

"You didn't have to take that job with the forest service. You could have spent the summer with me. You were abandoning me. I was mad, but I didn't realize it would hurt so much after we broke up," she said and began to wipe the tears with her hands.

Despite Greg's longing to hold her comfortingly, he

remained where he was and watched her weep. She pulled her hands away from her face and gave him a sorrowful expression. "Rene's changed. He's nothing like he was in school. He'll never let me go back to school, Greg. I can't even go to my parent's house without him counting the minutes and threatening to hurt me if I lie about where I am. He scares me."

For a moment, Greg watched her compassionately. "My sister said he was bad news now; I didn't believe her. Is he?"

Tina lifted her chin and pulled down the neck of her shirt. Her throat was reddened but not bruised. "Do you see anything?" she asked.

"A red mark," he answered.

"He strangled me before he left tonight, here," she said and pulled up her shirt, revealing a large bruise on her left ribs. It was still quite sore. "That's where he kicked me yesterday."

Greg's face revealed his shock. "Rene did that? Why don't you leave him? Tina..." he was lost for any words to say.

"I can't. Rene threatened to kill me if I did. And..." she paused to bite her bottom lip in fear, "I believe he would."

Greg was stunned. "Do your parents know?"

Tina shook her head. "I've never told them. They've asked me about some bruises on my arms, but I've always denied it."

"Why in the world did you start dating him anyway?" Greg asked, sounding troubled. "Rene was a friend of mine, but he was the last person I ever thought you'd date. You had nothing in common with him, Tina."

She touched his hand softly. "We had you in common."

"Me?" Greg asked, not understanding.

"Nothing was the same after you left. You were my rock, Greg. I loved you so much and you weren't there for me. I never imagined anything could hurt so much." She reached over to the coffee table for her cigarettes, lit one, and breathed in the smoke. She glanced at the clock. It was eleven-forty. She continued, "After you left, I quit going to church and started partying with Rene and his friends. He understood what I felt because you were his rock as well. One thing led to another and here I am, exactly what I never wanted to be. I even began smoking," she said, lifting her cigarette.

"You broke up with me, Tina. I was the one heartbroken." He paused momentarily. "I was hoping there would still be time for us, but then I heard you married Rene. I couldn't believe it. I put my focus into school and football and spent my summers in Idaho. I wasn't necessarily avoiding you, but if I ever saw you and Rene together, like I did today, I wouldn't know what to say. Congratulations, perhaps, but I wouldn't have meant it." He leaned towards her and touched her feet which stuck out of the blanket. "You deserve better than this. Move back in with your parents and divorce Rene. Any man that hits a woman is not the kind of man you want to live with, so end it now before it gets even worse and harder to leave. Your life is not over, but if you live like this, it might as well be. Grab some things and I'll walk you over to your parent's house. I love you too much to see you living like this, Tina."

Tina's breathing grew more profound with each breath. "You don't know him anymore, Greg. He's changed."

"I can see that. But you can't allow him to hurt you and keep it a secret. Does anyone else know?"

Tina tightened her lips and shook her head slowly.

"Why did you tell me?' Greg asked curiously.

"Because you've always been my closest friend. If I can't trust you, then there's nobody in this world who I can trust."

"Tina, you can't keep this a secret anymore. Talk to your parents and move in with them, or call the police, but don't be quiet. It's remaining silent that creates the prison you live in. Trust me, my friend. The first step to making a better life for yourself is getting away from being abused."

He took hold of her feet and set them on his lap to massage them. "You're worth more than that."

Tina's attention went to the TV. The countdown to midnight was less than twenty minutes away. She turned back to Greg. "If I divorced Rene, and I am, is there any chance of us getting back together?" she asked tentatively.

Greg frowned. "I don't know. What I do know is that you need to stand up for yourself, first and foremost."

"Is that a no?" she asked sadly. Her eyes grew moist as they watched Greg rubbing her feet. "You were always my rock, Greg. I felt safe in your arms. I knew nothing could hurt me when I was with you. I don't have that anymore. You're still the only one that makes me feel like that. I know I messed up, but is there any chance of us getting back together?"

Greg took a deep breath and looked at her feet on his lap. It was a line he had already crossed that he never should've allowed happening, even though it was his own doing. He peered into her eyes. "You're married to Rene, Tina. I love you, and I probably always will love you, but I can't answer that question. Before you even consider asking that, you have other things to consider, like your family and future. I'll always be your friend and that's where we need to begin," he said gently. He laughed slightly. "I shouldn't even be rubbing your feet."

"So, holding me for a few minutes is out of the question?" she asked softly.

His reply saddened her even more. "If I hold you, I might not let you go," he said and moved her feet off his lap. He stood up. "Can I use your bathroom?"

"Sure, it's through the kitchen. The first door on your right."

The bathroom was small and outdated but was clean for the most part. Greg washed his hands in the sink and looked into the mirror. He took a deep breath and decided it was time to leave. He had not planned on coming home during Christmas break to win back his old girlfriend. It was time to go before the temptation to hold her, even for just a moment, became too much. She was married now, whether happily or not, it didn't matter. She was still married. It was a line he would not cross.

As he reached to unlock the bathroom door, he heard Rene and his friends enter the house. Rene immediately said to Tina, "I told these guys you'd be sitting on your ass while the house is a mess. It's always a mess! What?" he asked harshly.

"Greg's here," Greg heard Tina say. She sounded very cautious.

"Where?"

Greg exited the bathroom and walked through the kitchen. Rene stood in the middle of the living room glaring down at Tina with his back to Greg. Two guys and a girl who Greg didn't know were with him. A thin, fragile-looking long-haired guy sat on the couch not far from Tina's feet. A more solidly built, clean-cut, and handsome Hispanic man stood just inside the door, with his arm around his girlfriend that stared at Greg.

Greg forced an uncomfortable smile. "Hey, Rene," he said. Rene turned around quickly; he stared at Greg with hostile eyes. "I just stopped by. It's good to see you," Greg said, reaching his hand out to shake.

Rene took a deep breath and shook his hand reluctantly. "What's up, man?" he asked quietly without any show of emotion.

Greg shrugged. "I thought I'd take you up on your invitation to stop by."

"Cool, but we're not having a party tonight. How long have you been waiting?"

"Oh, not long, twenty minutes or so. How are you, Rene?"

Rene lowered his head and nodded. "Good."

"That's good. So who are your friends?" Greg asked, glancing at Manny and Stacy, who stood by the door. Manny watched Greg suspiciously.

"That's Manny, Stacy, and Jessie. This is my old pal, Greg. You guys need to take off. I'll catch you all tomorrow."

Jessie stated, "I thought we were going back to the bar?"

Rene answered Jessie. "Go without me, Jess. I'm not feeling so well."

Manny took a deep breath. "Well, can I get that shirt you borrowed?" he asked intentionally, with a nod towards the bedroom.

"Yeah, come on back with me," Rene said and stepped past Greg irritably. Manny followed Rene to his bedroom.

Greg stood uncomfortably in the living room while Stacy and Jessie waited impatiently for Manny to return. Tina remained on the sofa, covered by her blanket. She reached over to the coffee table to get her cigarettes. Her hands were shaking in the uncomfortable silence. Before long, Rene led Manny back into the living room, saying, "I'll wash that shirt, Manny. I forgot I wore it yesterday."

"So, what's up?" Rene asked once his friends had left. He intentionally stepped in front of Tina to block her view from Greg.

"I was walking around town reminiscing a bit and thought I'd stop by. Other than that, I'm heading back to Idaho on Tuesday."

"Reminiscing, huh?" Rene asked with a sinister tone while staring at the floor, nodding. He raised his head and met Greg's eyes evenly. "That's cool, man. It's good to see you, but we're calling it a night. You take care." He put out his hand to shake again.

Greg shook it. "Okay, you take care," he repeated to Rene. He looked at Tina. She was avoiding eye contact with him. "Take care, Tina."

"You too," she answered quickly.

Rene walked over and held the door for him. "I hate to be rude, man, but I've had enough for one night."

"Not a problem," Greg said and paused in front of the TV to look at it. The New Year's Eve countdown had reached its pinnacle of the celebration on TV. It was quickly followed by the sounds of fireworks, yells, and whistles from around town. He offered a smile as he turned towards Tina, "Happy New Year, Tina."

"You too," she said nervously.

Rene stood in the opened door, watching Greg walk up their short driveway and turn onto Sixth Street before he closed the door.

Greg paused at the end of the driveway and turned back toward the house. He stayed hidden in the darkness while he waited to see if he could hear anything. It didn't take long. Almost immediately, he heard Rene shout accusations at Tina. Her urgent cries of defense were meek and barely audible at first but grew in intensity with the volume of Rene's rage. The covered windows blocked any view of what was happening inside, but her terrified cries made it clear that he was hurting her.

Filled with a wave of gut-wrenching anger that he'd never felt before, Greg burst into the living room. Rene pulled Tina onto the floor and sat on her chest with his hands around her throat, strangling her. Greg grabbed Rene by the hair, pulled him up off her, and then pushed him into the wall. Rene immediately came at Greg with nothing less than absolute murder showing in his eyes. Greg threw a quick left jab into Rene's mouth and followed it with a powerful overhand right that knocked Rene to the kitchen floor. Greg pointed at Rene, "Stay away from her! Don't you touch her again!" Greg shouted with some fury of his own.

Rene wiped the blood from a split lip before rising to his feet. He moved quickly towards his bedroom.

Greg approached Tina, lying on the floor in a fetal position, holding her throat while sobbing uncontrollably, He knelt and touched her shoulder. "Come on, Tina; let's get you out of here. You'll be all right." He took her soft hand in his and gently helped her up. She wrapped her arms around him and sobbed into his shoulder. "Come on, let's get your shoes on," he said, breaking the embrace.

Rene appeared in the kitchen entrance holding a black

.32 caliber semi-automatic handgun. "You're not taking her anywhere!" He pointed the pistol at Greg.

Greg froze in disbelief. Rene's cold eyes left no doubt that he intended to kill him. Time stood still momentarily, which was good because his time was running out. The terror he felt demanded some immediate action because he would not go down without a fight. Greg quickly pushed Tina away and then sprung forward, reaching for the pistol. The pistol fired, the bullet grazed Greg's left ribs and ricocheted into the wall.

Greg grimaced in pain as he pushed Rene into the kitchen, forcing the pistol up into the air by grabbing Rene's right wrist with his left hand. Greg's left side burned, and he could feel the blood running down his side as he wrestled with Rene to keep from being shot in a more vital area. Tina screamed and ran out of the house in terror.

Greg tripped Rene down to the floor and focused on controlling Rene's gun hand as he lay on top of Rene and maneuvered his body to straddle one of Rene's legs. Rene saw Tina run out of their house and, desperate to free himself from Greg, brought his knee up hard into Greg's groin. The unexpected blow sent a burst of pain into Greg's stomach and took the wind out of him. His left hand loosened just a bit on Rene's wrist, but it was enough for Rene to break Greg's grasp. Rene immediately pointed the gun at Greg's body and pulled the trigger. The weapon exploded at point-blank range into Greg's left thigh. He yelled from the pain and quickly rolled off Rene and held his leg while he rolled back and forth on the floor. Rene got up quickly and ran after Tina.

Tina had run as fast as she could with her bare feet, through the rain and cold streets the three-block distance to her parent's home. She knew Rene was running behind her and catching up fast. With her parents' home in view, she glanced back to see Rene quickly gaining behind her. Screaming for help, she cut across her parent's yard and jumped up onto the front porch and banged on the door while screaming. Suddenly, Rene slammed Tina into the door with all the force he could and then slung her off the porch into the wet grass of the yard like a trash bag. Enraged, he followed and kicked her as hard as he could in the ribs while yelling curses ferociously.

The front porch light came on and the door opened. Tina's father, Art, stepped outside in a pair of sweats. Seeing his daughter being beaten, he leaped off the porch to intervene. Rene turned his attention to her enraged father; he raised his pistol and pulled the trigger without saying a word. The bullet hit Art in the chest; he stopped and looked at Rene in horror. Rene fired again. This time her father fell backward to the wet ground. Art's startled wife stepped out onto the porch to see what was happening; horrified, she ran inside to call the police.

Tina lay in the grass, wailing after witnessing her father being shot. She tried to crawl to her father as she called to him, but Rene stopped her, aiming the pistol carefully at her head. "It's your fault!" he yelled. "It's your fault that he's dead!"

Tina stared at Rene, knowing her life was about to end. She slowly crawled backward without taking her eyes off the gun. Her agonizing cries, pleads, and screams were going unheard. She could see the dark and murderous eyes of Rene staring down the barrel of the weapon, stalking her with a touch of a satisfied smile mixing with his snarl. She knew her life was over and waited for the expected bullet to pierce her skull right between the eyes where he was aiming.

"It's over, Tina. You made me kill your father, and now I have to kill you. I've never been happier to do so."

Tina closed her eyes and wept while waiting for Rene to pull the trigger. Out of nowhere, Greg ran across the yard and made a diving tackle that drove Rene's body forcefully into the grass. The handgun fired upon impact, sending the bullet harmlessly into the ground.

Rene dropped the gun as he made contact with the

ground. For a moment, he had no idea what force had hit him, but once on the ground, he realized it was Greg. Rene pushed himself up in a fury and tried to get away from Greg by throwing his elbow towards Greg's head. It didn't work. Greg shifted his weight to one side, maneuvered Rene to his back, and quickly sat on Rene's chest. Greg's left leg burned severely where the bullet was lodged, and he swore one of his ribs was broken where the bullet struck his ribs that brought a near-crippling amount of pain through his chest with every move he took. Rene tried to lift his hips off the wet ground forcefully to knock Greg off balance and off of him, but despite the pain in his thigh, Greg quickly slid his feet under Rene's lifted hips to hold him perfectly contained between his feet and his torso. Rene's only defense was his hands and trying to hold Greg close to minimize the effect of any downward strikes. Greg swung two hard and fast solid blows to Rene's head that stunned him enough to drop his hands, leaving Rene defenseless. Greg grabbed Rene's hair with his left hand and hit him repeatedly with his right fist until Rene's face was covered with blood, and he was barely conscious.

Greg stopped hitting and released Rene's hair when the pain in his ribs had become too much. With a pain-filled grimace, he lifted his head just as a camera flash took his picture. Another followed it.

Sirens could be heard approaching while a local man named Dave Simpson, who lived just down the street and worked for the county newspaper as a photographer, took another picture.

A crowd of concerned neighbors swarmed around Tina and her mother as they wailed near where her father lay. Two neighbors who were both volunteer firemen did what they could with him, but neither had any equipment. They and Police Chief Harry Bishop tried to save the man's life. Many more sirens were heard, and momentarily the Middleton volunteer medics arrived to take over the rescue attempt of Tina's father. Harry Bishop walked over to Greg just as the other officers arrived and took Rene into custody. Dave Simpson took a picture of Chief Bishop and the other officer taking blood-covered Rene to the car.

An ambulance arrived to rush Tina's father to the hospital. Another ambulance arrived to take Greg. He had been grazed by one bullet that broke a rib and hit solidly with another bullet that penetrated the bone in his leg. It should've been painful to run, but he hadn't felt a thing while running the three blocks after Rene.

At the hospital, Tina's father died in surgery from his wounds. Four days later, Greg stood painfully at the funeral with his crutches to allow his leg to heal. His discomfort was put aside momentarily to attend the funeral of a good man and the father of the woman he loved. Greg held Tina lovingly while she sobbed into his shoulder. Dave Simpson took a picture, and the story of the college football star sacrificing himself to save an abused wife from an enraged murderer made headlines around the state.

Six months later, Greg sat with Tina and the rest of the Stewart family on the wooden benches in the courtroom, waiting for Rene to be brought in to be sentenced in the court of law. The media had made Greg into a hero, as they told the story of the star Boise State linebacker being shot twice while saving an abused wife from her enraged husband's murderous rampage. The story of the two high school best friends who loved the same young woman had been of great human interest. But to hear the rest of the story of one's great success with a promising future and the other's fall into drug abuse and life as a meth dealer had become national headline news. The trial of Rene Dibari was just shy of a media circus, as local and national news stations reported on the domestic dispute that erupted into the murder of Art Stewart and the attempted murder of both Tina and Greg.

Rene had been found guilty of Murder in the Second

Degree and two counts of Attempted Murder. Now once again, the media hovered in and around the courtroom, waiting for the sentencing of Rene.

Tina cuddled closer to Greg's arm when Rene was brought into the courtroom. His wrists were shackled around his waist and two guards guided him to the defense table, where his lawyer, a local public defender, waited for him. Rene glanced over towards Greg and Tina with his fierce sneer when he entered the courtroom. They were sitting close together, holding hands. He could see how afraid she was of him, and it gave him a touch of pleasure. Tina had filed for a divorce which was finalized two months before. She had full custody of their daughter and as of the moment, he had no right to see her. Karen was not in the courtroom yet again, and Rene knew he might not see her for another few months at least, as his lawyer had promised to help him get visitations to see his daughter. Rene felt the only absolute satisfaction was knowing that Greg would miss a good portion of the football season due to the .32 caliber bullet that ripped through his thigh muscles and splintered part of his bone. According to the reports that Rene had heard, Greg wouldn't be the star player anymore and probably put an end to any NFL aspirations. Rene sat with his lawyer and turned his head just enough to look back at Greg. Greg wrapped a protective arm around her shoulders while keeping his eyes on Rene. Rene smirked wickedly and shook his head with disgust.

Rene stood while the judge quietly entered the courtroom. He took a seat as the judge read through some paperwork and spoke with the lawyers. Before the sentencing took place, the victims had the opportunity to address Rene and let him know how his choices had impacted their lives.

Tina's mother was the first to speak and poured her anger and hurt out as she spoke of her late husband. Rene had kept his head down and showed no remorse for the life he had taken from the family. While she grieved, Rene's face was stone cold with neither a smile nor a frown with dark eyes that revealed nothing.

Tina walked over to the witness seat where the microphone was and sat down gracefully. She was dressed in a new yellow summer dress and appeared renewed, rested, and beautiful. Her hair was long and fell with new life and waves below her shoulders. Her eyes shined like they had years before and had a certain joy within them, despite the obvious anxiety she revealed about speaking. She held her single piece of paper in her shaking hands. She then glanced at Rene, and his head lifted with interest, and a slight smirk spread the corner of his lips as he waited for her to speak.

Her voice cracked as she said, "I won't say too much. You have taken my father away from my mother, sisters, and me. We all have to forgive you for that so we can move forward, but no one needs to forgive you more than I do." She stopped as Rene raised his eyebrows at her sarcastically. She continued with growing strength in her voice, "I am moving on while you're going to prison. That is my revenge, Rene. I am forgetting about you. You took my father away from me, but you also took your daughter away from you. So while you are rotting away in prison, do know that I will be living freely and happy because I forgive you. You will be forgotten by Karen and by me. That's all I have to say; have a good life, Rene, because you will never see me again."

Rene's sarcastic smirk changed slowly to anger as his lips grew tight and his eyes burned hotter. Though he remained seated, calm, and quiet, he appeared like he could explode any second while he watched Tina take her seat next to Greg. His breathing grew strained, while his jaw clenched with a twitch to his upper lip when he was asked to stand with his lawyer to hear his sentence. His eyes stared straight ahead as though he could see through the judge.

The judge sentenced Rene with a voice of authority, "Rene Dibari, you have been found guilty in a court of law. You are hereby sentenced to serve no less than a life sentence in the Oregon State Penitentiary without the possibility of parole. Bailiff, take him away."

Rene stood momentarily as the cries of his mother filled the courtroom. When the bailiff stepped near to take hold of his arm, Rene kneed the bailiff in the groin and turned to face Greg and Tina. He ran forward and tried to leap over the wooden rail, that separated the spectators from the trial lawyers, to get to them. Rene was pulled backward by another officer and quickly detained by three officers who fought to control him. They stood him up and dragged him out of the courtroom by his arms. He screamed with an animalistic expression taking over his face, "I'm going to kill you, Greg! When I get out, I'm coming for you! This is your fault, Tina! I'm going to hurt you when I get out! I'll kill you both! I'll see you again, Tina, I promise you that! Karen will never forget me. She's my baby!" he screamed as they dragged him out of the courtroom. The door closed behind them.

The news media captured every word on film. They also caught the loving embrace between Greg and Tina. It was finally over.

CHAPTER 1

15 YEARS LATER

GREG SLATER STEPPED OUT OF THE SHOWER AND DRESSED IN slacks and a button-up tan dress shirt for the day. It was Tuesday morning and he had to be at the school by seven-thirty to supervise the halls at the Middleton High School. He sat on his bed and put on his socks and shoes before going downstairs to eat breakfast. He wasn't in a good mood, as he and his wife, Tina, had argued the night before. The dispute had not been settled and still lingered that morning. Tina had ignored him this morning and was downstairs slamming the pans around while she made breakfast for their three kids. Greg had gone to bed angry and was quickly becoming aggravated by Tina's attitude before this day even began.

Greg combed his hair and was putting on some cologne when Tina quickly entered the bedroom. She was in her white bath robe and glared at him with angry blue eyes. "I have to be at the office by nine today. I sure hope you and the kids didn't take all of the hot water again. I told you yesterday that I have the floor this morning. You should've known that I'd like to shower too. You and the kids do this to me every time. You need to tell the boys to quit showering in the mornings. They don't need to," she spoke with irritation in her voice.

"Fine, I'll tell them, but you could tell them that too."

"You're their father; it's your job to tell them! For crying out loud, Greg, is it too much to ask for you to think about my needs? You have no consideration for me at all."

Greg grimaced. "You had the opportunity to shower before the kids were even up this morning, but you chose to sit downstairs and drink coffee for half an hour."

"You know what?" Tina asked scornfully, "I am sick of you degrading me."

"Degrading you?"

"You know what I mean! If I want a cup of coffee in the morning, I shouldn't have to get up at five in the morning. But maybe I will since you're not considerate enough to think of me!"

Greg grinned in exasperation. "I'll have to work on becoming more considerate. Especially since this has never been a problem before."

Tina stood near the foot of the bed, astounded by his reply. "What?... You're being inconsiderate to my feelings? Oh, it's an ongoing thing, Greg. You just don't see it because you're so wrapped up in yourself. It's always about you. Always!"

Greg took a deep breath to control his growing frustration. "What are you mad about? Last night it was one thing, the day before was something different. You haven't been the same in over a month. Maybe if you came to church with us, you'd feel better."

"You just don't get it, do you?" she asked with a scornful glare.

"No, I don't." He shrugged and sat down on the edge of the bed.

"Well, maybe you will when it's too late. Why don't you think about it for a while? You're such an ass. Now I have to jump into the cold shower and get ready for work. Oh yeah, I work too, don't I?" She continued to glare at Greg for a moment and then walked into the bathroom with a disgusted scoff.

Greg lay back on the bed and stared up at the ceiling. He took a deep breath and exhaled. He turned his head to see Tina standing in the bathroom doorway with her hands on her hips with the same scowl on her face. "And another thing, I'm not making dinner tonight. You can when you get home. I'm sick of having to work all of the time and come home to a messy house and make dinner while you're out enjoying yourself."

Greg chuckled as he sat up. "Fine. I'll make dinner, and I'll make sure I don't enjoy it."

Tina shifted her feet to lean on the doorjamb. "Do you think it's funny that I feel disconnected from this family?" she asked, appalled. "Maybe I just feel second best to your students, your football team, wrestling team, and whatever else you're doing. You have no more time for me. But don't worry, someone else will if you don't. I know where I stand in this house."

Greg stood up and walked over to her. "Tina, if I've made you feel second to anything, I am sorry." He hugged her. Her arms remained at her side as she turned her head when he tried to kiss her. She displayed no sign of affection. "I love you, Tina. I would never intentionally hurt you."

"Yeah, right. I love you too," she said without emotion. She turned away from him to break loose from the hug. "Have a good day with your precious students."

"What the hell's wrong with you?" Greg asked angrily.

"Nothing," she replied sadly. "I have to get ready to go and so do you."

Greg shook his head with a heavier dose of frustration than the day before. "Fine. Have a good day," he said and turned to leave the room. He stepped back towards her. "I don't know what's wrong with you, but it's not my job. I'm a teacher, Tina. That's what I do, and you've never had a problem with it until recently. You quit coming to church and have become critical of everything I do or say since then. Maybe you need a cold shower to wake up because quite frankly, I'm getting sick of it!" he said irritably, though he kept his voice down so the kids wouldn't overhear.

"Me too!" she answered quickly. "You have no idea how sick of it I am."

CHAPTER 2

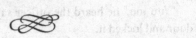

AFTER FIFTEEN YEARS IN PRISON, RENE DIBARI HAD GOTTEN accustomed to the daily routine of hearing the clanging of the iron-barred doors opening and closing. He was used to the voices that echoed out around him and the guard's watchful eyes upon him. He had gotten used to the life of prison rules and earned respect within the prison walls. He had his share of battles and was still alive and well as he walked down a two-toned painted corridor. The top half of the wall was a high gloss yellowish-white, while the bottom half was painted puke green. He breathed in deeply as he stepped confidently towards a swing-out iron-barred door guarded by a stern-looking security officer with a muscular frame and brown hair in a military crew cut. His hardened expression matched his eyes and tough demeanor.

"Where's your escort?" the security officer asked curtly. He continued with the same short, authoritative tone, "You're not supposed to be in here unescorted."

Rene shook his head and said impatiently, "Buddy, I don't have time to wait for him to get off the pot. I have three more inspections to do today and one of them's in Portland. I'd like to be home in time for dinner if you know what I mean."

The middle-aged officer was irritated by an outside

vendor not abiding by the rules. He spoke harshly, "You're lucky to get out of here at all unguarded. Do you understand me?" he asked impatiently as he opened the door. "Stay with your escort next time!"

"Will do," Rene said as he walked past the guard. "Have a good day."

"You too," he heard the officer say as he closed the iron door and locked it.

Rene walked casually towards the last locked door. He carried a clipboard and a small nylon tool bag holding a few hand tools and a couple of meters of some sort. He wore tan slacks with brown loafers and a pressed blue and white pin-striped, long-sleeved dress shirt with the top two buttons left undone. A white square card badge on the left lapel indicated that he was the State Boiler Inspector. The badge had a small photo ID of a man named Gary Baugh. So far, not one of the guards had looked close enough to notice that Rene Dibari appeared nothing like the man in the photo. Rene had left Gary Baugh's lifeless body behind the storage tanks in the boiler room, alongside the corrections officer who had been escorting him through the North Sector A Utilities Building. The utility building was separated from the general population and rarely had any prisoners in the area, except for an occasional trustee on the maintenance program. Rene had been sent there to buff the corridor floors, which he'd done many times before.

It wasn't planned; in fact, he had never even considered such an idea before the opportunity was presented. He was buffing the floor when he watched one guard escort the inspector into the boiler room. The boiler room door normally would've closed and locked behind the guard, but the tension on the hydraulic door closer failed to close, leaving it unlocked. Rene acted quickly by using the sound of the buffer to cover what noise he might've made as he slipped into the boiler room behind them. Inside, a twenty-four-inch heavy-duty pipe-wrench was hanging on the wall by the main water shutoff. Using the pipe wrench like a baseball bat, he swung it with all his might and hit the guard in the back of his head. The guard was driven forward immediately to the concrete floor, lifeless while his blood flowed out of the head wound and rolled across the floor.

Gary Baugh, the state inspector, reacted in terror and quickly backed up against the wall with his hands out protectively in front of him, pleading with Rene not to hurt him. His pleadings turned to horror when Rene ordered him to remove his clothes.

"Oh, please no," Gary began to weep. "Please, I don't want to..." he begged.

The weakness of his terrified tears was nothing Rene had not seen within the prison walls before. Weak, yellow-spined cowards deserved no mercy. He had no respect for weakness. Rene shouted urgently, "Get them off! I'm not going to hurt you; I just want your clothes. Now hurry up!"

"You won't hurt me?" Gary repeated through a quivering voice.

"Not if you hurry. Come on! There's not much time!" Rene ordered urgently.

Under the pressure of Rene holding the pipe wrench like a baseball bat, Gary undressed and laid his clothes on top of one of the backup boilers. When he stood in his underwear, he stared at Rene with great anxiety. His heart pounded harder than it ever had before with the absolute terror of what stood before him. Of all the fictional movies he'd ever seen or stories he had heard, not a single one compared to the nightmare he was facing. Jarrod, the young guard that lay dead not six feet away, told him about his new infant daughter, and now he was dead. Unprotected and isolated in a locked room with a murderous convict, Gary feared the worst. In the best scenario, he would be raped by another man, and there was nothing he could do about it except beg, but at least he might survive. Standing helpless in his underwear, it took all he could do not to break down and sob like a child. "Please... Don't hurt me."

Rene pointed. "Turn towards the wall and get to your

knees. Come on, hurry up! Put your hands behind your back."

Gary paused and gasped through uncontrolled breaths, "You said you wouldn't hurt me." His face contorted into sobs.

"I'm not! I'm tying your hands, so you won't ruin this. Now get down, or I will knock you down. Your choice!" The evil in Rene's eyes showed absolutely no hesitation to swing the pipe wrench if Gary did not do as he was commanded.

Gary cautiously turned around and got to his knees. He placed his hands behind his back. He spoke through his shaking voice, "Please...I have a family. I..."

"So do I," Rene said with a sneer. He stepped forward quickly and swung the pipe wrench as hard as he could at the back of Gary's head. It connected with a solid blow. Gary's body fell forward, twitching, with his eyes still open. Blood poured from the back of his head onto the concrete. Quickly, Rene pulled both the bodies into the small workspace behind the four hot water storage tanks. He then stripped out of his blue jeans and issued shirt and put on Gary's clothes. Gary's pants were a little too big, but he tightened the belt to hold them in place. He found a pocketknife, a wallet with a little cash, a pack of gum, some change, and a set of car keys connected to a black push-button mechanism that read "Jeep" in the pants pockets. He had also taken Gary's wristwatch, eyeglasses, and his tan hat with a company logo on it. Once Rene was dressed, he grabbed Gary's clipboard and a small bag of tools. And after taking a deep breath, he opened the door, shut off the buffer, and pushed it into the boiler room. He considered washing the blood off the floor with a hose, but he was pressed for time. His supervisor could come to check on his work at any moment. He only had one shot at making his escape attempt. He had to try it now! What's the worst that could happen? He was already in prison.

He was reprimanded for leaving his guard escort at the

first locked corridor door but now he was nearing the second locked door, which was the one that opened up to the main offices and public corridor.

Behind this door was his freedom if he could get past the guards. Two guards sat in an office on the other side of a wall and watched Rene walking towards them. He stopped at the electronic solid steel door with a wire mesh window in its center. The guard spoke through an intercom, "Come on through." The door is unlocked.

Rene stepped through the door and was at a counter where one of the guards held out a log sheet for him to sign out on the clipboard. "Sign out here. Mike will be here shortly to talk to you," the guard said of the prison's operations director. "You can have a seat if you want. I'll let him know you're done. He shouldn't be long."

Rene asked with a hint of urgency in his voice, "Is there a bathroom somewhere? This place scares the crap out of me."

The guard smiled. "Down the hallway, it's in the main lobby."

Rene left his clipboard and tool bag with the guards and walked quickly down the corridor towards the restroom. He walked into a large entrance lobby that had a receptionist behind a glass front window. Two guards were standing nearby and appeared to be more at ease than any other guards inside the prison. Rene could see the daylight through the front door windows and the wet pavement of the parking lot not too far away from him. He took a deep breath and forced himself to keep calm as he walked casually by the guards. He expected the alarm to sound at any given second. If the alarm sounded, the guards would order everyone in the lobby down on the floor. Every door and gate inside and outside of the prison grounds would be secured. No one would leave the prison grounds until who or what they were looking for was found. Not even visitors in the lobby would be free to leave until prison officials could positively identify them. Rene would be caught just feet from freedom.

Nodding nervously to a guard and walking out of the front doors of the prison, he stepped outside into the late October air. He squinted his eyes and searched the parking lot for a Jeep of some kind. The cool air chilled him as he forced himself to remain calm and casually pull the keys out of his pocket. Rene hit the red alarm button and to his right, a blue Jeep Liberty sounded its horn and lights in a visitor's parking space. Alarmed and nearly panic-stricken, he quickly hit the alarm button again, not knowing what else to do. The cars that Rene drove before his arrest didn't have alarm buttons. He breathed quickly and glanced around him for any guards that might've come running out after him.

None did. Rene walked purposefully towards the Jeep, restraining himself from the urge to run as fast as he could to get into it. Everything within him wanted to run as fast and far as he could, but he knew he could not without drawing attention to himself, and the last thing he wanted was a guard's attention. Pushing a button that showed an unlocked padlock, the doors automatically unlocked. Climbing in behind the driver's seat, Rene put the labeled Jeep key into the ignition and turned the key. It started up immediately. The radio came on to a country music station, and a continuing beeping with a seatbelt light on the dash flashed before his eyes. Putting on his seat belt, he watched the prison's front door nervously. He put the automatic lever into reverse and backed up slowly, careful not to back into another vehicle while in the prison parking lot. He put the Jeep into drive and pulled forward carefully, as it had been many years since he had driven a car. Rene nervously stopped at a stop sign and turned towards the main gate of the prison's outer perimeter. His breath quickened when he saw the guard in the main entrance watching him drive closer. The guard did not attempt to stop him, and Rene drove past the guard with a casual wave. Turning onto the main city street and pressing on the gas pedal to pick up some speed, Rene mixed with the other city traffic.

Rene yelled out in disbelief and then laughed. He had escaped from prison without even planning to. He had heard of many elaborate ideas and schemes to escape from his fellow inmates, but few were ever attempted and those that were had failed miserably. Prisons were not easy to escape from because the prison security system had evolved over the years, and now it was nearly impossible to escape. He was told by another inmate once that it would take a magician to escape from prison and a highly talented magician at that. Rene didn't use any magic and he wasn't a magician. He had reacted to a moment's opportunity and with another man's clothes, including Gary Baugh's photograph pinned to Rene's chest, he had merely walked past the guards. The very irony of it, Rene couldn't get over. It made him laugh. Soon though, they would notice a missing guard and would lock down the prison. He was just lucky it hadn't happened while he was still there. It would happen anytime now, and he needed to stay ahead of the law while he could. He needed to disappear and quickly. He didn't have much time.

CHAPTER 3

RENE DROVE SLOWER THAN MOST OF THE TRAFFIC THROUGH the light rain that fell on the road. He didn't want to cut his escape short by foolishly speeding or getting into an accident. Despite his instinct to run as fast as possible to get away, he kept his speed below the posted limit of thirty-five miles per hour and made his way through Salem towards the city center.

He kept the radio off so it wouldn't distract him from his careful driving and kept his eyes open for any sign of the police or the sound of sirens. The amount of traffic was overwhelming, and it wasn't even the noon hour yet. He knew at noon the traffic would increase as people went to lunch. He watched the road signs, traffic lights, and the other cars like a sixteen-year-old boy who had just gotten his license and was driving alone for the first time. With very similar skills as a new driver, he drove through the traffic and stop lights while looking for some place to leave the Jeep and disappear into a crowd. He passed businesses and shopping centers, but it was a four-story parking garage in the center of downtown that caught his eye. Pulling into the entrance, he stopped at a gate that blocked the access. It wouldn't rise until he took a ticket from the dispenser, stamping his time of arrival. He chuckled as he pulled forward, knowing he would not be paying for the hourly parking rates. Rene found a good parking space on the third level and parked the Jeep. In the semi-darkness that filled the parking garage in late October, he didn't expect the Jeep to be discovered for at least a day. Looking through Gary Baugh's wallet, Rene found thirty-six dollars in cash and two credit cards. Nothing else in it interested him, including Gary's wallet-sized family photo and the individual school photos of his young sons. Rene emptied the wallet of its identifications, including the credit cards and pictures; leaving the cash in the wallet it went into his back pocket. Searching the Jeep, Rene found another dollar-sixty in change, a pair of dark sunglasses, and a black jacket, which he put on as he abandoned the Jeep.

He walked to an elevator with glass windows and rode down to the first floor. He had noticed as he rode down, the many orange and red leaves that still hung onto the well-groomed trees lining the street. He hadn't seen such a simple pleasure in fifteen years, except in magazines, TV, and the calendars that hung on his cell wall over the years. As the elevator door opened, he stepped onto the public sidewalk of downtown Salem. He walked to a crosswalk where other people waited for the light to change. When it did, he crossed the street with the others who had some-place to go. Unlike them, Rene had nowhere in particular to go, except away from the parking garage. At the next corner, he again waited for the pedestrian light to change. He watched anxiously as a police car drove past him. The police officer didn't even look at him. At the moment, he was an unsuspicious civilian, but it wouldn't last. By now, he knew they were looking for the missing guard, and if they hadn't found him yet, they would soon. The prison might have been already on lockdown until they found him. He wouldn't have much time until his name and picture would be plastered on the TV for any and every civilian to see. The local police would be notified first, and then any police officer passing by him could end his escape just that quickly while he stood on the corner. He needed to find another car and disappear. He put six blocks between the Jeep and himself as he walked casually towards the water-front of the Willamette River. He was leaving the business and shopping area of beautiful downtown Salem and entered the more barren industrial area of the waterfront. He wondered if it was wise to do so, as it made him more noticeable. He was the only man walking on that side of the street for the entire block and there were very few others walking that he could see. He felt like the focal point of every car that drove by. He turned around and walked back towards the city center and the pedestrian foot traffic he could mix in with.

In the distance, he heard sirens, and he quickened his pace. The sirens grew louder as he came to a corner of a busy one-way street. He pushed the pedestrian crosswalk signal button and stood at the corner, waiting impatiently as the sirens grew louder. It was then that he noticed an older silver Buick Lesabre parked on the side of the road. It was a block away with its emergency lights flashing and the trunk opened. A tall and thin elderly gentleman stood beside his car helplessly after trying to get his spare tire out of the bottom of his trunk. Impatiently, Rene watched the oncoming traffic and darted quickly across the three-lane street when there was space between the traffic. Quickly, as though he was in a race to reach the stranded senior citizen before the police reached the corner, he walked the distance to the old man's car.

Rene offered a helpful smile as he approached the neatly dressed silver-haired gentleman. "Sir, can I help you?"

The friendliness of the older man showed in his cheerful smile. He had neatly-cut silver hair and wore glasses on his thin but healthy face. "Would I ever be thankful! I just can't lift the spare out anymore. I tried, but..." He shook his head with a smile. "I guess I was just waiting for a strong young man like you to come by and help out an old fella like me," he added with a humorous grin.

"Well, I can certainly do that," Rene said. He reached into the trunk and effortlessly pulled the spare tire out; under the tire, he found the jack and lug wrench. He turned around and watched as a police car sped by the intersection with its lights flashing in a hurry to get somewhere. Rene carried the jack and lug wrench to the front passenger side tire and got down on his knees to set the jack under the frame and loosen the tire's lug nuts before he lifted the car's weight off it. He smiled to himself as he considered it had been fifteen years since he'd driven a car, but he had never forgotten how to change a tire.

"I'm sorry about you getting your pants wet," the old man said empathetically. "I hope you aren't putting yourself to too much trouble. I canceled my Triple-A membership just two months ago. I'll have to join back up," he said with a half-smile.

"It's no trouble at all, sir," Rene said without looking up.

"I appreciate it," the man said and added to make conversation as he watched Rene. "The darn rain's getting cold, isn't it?"

"Yes, sir," Rene agreed. When he had finished changing the tire, he put the flat tire in the trunk and closed it. "There you go." He wiped his wet hands on his pants. He was wet from the slight drizzle of rain that stayed consistent through the gray and hazy day.

The elderly gentleman opened his wallet and pulled out a twenty-dollar bill. "My thanks to you. I appreciate what you've done."

Rene shrugged and took the twenty. "Thank you, but I'd rather get a ride if I could. My Jeep broke down a few blocks over. I was walking by when I saw you."

"Oh, yes, sir! Just hop on in and I'll give you a ride. It's the least I could do after you helped me out."

"Fair enough," Rene said and happened to look up at cross street traffic as it passed. No one seemed to notice him. He smiled to himself and climbed into the passenger seat.

CHAPTER 4

THE RINALDI CAFÉ WAS A 1950's STYLE HAMBURGER restaurant with all the appeal and nostalgic glamour of a time long past. The black and white tiled floor was waxed to a high gloss and the red vinyl bench seats were surrounded by chrome trimmed white tables. Photos of the restaurant from its early days lined the walls, as did Elvis Presley memorabilia. Though many years had passed since its original opening in 1956, the family recipes had not. It was the best hamburgers and fries in the city of Ridgefield.

Tina Slater sat in a booth and took a drink of her home-made chocolate shake. Her burger was mostly eaten along with the fries, but she dared not eat all her lunch in the presence of her lunch date, Ray Tristan. Ray was a financial lender with a finance company who had asked Tina out for a business lunch.

As a Realtor, Tina was treated to many free lunches annually by a wide selection of lenders who sought her business. A realtor would often recommend a loan officer to their clients when buyers showed some interest in buying a home. Tina referred almost all her clients to a select few lenders depending on their credit and other financial needs. It was strange how a few of those lenders treated her to lunch and asked for her business, but those same lenders never referred their potential buyers to her. In the last six months, Ray Tristan had referred four buyers and a seller to Tina. He had become Tina's primary lender and the more they worked together, the more loyal she was to him and their working relationship.

Tina was dressed in a black business suit with a white blouse. Her straight light-brown hair was styled at neck length and appeared entirely professional, with her bangs slightly off to one side. Tina had beautiful dark-blue eyes and a thin but oval-shaped face with soft lips. When she smiled, it was similar to the sunshine breaking through the clouds. Her smile could draw the warmth out of the coldest hearts; however, it wasn't seen too often. Tina was a serious-minded woman who had no tolerance for nonsense, gossip, or idle chit-chat. She was strictly business and seldom brought up any subject during lunch dates other than business. It had taken four months for Ray to get Tina to start talking to him like a friend rather than a business associate. Of course, they didn't have lunch every day, but they now had lunch once a week instead of once a month.

Ray Tristan was tall and physically fit. He kept his dark brown hair well-groomed and short, with a clean-shaven face. He was thirty-eight years old, handsome, divorced, and active in the community at many levels. Ray was successful in his profession and well known around the community partly due to his aggressive advertising. Ray advertised his winning smile on local restaurant menus and grocery store shopping carts, along with the local newspaper. It was hard not to recognize him as he drove through town in either his red Porsche 911 Carrera or his green Jeep Wrangler, depending on the weather. Today his Porsche was parked outside of Rinaldi's. He was dressed in light tan slacks and a green and white striped shirt with a green tie. Ray looked at Tina fondly. "You have a bit of mustard right here." He touched the corner of his mouth.

She wiped it off with a napkin. "How's that?"

"Perfect."

"Thank you. I wasn't aware that you were in a band?" she asked more than stated.

Ray nodded. "Yeah, back in my twenties. It was no big deal, really; we played in a few bars and small auditoriums."

"Well, tell me about it. What did you play?" Tina asked, with her elbows on the table. She rested her chin with interest onto her folded hands.

Ray grinned in hindsight. "Our band wasn't very good." He laughed. "We played classic rock mostly, some alternative, and then we really killed ourselves by playing 80's pop-rock. It was fun, but it wasn't paying the bills. That's where I met Marcy, my ex-wife. We were playing in a Portland bar when I met her. After we got married, I had to get a real job, as they say. One year later, we got divorced," he finished with a smile. "So, I learned a valuable lesson, don't marry someone you met in a bar."

"What instrument did you play?" she asked with an amused expression.

"Drums. I was the drummer."

"Were you the bad boy of the band? I heard once that the drummers are usually the bad boys. That's why so many girls are more interested in meeting the drummers." She held up her hands in defense. "I don't know if that's true, but that's what I heard."

"They might've been interested if I was any good, but I wasn't. Trust me when I say we sucked."

Tina laughed.

Ray continued, "What about you? Did you ever hang out with the bands when you went to the bars?"

Tina shook her head. "I never went to bars."

"No?" Ray asked. "What kind of goofy things did you do in your twenties? You must've done something that you hate to admit."

Tina frowned thoughtfully. "No. I told you about my first husband and my father being killed. After that, I ended up marrying Greg and have been raising kids ever since then. I didn't have the opportunity to go out and enjoy my youth as carefree as you did. But my biggest regret and the only thing I hate to admit is marrying my first husband."

"That's understandable," Ray said softly. "As much as you hate to admit it, you have to admit one good thing came from that horrible experience; your beautiful daughter. I saw her picture in the paper last week. She sure looks like you."

Tina smiled proudly. "Yeah, she does. She is a beautiful girl."

"Absolutely," Ray agreed. "The article said her volleyball team has already won the division. So they'll be going to Corvallis for the state tournament next week. That's awesome. I don't know how you have time to do it all: real estate, wife, mother, football, volleyball, and everything else."

Tina tilted her head while taking a deep breath. "I'm a busy girl."

"Indeed. Were you a star athlete in school too?"

"No. I was barely coordinated enough to do a jumping jack in P.E. All of my kids get their athleticism from Greg. He was the star athlete."

"I find that interesting. As competitive and determined as you are, I would've thought you were very athletic. Especially considering how much sports consume your life nowadays, huh?"

Tina nodded. "That's true. I've got two boys playing football and Karen playing volleyball. I have three games a week to watch right now, and then come girls' basketball and wrestling, then softball and baseball. It's a constant run to this game and run to that one." She sighed tiredly with a soft yet sincere expression. "Don't get me wrong, I love watching my children compete with whatever they're playing, but sometimes I'd just like to take a break from it. It's year-round in our household. Karen plays softball all summer on a traveling team and has basketball and volleyball camps. The boys play baseball and wrestle until football starts again. Trust me when I say I'd like to have a break sometime."

"And your husband's the coach too?"

Tina smiled sadly. "Yip."

"You don't seem so excited about that," Ray suggested.

Tina twirled the straw around in what remained of her shake thoughtfully. "It's what he always wanted to do. It's what the whole town wanted him to do. But from mid-August through February, I don't see him much. Sports take up so much of his time. During wrestling season, I hardly ever see him. It's amazing how much time high school athletics consume. As I said, I'd like to have a break, but I don't see one coming for a while. Our house is constantly busy. And sometimes my family doesn't understand that I have things to do too. I have work to do, bills to pay, and dinner to cook…" she stopped talking and shook her head with frustration. "I'm sorry to bore you with all this."

He listened attentively to her words. "You never bore me; I think it's impossible for you to bore me. You have an incredible life, a bit busier than most, but an incredible life just the same. Enjoy it, my friend, because someday you'll miss it. Now I have a boring life."

Tina laughed. "Yeah, between golfing and skiing, you must get bored," she said skeptically.

He adjusted to a more comfortable position in the bench seat, casually resting his knee against hers underneath the table. "I do have a boring life," he repeated. For the first time, she did not move her knee from his when they touched. It was small and almost insignificant, except it indicated her interest in him had grown over the past month of weekly lunches and frequent conversations on the phone and social media. Her willingly keeping her knee against his opened the door to the next level of their growing relationship. He leaned forward a touch looking into Tina's eyes. "I wait all night for a friend to text me, but she never does. That's how boring my life is."

"I do too," she said with a flirtatious wave of her hand. "Unless you're talking about someone else?"

He lowered his voice, "No, there's only one person who I look forward to talking to and that's you." He gazed affectionately from across the table.

Tina smiled innocently and put the straw to her lips to suck the chocolate out of the straw. She removed the straw from her lips and set it back in the glass before licking the cold moisture from her lips. She was about to say something when her phone rang. Reaching to her hip, Tina pulled her phone out of her phone case while moving her knee from his as she shifted in her seat. She frowned at the screen and set the phone on the table without answering it. "It's my mother. She can leave a message," Tina said and put her focus back onto Ray.

Ray gave a wry smile. "So that's why you never answer my calls."

"I answer your calls, thank you. There are some people who I do answer when they call."

"And I'm one of the lucky ones?"

"You are," she said with a definite tone. The phone quit ringing and quickly her mother called back when it went to voice mail. Tina frowned with a bit of annoyance. "Excuse me," she said to Ray and answered the phone. "Hello, Mother," she said without any enthusiasm. Her expression soon changed to concern and then to distress. "What?" she shouted in alarm. "Okay, my lord... Today... An hour ago? No, no. I'll be over in a few minutes. No, I'm... No, I'm... okay. I'll be there. I'll call Greg... Okay, I love you too. Bye, Mom." Tina gazed at Ray with a puddle of frightened tears gathering in her blue eyes.

Ray was concerned. "What's wrong?"

Tina hesitated, unable to form the words. She stared at Ray and silently shook her head, greatly troubled. "Rene escaped from prison," she said softly.

"Who?" Ray asked.

Tina's mouth twisted strangely as she replied, "My first husband."

"Oh! Oh, that's, that's...wow."

"Exactly," she said and sighed. "I'm sorry, Ray, I have to cut this short. I can't believe this. I have to go see my mom."

Ray walked Tina out to her blue Mountaineer and stopped short of the car door. "If there is anything I can do, let me know, even if it's just needing to talk at midnight or three in the morning. Feel free to call me because I'm here for you, Tina. I'll do anything I can for you."

Tina stood in the slight rain with her hair getting wet. "Thank you," she said. She was hesitant to speak.

"What is it?" he asked.

Tina's face revealed a growing fear that was starting to consume her. "I'm scared."

"Come here," Ray invited while extending his arms. She went forward into his arms and wrapped her arms around him. He held her tight while swaying to the left and right. "They'll find him in no time. If you get scared, give me a call." Ray placed his hands on her cheeks and moved her back enough to look into her eyes while her arms were still around him. "You're a beautiful woman, my friend. And you know I wouldn't let anyone hurt you. So if you need me, you know I'm here, right?"

She nodded with a sincere little smile of appreciation while she gazed into his eyes. She suddenly realized they were in a public parking lot alongside a busy road with his hands caressing her cheeks and her arms around him affectionately. She stepped back out of his reach and turned away from him. "It would be just my luck if someone I knew saw us," she said nervously.

Ray shrugged. "What if they did? It was no big deal. Now, if I would've kissed you, that would be hard to explain."

"I'm married, Ray."

Ray shrugged his shoulders. "You need to go see your mom. Don't hesitate to call me, okay?"

"You're a great friend, Ray. I'll see you later."

"Anytime, Tina. I mean that. You call me anytime and I'll be there for you."

"Thank you," she said and lingered a moment as if she wanted to say more. "I have to go. I'll talk to you later," she said as she opened her car door to get in.

"Call me," Ray said with concern.

Tina smiled uneasily. "I will." As she drove out of the parking lot, she could see Ray standing in the rain watching her leave. She felt a slight grin grow on her lips. Ray was a good friend.

CHAPTER 5

RENE DROVE THE SILVER BUICK LESABRE SOUTH DOWN I-5 AS he drank a soda and ate a bag of chips. He had forgotten how delicious both were individually but having them together was a long-forgotten delicacy. He listened to a public talk radio station as he headed towards Eugene, an hour south of Salem. He drove with the cruise control set at the speed limit. He hadn't seen one patrol car since leaving Salem, however, the signs posted did alert the drivers to the possibility of the police monitoring the Interstate by air patrol.

His escape was being broadcast over the radio, which left no doubt that his prison photograph would be shown on every TV news channel soon, if not already. The law officials were looking for a blue Jeep Liberty with a specific license plate number at the moment. Sooner or later, they'd be looking for a silver Buick Lesabre when they found the body of an older man named Jack Miller in a pond just outside of the Salem city limits.

Rene took an exit off I-5 and drove into the Eugene Mall parking lot. Again, he searched the car finding only minimal change before entering the mall itself. The mall was decorated with the usual Halloween witches, black cats and other macabre horror set out in front of the stores. With the money that he had forced Jack Miller to withdraw from the ATM, Rene bought a cheap pair of tennis shoes to relieve the uncomfortable shoes he had taken from Gary. He bought a pair of blue jeans, a T-shirt and a sweatshirt. He went into a hair salon that sold wigs, and under the pretense of a coming Halloween party, he bought a long black-haired wig. It looked convincing once the lady showed him how to wear it without it coming off. He bought a small bottle of hair conditioner and a brush, which he had placed in a small bag. The wig he put in his clothes bag and walked out of the mall.

Rene thanked old Jack Miller for his monetary contribution of five hundred dollars. In prison, Rene got to know many thieves, robbers, and various types of criminals who had told him some of the tricks of the trade and some of the things that the police could trace and use to locate the perpetrator. The world had changed since Rene lived in it. There was much that he didn't know about that could be used against him. Rene decided only to use what he did know and leave the technology alone to avoid any unknown risks. He understood well that the mall contained cameras that had him on film. The parking lot as well had cameras watching it. He knew that as soon as Jack's car was found, he would be traced throughout the mall by the police watching the film. Knowing he would eventually be tracked to the mall; he kept his head down and all of his purchases in their bags and out of sight.

He walked away from the mall towards a small corner gas station and went into the public restroom on the backside of the building. Inside he changed out of Gary Baugh's clothes and into his new ones. He was relieved to put on his new shoes, and he tossed Gary's clothes into the garbage can. When he was satisfied that his wig appeared authentic and was securely on his head, he walked out of the restroom and away from the gas station across a grass field back towards the mall parking lot along the highway. He had seen a commercial truck stop offering fuel, showers, food, and gift store along I-5 not far from the mall. He had walked quickly across the far end of the mall's parking lot, crossed a small ravine with a creek, and entered the property of the truck stop. The truck traffic along I-5 is heavy, and as he expected, as one truck pulled off the highway, another would be pulling back onto it. Rene watched an older truck driver walking back to his semi and followed him to his Freightliner.

"Hey!" he called as the driver was climbing up into the cab of his truck. "Are you going north?"

"Yeah. Why?" the man asked.

"Can I get a ride? My lady and I got into a fight, and she left me! I'm not playing her game anymore, so if I could get a ride to Portland, I'd appreciate it," Rene asked quickly while the driver took his seat and closed the door.

The driver rolled down his window. "I'm not stopping in Portland. I'm driving straight through to Seattle."

"Yeah, but it's already almost three o'clock and by the time you get to Portland, won't the traffic be slow enough for me to jump out? It'll be rush hour, won't it?"

The truck driver chuckled. "Probably, come on in."

Rene ran to the other side of the Freightliner, climbed in, and closed the door. He reached his hand over to introduce himself. "My name's Johnny Gibson. I'm a guitarist in a rock band. What's yours?"

"Richard."

"Thanks for the ride, Richard. You don't know how much I appreciate it," Rene said honestly. He crossed his legs comfortably and relaxed. "Yes indeed, Richard, my wife's going to be surprised to see me."

CHAPTER 6

COACH GREG SLATER BLEW HIS WHISTLE, STOPPING THE PLAY short. He was irritated that it was taking so many tries to get the play right. "Come on, Moore! Ace right 28 Sweep, you are pulling, huh? It's a trap play; it won't work if you, meaning you," he grabbed Moore's face mask to get his attention, "aren't pulling to the right! Where's your head today?"

"I don't know, Coach," the junior left guard replied through his mouthpiece.

"Get your mind off of Suzy and pay attention to the play call!" Coach Slater said impatiently. He added to his entire team, "We've got a tough game Friday night. Trust me; the Bulldogs aren't coming here expecting to lose. Every play we mess up ourselves can cost us the game, and we can't afford another loss. If you guys want to reach the playoffs, then we have to win Friday night. So forget about your dates to the Halloween dance and pay attention to your assignments on every play! That means listening to the play!" He finished with a stern look at Bruce Moore in particular.

"Coach," the quarterback, Ross Greenfield, said with a slight chuckle, "Moore doesn't like Suzy; he likes Karen." Bruce's eyes widened in surprise as his round cheeks flushed red. Karen was Coach Slater's daughter. Some of the boys laughed.

"Shut up, Greenfield!" Greg snapped without any humor in his voice. "Ace Right 28 Sweep. Let's go!" He blew his whistle and stepped back to watch with his two assistant coaches.

The Middleton Giants weren't necessarily a state power-house football team, but they were usually in the running for the league title. Three teams generally battled for the league title and second place, which went to the state play-offs. Those three teams were the currently undefeated Brouwer Bulldogs, the Neeld Lions, and the Middleton Giants. The Bulldogs were leading the division now, and Neeld was one game behind them with one week left in the season. The Neeld Lions had beaten Middleton earlier in the season by a single touchdown, which was the only loss Middleton had. With one week left to play, it was a who's who to see which two teams represented their league in the playoffs. All eyes would be on Friday night's game to decide who would go to State, and it irritated Coach Slater that his players would giggle like schoolgirls over a boy's crush on his daughter.

He blew his whistle. "Better! Way to get the block, Moore. This play will score every time if everyone does their job. Let's run it again!"

"How many times are we practicing it?" one of the players named Curt Simpson complained as he took his position on the line.

Greg eyed his offensive tackle harshly. "Just like wrestling, repetitive motions over and over again create fluid actions in the field of play. Huh, Curt?" he asked his starting tackle and state-ranked heavyweight wrestler.

"Yes, Coach," he replied, knowing he was reprimanded.

"Let's run it again!"

"Coach," Greg heard from the sideline. It was the Middleton Police Chief, Harry Bishop. He was standing on the newly asphalted track that circled the football field. His blue and white patrol car was parked by the stadium's entry gate.

"Ohh, busted," one of the players commented playfully. Other players followed with similar lines.

Greg scowled at his players. "Let's get going, guys, come on!" He turned to his assistant coach Travis Lyman. "I'll be right back. Keep running this play until then," he said and walked over to Harry. "Hello, Harry, what can I do for you?"

"I'm sorry to disturb your practice, but what are you doing here? Shouldn't you be with your family?"

"Why would I be?" Greg asked, furrowing his brow questionably. A wave of fear began to spring through Greg's spine as the thought of Tina being in a car accident came to mind. The loud emergency alarm that sounded like a World War II air raid warning sounded earlier throughout the town. It alerted the volunteer fire department of an emergency call. "What are you talking about?" Greg asked. His voice showed a trace of his growing anxiety.

"Rene escaped from prison this morning. Didn't you know that?"

"What?" Greg asked with surprise. "How?"

Harry shrugged. "Apparently, he was part of an in-house maintenance program for the inmates. He was waxing the floors in a restricted area that his supervisor left him alone in, which he'd done numerous times before apparently. Anyway, today, the state boiler inspector came into the prison, and Rene apparently bludgeoned the guard and the inspector to death. He put on the inspector's clothes and walked out." Harry paused for a second. "He walked out and drove away in the inspector's car. But it's still early, and they have a description of the suspected vehicle. It's just a matter of time, Greg. Usually, these situations are swept up and have the suspect back in custody within hours."

"How?" Greg gasped, perplexed. "How can he just walk out of a maximum-security prison, Harry?" he asked anxiously. "Have they found him?"

Harry shook his head. "No, not yet. That's why I am

surprised to see you out here. I would've thought you'd be at home with Tina. You haven't heard about this?" Harry asked in disbelief.

"No! What time this morning did he walk out?"

"A little before noon."

"It's now four-thirty and I'm just hearing about this? He could already be here!" Greg stated irritably.

"Oh, I wouldn't think he's coming back here," Harry said confidently. "He's just gotten a dose of freedom after all of these years. He's going to run to Mexico or somewhere sunny. This is the only chance at freedom he's ever going to have; I don't think he'll waste it to come back to Middleton."

Greg shook his head in disbelief. "How does anyone just walk out of prison? Especially someone convicted of murder! For crying out loud!"

Harry opened his hands with a slight shrug of his shoulders. "I don't know. I know there's going to be an investigation into just that. As you can imagine, the prison's got a lot to answer for, and the media won't be kind. Which reminds me; don't be surprised if the news channels show up at your house. I just saw a news van pulling up at the park downtown."

Greg felt the air leave his body. "Have you told Tina yet?"

"No, but the state officials would've contacted her immediately."

"Thanks for letting me know, Harry. My phone's been off all day. I don't use it unless I need it," he explained. "I guess I better run home and tell Tina if she doesn't already know. So in your opinion, you don't think he'll come back here?" He observed Harry's expression looking for an honest answer.

Harry shook his head reassuringly. "Middleton has nothing to offer him. He's looking to escape prison, not go back to it. Go home and be with Tina. She's probably feeling a bit anxious if she heard. And I'm sure she has."

CHAPTER 7

GREG HAD GONE TO THE LOCKER ROOM TO GRAB HIS briefcase of class assignments to correct, and his clothes. He turned on his cell phone as he left the locker room office, he had five missed calls and three messages. Two of the missed calls were from Tina, but all three messages were from concerned family members. Tina had not left a message. He called Tina's cell phone but got a call-waiting signal. He ended the call and redialed as he walked towards his gray Dodge Ram truck across the parking lot. Again, he got the call-waiting signal. He pulled out of the back parking lot and drove around the front of the school and was surprised to see a van from Channel 5 News was parked in front of the school.

At the corner of the school, he turned left onto Vanderveld Road. It was a country road that dipped down over a bridge and then as it came back uphill, it curved sharply to the left. The next several miles of Vanderveld Road was perfectly straight, with flat crop fields on both sides of the road. An occasional farmhouse was scattered here and there, but primarily it was fields and working farmland. A mile and a half outside of Middleton, Greg slowed down to turn into his driveway on the left side of the road. He had five acres of land that fed his single steer and Karen's horse. Their property line was thick with briars and shrub trees along the fence lines, but their small farm was set alone surrounded by the barren fields of a harvested wheat crop. The nearest neighbor was more than a half-mile away. A white news van with a satellite dish on its top from Channel 9 News was parked on the road's shoulder across from their old white two-story farmhouse.

As Greg parked his truck beside Tina's Mountaineer, he noticed in his mirror the male reporter and his cameraman hurrying to cross the road to interview him. He grabbed his briefcase and duffel bag as he got out of the truck.

"Greg, you are Greg Slater, right?" the reporter asked as he approached. Greg recognized him from watching the news as John Travis. He was a clean-cut and persistent middle-aged man. The camera's light turned on as John continued. "Greg, my name's John Travis of Channel 9 News. I'd like to ask you about Rene Dibari's escape and how it's affecting you and Tina tonight?"

Greg shook his head and held up his hand to block the camera's light from his eyes as he walked towards the front door. "I don't have anything to say at the moment," he said without slowing down.

"Are you concerned that Rene might come back here? As you remember, he threatened to do so if he ever escaped. Is there any threat to your family?" John asked as Greg reached the front door.

Greg spoke to John kindly, "I'm sure there's not. Now please move back off of our property." He unlocked the front door and stepped inside.

"Greg, how's Rene's daughter taking the news?" was the last question Greg heard before he closed the door.

Tina stood in the middle of the family room watching Channel 9 news. The moment of Greg coming home was not on live TV. She was on the phone with an alarmed expression on her face. "Hold on, Mom. Where are the kids?" she asked Greg urgently.

"They're at practice," Greg replied. "What's the latest

news? Have they found him?" He set his briefcase and duffle bag down before walking around the entry half wall and into the large family room.

"Practice?" Tina gasped. "Why didn't you bring them home with you? For crying out loud! Rene's loose somewhere, and you left Karen at the school? Are you out of your mind? Go back and get our kids. You can't leave them there!" Her eyes glared at him the same way they had earlier that morning.

"They're at practice. The kids are fine. I'll pick them up when practice is over. There's no reason to panic."

Tina covered the speaker of her phone and spoke quietly yet vehemently, "Go get my daughter now! I don't want her alone until Rene's caught!"

John Travis knocked on the door.

Greg spoke quietly as not to be heard. "She's at volleyball practice."

"I don't care about volleyball practice! Go get my daughter. If you'd keep your phone on, I could've told you to bring her home. I don't even know why you have a phone; I can never get a hold of you."

"I can't answer my phone in the middle of class. You should've left a message or answered your phone when I called you back a few minutes ago."

John knocked on the door again. It was the only reason Tina didn't lose her composure and begin to yell. Her eyes held the venom as she sputtered, "I'm talking to my mother! She's very upset, as you might imagine if you weren't so damn self-centered. Now go get my daughter, dammit!"

"Fine, I'll go get the kids. You talk to your mom," he said irritably and walked to the front door. He opened it.

John Travis stood there with the camera on Greg. "Greg, if we could just have a moment..."

"Get off my property!" Greg demanded. "This is private property and you're trespassing. Don't come near our house again, or I'll call the police. Get out of my way!" he said as he brushed past John Travis. Greg turned around to face him.

"Get off of my property and stay off of it!" He turned back and walked quickly to his truck.

Greg drove to the school and parked in the back parking lot like usual. He walked out to the varsity football practice, called his team together, and had the players take a knee to explain what had happened. He told his son, Robert, to skip showering and get dressed so they could go home. Greg then approached the junior high wrestling coach and gathered his other son, Samuel. Both the boys were to meet him in the gym when they were ready to go.

Greg walked into the gymnasium, where the Middleton Volleyball team was nearing the end of practice. Instead of interrupting, he took a seat on the bottom bench of the bleachers. The gymnasium was a large hardwood floor with the usual athletic lines and basketball hoops at both ends. At the moment, a volleyball net stretched across the middle of the floor. A new scoreboard was mounted at one end of the gym and the other end were five large banners representing the other teams in their league, such as the Brouwer Bulldogs with a large orange and black bulldog snarling with large, sharp teeth. The Neeld Lions banner had a yellow and blue lion with a fierce glare and sharp claws as it pounced seemingly out of the banner.

Straight across from the bleachers hung red banners across the top of the wall with white writing that gave the years that each sport had won the league championship. State championship banners hung alongside the league championships for each particular sport that had won a state championship. The Middleton football banner had numerous league championships but only five state championship years on a banner beside it. The most successful sports were volleyball and wrestling. Both of those athletic teams had multiple league and state championships on their banners.

Greg held a particular pride in growing up in Middleton

and playing football in two state championship seasons. He had also wrestled on a state championship team and won two state titles himself. He was now the head coach of both the sports that he had loved and excelled at. However, his greatest pride wasn't looking at long ago successes that hung in the gym or that set behind newer awards in the school's trophy case in the main hallway. His greatest pride was watching his children excelling on their own in the same school he attended.

"Hello, Coach Slater," a young eighth-grade boy said as he walked by with an extra strut for the ladies at practice.

"Hello, Kevin," Greg said. He placed his hands behind his head and reclined against the next bench to watch the girls finish up. He would have pulled Karen from practice and gone back home, but he didn't want to reveal a sense of panic to his kids. He sat patiently and waited.

Karen Slater expertly lowered her body to dig out the ball and stepped back to watch her teammate set the ball while a third hit the ball over the net. The process was repeated somewhat the same, as the girls worked the ball back and forth over the net, under the critical eye of their coach.

This year's volleyball team was nearly undefeated and had already won the league championship with one season game left to play. They were practicing for the State Championship Tournament in Corvallis the following week. Karen was a big part of the team's success as the team captain and star athlete. Karen was much more valuable than just a good athlete; she kept a winning attitude and encouraged her teammates rather than condemning them when they made a mistake. Karen was a leader with a reassuring smile that encouraged her teammates to keep smiling and striving to win. She was the kind of team leader that coaches of every sport loved to have, hardworking, dedicated, athletic, and teachable. Many kids had the same natural athletic ability as Karen; some even had greater potential and instincts for the sport they played but fell short on heart, dedication, and, tragically, home support. Often those kids were lost along the way, and less naturally talented athletes excelled with hard work and earned college scholarships.

Every day, Greg tried to encourage his students and athletes to apply themselves and remain focused on the things in life that build a career, such as academics, athletics, and making responsible choices in their personal lives. Some students listened, some even paid attention, while others fell along the wayside. It could never be said that he didn't care about the Middleton youth. However, he was only responsible for his three children, Karen, a senior, Robert, a freshman, and Samuel was in seventh grade. So far, he and Tina had created a stable and loving home where their children learned priorities in their lives, God, family, education, personal responsibilities, commitments, and finally, friends. Greg took his responsibilities as a husband, father, teacher, friend, and coach very seriously. He knew firsthand just how easy it is for someone with great potential and an unlimited future to lose it all too quickly. Rene Dibari was Greg's friend and had every opportunity that Greg had, except for one. Rene's parents never encouraged him. They only discouraged him.

Being a parent of teens himself, Greg knew it was hard enough to encourage a teenager and keep their self-confidence up when all around them they are being put down. It is a vicious cycle of ups and downs and without a parent's approval and encouragement, what chance do some kids have? Every human being desires to be accepted by others and have a place where they fit in with good friends, but it is nearly an obsession for teenagers. It is a need that should be satisfied in their own home by a support team of the family that will always be there to accept and love them. Some homes offer no such warmth or loving-kindness, only wrath, violence, and soul-destroying words day after day. Greg had witnessed it all through high school at his friend Rene's house. He still saw it year after year in some of the students at Middleton High School. Greg had seen what poor parenting could do to a good friend of his; he also knew the same could happen to any one of his students that he spoke to every day. He also knew an honest compliment and an encouraging word could be long remembered in a student's life.

"Hi, Dad, what are you doing in here? Did you end practice early?" Karen asked as she walked over to Greg with her best friend beside her.

"No, I came to pick you and the boys up." He stood up from the bench seat of the bleachers.

Karen frowned. "Amanda and I were going into Ridgefield to look for Halloween costumes for the dance. Mom already said I could." Karen stood about the same height as her mother at five foot five inches tall with a thin but athletic body. Her shoulder-length brown hair was straight and in a ponytail at the moment, as she stood in her practice shorts and a T-shirt. She had beautiful big brown eyes and usually had a quick smile on her attractive face.

Greg shook his head without a smile. "No, you need to come home."

"Why, is something wrong? We're just going to the store, nowhere else."

Greg took a deep breath. "Rene escaped today. They don't know where he is. The media is already here at the school and at home. I need you to come home with me."

"Who's that?" Amanda asked with a questionable expression on her face. She was Karen's best friend.

Karen answered, more aggravated than concerned. "My biological father," she replied dryly.

"Oh, my gosh!" Amanda exclaimed.

Karen was unconcerned. "So? He's not coming here. Why can't I go to Ridgefield? It's not like he's waiting outside or anything."

Greg shared her reasoning, but for Tina's sake, he said, "I'm sorry, Karen, but you need to come home. He may not be outside, but the media is. Your mother wants you to come home now."

Karen was irritated. "Did you stop practice because of him escaping? Please tell me you didn't."

Greg smiled appreciatively. He loved her dedication to whatever she was committed to doing, and she gave her all to be better than the day before. She reminded Greg of himself sometimes. "No, I left to check on your mother, but practice is still going on."

"Is Mom scared? Is that why I can't go?"

"Karen, I said you're coming home. I don't need to explain further. Go get your stuff and let's go."

Karen rolled her eyes and turned away, followed by her friend. She turned back to Greg. "All of the good costumes are going to be gone if I can't go tonight. I have youth group tomorrow night and a game Thursday night. Tonight's the only night I can look for a Halloween costume for the dance, Dad. We planned it already with Mom."

"Whaa, whaa," Robert Slater said mockingly as he walked across the gym floor. He had changed into his clothes. He carried a backpack with his homework inside.

"Shut up, Robert!" Karen exclaimed, growing angry.

Robert laughed. "Hey, Amanda, are you going to ask me to the dance?"

Amanda shook her head without interest. "I think not."

Greg spoke, "I'm sorry, Karen. We'll have to figure that out later. Right now, you're needed at home. And Mom's waiting, so we need to go." He turned to Robert. "Where's Sam?"

"He's getting dressed. So how am I supposed to start in Friday's game when you pull me from practice? You're doing me a disservice, Dad; you should start me on varsity to make up for it."

Greg answered his son, "I really should, but I need to save you for the fourth quarter like all JV players."

"Come on," Robert pleaded.

Greg watched Karen walk into the girl's locker room

and realized for the first time how much she resembled Rene. She had his deep brown eyes and his quick wit. She shared some of his physical characteristics, such as how she walked, and her facial expressions were reminiscent of his. Momentarily, Greg felt a pang of sadness as he remembered the many good times he and Rene had together.

Greg met Rene on the first day of school in his seventh grade P.E. class in this very gym. They had almost gotten into a fight when Greg was getting a drink at the water fountain, and Rene pushed his head down into the water. Greg and Rene were both new students at Middleton and Rene was trying to make friends at Greg's expense. However, it had backfired, and they were quickly at odds but became best friends through junior high football season. There was no part of the gym where Greg couldn't think of a memory with Rene. They wrestled every home match in the gym, watched basketball games, went to dances in the gym, and created memories that would last a lifetime. They shared a lot of laughter in those years, but that was a long time ago. Rene was a good friend with a promising future until he traded it for a life of alcohol and drugs. What happened to Rene is what motivated Greg to reach as many of his students as possible, encourage them to seek higher expectations of themselves, and give one hundred percent to everything they do. It was especially true with his own kids.

CHAPTER 8

THE MEDIA HAD JUMPED ONTO RENE'S ESCAPE, MAKING IT THE top news story of every channel. The house phone had begun to ring, as well as Tina's cell phone with reporters from every form of media, TV news, newspapers, and radio news stations, all hoping to get an interview with Greg or Tina. Two mobile news vans were parked outside of their home, and another was giving a live report from the high school. The evening had erupted into an unexpected media frenzy as they'd never imagined since the sentencing of Rene fifteen years before. They had refused to talk to the media, despite the multiple tries by the news crews to contact them. They were locked within their home like prisoners because reporters swarmed to them like flies. When Greg and his kids returned home, they were pounced upon with the camera lights and two reporters asking questions as Greg walked with the kids to the front door. Now they dared not to step outside again. Every local channel told the same story, the details of what was known about the escape. However, Channel 5 broadcast live from the prison about the escape, while another crew reported live from the Slater's home about Rene's backstory involving Greg and Tina. Channel 7 broadcast live from the parking lot where they found Gary Baugh's Jeep and from

Middleton High School, where all the persons involved went to school together and where Greg now taught. Channel 9 broadcast live from the Slater's front yard and downtown Salem, Rene's last known location.

Inside the Slater's home, all the window blinds were closed as they watched the news, turning from channel to channel to see what was being said. Nothing new was known beyond finding the Jeep, and with nothing new to report. They reminded the viewers of that New Year's Eve fifteen years before, when Art Stewart had been murdered trying to protect his daughter, and Greg ran three blocks with a broken rib and a bullet in his thigh to save the life of the girl he loved, Tina Dibari, Rene's wife. The news resurrected the footage of the vicious threats Rene made at the sentencing hearing and replayed it repeatedly. It wouldn't be a story if they didn't mention that Greg had married Rene's ex-wife and raised Rene's only daughter in Middleton, Oregon. It was the same town they had all grown up in, and where Greg was now a teacher and football coach at the local high school. They even showed their home live on TV while the reporter stood in front of it and retold the same story again.

Tina was talking to a neighbor down the road on the house phone before hanging up. It immediately rang again. "Hello," she answered. After a short pause, she said, "I have no comment, thank you." Frustration was evident in her voice as she hung up the phone. Her father's picture had been shown on TV, as well as the sound of Rene's voice screaming through the footage shown from the courtroom years before. Tina was suddenly transported emotionally back to the day her father was murdered, and the emptiness of his presence consumed her. She remembered clearly the horrified expression on her mother's face while they kneeled over her father's body in the rain while Greg battled Rene to save her life. It started as just another hopeless day in her life until she and Rene had run into Greg outside of O'Leary's Market. An invitation to a small get-together at their house had turned into a nightmare. For so long, it haunted her to think that opening the door to let Greg into her house led to her father's death. She knew it wasn't Greg's, or her fault. The blame rested solely on Rene. However, it had taken years for her to release the guilt that she had lived with and get to a point where she could put that day behind her and celebrate New Year's Eve again. It was fifteen years ago, and all the heartache she had struggled through was brought back with full force at the sound of Rene's rage-filled voice in the courtroom. The unsettling truth was he was free, and no one knew where he was. She watched another clip of Rene threatening her while being dragged out of the courtroom. Tina knew him better than anyone, and she knew he was coming to find her to keep his promise. It terrified her completely and thoroughly. Wordlessly, she looked at Greg, and silently he walked over to her and put his arms around her. "I'll answer the phone from now on," he offered, sensing her frustration with the phone calls correctly but missing her deepest fears completely.

She put her arms around him for the comfort it brought. "I wish the police would hurry up and find him, so they'd leave us alone!"

"They'll leave eventually."

"Yeah, but I don't want my life broadcast on TV, Greg." She broke from his arms and took a step away. "I don't want Rene to see where we live or to see Karen on TV. I don't want him coming here, and if he sees that film of Karen on TV, he's going to come here!" Tears filled her eyes as she pointed towards the front of the house. Her chest heaved with every word while her hands shook uncontrollably. Her worst fears seemed to be unraveling before her very eyes. "They're telling him and everyone else everything about us, Greg! Where we live, what we do for a living, our children, they even showed Karen on the news! For crying out loud, is there no such thing as privacy anymore!"

"Tina, try to relax. Harry has his officers looking out for

us. We'll be fine. They'll find Rene soon enough. He has nowhere to go," Greg tried to calm his wife.

"Lord, I hope so. Jesus, please let them find him quickly," she prayed quietly.

Tina grimaced at the sound of the phone ringing. Greg answered it. "Hello...Oh, Pastor Dan...yeah, come on over. I just ask you not to mention Tina or Karen when the reporters surround you...Okay, I'll see you in a few, bye." He hung up the phone. "Pastor Dan's coming over," he announced.

The news was showing a photograph of Rene taken from the prison identification file. He was middle-aged and had short black hair that was greased thickly and combed straight back over his head, with a medium-length goatee and a menacing sneer on his toughened face. The innocence of Rene's youth had grown as dark and bitter as the eyes that stared into the camera with a cold and emotionless glare. Rene's neck and shoulders appeared quite muscular, with evidence of the green ink typical of prison tattoos. Although they had shown the same photograph throughout the day, it still sent a cold chill down Tina's spine. He looked like a dangerous caged animal just waiting to be released. And most terrifyingly, he was.

"Ooh, he's ugly," Karen said, unaffected by the photograph. She was sitting in a recliner watching the news. She stood up with her usual light-hearted smile on her lips. "I don't think Rene's my father. Did you and Dad have something going on when you got pregnant, Mom? Because I get my good looks from you and Dad," she finished with an accusing nod of her head. "You and Dad did, huh, Mom?"

Tina smiled slightly, despite her growing anxiety. "No, sweetheart, I'm afraid Rene is your biological father."

Karen shook her head doubtfully. "I don't believe it. Dad, you and Mom, had something going on, huh?"

Greg shook his head with a slight grin. "Unfortunately, not."

"Oh well, you're my daddy anyway," she said with a

cheerful shrug and walked into the kitchen, texting on her phone. She asked loudly from the kitchen, "Dad, have you fed Candy tonight, or are you too scared to go to the barn?" She giggled to herself. Candy was the six-year-old bay mare that she used as a show horse for her 4-H group. She rode Candy in parades during the summer months, when not riding around the farm or town. Karen loved to ride whenever she could.

Greg chuckled. "No, as a matter of fact, I haven't. Will you come out there with me?"

"Sure, I'm not afraid."

Twelve-year-old Samuel Slater was sitting quietly at the dining room table with his homework laid out before him. He hadn't done any of it, as he'd been preoccupied with the news and the overwhelming realization that his family was the focus of every news channel. He could see the TV clearly from the table and hear the conversations around him. It overwhelmed him, but it was the photograph of Rene that scared him the most. It made Rene Dibari a real man and a real threat that petrified him. Listening to Karen's light-heartedness towards the situation was more than Samuel could stand. He glared at his older sister and shouted fearfully, "He's your father. He won't kill you, but what about the rest of us, huh? He's going to kill Mom, Dad, Robert, and me!" His eyes suddenly grew thick as a puddle with tears. He stood up quickly to walk towards his room.

"Samuel," Greg said with a mixture of concern and surprise. "He's not coming here." Greg stepped over to his son and caught him by the shoulders gently. Tina watched quietly but covered her mouth emotionally at the sight of her terrorized boy.

Karen stepped out of the kitchen holding a celery stalk in her hand. There was a perplexed expression. "He's not my father, Sam. I have nothing to do with him!"

"Yes, he is!" Samuel yelled at her. "You're the only reason he'd come here. Mom just said so. If he kills Mom, it's your fault!"

Karen responded quickly by shouting, "He's not coming here, Sam! He's not my father; I don't even know who he is, so why are you blaming me? I have nothing to do with him!"

"Yeah, you do!" Samuel persisted.

"No, I don't! I've never even met him, you idiot!"

"Don't call me an idiot!" Sam yelled.

"Stop it!" Greg yelled over his two kids. "Both of you, stop it!" The last thing he wanted was to give the news reporters something else to report as they waited outside. He knew they'd love to listen in and broadcast the kids fighting live on the air.

"No, Dad," Samuel said fearfully. He pointed at Karen and explained as a tear finally fell from his eyes. "He's a killer, and he could come to our house because of her!"

"He has no reason to come here!" Karen explained heatedly. "What do you want me to do about it anyway, Sam? You're so stupid!" Samuel's thick tears fell from his eyes, but just beyond the tears, she could see the panic in his eyes. Karen paused just long enough to recognize that her brother was afraid, but she was being blamed for something she had no more to do with than Samuel did. It wasn't right, and she wasn't going to put up with it.

Samuel continued, "And your father's a murderer!"

"Maybe he'll kill you!" Karen spat out like a lethal poison in response.

Greg pointed his finger at Karen and yelled, "Enough! Don't you ever talk to your brother like that again!"

"But..."

"Shut your mouth!" He warned her with a pointed finger. He turned towards Samuel to speak.

Karen couldn't resist. "He's the one attacking me!"

"I am not," Samuel replied quickly.

"Of course, you are! What else would you call it?"

"Well, Mom said it's your fault!"

Tina was shocked. "I said no such thing!"

"He's not coming here!" Karen yelled, losing her composure while her eyes filled with tears of frustration. Rene was a stranger and would have no reason to come to Middleton. Even if he was her father, he didn't know her, and she didn't care about him. To think he'd come to their house to meet her or to keep an old vendetta was ridiculous. He was running for his life, just like her dad had said.

Greg turned Samuel towards the couch in the family room. "Go! Don't say another word, Sam, and go sit down, right now!" He paused as Tina put her arm around Samuel and escorted him into the family room to sit down by him. Greg looked at Karen disapprovingly. "He's scared, Karen. You should be old enough to recognize that and reassure him, not argue with him."

Karen spoke openly, "He's saying I'm to blame if Rene comes here, Dad. How would you feel? I don't even know who he is, but suddenly there are TV cameras outside, and I'm *his* daughter! I'm not his daughter, Dad. I'm your daughter," she said with thick tears falling from her eyes. She turned her head to hide them and crossed her arms. "I find all of this ridiculous!"

Greg stepped forward and put his hand on her shoulder affectionately. He turned her chin to look at him with his other hand. Her eyes were wet with thick tears that she quickly wiped away. "Listen to me, sweetheart, you are *my* daughter and I love you very much. There's nobody in this world that can tell me you're not. You're my only daughter and I'm very proud of you. Don't ever forget that." He hugged Karen. "Don't let Sam coerce you into a fight. He's just scared at the moment, sweetheart," he said while holding her.

"Are you scared, Dad? Do you think we have any reason to worry?" she asked as he ended the hug. For the first time, a look of genuine concern crossed Karen's expression.

"Scared? No," he answered. "But it is unsettling to have him out there somewhere. He is a murderer, Karen, but I don't think we have anything to worry about."

"Mom's scared."

"She is. In fact, let's take this conversation into the

family room so Sam can hear it too. But don't argue with him. With all of the news and commotion going on, how can he not be afraid? Give him some grace, and let's discuss it."

"I'll try, but if he attacks me..." Karen said through a mischievous smile. She was comforted by her father's reassuring words and embrace.

Tina sat on the couch with her arm around Samuel's shoulders. She spoke to him softly, trying to reassure him that there was nothing to worry about. However, her doubts and fear spoke louder than her calming words. Tina was relieved to see Greg and Karen walk into the family room with a sense of strength evident on their faces. For a moment, Tina was envious of her daughter's relationship with Greg. She knew Karen found her strength in Greg; he kept her safe, and she could rest in that. Tina looked to Greg for the same sense of security and felt a certain comfort when he sat down on the other side of Samuel on the couch. "Hey, big guy, how are you doing?" He gave a soft slap to Samuel's leg as he asked.

Karen sat down in one of the two recliners. She kicked her legs over the side of the armrest to face her family on the couch.

"Fine," Samuel replied while staring at the floor.

Tina spoke, "He's worried that Rene will come here to hurt us." Her blue eyes revealed her anxiety. She needed to hear some comforting words of reassurance from Greg herself. She needed him to protect her as he had all those years before to make her feel safe in her own home.

Greg paused when he gazed into Tina's eyes. It had been a long time since she had looked at him like that. He offered her a soft loving smile and then spoke confidently, "I was just telling Karen that I don't think we have any reason to worry about him. Right now, he's hiding from the police. That's what he's doing. He won't come back to Middleton, he'd be recognized immediately, and he knows that. So he has his plate full just trying to figure out how to get out of Oregon. Rest assured, we're the last thing on his mind."

Samuel was unconvinced. "We're on TV, Dad. If he sees us, he'll think about us. Mom said so."

"Son," Greg said softly, "Rene's running from the law. The last thing he wants is to go back to prison. If he comes here, he'll go back to prison. There are too many people that know him here."

Samuel shifted in his seat and said, "He wanted to kill you and Mom. I saw it on the news." His voice shook with anxiety.

"That was a long time ago, Sam. We have nothing to worry about, Son."

"Mom's worried! If we don't have anything to worry about, then why is she worried?" he questioned quickly.

Greg took a deep breath. "Because of what happened in the past. It's the past that's scaring her. Trust me, Sam; you have nothing to worry about."

The sound of someone dashing down the stairs ended as Robert jumped off the last few stairs. "Worried about what?" he asked no one in particular. He had showered and changed into a pair of sweatpants and a gray Middleton wrestling T-shirt with the sleeves cut off. Robert had just turned fifteen, and though he was only a freshman, he was quite muscular for his age. It was a benefit of having the football and wrestling coach as his father. They had spent a lot of time together in the weight room and on the wrestling mat.

Samuel answered his older brother, "Rene Dibari coming here to kill us."

The doorbell rang. "Oh, Sam," Robert said, fearless of Rene's escape, as he went towards the door. "Dad will kick his ass if he showed up here, just like he did the first time. So relax." He opened the door carelessly. "Pastor Dan, come on in," he said enthusiastically and held the door open a moment longer to flex his biceps in case the news channels were reporting live.

Pastor Dan Carter was in his mid-fifties with short, balding brown hair, a touch of gray around the edges, and a clean-shaven round face. Beneath his silver-rimmed glasses, his blue eyes revealed a quick wit and a joyful sense of humor. He was of average height and overweight by most standards, with a large belly. As always, Pastor Dan carried his Bible and offered a pleasant smile as he came inside. "Hello, everyone."

"Come sit down, Dan. Take the recliner there." Greg pointed to the recliner beside Karen. The two recliners were separated by a small table with a built-in lamp. Greg continued as Pastor Dan sat down. "We were just trying to talk to Samuel; he's afraid Rene will come here."

"Oh," Pastor Dan said, losing his smile to show some sincere concern, as he sat down comfortably. "That is a scary thought, but I wouldn't worry too much about that, do you know why?" he asked Sam.

Samuel shook his head wordlessly.

"Because with all of the news attention being brought to Middleton and especially your family, there's no way he'd show up here. He'll be arrested pretty soon, and this will be over."

"What if it's not, though, Pastor Dan?" Sam asked.

Tina added, "That's kind of my question too. If they don't catch him, I will never feel secure as long as he's out there somewhere. I'm sitting here trying to reassure my son that we have nothing to fear, but I think I'm more afraid than Sam is. I know what Rene is capable of, Pastor Dan. I've seen it." she said with a breaking voice and tears filling her eyes. She knew Pastor Dan thought she was referring to the night her father was killed or the spousal abuse she suffered. However, she was thinking back to a particular August afternoon many years ago when Rene took her along with him and Manny to go swimming. Tina sat in the backseat next to Karen's car seat while Rene and Jose went to pick up a young man Tina had never seen before named Tim. Tim was hesitant to get into the car, but after seeing

Tina and a baby in the backseat, he relaxed and got inside the car with them.

Rene and Manny offered Tim a beer as they drove out of town towards the river. They found an isolated gravel pullout along the road and walked down through the thick brush to the river. There was no warning, and there was no sign of its coming when Rene turned around and hit Tim with a stunning blow to his face. Tim fell to the ground immediately and covered up to block Manny's kicks as best he could. Rene kicked him a few times too, and then ran up to the car and came back down with his wooden club that Rene had drilled the center out and melted lead into the hole. He began to beat Tim with the club on the arms, legs, ribs, and once on the head before Manny pulled him back to stop Rene from killing him. Tim was left bleeding on the riverbed with a broken arm and possibly other broken bones. He was in so much pain that he wasn't even trying to protect himself anymore, let alone move. Tina watched in horror while she tried to hide her daughter's eyes from the brutal beating. Rene grabbed a half case of beer and walked back towards where Tina held their daughter.

Rene said, "Maybe you are worth something. He wouldn't have gotten into the car if you weren't with us." They drove away, leaving a young man named Tim to suffer on the riverbank alone. Tim survived; the newspaper reported that three Mexicans had beaten him in a racial attack. It was the only time Tina had witnessed Rene's brutality toward someone other than herself, but she knew there were other victims. She occasionally heard about his brutality from others and saw his blood-stained clothes sometimes in the laundry.

Pastor Dan frowned in thought and then answered Tina, "I think it's perfectly natural to be afraid under the circumstances. It's a threat to the security of your home, and when the security of your home is threatened, everything else no longer matters, does it?"

Tina shook her head. "No," she admitted. "This morning,

I was stressed about a sell that may not close; I couldn't care less about that right now."

Dan nodded. "The epicenter of our lives is security. We grow up and invest in our futures just so we can build our home, and our lives revolve around our home, meaning, our family. When our family is threatened, like yours is, it's natural to become afraid." He paused for a moment. "I mean, it's natural to fear, but as a Christian, you should know that the Bible says God will protect His people. Jesus said He is the good shepherd, and He will protect His sheep. As Christians, we are watched over, protected, and even commanded not to fear because He is with us. I once heard a great quote that says, 'fear is the opposite of faith.' So, Tina, do you believe the Lord could protect you if He wanted to?"

"Yes, of course, but what if…" she stopped as she considered Samuel. "I do."

Pastor Dan looked at Samuel. "What about you, Sam? Do you believe Jesus could protect your family?"

Samuel answered with a quivering voice, "I guess, but he's invisible, and Rene isn't."

Pastor Dan tilted his head thoughtfully for a moment and then opened his Bible. "Well, Sam, I want to read you a couple of verses that I think might help bring you some comfort. Listen to this out of Second Kings Chapter Six, verses fifteen through seventeen.

'When the servant of the man of God got up and went out early the next morning, an army with horses and chariots had surrounded the city. "Oh, my lord, what shall we do?" the servant asked. "Don't be afraid," the prophet answered. "Those who are with us are more than those who are with them." And Elisha prayed, "Oh Lord, open his eyes so he may see." Then the Lord opened the servant's eyes, and he looked and saw the hills full of horses and chariots of fire all around Elisha.'" Pastor Dan closed his Bible and explained, "You see, Elisha and his servant were surrounded by an entire army sent to retrieve them. That would be scary to almost anyone, but not Elisha, because he knew God was protecting them, just like he is you. Yes, our Lord is invisible, but so is the wind. We know wind exists, though, don't we, because we can feel it and see what it does all around us. The exact same is true with the Lord; we can see what He's doing around us, and we can feel what he does to us inside. The evidence is the same."

"Hmm, I never thought about that," Samuel said thoughtfully.

"My friends," Pastor Dan continued, "I knew coming over here that there would probably be some anxiety over Rene's escape. I wanted to offer some Bible verses that you might take refuge in, and there are many to choose from. I chose the story that I read as a visual reminder that God is invisible, but He is still there. Just because it looks like we're alone doesn't mean we are. Even when it feels like we've been abandoned by God, it doesn't mean we have been. God promises never to abandon His children, not even when we abandon Him," he said with a gentle gaze towards Tina.

He continued after a short pause, "Jesus said He is the good shepherd, and we are His sheep. A good shepherd will protect the sheep; that's why the shepherds are there, to begin with. So when the wolf comes knocking, you can be sure that the Lord is there. His sheep can rest easily because Jesus is the shepherd. Trust me, our Shepherd doesn't sleep, and He has his eye on you. So, rest in your Lord and relax. Faith and fear don't mix. It's like saying, 'I'm going to go clean my hands in the sewer pond before dinner.' No, 'perfect faith casts away fear.' Now, how about we pray and ask the Lord for His protection and peace upon your family."

CHAPTER 9

RON MYERS WAS EIGHTEEN YEARS OLD AND A SENIOR AT Middleton High School. He lived with his mother in a small two-bedroom trailer house on the east side of town, near the sewage ponds along the river. They lived in a small lower-income mobile home park filled with single-wide trailers with built-on carports. Ron parked his 1972 Datsun 510 Wagon under their carport, to use the outside lights to finish tightening the battery cables and protect him from the rain. He had to remove the battery to tighten the alternator belt, which regularly loosened every few days. With his hands slightly greasy, he finished the last drink of beer before tossing the empty can into a corner of the carport. Three black garbage bags filled with cans and bottles were piled in the same corner.

Ron closed the hood of his car and lit a cigarette and breathed in the smoke while he stared at his car. It was fifty years old and, therefore, a classic. It was bright orange with black interior, and aside from a few dings and tears, it was a beautiful car. He bought it for less than a thousand dollars that he earned, and he loved it. No one else had a car like it and probably hadn't in many years. He worked every Friday night through Monday night at a gas station in Ridgefield to pay for his car and other areas of entertainment. He had no interest in after-school activities. Ron didn't have any great affection for school at all. He enjoyed very few classes and had never made many friends. Middleton was a small-town school with many little tight-knit cliques that mingled within a larger social circle that rarely accepted outsiders into their group of friends. Ron had moved to Middleton as a freshman and learned immediately that he wasn't accepted. He wasn't outgoing, he wasn't athletic, and his family wasn't from Middleton. The other social outcasts welcomed Ron at Middleton High, and those were his friends.

Ron wasn't a bad-looking young man; he was about five foot nine inches tall with an average build with more flab than muscle tone. He had curly light brown hair that fell over his ears and a mustache, which appeared to be more like peach fuzz than whiskers. His face was rounded, but his lifeless dark brown eyes revealed his indifference to the world around him. Though indifferent and embittered, his eyes were his most prominent feature.

Ron looked out to the private trailer park's gravel driveway and saw his friend, Eddy Franklyn, walking in the rain towards his house. Eddy was a few inches taller than Ron but so thin he almost appeared fragile. Eddy had long light-brown hair that fell to his shoulders like a wet noodle. Eddy's clean-shaven face was long, narrow, and appeared sunken by malnourishment, though most people considered it was from the drugs he was known for using.

Eddy walked under the carport and pointed back towards town. "Dude, there's a news channel at the school. I wonder what that's about?"

Ron shrugged. "Probably the football game Friday night. So what's going on?"

"Yeah!" Eddy exclaimed. "You're probably right. Hey, dude, I scored some weed from my old lady if you want a hit."

"Awesome. Come on in," Ron said and led Eddy onto the small porch and into their trailer home.

"Where's your new dad?" Eddy asked with a laugh.

Ron gave Eddy a threatening glare. "Don't say that again; don't even joke about it!"

Eddy laughed. "I was kidding! Where is he, though? He doesn't like me much, you know."

Ron opened the fridge and pulled out two more cans of beer. He handed one to Eddy. "Jeff went to Ridgefield to pick up my mom from work; they must've gone to the store on the way home," Ron said and took a drink. He sighed. "I hate that guy. The longer he's here, the more I hate him. He doesn't like me either."

"I don't know what your mom sees in him," Eddy stated while he pulled a small amount of marijuana in a plastic bag out of his pants pocket along with a small blue metal pipe. The burn marks around the bowl proved it was used often.

Ron nodded towards the door. "Let's take that out back behind the carport. If Jeff smells it, he might use that to start a fight. We're drinking his beer, so he's going to be mad anyway, but…"

"I get it. Let's go, man. I don't want big old Jeff catching me drinking his beer," Eddy said and moved to the door, followed by Ron.

Ron's mother, Wendy Myers, worked on the assembly line of a manufacturing company in Ridgefield. She had divorced Ron's father many years before and since then had multiple boyfriends. Most of her boyfriends moved in with her and Ron. It never failed that almost all of them turned out to be alcoholics with a bad temper once the newness of the relationship had worn off. Inevitably, the arguing progressed to shouting and then to physical fighting. Ron had come to his mother's aid many times to protect her from the men she brought home.

Like usual, Wendy met Jeff at the bar and brought him into their home. He was a big burly man with a large belly and jet-black hair and beard. He was a truck driver by trade but no longer drove due to his disabled back. Jeff now collected his disability checks and lounged around their house drinking beer and taking his prescription drugs. Like so many of Wendy's boyfriends, Jeff was becoming more controlling over their home. It was getting to the point where Ron could hardly stand living in his own house, but despite his multiple arguments and pleas, Wendy would not risk losing the love she swore she'd finally found. It appeared Jeff wouldn't be leaving anytime soon.

The impatient honking of a car horn brought Ron from behind the carport to the driveway. On the main road, Jeff sat in the driver's seat of Wendy's red Pontiac Firebird with his window rolled down. He yelled impatiently, "Get that piece of crap out of my driveway! Hurry up." He rolled the window up and spoke heatedly to Wendy, words that Ron couldn't hear.

"It's not your driveway!" Ron shouted irritably and then climbed into his car and backed it out of the carport to park his car on the gravel road. He stepped out into the rain and walked towards the carport where Jeff was opening the trunk. His mother, Wendy, was standing beside him. She was five foot eight with a full figure, though still shapely in her tight blue jeans and snuggly-fit, button-up red flannel shirt. She had shoulder-length brown hair with frost highlights and an oblong-shaped face that was fairly attractive, despite looking older than her thirty-seven years of age. The years of smoking, drinking, hardship, and abuse had left their toll in her hazel-colored eyes. She appeared tired and worn down by a life of defeat and disappointment. As a result, she seldom smiled without a drink in her system and a cigarette in her hand. Bitterness laid heavily in her eyes as she looked out on the world.

She turned to Ron. "Why are all the news channels in town? Did something happen?"

Ron shrugged. "I don't know." He was irritated by Jeff already.

Jeff reached into the trunk and grabbed his case of beer. He turned to Ron. "This parking spot is for your mother's car, not yours, got it? Now carry the groceries in and help put them away," he ordered and carried the beer inside.

"You know better than to park your car here," Wendy said quietly. "I need to know what's going on. I saw a news lady talking live by the high school and another one downtown. Something's happening," she said with a sense of excitement in her voice. She walked quickly inside, carrying her purse, lunch box, and grocery bag.

"Help me carry these in," Ron said to Eddy. He grabbed two plastic grocery bags.

Wendy had already turned on the news and was standing in the middle of the small family room. Jeff sat on his favorite end of the sofa with a beer and a cigarette, watching the news as well. Ron and Eddy busied themselves putting the groceries away when they heard the word "Middleton" being spoken on the news. Ron asked from the kitchen, "Are they talking about the football game?"

"No," his mother answered with her attention on the TV.

Jeff answered Ron with disgust evident in his voice, "If you weren't such a candy ass, you'd be playing on the football team."

"Like you?" Ron asked equally sarcastically.

"Yeah, like me. I wasn't afraid of getting hurt on the football field. We were men back when I was your age. Now you guys are a bunch of dancing..."

"Don't!" Wendy warned, glaring at Jeff with a pointed finger. It was an argument she had heard fifty times before and didn't want to hear it again.

Jeff changed his phrasing. "Well, it's true. We were men back then. Now all these kids are sissies!"

"What happened?" Ron asked pointedly, "You're not much of a man now."

Jeff cast a hardened glance towards Ron. "I fell off the trailer of my truck, you little smart-mouthed bastard! I broke my back. That's what happened, you disrespectable little..."

"Stop it!" Wendy lashed out, "I'm trying to hear this. Ronny, do you know who they're talking about?"

Ron and Eddy stepped into the living room and listened to the news anchor tell the story about Rene Dibari's escape from prison and the history of his crime in Middleton fifteen years before. The news anchor revealed that the former Boise State football star whose career was ended by Rene was now married to Rene's ex-wife and raising Rene's only daughter in Middleton. Though the reporter didn't mention Karen's name, she did say that Tina was a Ridgefield realtor and Greg was now the head coach of the varsity football team.

"Daaamn!" Ron said and then laughed. "Did you know Karen's not Mister Slater's daughter?" he asked Eddy.

Eddy shrugged. "No."

"Do you know her?" Wendy asked.

Ron spoke through a mischievous grin, "Yeah, I know her. She's the biggest bitch in school. Miss Perfect isn't so perfect after all." He laughed. "I can't wait to see her tomorrow!"

"Is she pretty?" Wendy asked.

"Beautiful," Eddy answered quietly.

"Oh, she's pretty, but she's stuck up," Ron offered with a touch of excitement in his dull eyes.

Jeff grabbed the Saturday paper sports section and opened it up. "Here is her picture, Wendy." He handed the paper to her.

Wendy stared at Karen's picture. It was a standard head and shoulder photograph of a smiling young lady with an article about the volleyball team. "Oh, she is beautiful! Much prettier than your Gina girlfriend and quite an athlete, too, it appears. You should ask her out, Ronny."

Eddy chucked. "He did. That's why he doesn't like her!"

"Oh," Wendy said sensitively.

"Shut up, Eddy! I wouldn't ask her out if she was the last girl alive. And Gina's my ex-girlfriend, Mom," he said of his off-and-on girlfriend, Gina Wickering. They had broken up again just a week before.

Jeff cast a sideways glance at Ron. "Unlike Gina, this girl's too good for you anyway. She's got a future ahead of her."

Ron glanced at Jeff with contempt and then back at the TV. "Yeah, I can't wait to see Karen tomorrow. I wonder if anyone knew about this?"

CHAPTER 10

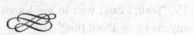

RENE DIBARI STOOD AT THE FOOT OF THE DOUBLE BED watching a nineteen-inch TV set on a narrow, badly stained three-drawer dresser. The 'Sanderson Motel' was a rundown den of cheap dirty rooms for twenty dollars a night used by the nearly homeless, prostitutes, pimps, and drug dealers. It was slightly hidden just off Portland's 82nd Avenue on a dark side street. It was the kind of place that contained a small bathroom, a double bed with quite possibly dirty sheets, two old, stained, cloth-covered chairs, and a three-drawer dresser with an old TV placed on top of it. The stale, musty odor of mold and cigarette smoke filled the room.

His new trucker friend dropped Rene off just a few blocks off 82nd Avenue on Interstate 205. For a while, Rene wandered, not knowing what to do now that he was mixing with Portland's rush hour traffic. He wore his long dark wig and new clothes, knowing he wouldn't draw much attention in the daylight hours, but with the gray day's light fading fast, he knew he needed to get indoors before the police took notice of him. He had money and ate a hamburger and fries before walking another few blocks to sit and rest at a covered bus stop. He was tired and exhaustion began to take over. At the bus stop, a woman wearing a fake leopard-skin coat and a high-cut skirt asked if he wanted to have a good time. She was a prostitute in her late thirties and had known a rough life, as it showed on her aged face. She had mentioned the 'Sanderson Hotel,' which was just around the corner if he paid for the room. Rene offered her an extra fifty dollars if she would rent the room in her name for the next five days. She did. When her services were rendered, she left his motel room with cash in her purse, and that was all that mattered to her.

Rene locked the door and removed the wig after she had left. He turned on the TV with interest in watching the news. The breaking story was his escape and the double murder of the corrections officer and the state boiler inspector Gary Baugh, whose Jeep Liberty was found in a Salem downtown parking lot. Little more was known of Rene's whereabouts, so with nothing more to report than the escape of an inmate sentenced to life in prison, the media focused on the backstory and went to Rene's hometown to interview the town's people and, most desirably, his ex-wife and daughter. Rene's chest tightened. He found his breath being sucked out of him as he watched his past come to life before his very eyes. Earlier footage showed his old friend Greg and his daughter Karen making their way towards the front door. The camera zoomed in on Karen, who tried to hide her face.

Rene watched his daughter walk quickly past the cameras and then glance back before stepping inside. He took notice of every detail of her face in the few seconds she was shown. She wore sweatpants and a sweatshirt with 'Middleton Volleyball' on the back with a volleyball logo between the words. Her brown hair was in a ponytail; she looked the part of a skilled and athletic volleyball player. It brought a proud slight smile to Rene's lips. When she turned to glance back at the camera, a quick glimpse of her face had stunned Rene. His baby girl had become beautiful. It took his breath away as he stepped backward in awe and sat on the end of the bed. The moment was quickly over, though, and the reporter asked Greg a question. Greg glanced into the camera with his stern expression before he followed Karen into the house.

Rene sat slack jawed at the foot of the bed, unable to breathe and filled with conflicting emotions that he never expected to feel. He was overwhelmed. He had expected his escape to make the news, but he never expected to see the coverage of his hometown or his daughter. Karen had grown up to become quite a beautiful young lady, but it wasn't him that got the opportunity to raise her. Greg Slater got the privilege of raising his daughter and knowing that filled Rene with a certain resentment that he hadn't felt that clearly in years. Throughout the rest of the night, Rene watched the news repeatedly, as much as he could on every channel that reported the story for another view of his daughter. Though he never saw a different clip of Karen, he did watch the same footage once more later that night.

By eleven, there was still nothing new to report about his escape. Another report unrelated but interesting to Rene was the concerned Salem family that said their husband, father, and grandfather, Jack Miller, was missing. The picture of Jack on TV showed a cheerful silver-haired gentleman with a friendly smile and joy-filled eyes. He disappeared after leaving his retirement facility in his silver Buick to go to an appointment, in which he had never returned. Rene toyed with the idea of calling the news to tell them where they could find him. But he knew he was better off if he remained invisible. Jack was a nice man, but he was a necessary means for money and transportation. Rene didn't want to kill him, but he was forced to as a means of survival.

Rene turned off the lights and lay on the bed with the TV left on. His thoughts were not on his escape or even guilt for the three men he murdered. He couldn't get Karen's facial features off his mind. He had loved a few people in his lifetime, but there was only one person who had never betrayed him. The only love he had left was for his daughter. It hit him with such force that it filled his chest with a strange and unexplainable pressure. He had forgotten how much he loved her. In a very unexpected powerful way, his love for her bloomed like a long-overdue seed sprouting after a fifteen-year drought. It broke his heart to not be a part of his daughter's life after seeing her again on the news.

Strangely, and ever so unlike him, he felt the hot tears run down his face. Painfully he realized, Karen would not have any memories of him. His daughter did not know how much she meant to him. Even so, he would mean nothing to her. Perhaps the most tragic of life sentences is a life spent loving someone so completely and thoroughly and never being loved in return. The tears that burned Rene's eyes were merely a drip of the painful loss and emptiness that swelled within him. There was no worse sentence in life than a life lived with unreturned love.

CHAPTER 11

THE KATHRYN E. RUPP REAL ESTATE OFFICE WAS ON THE corner of First and Pilcher Streets in the heart of Ridgefield's beautiful downtown historic district. The location couldn't be better as the downtown business association worked hard to attract tourism to its many stores and businesses. Though once known as a sleepy farm town, Ridgefield was now becoming a first-class community known for its many wineries and up-scale fine dining restaurants and inns providing all the amenities for the tourists who came to taste the various wines. The green vertical rows of vineyards replaced the wheat and hay fields that once covered the low-lying rolling hills with the golden evidence of a successful crop. The fertile ground and mild climate of the Willamette Valley, matching that of France, made for the perfect conditions for growing Pinot-Noir grapes to produce first-class Pinot Noir wine. To many wine connoisseurs, the Willamette Valley's Pinot-Noir surpassed Nampa Valley's and matched, if not surpassed, some of France's own finest wines. Investors and wine enthusiasts had brought new life into Ridgefield's economy, and even third-generation farmers were now leasing out fields to the grape growers. For others lucky enough to own property or other small communities, housing developers were buying up their fields bordering Ridgefield to annex into the city limits and build on to meet the demand for a quickly expanding population. Ridgefield had evolved into a beautiful community and a popular retirement destination with a wide range of tasting rooms, upscale shopping, and coffee houses taking over its once blue-collar historic downtown.

Tina Slater was a respected name in the real estate market. Being right in the middle of historical First Street's busy foot traffic, she had every opportunity to make her name a community staple when it came to buying or selling a home. She was known for being forthright, honest, and a true fighter for getting her clients' homes for close to their desired price. Tina was all business; it was what she knew and enjoyed about her profession. Generally, she strolled into her office with a smile for her co-workers and a determined expression when she sat down at her desk. However, on this day, she lacked both the smile and the focus of her determination. She was visibly troubled, withdrawn, and frightened. Rene's murderous escape from prison had shaken her foundation to its core. She could not get Rene off her mind. She knew his criminal mindset better than anyone else, and despite what Greg and the police said, it would surprise her if Rene did not try to find her. With that expectation stirring in her heart, she found herself looking at everyone that passed by her office windows with the slight relief that it wasn't Rene. She expected to see him looking at her through the window at any moment. Salem was twenty miles or so from Middleton and twenty-five miles from Ridgefield. Rene could walk that distance in one night if he wanted to. While Greg slept peacefully and was confident that Rene was running for the Mexican border, Tina couldn't sleep. Rene was free, unaccounted for, and had nearly sixteen years of rage built up within him and had the opportunity to avenge it. She couldn't imagine him turning away from a chance to hurt her. She had seen his violent side and the insidious means by which he set up his victims. He was cold, calculating, and an opportunist whose criminal mindset reasoned well under pressure. She could not imagine him becoming overwhelmed by being outside and giving up, or as Greg seemed to think, being lost in the modern age of technology. Greg reasoned that Rene would be caught anytime, but Tina wasn't so sure about that. Rene was street-smart and knew how to remain unnoticed and under the police radar. He had done it for the whole time they were married while running drugs and collecting from those who owed. He had outwitted the police back then, and she wasn't so sure he wouldn't do it again, at least for long enough for him to find her.

Despite Pastor Dan coming over to their home and trying to comfort her worries, and despite the extra patrols around their isolated home by the Middleton and county police departments, Tina had slept very little. Every creaking sound and every stirring of Greg's sleep suddenly jerked her awake in a new moment of panic. It had been a long night, and she was tired. But the fact was until Rene was found, she could not let her guard down.

To her relief, there were no news vans outside of her house that morning. She didn't want her face shown on TV being identified as Rene's ex-wife. She had worked too hard over the years to have her past dug up and relived for the world to see. She was already horrified to see their home being shown on the news. Even though she was not shown in any new footage, every channel showed clips of her from the sentencing trial years before, and her name had been mentioned throughout the night. Everyone in the county would know that she was once married to Rene Dibari. Worse than blemishing her reputation, she was furious that Channel 9 News showed footage of Greg and Karen walking into the house. It angered her that whatever privacy they might have had was now made public for everyone to see. If Rene had watched the news, he'd know exactly what Karen looked like and where they lived. It had been nearly sixteen years since she divorced Rene. It was a part of her life that was so long ago that to most people in Middleton, it had become a vague memory. It would have been for Tina as well, except for the loss of her father, which never seemed too far away. Every New Year's Eve at the stroke of midnight, Tina's heart ached for her dear father. Like anything, time heals the wounds and leaves a scar of memory to endure. She had come to forgive any role she may have played in his death, but she still missed him dearly. It was an uncanny sense of déjà vu to hear the reporter mention her father's name with Rene's again on the evening news. It resurrected and refreshed the agony of loss and the surreal emotion of disbelief and fear that once consumed her life. It felt like stepping back in time to relive the worst days of her life, and once again, the entire world was watching through the media. The media mentioned the murder of her father, but how many times did she have to hear that Greg's future NFL hopes were ruined because of his sacrificial efforts to save her? It was all over the news, again. They made Greg sound like the victim, while she was the cause of his ruined dreams. Tina was simply referred to as Rene's abused wife.

She sighed as she read another article in the day's newspaper.

"Tina Slater, a successful realtor in Ridgefield, was once the wife of Rene Dibari, the convicted killer who ruined the future hopes of Boise State's star linebacker and NFL hopeful, Greg Slater. Greg had shown great courage to intervene in the savage attack, which left Tina's father, Art Stewart, lying dead from two bullet wounds not ten feet away when Greg heroically dove into action to save Tina Dibari's life. Despite receiving two point-blank gunshot wounds himself to the ribs and upper thigh, Greg single-handedly disposed of the murderous Dibari until police arrived."

It amazed Tina how the story always focused more on Greg's loss of a possible football career than the loss of her father. It was offensive, like a slap across her family's face. Her father was murdered trying to save her, but the top story was about Greg's possible future? What about her mother's future or her sibling's, or that matter, her own? It was an aggravation that still fumed within her now that the story had been resurrected. Greg, to his credit, had always been disappointed in the news coverage and when asked about his misfortune, he shook it off with a smile and replied, "I have the girl." It had constantly been Greg's response, and he had never shown any regret. He'd been constant in his modesty and never fed the flames of his heroics to gain notoriety. He had never once indicated in any way, shape, or form that he had any interest in the NFL or ever wondered what could have been if he had walked away that night. Tina asked him while they watched a professional football game one Sunday if he regretted not having the chance to continue his football career. Greg had answered, "I am where I am meant to be, doing what I am meant to do, and with who I was meant to be with. How can life get any better than that?"

She tried not to let the article and the news reports get to her, but it still ate at her like a gnawing rat in the wall. She understood the human interest in a hero's story, but it seemed to her that sacrificing your life to save your daughter was more heroic. The truth was Greg could have walked into training camp if he had desired to. He wasn't crippled, and he recovered well. If the truth were told, it would simply be he had no desire to play professional football. He loved to teach and enjoyed coaching far more than playing.

The way the media spun the story, it begged the question, with so much tragedy that night because of her, was her life worth saving? The local news sure seemed to question that while demonizing her, unintentionally, of course. The article and many others like it made her question her worth. She knew for a fact that her story would never have gotten the publicity it did if Greg hadn't been there. Even if Rene had killed her and her father both, it would not have gotten the same media coverage without the heroism of Greg.

Tina had never hidden the fact that she was married to Rene, but she preferred not to talk about it. However, she was already sick of hearing the; "I didn't know you were married to him" comments by her co-workers and other realtors around town. Some of them just wanted to hear the gossip so that they could share it; others seemed to thrive on her troubles and enjoyed seeing the adversity in her life, while a few were sincere when they offered their comforting words. Nonetheless, Tina couldn't hide from it, and she had work to do. The last place she wanted to be was alone in that big old country home. She was tempted to take her family on an unexpected vacation to the coast until Rene was captured, but there was no telling how long that would be, and she knew Greg and the two older kids would refuse to leave with a big football game coming up. By all the evidence so far, the police figured he was probably still in the local area but suspected he'd head toward California to get across the Mexican border for reasons they never disclosed. She could only hope so, but it didn't calm her nerves. Rene had sworn those years ago to get even, and now that he had the chance to do so, she wasn't so sure he wouldn't take advantage of it even if he had a free flight and million dollars to spend in Mexico.

A text came over her phone; Ray Tristan wanted to know if she was at her office. She texted back. Her office extension began to ring.

"Kathryn E. Rupp Real Estate Associates, this is Tina. How may I help you?" she asked with a small knowing smile.

"How about joining me for lunch? I went to that new little bistro last night and would love to take you there."

"I haven't been there yet. Is it any good?"

"Fantastic. Are you free about one?"

"Sure."

"I'll pick you up then. So how are you feeling today, any better than last night?" Ray asked quickly.

"No, not really. There's always the thought of Rene showing up anywhere at any time. I wish I could show you what he looked like when he was sentenced. He was so filled with rage; he would've killed me if he could've. He said he would if he ever got out. And now he's out. They think he may have gone to California, but he could be anywhere. It's pretty frightening."

"I saw it on the news. You mentioned last night that Rene would recognize your house. That would be scary. I don't think I'd feel very secure there, especially since they don't know where he is. I don't want to scare you, nor do I want to sound out of line here, but your husband should not be putting your safety above his football game. I could move into a hotel and let you use my house if you want a safe place to stay."

Tina smiled appreciatively. "Well, thanks for the offer, but I have to stay close to my children."

"And Greg?" he asked.

"Yes, him too," she said with less enthusiasm in her voice.

"I don't want to pry, but doesn't it bother you a little that Greg would be okay with keeping your family there during this potential threat? I know I'm concerned myself, so I can't believe he'd even take that risk. I know he's a tough guy, and all, but I'd never leave my family open to chance Rene stopping by. Forgive me for carrying on, Tina. But you're my friend, and I wouldn't want to see anything bad happen to you."

His sincere caring touched her. "Thank you, Ray. I appreciate it. And yeah, it does bother me. I guess I never figured a football game was more important to him than his family." She sounded bitter and then added in a kinder tone, "Well, that's not fair; he thinks Rene is running for his life to Mexico."

Ray spoke hesitantly, "Oh, he could be, I suppose. Personally, if I were Greg, I'd take your family to Disneyland for a week. Anywhere would be better than staying there waiting for Rene to show up possibly. I'd consider taking your kids and disappearing for a week, Tina. You could hide out at my place if you'd like. I also have a buddy that has a beach house that you could use probably. And just as a second thought, if your husband is putting a football game before your safety, it might indicate his priorities. But you know, we'll talk about that over lunch, my treat. I'll pick you up at one."

"Well, I don't want to bad talk, Greg, so I shouldn't have said that. Maybe he's right, and we have nothing to worry about. My imagination is probably just getting the better of me."

Ray chuckled lightly. "But you don't believe that do you?" It was more of a knowing statement than a question.

"No," Tina replied after a slight pause. "I don't," the sound of defeat was in her voice.

"Then why do you want to stick up for a guy who is putting your family at risk?"

Tina sighed heavily. "I don't know. He's my husband, I guess."

"He may be your husband, but I don't think he has your best interest in mind. I mean, think about it. He's risking your life for a football game. It doesn't sound like love to me, which is supposed to mean putting you first, especially in a situation like this one where your life is in danger, perhaps. I don't know, my friend, all I know is time changes people, and sometimes those changes become so self-oriented that they become blind to what they have. You deserve more, my gosh. You deserve to be kept safe. But we'll talk about it more over lunch. I will pick you up at one. How does that sound, Missy?"

"Missy...?" she asked curiously. "Is that one of your girlfriends by chance?" she asked with a light uncomfortable laugh

"I don't have any girlfriends, but I do have one good friend. And, Missy, I'll see you soon."

"Okay," she said awkwardly and hung up the phone. Her smile faded as her thoughts went to Ray's words.

CHAPTER 12

KAREN SLATER SAT AT HER DESK DURING THIRD-PERIOD English Literature class and tried to focus on the assignment at hand while Missus Higgins lectured in front of the blackboard. Usually, an interested and studious student, Karen could not pay attention. Her mind was on the news reporters that had invaded their town and especially her life. A Channel 9 News van was parked outside the school. The reporter had interviewed numerous students about Rene's escape but was more interested in asking them about Karen. Her friends said the reporter wanted to talk to Karen about her father. It left an uneasy feeling in her stomach, slightly anxious and certainly offensive because the only father she knew was her dad. She didn't care about Rene Dibari; he was nothing more than a title with a name.

"Hey, Dibari," a clean-cut senior named Chris Willis whispered from two desks away. He had short light brown hair and a playful grin on his oblong face as his blue eyes watched his friend's reaction closely.

Karen turned around quickly with a fierce glare. She did not attempt to whisper as she spoke loudly, "My name is not Dibari! I don't even know the man, Chris, and I don't think it's funny!"

Missus Higgins stopped talking and peered at Chris with annoyance. "Chris, have you got something to say?"

Chris shook his head while his cheeks reddened.

"Certainly, you must," Missus Higgins pressed. "Miss Slater," she emphasized, "deserves an apology for that immature and insensitive remark. I expected more out of you, Chris. So would her father...Coach Slater."

Chris nodded somberly. "I'm sorry, Karen. I was just joking."

"It's not funny," Karen said with a hint of a tear in her big brown eyes. She hid her emotions as she rested her face on her hand with a downward gaze.

"Listen, everyone," Missus Higgins said, "I know it's odd and maybe even exciting to have a TV news team parked outside of our school and having the opportunity to be seen on TV. However, nobody in this school has done anything to merit this kind of abuse of privacy. Nor does anyone deserve to hear snide, little remarks that are hurtful and degrading, even when they're covered innocently enough by the sweet little catchphrase, 'it was a joke.' Stop it!" she finished sharply just as the bell rang to excuse the class.

Chris Willis closed his binder and quickly left the classroom red-faced.

Karen closed her organized notebook and walked out into the crowded hallway under the eyes of the many other students. There was no hiding the fact that the attention was on her. Every pair of eyes she glanced at were fixed upon her. She was the center of attention and gossip, for that matter. Whispers behind her back and statements directed at her increased her anxiety as she tried to walk to her next class.

Ross Greenfield, the football team's quarterback, walked towards her with an excited smile. "Hey, Karen, watch Channel 9 News tonight, they interviewed me, and I complimented you and your dad."

Karen stopped and said through a scowl, "Rene is not my

father!" Her eyes were wide and penetrated Ross like a red-hot branding iron.

Ross was taken back by the ferocity of her glare. "I wasn't talking about him. I'm talking about your dad, you know, Coach." He gave her a second look. "Are you all right?"

"Fine," she quipped irritably and kept walking.

Karen's fourth-period art class was an elective that she shared with students in other grades, which was made apparent when two freshman girls widened their eyes and whispered when she walked in. The classroom was at the school's front, overlooking where the two news crews waited in their vans to give the newest updates as the day rolled on. With distaste, Karen glanced at them through the window and took her seat, simmering underneath her calm demeanor. The pressure of having the stigma of a convicted killer's daughter was shameful enough to deal with without everyone knowing about it. Like any other small town, there were few secrets in Middleton. Most everyone who had been in Middleton for a while knew she was Rene's daughter, but it was a fact that was quickly forgotten. Even in the gossip hub of all small towns, it was like a touch of dust on a piano key. It simply didn't matter.

The high school was no different from the local store where the old-timers sat and gossiped; however, most students had no idea that she was not Greg's biological daughter. Somehow, the escape of Rene Dibari had revived a spirit of excitement into Middleton, and everyone was talking about the center of the media's current attention: Karen. For the first time in her life, Karen felt like an outsider at Middleton High School. Everyone seemed to be pointing at her and taking a step back to gawk at the daughter of the escaped killer. Yesterday, Greg was her father, and she was just Karen Slater. Today, her identity had changed to Rene Dibari's daughter. For the first time, her life was thrown into disarray by the confusion brought to her identity. She could not remember when she didn't have Greg as her dad nor his loving arms there to pick her up when she fell. She had always known the security of her father's love and his encouraging words when she struggled in any area of her life. He was her number one fan, and he was the one she hated to disappoint the most. She had a wonderful childhood and every opportunity that a girl could have. She knew exactly how lucky she was to have the parents and home she did. Within the last twenty-four hours, the surreal changes and attention brought to her front door were incomprehensible. A felon she had no memory of had escaped and everyone was calling him her father, but the only father she knew was her own. Rene was not him; Rene Dibari had absolutely nothing to do with her!

"Hi, Karen, how are you?" Bruce Moore sincerely asked as he came into Art class. He was a big kid at five feet nine inches tall and one hundred and ninety pounds. Bruce was the starting right guard on the football team's front line. He was also the younger brother of Karen's best friend, Amanda. It wasn't a secret that Bruce had a long-lasting crush on her, but Bruce was more like a brother to Karen than someone of romantic interest. Bruce had short dark hair and a round face with an acne problem, but he was one of the nicest and caring young men Karen had ever known. Karen just nodded with a sad smile to her friend. He knew her well enough to know that she wasn't okay but didn't want to talk at the moment. He was just that kind of friend.

More students entered the classroom, but Karen felt a sinking feeling overwhelming her when Ron Myers walked in with a broad smile. Ron was the one young man in the Middleton High School that she despised the most. Ron was a senior with a low moral conviction, that went out of his way to irritate her. He had been given multiple warnings and even suspended for his persistent sexual and perverse harassment. No matter how often he was thrown out of class, sent to the office, or disciplined with suspensions, he continued to harass her, without caring about the consequences. She closed her eyes in frustration when she saw him smiling at her like a funeral director who'd gotten his first death call in months.

Ron walked over to the front of her desk and knelt to look at her at eye level.

"Not today, Ron, please," she said quietly, avoiding his eyes.

He chuckled. "So, Daddy couldn't wait for parole, huh? What do you think he'll do when he comes home and finds Coach Slater in bed with his wife?"

Karen stood up quickly, shouting, "He's not married to my mom, you ass! Stop calling him my dad!" Her eyes were full of tears as they burned into Ron. "Why don't you leave me alone."

For just a quick moment, Ron was surprised by her response. He stood slowly, taking pleasure in watching the thick tears build in her large beautiful brown eyes. "Wow," he said softly, "killing does run in the blood! It looks like you could kill me as easily as your daddy killed those two men yesterday. Are you a daddy's girl? A murderous vixen?"

Karen's face contorted. She couldn't quite catch her breath, and her chest began to hurt. "You..." she said with frustration, but she couldn't continue. She stared in horror at the joy that showed on Ron's face. She shook her head slowly. It was unimaginable that someone could find joy in the misery that she felt. A tear dropped from her eye.

Bruce Moore left his seat and quickly approached Ron. He spoke firmly, "Go sit down, Ron. Don't say another word to her."

"Or what?" Ron asked with an arrogant shrug.

"I'll kick your ass!"

"Yeah, right," Ron answered sarcastically. He ignored Bruce and spoke to Karen, "When your daddy gets a hold of your mom, it'll probably be the first real man she's had since your daddy left."

"Shut up!" Karen shouted. She could no longer control her emotions as she broke into tears. She quickly grabbed her notebook and ran out of the classroom, passing the teacher as she entered the room to start class. Missus Pfeiffer, an older lady in her sixties, paused to watch Karen run by in tears and was just about to call after her when a sudden commotion exploded inside the classroom. Bruce Moore called Ron Myers a few choice words and then quickly shoved him with enough force to send Ron into a desk and then onto the floor. Ron got up quickly and returned the verbal attacks as he approached Bruce, red-faced and angry.

Bruce, usually a well-tempered young man with a gentle nature, unleashed his temper, and with a powerful right fist, he knocked Ron off his feet and into another desk. Ron stayed where he was, cupping his hands over his nose as it bled. "Leave her alone, you son of a…"

"Stop it, Bruce!" Missus Pfeiffer shouted, interrupting him. "What's going on here? Kayleigh, go get Principal Bennet!"

Bruce continued to stand over Ron and yelled, "I'll beat the hell out you! Just shut your mouth and leave her alone!"

CHAPTER 13

KAREN SAT IN A CHAIR FACING PRINCIPAL STEVE BENNET'S desk. She wiped her eyes while she finished with their conversation of what happened in Missus Pfeiffer's art class between Ron Myers and Bruce Moore.

Principal Bennet was in his fifties, tall and thin, with short brown hair balding on top, and wore glasses on his thin face. At first sight, he may not have appeared to be an intimidating authority figure, but his eyes could turn as hard as steel when it was needed. He sat behind his desk with a serious countenance while he listened to Karen. His eyes occasionally darted out of his office window into the main office where Ron and Bruce both sat waiting. Bruce fidgeted nervously, while Ron waited much too casually and unconcerned. "I think we're done in here, Karen. You can go back to class unless your dad has something more."

Greg shook his head as he stood up. "Come here, kid," he said and hugged her tightly. "You go on back to class and don't worry about guys like Ron. They're just aching to make anyone as miserable as they are. Don't fall for it, sweetheart. You are my daughter and I love you. There's nothing these kids can say that will change that. Okay?"

Her lips squeezed together emotionally in his comforting arms. "I love you, Dad." Karen left the principal's office and said to Ron under her breath, "Jerk," as she passed by. In response, he smirked and licked his lips in a sexual manner.

Greg was watching from the door when Ron licked his lips. "Myers!" he shouted with a glare. "You get in here! You too, Bruce." The two boys took a seat quietly while Greg closed the door. He leaned against the door with folded arms and a scowl as he watched Ron irritably.

Principal Bennet leaned forward over his desk and spoke first, "You're both going to be held accountable for your actions today. Mister Myers, I cannot believe you would be so callous to say something so inexcusable to anyone. Your actions are beyond apologizing, and I will call your mother to request a meeting with her to discuss your future here at Middleton High. I cannot allow you to continue to harass Karen or any student any longer. You've had multiple warnings and suspensions going back to early last year, and you don't seem to care. You have crossed a line this time that I can't overlook, but we'll talk more about that with your mother here," he finished pointedly to make his point clear.

He then turned his focus to Bruce Moore. "Although I understand your frustration, Bruce, I cannot allow you to beat up another student. Both of you are suspended for three days and will not be allowed to participate in the game or Halloween Dance Friday night."

"What about the game?" Bruce asked suddenly. He stared at Principal Bennet with tears moistening his eyes. "I have to play!"

"You are suspended. That means you won't be playing in the game, nor will you be allowed to watch it. Neither of you will be permitted on school premises this weekend. I'm sorry, Bruce, but you made your choice."

"He was harassing Karen!" Bruce raised his voice defensively. "This isn't fair! Ron was making Karen cry. What was I supposed to do?"

Greg stepped forward. "May I speak frankly?" he asked Principal Bennet.

"Absolutely."

Greg's disappointment in Bruce was evident on his face. "Bruce, you know the rules and the consequences for breaking them. I appreciate your wanting to stick up for my daughter. I really do. But I can take care of my daughter. I needed you on the field Friday night, Bruce, not fighting my fight in Art class."

Bruce's eyes teared painfully. "Coach, this could be the last game of the season. I don't want to miss it. Mister Bennet, can't I have Saturday school instead? I'll spend the next three weeks in Saturday school. Mister Bennet, please, I can't miss the last game of the season. Coach, I was just trying to do what was right," he finished emotionally to Greg.

Ron Myers rolled his eyes and laughed quietly while he sat beside Bruce.

Principal Bennet answered with finality. "I'm sorry, Bruce, I really am. But you are suspended. You can leave the school premises immediately; we'll see you on Monday."

"Coach, can't you do something? It's the last game of the season! I don't deserve to miss the game. He deserved to get his ass kicked and you both know it!" Bruce stood up quickly and pointed his finger at Ron. "If I see you off of school grounds, I'm going to beat the crap out of you!"

Ron shrugged carelessly. Though a twinge of concern flickered in his eyes, he struggled to keep his careless demeanor.

"Bruce," Greg said, "I'm sorry." It was his parting words as Bruce tightened his lips and fought the tears that clouded his vision. He nodded and left the principal's office, closing the door behind him.

In the momentary silence that followed, Ron began to fidget under the gaze of both men. Principal Bennet spoke first, "This involves your family Greg, why don't you speak your piece. Just keep it professional," he emphasized with a nod.

Greg sighed. "Ron, I have tried for years to reach you. I have tried to help you with your studies and encouraged you to join my football and wrestling teams. I have done all that I know how to do to help you, including standing up for you when no one else would to keep you in school after last year's stunt in the gym. And yet, you don't give a rat's ass about that at all. You have insulted my daughter, me, and my family. Do you not understand that Rene is a dangerous man? He's already killed two men just to get out of prison. It's hard to say what he'll do now that he's out. My family could possibly be in danger. Do you find that funny, Ron?" Greg asked intentionally. He leaned forward slightly towards Ron before continuing, "Ron, I have always wanted to help you because I thought you were a good-hearted young man with a lot of potential. After your comments today, I'm beginning to have my doubts. Quite frankly, I'd like nothing more than to take you onto the wrestling mat myself, but I cannot do that. I can protect my daughter from being harassed by you, though." He paused. "I've been your biggest fan here, Ron. But I won't be standing up for you this time. I am sick of it!" Greg nodded towards Principal Bennet and said, "He's all yours."

Principal Bennet asked, "So do you have anything to say, Mister Myers? Because I'd really like to understand why you'd say something so terrible?"

Ron gritted his teeth upset by what Greg had said to him. "I hope Rene comes back and kills you all."

Principal Bennet spoke loudly, "Let's go! You need to leave the school premises right now! You are expelled until further notice. Get up and let's go!" he said commanded as he grabbed Ron's arm and yanked him to his feet. "Believe me; I will be contacting your mother as soon as I can!" Steve Bennet physically escorted Ron out of the office and off the school grounds himself.

Greg stayed in the office and waited for Steve to

return. Ron Myers was one of those kids that could do so well if he applied himself but lacked discipline. Ron was walking down the wrong path. Greg wished he would have been a more positive influence on Ron but failed to connect. It wasn't for his lack of trying, though. A teacher can try to make a difference, but some kids couldn't care less.

Principal Bennet walked back into his office and closed the door. "That kid is trouble. There's always one or two, but he's trouble." He looked out the window with growing frustration. "Look at him over there talking up a storm to that reporter. He's getting even with us for expelling him, is what he's doing."

Greg stood up and peeked out the window to see Ron talking to the news crew across the street. Ron was animatedly expressing himself by pointing angrily at the school and other hand gestures. It appeared that the middle-aged reporter John Travis from Channel 9 News was interested in Ron's story. He had the cameraman get his camera ready to interview Ron. It wouldn't be a live feed but taped to edit and show later.

Steve walked behind his desk and sat down. "This media circus is so distracting. I can promise you that every classroom with windows facing the front of the school is sidetracked right now by the sight of Ron talking to that reporter. That proverbial fifteen minutes of fame is a big deal around here today. I can only imagine what he's telling them. I suppose we'd better watch the news tonight and find out."

Greg spoke slowly, "They want to talk to me. I wonder if they'll leave the school perimeter if I promise to give them an interview after practice tonight. There's no reason for us to reward Ron by letting him trash talk us, is there?"

"Huh? Where are you going?"

"To make a deal."

Principal Steve Bennet watched from his office window as Greg approached the news van preparing to interview

Ron. The reporter, John Travis, stopped Ron's interview and walked towards Greg Slater in a hurry.

Principal Bennet watched Greg talk to John for a few seconds, and the cameraman lowered his camera. They talked a bit more, shook hands, and separated.

After talking to Greg, the news crew passed by Ron carelessly and got into their van and drove away. Ron angrily flipped his middle finger up at Greg while yelling a long line of obscenities. Greg ignored him and walked back towards the school.

Greg stepped into the office a minute later and said, "I have a live interview at six o'clock on Channel 9 News. Ron won't be on TV after all; he's a little mad about that," he finished with a satisfied smile.

CHAPTER 14

THE BODY OF JACK MILLER, THE ELDERLY MAN, REPORTED
missing the night before on the news, was found by a couple
of teenage boys skipping school at a small recreational pond
outside of Salem. The eighty-six-year-old's car was still
missing and was likely stolen by the murderer. Jack Miller
had been bludgeoned from behind. Suspicion automatically
fell on Rene Dibari. Much of the afternoon's news breaks
were about finding Jack Miller's body and the hunt to locate
his missing silver Buick Lesabre and the possible connection to Rene Dibari. Speculation abounded, but most law
enforcement agencies agreed that the cause of death
matched Rene's other two victims precisely. It was a potential step closer to finding their escaped murderer.

About five-thirty that afternoon, Jack Miller's car was
found in Eugene. It was a break in the case that the media
was frantic to report. The search for Rene was now focused
on the Eugene area. It was reported that it was very likely
that Rene had carjacked another victim from the mall
parking lot. They urged anyone with a suspiciously missing
friend or family member with a vehicle to notify the police
immediately. Amidst all of the updates, Channel 9 News
announced that they would have an "exclusive live interview with Greg Slater on the six o'clock news".

Rene Dibari paused from his channel surfing and laid down the remote to not miss that interview. A surge of resentment swelled from deep within to bring a dangerous scowl to Rene's face. His heart beat a touch harder while his breathing grew more profound. The very sound of Greg's name lit a fuse of hatred that burned long and deep. Rene would watch channel nine for the rest of the night to ensure he didn't miss the interview with Greg. He wondered where the discussion would take place, inside of his home or outside of it. He had seen their house on the news the night before. It was a house that Rene knew well; it belonged to his high school girlfriend, Lisa White, many years ago. He knew precisely where they lived, about a mile and a half out of town on Vanderveld Road. Life must have been treating Greg and Tina well for them to buy the old White property. It was an old four-bedroom farmhouse with some acreage and a large old barn behind the house. Rene remembered the place quite well. Lisa's parents had forbidden her to see him, so he had spent many nights sneaking around to get into Lisa's bedroom.

At five-forty, local breaking news interrupted the national news. The news anchor announced for the sixth time that the silver Buick Lesabre belonging to murder victim Jack Miller had been found abandoned in the Eugene Mall parking lot. No trace of Rene Dibari had been found, but law enforcement agencies were viewing video from the mall cameras. The news break was cut back to the national news.

Rene had ventured out from the motel that morning to walk to a nearby market. The less he was outside, the better off he was, but he still had to eat. He had paid for five days at the motel, but he needed to decide what to do next. He had a chance to remain free, but he needed to figure out how to escape the law and begin a new life with a new identity. He was in Portland within easy access of I-5 North to Canada or South to Mexico. He could hitch a ride East on I-84 to Idaho and beyond as well. He had options he could use, but the question he didn't know the answer to was which direction to go with the least risk of being caught. He could try to stay unnoticed and live in the lower ends of Portland, or he could run to another large city and try to mix in with their underground homeless, but the fact is, it's nearly impossible to outrun the law for very long. So far, he'd been able to get away and stay hidden, but there was no promise that someone didn't recognize him at the local store and call the police already. To remain hidden meant living in a cage with the fear of being caught. He had found a temporary place to hide, but he couldn't stay too long. This motel was bottom of the barrel, but everyone who had seen him could potentially recognize him. His old friends couldn't be trusted, and strangers were as loyal as enemies. His mother lived in Portland, not too far away from where he was, but he would not risk contacting her. Undoubtedly the police would be monitoring her home for him to do just that.

He would have to run, but to where he didn't know. He would have to change his identity, but he didn't know how or who could help him acquire the needed documents to appear legal. It was perhaps reasonable that a man with a new identity could live in a small town somewhere and work under the table for a living. He would never get wealthy, but at least he could be living as a free man. He needed to find someone who could help him with those arrangements. In the meantime, he would have to find the prostitute that rented the room for him and pay her to rent it for another week.

Channel 9 News started at six o'clock with an immediate report on the finding of Jack Miller's body in a Salem pond, and the breaking news that they had just found his car in Eugene within the last hour. They were able to verify that Rene Dibari was with Jack Miller in a photo taken at the drive-through ATM. Nothing more was reported than earlier, except that more updates would be reported as the investigation continued. Before long, the news anchor said.

"We take you now live to the Middleton High School football field with reporter John Travis."

"Hello, Kayleigh. I'm standing with the Middleton head football coach, Greg Slater. As many of you know, Greg is Rene Dibari's ex-friend and is now married to Rene's ex-wife. Greg, I'm sure that Rene's escape has been extremely difficult for you and your family. Just so the viewers understand, you were the hero when you intervened in a murderous domestic dispute. Your future father-in-law was murdered, and you stepped in to save Tina, who was Rene's wife at the time. You had been shot twice by Rene, yet you still courageously fought and beat Rene Dibari on that fateful night until the police arrived. Your testimony helped put him away for life, and then you married Tina. It was an amazing love story back then, I thought, and it still is now. Greg, learning that Rene has killed his third victim how is his escape and unknown whereabouts affecting your family?" Rene watched closely.

Greg stood in the end zone in front of the scoreboard, under the field lights. It was drizzling, and Greg was dressed in red and white weather-resistant athletic wear. He wore a Middleton Football hat that dripped drops of rain off its bill. Greg appeared in good health and had an essence about him that exuded confidence. Greg nodded as he pressed his lips together in thought. "Of course, there's a concern. It throws the sense of security of our home a bit out of whack, but we're dealing with it all right. I just want to send my condolences to the families that Rene's stolen someone's life from. Our deepest heartfelt prayers go out to them."

John Travis asked, "So, Greg, nobody knows Rene Dibari more intimately than your wife and yourself. Were you surprised to hear that he had escaped? And secondly, at the sentencing trial fifteen years ago, Rene caused quite a scene as he was being drug out of the courtroom, swearing he'd get revenge if he ever got out of prison. Do you have any fear that he'll come after you?"

Greg shook his head. "No, I don't fear him coming after my family or me. I think he's got bigger issues on his plate at the moment, such as where to go. It sounds like he's heading south, but," he shrugged, "where's he going to go? He's an escaped felon. He can't go anywhere. He can't possibly think he can outrun the police and outsmart the FBI. He's been in prison for fifteen years. They'll find him in a day or two."

"We heard from a student today that Rene's biological daughter has been harassed by other students since Rene's escape. Can you give us an idea of how she is handling his escape? According to one student I talked to earlier today, nobody knew she was Rene's daughter. I understand she is very upset. Was she aware that Rene was her father before yesterday?"

Greg appeared to be taken off guard and quickly irritated. "Let me assure you that she is doing fine. She has always known that Rene is her father, but she has had no contact with him since she was two years old. He has no part of her life. The only thing that upset her is the ignorance of that young man that you talked to."

"Coach, I want to thank you for your time, but before we go. I want to say that you're hosting the Brouwer Bulldogs this Friday night for the league championship game. With all of the media about Rene and your family, how are your players able to stay focused on the undefeated Bulldogs?"

Greg smiled easily. "We are preparing to play a tough opponent. The bulldogs are a great team and they're not coming here to lose. But we're fighting for our lives. We have to win to make the playoffs. So it's all or nothing. It's going to be a great game, John."

"That's Halloween night, here in Middleton at seven o'clock," John said into the camera. He then asked, "Greg, if you could say any one thing to Rene, what would it be?"

Greg looked into the camera. "Good luck."

"This is John Travis, live from Middleton. Back to you."

Rene stared at the TV. Greg was right about one thing;

he didn't have anywhere to go. His face was on all the TV stations, national news, and most wanted shows. He would never be able to start over again, even if he had a new identity. Who was he kidding? He was doomed from the very beginning. He was only free until they tracked him down; his freedom wouldn't last. He had a decision to make, which was reduced to what did he want to do the most before he went back to prison? He wanted to make the most of his time before going back to prison for the remainder of his life. If there was just one thing he could do that would last a lifetime and make his escape from prison worthwhile, what would it be? He would never be free again, and with all of the choices a man could make, his was easy. He wanted to see his daughter and visit some old friends; and satisfy every ounce of his thirst for vengeance. He was going home.

CHAPTER 15

TINA STOOD IN FRONT OF THE STOVE IN THE KITCHEN IN A black skirt and red blouse, watching a pot of boiling water and spaghetti sauce for dinner. Her jaw tightened and her thin lips pressed together in annoyance.

"Spaghetti! I thought you said we were having pork chops tonight?" Samuel asked, disappointed. He was looking with distaste at the noodles as they boiled.

"I never said that," Tina answered flatly.

"Yeah, you did last night. I don't like spaghetti, Mom. You know that. Are you making garlic bread, at least? Please tell me you're making garlic bread."

"No," is all Tina said.

"You're not? Why not? I'm starving and there's nothing to eat."

"Grab an apple, Samuel."

"I don't want an apple! I'm hungry, Mom. An apple isn't going to fill me up, and you know I don't like spaghetti. What am I going to eat? You're not making garlic bread."

"I'm making spaghetti, Sam. Take it or leave it but quit whining! I am not in the mood." Her eyes warned Sam not to continue.

"In a mood for what, to cook something good?" Sam challenged his mother.

Tina turned, suddenly grabbing a glass bowl off the counter and throwing it across the large kitchen at the wall; it shattered upon impact. Tina shouted, "Go to your room, Sam! Just get the hell away from me! And don't come back downstairs until your father's home." Sam stood in startled awe. His mother had never thrown anything before.

"Get out of my sight!" she yelled with her angry blue eyes burning into him.

Sam replied meekly, "I'm just hungry, Mom."

"I don't care! Now go!"

Sam stormed toward the stairs; the sound of his bedroom door slamming shut followed shortly.

Tina reached for her phone that was still attached to her hip and text messaged someone with urgency. A few moments later, a text came in and she opened it quickly. She text again. Her phone rang. "Ugh! My son Sam is driving me nuts. It's not like I don't have enough already on my mind. The last thing I want to hear is a thirteen-year-old boy whining... No, he didn't have wrestling practice today, the coach is sick or something, I don't know." She paused to listen as the voice on the other end of the phone spoke. For the first time since she had gotten home, she smiled.

She spoke with a lighter tone, "Nobody understands that more than I do, believe me. With all of the things happening right now, I can barely think. Did you see Greg's interview on the news?... No, you didn't miss anything. I just hope Rene missed it too. ...I know." A pleased grin spread across her face revealing her beautiful smile. It faded just as quickly as Greg's truck lights shined in through the window. "Listen, I'll talk to you later, Greg just pulled in... I promise I will... okay, bye," Tina said with a smile and replaced her phone on her hip. She immediately grabbed a strainer from the cabinet and poured the noodles. The front door opened, Robert, Karen, and Greg all came walking in.

"Mom, where's dinner?" Robert called out as he carried in his backpack, tossed it on the living room floor, and turned the TV to Channel 9 News. Karen took her backpack immediately upstairs to her room.

Greg wandered into the kitchen, carrying his case of homework to correct. "What's this?" he indicated to the broken glass spread across the kitchen floor.

Tina scowled. "Your son pissed me off. That's what!"

Greg frowned. "So you threw a bowl at him?"

"Not at him, but yes, I lost my temper and threw the bowl. He has no reason to come in here and bitch about what's for dinner again and again. I've had enough," her tone was restrained as if there was a greater force just waiting to burst free.

"Where's Sam, in his room?" Greg asked while he squatted down to pick up the larger pieces of broken glass.

"Mom," Robert asked as he came into the kitchen. "Did you record the news? I wanted to see Dad's interview."

"No, I didn't. I can't be expected to do it all around here, now can I?"

Greg gazed at her curiously. "I didn't know you did. Did you watch the interview?"

"Yes, I did."

Greg stood with a handful of broken glass. "How'd I do?"

Tina's fury was unleashed, "Why didn't you just invite Rene to dinner, Greg? You are such an idiot, I swear! Why would you give an interview to those blood-sucking vampires, Greg? All you did is make us a target."

"How so?" Greg asked skeptically. He tossed the glass into the garbage underneath the sink.

Tina stepped inches from Greg's face and spat out, "Rene knows you're the Middleton football coach now, you idiot! Between your stupid football players and you, you've challenged him to come here! Did you hear what Ross said?"

Greg frowned. "No, what did Ross say?"

"He said Rene wouldn't come back here because he'd be too scared you'd kick his ass again! They bleeped that out, but that's what he said. It's a challenge and Rene has never walked away from a challenge," she said heatedly with frightened tears clouding her eyes.

Greg chuckled. "Rene's long gone, Tina. Haven't you heard they tracked him to Eugene? He'll be picked up in California or somewhere."

"He hasn't been yet, Greg! He's still out there, and you're mocking him on TV!" she yelled loudly.

"I didn't mock him. I simply told the truth. He has no reason to come here, Tina, so quit worrying about him doing so. He went to Eugene, that's what eighty, ninety miles south from here. Rene's making a run for it, just as I said he would. He isn't coming a hundred miles back up this way because of an interview he didn't see. Relax. He's already in California by now, a long way from here. As the police said, he doesn't want to go back to prison. He's running for his life."

Tina spoke quietly, "It's just like Ray said."

"Ray, who?" Greg asked curiously.

"Ray Tristan. A lender I'm working with on a deal."

"What did he say?"

"It's on the news, Greg! You're on the news! I don't have any secrets because it's all on the news. My life is on the news!" She was getting louder. "It doesn't take a brain surgeon to figure out I'm under some stress, except for you. You just don't seem to get it at all!"

"What are you talking about?" Greg asked, growing irritated. "I know that you're worried. So what am I not getting?"

Hostility filled her eyes. "Rene killed my father, Greg. You were there. I would've thought you might've considered that before you took it so lightly that Rene's out there somewhere. You know what I'm afraid of, but you are not sympathetic whatsoever. All you care about is your stupid football team. I need you here when I come home from work, but I'm here alone for a good hour or two before Samuel comes home. You won't even leave practice for me. What if Rene was here waiting for me?" She paused and then continued, "I am taking the kids and going to a client's beach cabin until Rene is caught. I want you to come with us, but it's fine if you don't."

"Do you want me to quit my job too? Come on, Tina, I'm the coach. It's not an option to come home early or to leave, for that matter. We have a game to practice for; you know that. We can't just put our life on hold and leave because Rene escaped. He's going south. He's not anywhere around here. Do you think you're taking Karen away until he's caught, with a game Thursday night and the state tournament next week? Do you think Robert will miss Friday night's game? Not a chance! You have nothing to worry about. Rene's gone."

"What about me?" she asked pointedly.

"What about you?" Greg asked with a shrug of his shoulders. "You're not making any sense, Tina. If you're afraid to be home alone, then visit your mom or someone. Come down and watch Karen practice or the boys and me. You don't have to be here. And you certainly can't expect me to stop practice so that you're not alone. But one thing you're not going to do is take the kids away for an undetermined amount of time for no valid reason. They'd fall behind on their schoolwork and miss the most important games of the season, and you can't do that to them."

"Fine!" she shouted irritably, "I will go visit someone. But I won't be in this house alone anymore, not until Rene's either dead or back in prison. So, if I'm late for dinner, don't blame me. Maybe I'll go out for a couple of drinks with Abby and Dawn tomorrow night. It's lady's night at the bar, you know."

Greg grinned. "No, I wouldn't know. I'm not real big on bars." He raised his arms to give her a comforting hug.

"No," she said and turned away from him. "I don't want to be hugged by you. I'm serious; I think I'll go to the bar tomorrow night."

Greg laughed lightly. "Sure."

Tina mixed the sauce with the noodles and set the large

container on the counter. "Remember, you're the one that told me to go do something, so if I come home late, don't be surprised. Dinner's ready. Get the kids to set the table."

Greg, Tina, Karen, Robert, and Samuel sat around the dining table waiting to eat. They were about to give thanks when Karen said, "Mom, why don't you say grace tonight."

"Why don't you, Karen?" she snapped bitterly.

Karen was taken back by her mother's sharp response. "You should. It might snap you out of your cruddy mood."

Tina pushed her chair away from the table dramatically and stood to leave.

"Where are you going?" Greg asked, frustrated.

"Upstairs. I've lost my appetite!"

"We're praying, Tina. Please sit down until after we pray," Greg said and waited expectedly. Tina sat down and waited irritably while Greg and the kids bowed their heads and prayed. Tina refused to bow her head but instead stared at Greg with a scowl on her lips. When Greg finished saying grace, Tina immediately left the table and wordlessly walked upstairs. She pulled her phone from its case on her hip before she reached the top stair.

CHAPTER 16

RAY TRISTAN SET A BAG OF GROCERIES ON HIS KITCHEN counter and set about to put them away. Although he had bought some groceries, he pulled out leftover Chinese takeout for dinner. He warmed up a plate of leftovers, carried it to his plush cloth-covered recliner, and sat down. He grabbed the remote and turned on his 72-inch high-definition TV. He turned it to the local news and took a bite of his dinner when his cell phone beeped. He read a text and raised his eyebrows with surprise, followed by a thin smile. He took another bite before texting back.

Ray was a financial lender with a good reputation for being active in many community services. He was respected by nearly everyone of importance in the community and most of his professional contacts in the housing market. He was friendly, caring, helpful, and quite handsome. He was in his late thirties, in good physical shape, and didn't have too many worries while enjoying his single life. Ray was a financially stable man and owned his nice upper-class middle-income home.

Ray was divorced and had no children. He did have every kind of toy a man could want and a healthy craving for excitement and adventure. He had girlfriends from time to time, but so often, the challenge of capturing the affections of the single women in his sights had proved to be too easy. Once the challenge is conquered, what is left to explore? He didn't believe in love necessarily; at least he didn't want any part of it if it did exist. He loved being single and the hunt for his prey more than the conquest itself. When searching for his next victim in a bar became too easy, he concluded that he needed to aim for a higher quality of game. The kind of prey that no one else could lay their hands on, the untouchable and forbidden type of prey that took time and skill to stalk, coerce, and finally capture as his own. He had aimed his sights on professional married women. He was no longer interested in seeking barflies that would hand themselves over to him at a first meeting, or a bitterly married woman seeking a liaison. He was seeking a married woman who was happily married and loved her husband. Ray wanted a challenge. He wanted to test his abilities and make the game more valuable and satisfying than the prize of claiming another man's wife as his own. It was a challenge to see if he could win the affections of a happily married woman away from her husband and willing to give herself to him. He had ventured into the game with two married women so far and was disappointed at the ease of his success. It never failed to amaze him how lavishing some praise and attention upon a woman could open the doors to her very soul. Mere words were often the candle that warmed the hearts of the most concretely married women. How deceiving it was that the least content and unhappily married women praised their husbands far more than anyone else just to convince the people around them, or perhaps even themselves, of how happy they were. Ray had found the first two of his married challenges unfulfilling.

He went back to looking for the next trophy to set his sights on. In his career field and community service, there were many options with potential; however, none of the other women had the same structural integrity that Tina Slater had. He had worked with Tina a few times over the past five years, and she was always professional and avoided idol chit-chat with strict professional courtesy. She was attractive, intelligent, business-oriented, married to a respectable man, a mother of three teens, and a Christian. She was the perfect challenge. In April, he set her in his sights and made his first play; he asked for lunch, and she politely declined his offer. She agreed to meet him for lunch on his third request, but the conversation was strictly business-related. After six months of courting her business and a word here and there of a personal nature, he had slowly become a trusted ally in her inner circle. He could tell by the ease of her smile and the words she'd share with him about her career, husband, and family. When she began to confide in him about work and then her husband, Ray knew he had succeeded in becoming her friend. He was now just a touch away from conquering his greatest trophy yet, Tina Slater.

Tina wasn't necessarily the most attractive realtor in Ridgefield, but she was the most – untouchable. She was the perfect game. He had played his part patiently, and it appeared to be working well. She was texting him more often, complaining to him about her husband. It had taken time, but he had maneuvered himself between their marriage without her even realizing it. It was paying off; she had just texted him to express her fury at Greg. Ray could not help but smile. He needed to finish the game strong, he texted her back; "Missy, I can't believe he'd say that to you, my friend."

The escape of Rene Dibari only helped to encourage her into his protective arms. It was interesting how sweet little whispers of doubt could drive a wedge through a once-solid marriage. To casually point out her husband's faults and fertilize his own yard with caring words somehow almost magically won her friendship and trust. It was so easy to create a crack where so many thought there was none. Marriages were fragile; a hunter on a quest knew where to set the snares and when to reel her into him ever so slowly. It had taken time, but Tina was ready to meet with him for drinks tomorrow night. It was time to take the next step and see if she was willing to take it further. He was willing to bet after one or two drinks, he could lead her to another level of intimacy. The foundation of their relationship was built on trust, but the motivation was her discontent with her husband. It would not be long until Tina gave herself to him entirely. She wasn't so untouchable after all. Ray read her following text. With a predator's smile on his lips, he texted her back. It was time to up the game.

CHAPTER 17

"No, MY MOM'S BEING STUPID. SHE WON'T LET ME GO anywhere alone now that Rene has escaped from prison," Karen said into her cell phone. She was in her bedroom sitting at her antique vanity, talking to her friend, Amanda. "No, she won't," Karen answered, "My parents are being overly protective. I'm surprised they're letting me go to youth group tonight without them. Of course, Robert and Samuel are both coming. That's the only reason I'm allowed to go, I'm sure...Alright, I'll see you there. See ya." She hung up the phone and began to apply a light touch of makeup to her eyes. She had just finished eating dinner and wanted to touch up before going to youth group.

Her phone beeped, indicating a text message. She didn't recognize the number.

She opened the message and read a one-word message, "Bitch."

Karen frowned with surprise. She texted back quickly, "I'm flattered, you loser." She didn't know who wrote it but guessed it was Ron.

Her phone beeped. "I'm sure you are flattered bitch."

She texted, "I am." And set her phone down to continue with her makeup.

Her phone beeped. She opened the message and read, "U R A Slut."

Karen shook her head with a questionable grin. She texted, "You should buy a dictionary and look that word up. You are obviously ignorant."

Her phone beeped. "You think you're so smart. I'll show you how smart you are soon."

Karen smirked as she texted, "How can your ignorance reveal my intelligence? OH, that's right, you already have!"

Her phone beeped. "You don't know who I am. I could be anyone."

Karen chuckled. She texted, "Ooh, scary thought, I wonder if you are someone. Losers are people too, they say."

Her phone beeped. "You won't be so funny when I find you."

Karen raised her eyebrows. She texted, "I'm at home but going to youth group soon. How can I not be funny while corresponding with a joke like you?"

Her phone beeped. "Bitch, I'll see you soon."

Karen texted, "Ok, I'll just keep my eye open for the biggest loser."

The phone remained quiet as she applied her makeup. She finished up and put on a jacket before leaving her room to go downstairs. Greg was sitting on the couch, watching TV while correcting his students' assignments. Both boys sat nearby watching TV as well.

"Let's go, guys," Karen said.

"It's not time yet," Robert added. He was interested in the show on TV.

"I want to go early. I need to talk with Amanda. Where's Mom at?" she asked, looking in the kitchen and dining room.

"Don't know," Robert answered, not taking his eyes off the TV.

"Around somewhere," Greg answered, looking up from his corrections.

Karen peeked in the office to no avail and then went into

the kitchen. She found Tina at the back of the house in the laundry room, leaning against the dryer, texting on her phone. The soft smile on Tina's lips disappeared when she saw Karen.

"What are you doing?" Karen asked.

"Oh!" Tina appeared to be startled. "Laundry, I came in here to do some laundry."

"Are you sure you're not texting your boyfriend or something?" Karen questioned.

Tina's face flushed as she put her phone back in the holder on her hip. "Don't be ridiculous, Karen. I was checking my email. I do have clients to take care of. So, are you leaving for youth group?"

"Yeah, in a minute, I just wanted to give you a hug and hope you feel better."

"Oh, thanks, Karen," she said and hugged her daughter.

Karen added as she let go of her mother, "You've been crabby lately, Mom. Is everything all right?"

Tina's shoulders slumped. "Rene's escape has me on edge."

"It's been since before that, Mom. It's been going on for a while. You just don't seem happy anymore. You used to be playful and laugh, but you haven't in a long time."

"I guess it's just my job, honey. The market has been bad for a while now. I suppose I'm just working harder to keep us afloat."

"You know, Mom, maybe you'd have more sales if you went to church with us more often."

A look of annoyance flashed over Tina's expression. "I have to work, Karen. If someone wants to look at a piece of property on Sunday, I have to show it to them. If I don't, someone else will."

"No one called last Sunday," Karen stated simply.

"I did an open house for Richard. I have to do what I can to keep busy in the housing market. You do enjoy driving your own car, don't you? I have to work to get paid, and sometimes that includes working on the weekends."

"It would be nice to drive my car to school," Karen said with annoyance since her mom brought the car up.

Tina shook her head. "Sorry, you know the rules. You left school without permission with the car, so now you don't drive the car to school."

Karen sighed. "I know. Anyway, Sundays are supposed to be our family day, and it seems like you go out of the way to do something else every Sunday. Even if you are home on Sundays, you don't want to do anything."

Tina was getting tired of hearing the same conversation. "Karen, what I do with my Sundays is my business," she said plainly. "If I don't want to go to church, then I won't go. I am an adult, not a seventeen-year-old girl. Don't you dare try to cast some juvenile guilt trip on me for trying to keep a roof over our heads. Don't you forget, young lady, that I'm the one that feeds you!" Her eyes bore irritably into Karen as she finished.

"I have to go," Karen said, sounding hurt by her mother's quick lashing. She expected her mother to stop her and apologize before she left, but Karen walked away without any word from Tina. "Let's go," she said impatiently to her brothers and walked to the front door. "See you later, Dad."

"Drive safely," Greg said and went back to grading papers.

Tina followed into the living room as the three kids left. She didn't sit down or show any interest in talking to Greg. She lingered momentarily without saying a word. "I'm going to take a hot bath for a while." There was no intimacy or flirtation in her voice.

Greg looked up at her through his reading glasses. "Do you want me to join you? The kids will be gone for an hour at least."

Tina shook her head with a touch of repulsion. "I don't think so, Greg. I'm much too tired to want to fool around. I just want to be alone for a while."

"Is something wrong, Tina?"

"My daughter's father escaped from prison, Greg. What

else could be wrong?" She held up her hands in frustration. "Isn't that enough?"

Greg set the papers down and stood to give her a hug she had denied him earlier. She pushed him away. "No, I don't want to be held. I just want to be left alone!" She walked towards the stairs.

"Tina..."

She could see the concern on his face, but she had no desire to talk to him. "I just want to be alone and relax in the bathtub, Greg," she said softly. She added with a hint of bitterness, "Maybe you could stay down here and protect me from anyone breaking in. Isn't that what a husband is supposed to do; protect his wife?"

Greg frowned with the hurt of being rejected by his wife again. There was much he could say about how distant she had been acting, but he responded sincerely, "You're safe. Go take a bath and relax for a while."

CHAPTER 18

The Middleton Christian Church youth minister sat on the carpeted floor of one of the classrooms with the teens who made up the youth group. Cory Higgins was a young twenty-eight-year-old with a passion for teaching the Word to the youth in particular. He held his Bible in his hands and opened it to Psalm 62.

"Listen to this Psalm, guys, Psalms 62: 5-8," Cory said. *"I wait quietly before God, for my hope is in Him. He alone is my rock and my salvation. My salvation and my honor come from God alone. He is my refuge, a rock where no enemy can reach me. O my people, trust in Him at all times. Pour out your heart to Him, for God is our refuge."*

Cory closed his Bible. "I love the fact that God loves us enough to send His son to die for our sins on the cross so that we can be with Him. I love that, but it gets even better; we become his children when we accept Jesus as our Savior and God becomes our father. But it gets even better; God promises to lead our paths if we let him, and God also promises to protect us, and that's awesome! God is our refuge, a place of hiding. A place of resting. We can take our troubles and especially our fears and hand them to Jesus. We can give them to the Lord, but then we must refuse to take them back. That means every time that fear begins to come back, we need to say, 'No! I have given it to Jesus.' We give it by faith, and we have to hold onto that faith because trusting in God without faith isn't trusting him at all. We must give our troubles to the Lord, and then doing our part, we trust and rest in Him. Jesus commanded us to, 'Do not fear.' But you can't do it without surrendering the issue entirely to the Lord and having the faith not to take it back. Picture an airplane. It takes two wings for it to fly, right? If we surrender our fears to Jesus on one wing and set our faith on the other wing, our worries will fly away.

"Throughout the Bible, God is continuously saying 'come to me!' He wants us to rely on him as if our lives depend on him because they do. The Lord doesn't want us half committed and faithless. He wants us to come boldly to his throne as his children, filled with faith and committed fully to him. If you don't want to live in fear and anxiety, here's the two-part secret; surrender everything to Jesus Christ and never abandon your faith in him.

"The proverbial wolf story can come in multitudes of ways, but hear this, when the wolf comes knocking, you can send him on a one-way flight to Jesus Christ. If you can remember that planes need two wings to fly; surrender and faith."

When youth group was over, the teens filtered into smaller groups of friends while parents were picking others up; Karen stepped away from her friends to approach Pastor Cory. She spoke quietly. "You were supposed to give the second half of last week's sermon about Apostle Paul. You changed it because of Rene escaping today, didn't you?"

Cory nodded as he glanced over at Samuel playing foosball with his friends. "Yeah, I did. Pastor Dan called me and said Samuel was quite upset by the escape. I hope my words bring him some reassurance that God is with him." He paused to look at Karen caringly. "So, how are you doing?"

Karen shrugged uncaringly. "I'm fine. I just wish the news would leave us alone. They're making a big deal out of nothing. I understand Rene escaping is a big deal and they should cover that story, but we have nothing to do with him escaping. Why do they have to stand outside of our house and tell the world I'm his daughter? One day everything is fine, and the next, I'm stared at and treated like a stranger by the other kids at school. Like I'm a freak all of a sudden. I'm just me! But now I'm Rene's daughter." A mist of water clouded her eyes. "I hate it."

"Of course," Cory said gently. "Karen, I can't even begin to understand what you must be feeling. There's probably a variety of emotions you must be feeling, but I do know this; it will pass. Just as soon as Rene is caught, the media will forget about you and your family. In my opinion, the only reason they're hounding your family is that at the moment, there's nothing else to talk about. Give it a day or two and things will start going back to normal," Cory said with a wave of his hand. "And the other kids will come back around as well; you just walk in your integrity, Karen. That's all you have to do."

Karen wiped her eyes quickly. "That's all I can do, Cory. I better get home. Thanks, Cory."

"My pleasure. Have a good night."

"I will. Robert, Samuel, let's get going," she called out.

"I'm not done yet," Samuel replied from his foosball game without looking at her.

"I don't care, let's go!" Karen ordered. She hollered to Robert across the room, "Robert, let's go."

"Wait a minute," Robert hollered back. He and his friends were talking to some freshman girls.

"No, now!" she tried to sound authoritative.

An eighth-grade boy came running into the church, dripping wet from the rain. "Karen, someone scratched up your car! They wrote some bad things!"

"What?"

Robert Slater sprinted outside quickly before anyone else could reach the door. Outside, the rain fell heavily in the parking lot lights. Karen's older tan Honda Accord was vandalized by someone scratching unmentionable words into the paint. Nearly every door and side panel either had deep scratches across the paint or a combination of words that were degrading and foul. Robert stood in his T-shirt and fumed. "If I find out who did this, I'm going to kick their ass!" he said heatedly.

Karen began to cry in disbelief. Her friend Amanda put her arms around her. "It'll be okay," Amanda kept saying.

Samuel came outside amidst the commotion. He asked, "Did Rene do it?"

"No! But when I find out who did, I'm going to hurt them!" Robert said.

Cory called the police.

Officer Steve Turley was thirty-one, with a square-shaped face and broad, muscular body. His eyes were light blue, hardened, and alert. Officer Turley had a military background which made him neither friendly nor unfriendly, just profession oriented. He had met Karen and the others at the church to investigate the vandalism to her car and wrote up a report. Under the circumstances of who she was and the search for Rene still active, Officer Turley called the Police Chief, Harry Bishop. Harry told him to follow Karen home and Harry would meet them there. Steve Turley spoke with Greg and Tina about the vandalism and the text messages on Karen's phone. It didn't take long for him to discover that the text messages were from Ron Myers' cell phone. With the information provided by Greg about Ron being expelled from school earlier that day and the text messages from his phone, suspicion and basic common sense pointed to Ron as the likely suspect. There was no proof at the moment, but there was probable cause. Both officers knew Ron personally and had little doubt of his guilt.

"We will go speak with Ron and see what he says, but, Greg, I can't promise that we can charge him. Without proof, our hands are rather tied," Harry spoke with pending regret.

"What about the text messages?" Tina asked heatedly.

"They're just words, I'm afraid."

"Come on, you have to know he did it! The same words he texted are scratched into our car. He's the only one who would do that, Harry!" she exclaimed.

"Tina, I know that. We can accuse him all night long, and we could arrest him with probable cause, but without proof that he did it, it may not hold up in court. No one saw anything, Tina, and I'm the kind of guy who wants proof because I want it to stick in the court of law."

"What if I saw him?" Tina asked angrily.

Harry peered at her quizzically. "Did you, Tina, really?"

"If it gets my car repainted and him thrown in jail, then yeah, I saw him!"

Greg shook his head. "Tina…"

"What, Greg?" she snapped. "Somebody has to do something. We can't let him get away with this! Enough is enough. First, it was what he did at school, in which, you did what exactly? Nothing. Then came the text messages, and now this! Come on, Greg, we have to do something!" She turned back to Harry and Steve. "Yeah, I saw him carving up my car!"

Harry spoke candidly, "I'm glad to hear that, Tina. That means we can charge him for it, and you can testify in a court of law. You'd then be committing perjury and arrested yourself while all charges against Ron are dropped. You might do a few nights in jail and would be sued by Ron for a sweet financial gain, I bet." There was no-nonsense on his expression. "Now, are you still willing to do that?"

Tina signed heavily and shook her head.

Harry continued, "Like I was saying, we will go pay Ron a visit and do what we can. I suggest you contact your insurance company tomorrow. I am sorry," he said and left the Slaters' home.

Upset, Greg turned to Karen. "Why didn't you tell us about those text messages?"

Karen gave a dismissive shrug of her shoulders. "It was no big deal."

"Obviously, it was, Karen!" Greg raised his voice. "No one has the right to call you a bitch or anything else! Especially when it's a number that you don't know, making the threats! You don't *ever* respond to someone you don't know! Am I getting through to you?"

"Yes, father," she replied sarcastically.

"Karen, I will take your phone away if you don't change your attitude right now!" Greg sternly warned. "It's not a game. Threatening texts and sex texts are not acceptable. Do you understand me?"

"I don't sex text!" she huffed as teenagers often do.

"I didn't say you did. I'm simply making a point that you need to tell us when this kind of thing happens!"

Tina shouted, "Enough! For crying out loud, Greg, she gets the point. I get the point. We all get the damn point! The question is, do you get the point? And I highly doubt you do!" Tina said, glaring at Greg.

Greg gawked at her with a perplexed expression on his face. "No, riddler, I don't get it. Why don't you explain it to me because I have absolutely no idea what you're talking about!"

Tina breathed heavily. "Of course, you don't. And you never will," she stated and walked away towards the stairs.

Greg shook his head with frustration.

Samuel asked gingerly, "What's wrong with Mom?"

Greg took a deep breath and exhaled. "She's just tired. By the way, Sam, don't shower in the mornings anymore. So go take one now."

"What? Why?" he asked, "That's not fair."

CHAPTER 19

A KNOCK ON THE DOOR STARTLED WENDY MYERS AWAKE AS she laid tiredly on her recliner. She opened her eyes with annoyance and focused her eyes on the clock; it was just after 9:00 p.m.

"Wanna get the door?" Jeff asked impatiently. He was sitting on the couch, watching a movie. His cigarettes and beer were on a side table next to him.

Wendy stood with irritation from her reclined position. She was in her bathrobe and was very tired. She opened the door, expecting to see one of Ron's friends but was alarmed to see Police Chief Harry Bishop and Officer Steve Turley standing on her porch. Both of their squad cars were idling beside their driveway.

"Hi," she said wearily. "Can I help you?" she asked.

Harry spoke, "Good evening, Missus Myers. I'm sorry to come by so late, but I'd like to speak with Ron if he's in."

"Ronny? Why, what did he do?" she sounded alarmed.

Harry shook his head. "Missus Myers, I'm afraid there's something I need to discuss with Ron. Is he home?"

"Yeah, come in," she said. She turned towards the hallway leading to the two bedrooms, quickly walked to Ron's room, and knocked before opening the door. "The police are here for you. What did you do?"

A moment later, Ron walked out of this room wearing a pair of shorts and a T-shirt. He had recently showered. "What's up?" he asked. Ron didn't like police officers in general, but he had a particular dislike for Officer Turley. The feeling was mutual.

Harry took a breath of the smoke-filled air. "Do you want to step outside so we can speak privately? Or would you rather speak in front of your parents?"

Ron quickly answered, "I live with my mom, Harry; you know that."

"What's going on?" Wendy asked.

"Yeah, what is going on?" Ron asked condescendingly.

"We got a call about some harassing text messages you sent to Karen Slater earlier this evening. I ran the cell number, and it came up as your phone. You did text those messages to her?" Harry asked.

Ron shrugged. "Yeah, but it was no big deal. I didn't mean anything by it."

Harry nodded. "I read through the texts, and it appears you were growing angry with her. Is that a fair assessment?"

Ron chuckled with a smile. "No! Karen and I are always talking to each other like that."

Harry frowned. "I'm surprised by that since you haven't texted her before tonight."

Ron widened his eyes as he explained, "I didn't say we text. I said we talk that way. At school, you know?"

"I understand you were expelled from school today for harassing her. Are you sure you're not a little resentful towards her? Was it her fault that you were expelled?" Wendy Myers stepped forward and physically turned Ron's shoulder to face her. "You were what?" she shouted angrily. "You were expelled from school, Ronny? For what exactly?"

"It was nothing, Mom," he answered, getting angry and defensive.

"What did he do?" she asked Harry heatedly.

Harry addressed Wendy, "Between seven and eight-thirty tonight, someone severely vandalized Karen Slater's car in the Christian Church parking lot while she was at youth group. We believe it was your son."

"What?" Ron asked innocently. "I was here all night!"

Steve Turley casts his eyes over to the couch. "Jeff, is that true?"

Jeff shook his head. "No, he was gone for an hour or so at about that time."

"I drove into Ridgefield to get some cigarettes. There's no crime in that. But I didn't scratch up her car."

"I didn't say it was scratched," Harry replied knowingly.

Ron was getting angry. "Well, you said it was vandalized. What other way is there? You can't paint it in the rain!"

"Was anyone else with you?" Harry asked.

"No, I was alone."

Jeff spoke from the couch. "You left here with Eddy."

"I took him home!" Ron snapped impatiently at Jeff.

"Eddy Franklyn?" Steve asked.

"Yeah," Ron said.

Wendy was growing impatient. "What did you do to that girl to get expelled, Ronny?"

"Nothing, Mom!" he yelled. "You guys are trying to set me up for something I didn't do! Maybe her father came to town and did it. Did you ever think of that?" he asked irritability.

A slight smirk appeared on Steve's lips.

Harry spoke evenly, "Do you have a pocketknife, Ron?"

"Yeah, I have a pocketknife. I have a hunting knife too. Do you want to see them?" he asked sharply.

"Do you carry a screwdriver in your car?"

"No!" Ron said quickly. His eyes widened with surprise.

"May I search your car?" Harry asked. The scratches on Karen's car were too deep and wide to have been made by a key or a knife. In Harry's experience, the scratches were done by a heavier and broader gauge steel object like a large standard screwdriver.

"No, you may not! Unless you have a search warrant, I don't believe you can either. You don't have any evidence that I did anything to her car, except text messages? I'm guessing you don't have any witnesses, or you'd arrest me. So no, I won't let you plant something in my car. I know you guys will go out of your way to help Coach Slater and his family, but you won't do a thing to help us. Karen can speed through town, and you just wave at her, but you guys will pull me over for a taillight out and harass me for an hour about it. No, I won't let you look in my car for anything unless you have a search warrant. I'm sick of being harassed just because I don't play football!" He looked his mother in the eyes. "I didn't do anything to Karen that everyone else wasn't doing. I got singled because I'm not an athlete. That's all!" he said irately. He spoke to Harry, "Are we done yet?"

Harry spoke, frankly. "I know you did it, Ron. I have absolutely no doubt about that. Unfortunately, at this time, I don't have any evidence."

"I didn't think so," Ron said victoriously.

"But," Harry continued, "there's enough probable cause that I could arrest you right now if I wanted to…but I'll wait. We're a small-town department, so we have the time to talk to every home on the street and news will get around. If anyone saw anything, they'll let me know. This isn't over, Ron. Missus Myers," he spoke to Wendy, "You may want to call the school tomorrow and talk to Principal Bennet in person. You folks have a good night." He stepped outside with Steve. When they were back at their cars, Harry spoke softly, "You know he's calling Eddy right now to get their story straight. Talk to Eddy anyway and see what he says. I'll see you tomorrow. Have a good night."

"Alright. This kid's such a punk," Steve said with disgust.

"We'll catch him," Harry said confidently. He slapped Steve on the back affectionately. "Have a good night."

CHAPTER 20

THE ONLY NEW INFORMATION ABOUT RENE DIBARI ON THE
eleven o'clock news was that he was still on the loose. They
had recapped the day's biggest story, which was finding Jack
Miller's body in a rural fishing pond and his stolen car
being found in the Eugene Mall parking lot. They broadcast
a short video segment from the mall parking lot that
showed Rene walking towards the mall entrance from Jack's
car. He was dressed in Gary Baugh's clothes and appeared
as normal as anyone else on the street. It was unnerving to
both Tina and Greg to see him walking free in the gritty
video image. The reporter announced that the joint efforts
of State and Federal agencies were viewing video images
from inside of the mall to trace his steps further. At present,
there was no evidence of his kidnapping or stealing another
car from the mall. The authorities suspected Rene was
possibly still in the Eugene area. They also highlighted the
interview with Greg and replayed it on Channel 9.

Since giving the interview to Channel 9, other news
channels and one National channel repeatedly called to
schedule an interview. Greg had declined them all so far.
His main concern was how it would affect Tina and the
kids. He didn't want any more publicity, as it had already
put enough pressure upon his loved ones. Tina was under a

lot of stress and Karen suddenly being thrust into the spotlight had taken her completely off guard to the unexpected reactions of her friends and schoolmates. Samuel was perhaps the most frightened of them all, but he felt more at peace after youth group. The car being vandalized left them disgusted and angry, but it had nothing to do with Rene.

Greg had said goodnight to Samuel and went downstairs to find Tina. She was in her office, a small den on the main floor that they had made into an office. She was sitting at the desk looking at new home listings on the computer screen when Greg walked in. "Are you coming to bed?" he asked softly.

"I have work to do," she said without looking up.

"Oh," Greg said and sat down in an office chair that sat in front of the desk. "This late at night?"

Tina moved her eyes to peer at him through her glasses. "Does it matter if I work late one night? It shouldn't really matter to you now, should it?"

Greg frowned. "I don't understand…"

"That's right, I'm the riddler now!" she spoke heatedly. She kept her voice low. "You stood on National TV and basically invited Rene to come here. You didn't ask me how I felt about it. You just did it. Why?"

"Because it was the only way to get them to leave the school, this whole thing has become a distraction to the students, staff and Karen's the one paying for it. You weren't there to see the hurt on her face today. And then to look outside and watch Ron Myers talking to the TV camera… you know darn well he's not painting an accurate picture of Karen or what happened. I agreed to the interview so that Channel 9 News would leave the school grounds for good. It wasn't national news, by the way; it was local."

"It doesn't matter! You care more about that school than you do me. You didn't ask them to leave us alone. When are you going to realize that your family should come first?"

Greg was frustrated. "My family does come first. I did that interview, so they'd quit hanging around like leaches.

I've said all I have to say. There's no reason for them to harass us anymore."

"No," Tina said irritably. "They still want to interview you, not Channel 9, but all of the rest. All you did was throw another piece of meat into the wolf pen, Greg! And it wasn't even for me; it was for your precious school."

Greg sighed. "It's our school, and it's where I work. I was protecting our daughter."

"By inviting Rene to come back here?" she asked quickly.

"I didn't invite Rene to come here!" Greg raised his voice irritably. "What I did do is solve the issue at hand. Sorry I didn't call you and ask for your permission. Next time I'll send them to your office, and they can distract your clients instead of our students!"

"Oh, that would be wise, wouldn't it, Greg? The other agents would really appreciate that. I don't want anything to do with them, period."

"And yet you'll sit in here pissed off at me for doing what I think is right? Come on, Tina!" He took a deep breath and spoke calmly, "I know we've got a lot on our plates right now with just Rene, but let's not fight about it. We need to get on the same page and show some stability for the kids and us. The last thing we need is to be at each other's throats."

Tina's eyes moved away from Greg to the wall and back to Greg. "Fine, but you need to start putting us first. When you start doing that, you might find a happier wife," she said with a hint of animosity.

Greg took a deep breath. He was growing frustrated by her tone. It was becoming a catchphrase she'd say more often but would never elaborate upon it to any length. "So, how can I do that appropriately?" he asked with a touch of unintended sarcasm. He rephrased his question after seeing her expression change at his tone. "I keep hearing that lately, but you don't explain how I can do better," he spoke sincerely.

Tina leaned forward over the desk to explain. "From

mid-August through November, all I hear about is football. You spend your time coaching and then correcting papers. From the moment football ends to February, I hear about wrestling day after day, and the tournaments last all weekend. I don't see you during wrestling season, except when you're correcting papers. Do you see what I'm getting at?"

"Tina..."

"No, let me finish! If you're not coaching, then we have to watch Karen play volleyball, basketball, softball, summer leagues, travel here, travel there. It's all about sports. And just when we might get towards the end, football season starts! You go to every sporting event at the school no matter what, even if our kids aren't playing. That includes school plays, choir concerts, and dances! Quite honestly, I'm sick of chaperoning dances at the high school gym. Perhaps I'm just sick of everything. Even when we could spend one day together, you refuse to miss church." She shook her head with tears in her eyes. "Where do I fit in? Greg, Rene's out there somewhere and you don't care one bit about the news camped outside of our front door or them showing our house on TV. But when they come to the school, Coach Slater comes to the rescue, just like you did for me...once."

Greg shook his head with a frustrated grin. "So, what do you want me to do, quit? I'm a teacher; that's what I do. It's never been a problem before, so why is it now? In the last month, in particular, you've been acting differently, so what is it? Are you seeing someone else?" he asked seriously.

Tina glared at Greg with disbelief and spoke with disgust, "Are you accusing me of cheating on you, Greg? That's what Rene used to do; are you going to start that too?"

"No, I'm not accusing you," he said sharply. "But something's changed in you and I don't know what. You don't want to come to church with us anymore. You don't want to do a lot of things with me anymore. You seem to grow more bitter every time you see me, and I don't know why. I've done nothing out of the ordinary to deserve it, but I am getting sick of it!"

Tina shook her head. "So am I," she said softly.

Greg stood up. "I'm going to bed. Do your work or whatever it is you're doing. I'll see you in the morning. Oh, and I'll make sure there's hot water for you in the shower in the morning," he said sarcastically and left the office.

Tina clicked onto her social media page and typed the words, "Joy comes in the morning." Within ten minutes, three of her friends "liked" her status. If they only knew the intention of her statement, her three "friends" probably wouldn't like it so much. Increasingly more often, the only place she smiled anymore was at work.

CHAPTER 21

Karen Slater stood in the senior's traditional hallway near a heat duct known as the senior heater, not far from the high school's main office. She stood with a small group of her friends, discussing the events from the night before. Her best friend, Amanda Moore, stood with her boyfriend, Ross Greenfield. He was a tall, athletic, blond-haired young man who was also the football team's quarterback. Along with them was Ross' best friend, Chris Willis, the star running back. All of them listened to their friend Karen intently. "But Chief Bishop said they couldn't arrest him because there's no actual proof that he did it," Karen finished sounding quite irritated.

"Here's your phone," Ross said, handing it back to her. He and Chris had been reading through the text messages. "We need to thump Ron around a bit," he said to Chris.

Chris nodded. "Oh yeah, he got Bruce suspended, and now this," Chris said, shaking his head. "The scum bag's asking for it."

"Losing Bruce for tomorrow night's game screws us big time. That right 28 ace sweep we've been practicing all week is useless without Bruce pulling. Now we have Tommy Lawrence starting varsity,"

Ross said with disgust, "He can barely do a push up let alone stop the bulldog defense."

"Can you believe that, starting a freshman on varsity?" Chris stated unhappily. "We outta kick the snot out of Ron for that too."

"No," Karen said, "you guys better leave him alone, or you'll be suspended, and my dad needs you two to play. He was mad about losing Bruce, but he'd kick your butts if you get in trouble for nothing."

"For nothing?" Amanda asked. "It seems to me that there are a lot of reasons to want to beat Ron up. If the law can't do anything, then someone else should."

"Chief Bishop said they'll keep talking to Eddy Franklyn. He thinks Eddy is lying and will tell the truth when he gets scared enough. Officer Turley, I think, is taking a personal interest in speaking to Eddy," Karen said with a slight smile.

Ross laughed. "Steve Turley will have Eddy talking like the weasel he is by the end of the day. Steve can be a mean guy when he wants to be. He's a lot more intimidating than the chief, in my opinion."

"Eddy hasn't talked yet," Karen said simply. She shrugged her shoulders and changed the subject. "One thing about our police department is they do care about the Middleton citizens. They've been driving by our house a lot lately since Rene escaped. Last night, I peeked out my window and saw Officer Turley parked across the road. They're taking the risk of Rene coming here very seriously."

Chris nodded quietly. "By the way, I just wanted to apologize again, Karen, for joking around with you yesterday. I am sorry. It wasn't funny."

Karen tossed a hand to brush it away. "Thanks, Chris. I forgive you."

"So now that Bruce is suspended," Ross spoke light-heartedly to Karen, "Who's taking you to the dance tomorrow night?"

"I wasn't going with Bruce."

"He likes you," Ross said with a smile.

"I don't like him like that," Karen answered.

"Hey, maybe you could go with Chris. We could double date and drive into Ridgefield afterward to eat something. It's going to be Halloween night, we might as well have some fun," Ross stated.

Chris shrugged uncomfortably. "How does that sound to you?" he asked Karen awkwardly.

Karen feigned great thought and then said, "Well...okay, but Bruce might get mad." Ross laughed, as did Amanda.

"Cool," Chris said. "We'll have fun. What are you dressing up as? The dance is a costume party, you know."

Karen raised her eyebrows as she explained, "I haven't had the opportunity to think about it, really. What are you planning to dress up as?"

Chris grinned, slightly embarrassed. "A pirate."

"Then I'll be a piratess."

The first bell rang, indicating they had five minutes until class started.

"I'll talk to you guys later," Chris said. He walked away with an excited smile. Amanda drew near to Karen and said quietly, "Ross told me that Chris really likes you!"

Karen's mouth opened with a reluctant smile. "Now that we have a date, you tell me that? It sounds like you and Ross set that up to me."

Amanda giggled mischievously. "Maybe a little."

Eddy Franklyn had noticed throughout the morning that the other students had singled him out for the vandalism of Karen's car. The gossip got around quickly that the police had questioned him. Three other students had asked him if he had scratched Karen's car. Each time he denied it and said he knew nothing about it. He was half honest, he hadn't scratched her car, but he watched Ron do it with a standard screwdriver. Eddy had tried to talk Ron out of vandalizing her car but he was determined to do it. Eddy's part was to keep an eye out while Ron proceeded to carve into the car's paint. It was good common sense that if he said anything except for what Ron told him to say, not only would Ron give him a beating, but he'd be just as guilty and liable as Ron. It was in his best interest to deny any knowledge whatsoever, especially since the police had come to his house the night before. He had no intention of saying anything more than he had already to anyone. It was all better left unsaid. Eddy didn't have any problem with Karen or her family. He thought she was not only beautiful but also very nice. He knew why Ron despised her, but it wasn't her fault. Ron had a serious crush on Karen for a very long time and though he'd ask her out, she'd always turn him down. To her credit, she was always sensitive and kind about doing so. It all came to a climax last spring at the May Day Dance when Ron asked Karen for a slow dance and accepted his invitation. As they danced, a slight struggle occurred and then turned brutal as Ron tried to pull her close and force a kiss while cupping her breast with one hand while being drawn close to him. She struggled and kneed him in the groin to break loose from his grip and then slapped him so hard across the face that it sounded louder than the music that played. Ron was promptly removed from the dance and faced expulsion from school. He was given a three-day suspension instead. Ron had never forgiven Karen for not only rejecting him but for humiliating him in front of the entire school. Sometimes even now, other students would make fun of him about that night.

Eddy was becoming more anxious from the accusations from even his good friends like Gina Wickering. Gina was an attractive girl with curly dirty blonde hair that barely touched her shoulders and large blue eyes on an oval face that might've attracted even the most popular of students, except for her undeserved reputation of having a sordid past. She had moved to Middleton one year before and smoked. That common link connected her to the other smokers, including Ron, who she began dating. Before she knew it, she had a long reputation of unknown sources that labeled her as a tramp to the other students without any evidence or getting to know her. She had become a friend of Eddy's. He knew she was far from what others thought of her. She liked to party, but her heart was as golden as any other.

As usual, they stood across the street from the school, smoking cigarettes during lunch, when Gina said, "I know Ron did it, Eddy. You don't have to lie to me. I know him too well and I know when you're lying, I can see it on your face. I know you were there. Did you scratch her car up?"

A friend or not, Eddy was taken off guard and suddenly angry at the common knowledge that everyone, including his friends, suspected him. He was mad at her for accusing him in front of their group of friends, and spoke heatedly, "I had nothing to do with it! I don't know anything about it, and I am tired of being blamed! I would not do that to her, so shut up, Gina!"

Gina grinned. "Oh, that's right, she's your dream girl!" she said mockingly of his long-time crush on Karen.

"Get lost, Gina," he had said and left his group of friends. Lunch was nearly over, and Eddy walked down the crowded hallway, still irritated with Gina. To add to what was becoming a bad day, he had an English class that he hated to go to next. Eddy was in no hurry for the lunch bell to ring, indicating it was time to get to class. He walked into the men's bathroom and took his standing position in front of a urinal.

A moment later, three guys walked into the bathroom and intentionally surrounded him as he relieved himself. Ross Greenfield, Chris Willis, and Curt Simpson all stood around him with no jesting in their eyes.

"What's going on?" Ross asked in an unfriendly manner.

Eddy glanced over his shoulder and turned back to finish up quickly. His heart suddenly pounded as he nervously buttoned up his jeans. "Ah, nothing. I'm finished," he sounded frightened. He stepped away from the urinal and turned to walk past the boys. He was stopped by the big palm of Curt Simpson's hand, pushing him back against the wall of urinals. He caught himself from falling into one.

"Where do you think you're going?" Curt asked, his voice was full of venom. He was the biggest student in school and definitely the toughest. Curt was over six feet tall and two hundred and thirty pounds. He kept his black hair cut short and combed to the side. He was an All-State lineman and a top-ranked wrestler for Coach Slater's wrestling team. Usually, Curt was friendly and gentle, but his eyes glared right through Eddy with no more concern than stepping on an ant.

Eddy was scared. "To class." His eyes began to mist over.

"Not yet, you're not!" Curt exclaimed. "What's this crap I hear that you scratched up Karen's car? What the hell's your problem, Eddy?"

Eddy shook his head. "I didn't! I don't know anything about it," he insisted and tried to walk quickly around the three boys.

Chris Willis grabbed him by the shirt collar, spun him around, and drove him five steps backward, slamming him against the wall. Chris held him there by the collar as he spoke through his gritted teeth, "We know you and that piece of trash Ron Myers did it! Don't tell me you didn't, or I'll kick your ass and then Curt will. We'll kick your ass every day until you tell the cops the truth. Do you hear me, Eddy?" Chris shouted before shoving Eddy into the wall again.

Eddy's eyes watered. "I didn't do anything, man. Honestly," Eddy pleaded with a shaken voice.

"Oh," Ross said, "I suppose just anyone could've carved up Karen's car for no reason, huh?" Ross said accusingly.

"I don't know..."

Chris Willis shouted, "Bull! You know I can't kick your ass right now, but I see you every day in town. I'm going to hurt you and Ron for what you two did to her car!"

Big Curt Simpson stepped forward and jabbed a pointed

finger into Eddy's chest. "Listen, you little pot-smoking greaser. I'll snap your little neck like a twig! Who did that to her car?"

Greg Slater had heard what sounded like an altercation in the restroom and stepped inside just in time to see Curt give Eddy a shove against the wall. Ross and Chris also helped corner, Eddy. "What's going on?" Greg demanded.

Ross answered awkwardly, "Hey, Coach."

"Don't hey coach me. What's going on?" Greg demanded again.

"Oh," Ross answered uncomfortably, "we were just talking to our buddy."

"Don't give me that, Greenfield. Curt?"

Curt Simpson lowered his head and spoke meekly, "We're just trying to get him to tell us what happened to Karen's car. We're just trying to help," he added quickly.

Greg sighed and shook his head with disgust. "This isn't how you help anyone, gentlemen. There's no proof that Eddy knows anything about what happened. You boys ought to consider that, but we'll talk more about this before practice in my office. We're not finished with this. Now apologize to Eddy and shake his hand."

Greg waited and watched as all three of his football players apologized and offered their hand to Eddy. "Now you get to class," he said and watched the three boys leave the bathroom.

Eddy remained against the wall, trying to avoid looking Greg in the eyes. Greg spoke softly, "Are you okay?"

Eddy nodded. He glanced into Greg's eyes and then looked away. He was nervous. "Yeah, I'm fine," he said quickly and began to walk away.

"Just a second, Eddy. I would like to talk to you for a moment."

"I have to get to class," Eddy said as the first bell rang.

Greg nodded. "All I want to say is if you do know something about Karen's car, I'd appreciate it if you told Chief Bishop or Officer Turley. Not because you like me or because of anything those guys said. I promise you; they won't bother you again in any way, shape, or form." He paused. "You should tell the truth because it's the right thing to do. That's it; it's just the right thing to do. For the rest of your life, you're going to make choices for every circumstance that you'll come across. Your reputation as a man will be built upon those choices, so if you lie once, then you'll have to tell another lie to cover up for the first lie, and pretty soon, you'll be lying to cover up all the other lies. Sooner or later, everyone will know you as a liar and won't believe anything you say. Or, you can be known as a good man, a man of integrity. It is much simpler just to be an honest man. A man of integrity, Eddy, is a good man. You most certainly can be that kind of a man. The only secret to being that kind of man is simply doing what's right," Greg said sincerely with a soft smile. "I trust you will be. Now you better get to class."

"Um, I will. Can you write me a note; I'm going to be late?" Eddy asked.

"You bet," Greg said and pulled out a pocket note pad from his shirt pocket and a pen.

"Mister Slater..."

Greg waited with the pen to the notepad.

"Nothing," Eddy said, changing his mind.

Greg finished the note. "Here you go. Remember, Eddy, it's your choice what kind of a man you're going to be. It's totally up to you."

"I don't know anything about Karen's car, Mister Slater," Eddy said uneasily.

Greg tapped Eddy on the arm. "Eddy, I care more about you becoming a man of integrity than I do about the car. Have a good day."

CHAPTER 22

RAIN FELL HEAVILY AS RAY TRISTAN OPENED THE PASSENGER side door for Tina to climb into his red Porsche quickly. When she was safely inside and reaching for her seatbelt, Ray gently closed the door and stepped around the car. "It's pouring," he stated as he got into the driver's seat and started his car. Absolutely pouring, we should have stayed inside for a few minutes longer," he said, referring to the restaurant where they had lunch.

"Yeah, it is," Tina said simply while Ray maneuvered through the parking lot to turn onto the street. The rain poured down, hitting the windows with large, heavy drops that quickly saturated the parking lot and ran heavily along the curb towards the storm drains. Tina's hair and suit jacket were wet from the quick run from the restaurant out to the car.

"Well, again, I'm sorry to hear about Karen's car being vandalized," Ray said as he drove towards First Street at the other end of town. "I have a buddy that I play poker with occasionally, who could give you a good deal on a new paint job. He owes me a favor or two. I could get you a great deal on having it re-painted if you'd like."

Tina scratched her neck lightly. "I'm sure our insurance will cover it."

"And they'll raise your premium too. My buddy could make it look brand new for, I don't know, a few hundred dollars, probably. As I said, he owes me a favor, so I can get it done fairly cheap. He's been out of work for a while now; I'm just trying to help you both out."

"You seem to have a lot of buddies. One with a beach house I could stay in and a car painter too, huh?"

Ray chuckled. "I'm in the money business, so I get to know people here and there. I like to help out my friends when I can. Let's just say it helps my business. Take you, for example, I've been sending you all of my new clients since August. It's been a little slow lately, but I send them to you," he said while he paid attention to the traffic at an intersection. He continued, "I bring business your way and you bring it back my way. We both succeed that way. It's the same with other people I know, I help them with a loan or anything really, and they pay me back when they can. Sometimes a favor is worth more than the money, such as Lionel's beach cabin is open this week; all you have to do is go. I can get the key at any time. And John can get that car painted in a few days, and your insurance will never know. So, if I can help, you let me know. I'll make sure you're taken care of."

She turned her body towards him in her seat. Her eyes gazed upon him with an adorning touch of a smile in the corners of her lips. "Why are you doing all of this for me, Ray?"

"Why?" he asked questionably. "Because I believe in loyalty, and when you're loyally sending your buyers to me, I return the favor." He gazed longingly at her. "You're my friend. I'll do whatever I can to help you, Tina. You mean a lot to me," he said sincerely. He added quickly, "But that's why I have so many buddies. I help them in their time of need, just like I want to help you."

Perhaps it was the rain, but as Ray turned onto First Street towards her office, Tina realized she had no desire to go back to work. "You know, Ray, I don't feel like going back to the office right now with everything going on. So maybe if you're not busy, we could go park somewhere and talk for a while."

"Absolutely!" Ray said with surprise. "I know the perfect place. Have you ever been to the nature preserve outside of town?"

"No," Tina spoke slowly as she watched her office pass by outside of her window. "It's raining, you know."

Ray laughed. "We're not going for a walk. It's just a nice place and usually empty, especially on a day like today."

"I've heard there were some nice trails to walk on, but I've never been there."

Ray drove back across town and left Ridgefield on a two-lane road that led out into the country past a thriving vineyard on a rolling hillside belonging to one of the many wineries specializing in Pinot Noir wine. Ray passed another vineyard with an ornamental gate and an advertised tasting room not more than five miles down the road. Ray slowed down and turned left onto a paved, narrow roadway with a small green sign indicating a park. He drove a hundred yards off the main road into a small parking lot surrounded by a forest of trees, underbrush, and a small flowing river separating the parking lot from the park with a walking bridge visible as the only means to cross over it. The parking lot was empty, as Ray had suspected it would be. He came to a stop facing the river and turned off the motor. The radio played lightly with a soft rock radio station that played love songs. Ray unbuckled his seatbelt and turned towards Tina in his seat. "On stormy days like this, I like to go home and turn on some music, make myself something to eat and relax. Put on my sweats, kick up my feet and just watch the rain fall out the window. It's nice to do nothing at all except watch the rain."

"You obviously aren't married," Tina said scornfully. "My life is far too hectic to enjoy a moment like that. The only quiet time I have is spent cleaning the house or making dinner usually, just before everyone gets home, and then it becomes chaos," she said with a defeated tone to her voice.

"No, I'm not married, but I was," Ray said. "Getting divorced was the best thing that ever happened to me. It was scary at first, but then came the joy of living after being in a dead marriage for so long. I say we only live once, so why bother staying married in an unhappy relationship." He hesitated a moment as she stared sadly out the window at the rain.

He continued, "Take you, for instance; you're married to a guy that has forgotten how wonderful you are. He doesn't care anymore if your hair looks beautiful or not, and I wonder if he'd even notice it if you had it done today. He puts sports ahead of you and your kids' safety, for crying out loud! You're miserable, and yet you are pouring yourself out to him daily to make your marriage work. For what, the kids' sake? I didn't have any kids, but if I did, I'd still want to enjoy my life. There's no reason to live in misery when you could enjoy living your life." He paused carefully, "Now, I'm not suggesting you get divorced or leave your husband, but I know you well enough to know that you're not happy and that breaks my heart to see because you are worth much more than that. You deserve to be happy. If your husband can't make you happy, then maybe," he paused to say softly, "I can."

She turned her head and looked at him, silently taken back by his words. Her eyes were clouded with tears.

He added gently, "I think I'm falling in love with you, Tina."

"What?" she asked with a concerned expression on her face.

Ray reached his hand over to brush some of the hair away from her face gently. "I'm falling in love with you."

Tina closed her eyes as a tear fell down her cheek. She looked away from him to gaze back out the window. "Ray, I'm not..."

Ray quickly held up his hands in a defensive manner. "I

know, you're married, and I don't mean anything to you. I'm sorry, Tina. I shouldn't have said anything. It's my fault, I'm sorry," he sounded disappointed.

Tina sniffled and turned to face him. Her mascara ran down her cheeks with her tears. "It isn't that you don't mean a lot to me because you do. But I'm married to Greg. He's my husband," she said softly.

Ray sighed heavily. "I know. Trust me when I say I never expected to feel the way I do about you. It's taken me by surprise, but I can't sleep knowing you're sleeping in your house with Rene out there somewhere. If he harmed you, I'd be crushed and I'd never forgive your husband for allowing anything to happen to you or your children. I care about you, Missy. I've never had a friend like you before and I doubt I ever will again." He looked into her eyes. "I don't want to scare you away, and I won't mention it again because I care about your happiness more than I do about anything else. I respect your values and won't pressure you in any way. If you want," he said slowly, "I'll quit wanting to see you all of the time," he sounded heartbroken.

Tina answered softly. "No, it's okay. I enjoy seeing you too. You're a good friend, Ray."

Ray leaned his head against the door window. "I hope so. You deserve a good friend, a better one than me."

Tina smiled appreciatively through her moist eyes. "I couldn't imagine a better friend than you," she said and leaned over to hug him. She held him tightly and closed her eyes. The temptation to kiss him welled up within her like a spark in dry tinder. For a moment, she was afraid to release the embrace in fear of giving in to her momentary desire.

Ray moved his hands to her cheeks and softly guided her face back to look into her eyes. He moved forward to kiss her. Tina pulled back slowly and broke the embrace. "I'm married," she said quickly. "I'm sorry, Ray, I'd like to, but I can't."

Ray frowned. "It's alright, I understand," he said, disappointed. He was quiet for a moment and then said, "Now I feel like an ass. I'll take you back to the office. Is there any chance that you still might want to meet me for a drink tonight? It's ladies' night," he added with a shrug.

Tina frowned. "I'm..." Tears clouded her eyes again. "Ray, I am married to Greg, but I feel like I belong to you, and I don't understand why..." Her bottom lip began to quiver with emotion. "I just need some time. Please take me back to the office; I can't handle this right now." She covered her face with her hands and began to cry softly.

Ray watched her with compassion. "I will when your eyes are dry, and you fix your makeup. I can't have you looking upset when you go back into your office. You're much too wonderful of a person to be so sad, Tina. I'm sorry for adding to your stress. It was never my intention to upset you."

She laughed heavy-hearted, "It's not you, Ray, it's me. I just need to figure everything out. Will you wait for me that long, just until I think everything over?"

"I'm in no hurry, my friend. Take all of the time you need."

"Thank you," she said and wiped her eyes.

Ray tapped her leg. "My suggestion is to come out for a drink and relax. You deserve an evening out alone and have a little quiet time and enjoy yourself. I know you're a Christian, but one drink isn't going to hurt you."

Tina smiled. "I don't know, let me think about it. I'll call you and let you know." She used the rearview mirror to fix her makeup.

"I will be waiting," he said as he watched her adoringly as she pulled the mascara out of her purse to redo her eyes.

CHAPTER 23

EDDY FRANKLYN WAS RELIEVED WHEN THE FINAL BELL RANG, ending school for the day. It had been an uncomfortable day. He had become the number one suspect to Ron's stupid idea of vandalizing Karen's car. The three guys that threatened him in the bathroom not only scared him but confirmed that he was the center of the school gossip. Karen was perhaps the most beloved person at the school, and he was being blamed for defacing her car. His classmates had never accepted him, but he had never felt more uncomfortable than he did today.

Mister Slater had always been a friendly teacher and had never judged Eddy like some of the other teachers did at first sight. Mister Slater was one of Eddy's favorite teachers, and he was sure glad to see him enter the bathroom when Mister Slater did. Eddy knew he had nothing to worry about even if he ran into Chris Willis or the others on the street in the middle of the night. One thing Eddy knew about Greg Slater was he was a man of his word. If Mister Slater said it, he meant it. He was just that kind of a teacher.

The words that Mister Slater had spoken to him about growing up to be a good man and doing what was right had sparked a sense of guilt, or envy perhaps. Eddy didn't want to live his life as a liar and thief. He didn't want to struggle with making a living when he graduated from high school, unable to get a decent job because he couldn't pass a drug test. Eddy didn't want to go to prison as his father had. Oddly, the words spoken by Mister Slater had struck a chord, a layer of hope that caused Eddy to think he didn't have to become a nameless nobody, except to the local law enforcement officers. Eddy could actually become a respected individual, a decent citizen, and a good man like Mister Slater. He didn't have to follow his father's footsteps or those of his other family members, who basked in the glow of welfare and parole while selling a variety of drugs on the side. He could live differently, and if he chose to, he could be as successful as he showed the determination to be. What once seemed nearly impossible was made relatively simple by living three essential words, 'Do what's right.'

The more Eddy thought about it, the more its principle broadened into multiple areas of his life. If he followed that advice, he'd never again feel the guilt of hiding behind a lie or the anxiety of the police showing up at his door. He'd never have to fear being arrested or failing a drug test on any given day. He would not fear the fears that now consumed him. Its simplicity was broadening, but then the question became who's to say what's right from wrong in the shaded areas of gray? His parents taught him right from wrong, but within some of their wrongs, exceptions were made for monetary gain or personal pleasure. To hear one thing and see another is all the right from wrong, Eddy knew. To lie was wrong, but to lie about stealing money out of his mother's purse seemed reasonable.

For his mother to condemn his theft of five dollars from her purse but purchase a new TV with someone else's stolen credit card was somehow acceptable. On the one hand, his parents bitterly condemned the police, but when a man named Bob came over with a baseball bat looking to settle a score with his father, they urgently called the police for their help. To cheat on your wife is wrong, but it didn't stop his father from venturing to Bob's wife while Bob was in jail. Or, for that matter, his mother's infidelity while his father was in prison. It just never seemed to stop. The consequences had repetitive effects, fighting, arguing, alcohol and drug use, crime, arrests, and bitterness at the police for their harassment and anyone else who had a better life than them. It didn't have to be that way. If his parents simply resolved to do what was right, it would change their lives around. So many of the circumstances that they went through were the direct consequences of their choices, few of them were doing what was right. Eddy could see it and somehow, it clicked. He understood what made the difference between Mister Slater and his father and its effect on their families.

Eddy walked along the sidewalk in a hurry to get across town to Ron's house before the break in the rain ended. He wanted to tell Ron what had happened that day and thank him for the trouble. He was afraid the police would drive up at any time and arrest him for the damage to the car; all they needed was some proof, and proof in a small town wasn't always hard to find. He had taken Mister Slater's words to heart, but he didn't want to take the chance of being arrested if he told the truth. Besides, staying loyal to his friend was the right thing to do. They were in it together, after all.

Eddy crossed Sixth Street and kept walking east on Church Street when he noticed an older, heavy-set man wearing a raincoat while walking his dog. The man was looking straight ahead at Eddy while coming towards him. Somehow Eddy knew the man wanted to talk to him and it brought an uneasy feeling that began to build within him the closer every step brought the two of them together. The uneasiness in his chest became a precautionary urge to cross the street and avoid the man walking his dog. Eddy did not recognize him, but he didn't like the odd feeling that he was getting about the man. Maybe he was an undercover officer and the little pug on a leash was a trained narcotics dog. It was unlikely, but the need for self-preservation and the unexplained anxiety that became a sense of panic urged him to cross the street. It became more frantic the closer the man came. Having a small amount of weed in a baggy in his backpack, Eddy stepped off the sidewalk to cross the street ten feet from the man.

"Hello, can I ask you a question?" the man asked with a friendly smile. His round face seemed to be genuinely friendly. He wore glasses and had a respectfully short haircut with the hair parted to one side. The man's eyes seemed to have a joy and life to them that seemed odd to Eddy.

"Me?" Eddy asked skeptically. "I suppose." He stepped cautiously back up onto the sidewalk to be off the road, even though very few cars were passing through the residential street. He had his guard up and looked around for a patrol car hiding somewhere.

"My name's Pastor Dan Carter. What is your name?" he asked, extending his hand out to shake Eddy's.

"Eddy Franklyn," he said, shaking his hand tentatively.

"I've seen you around town before, but it's good to meet you, Eddy. Let me ask you something if you were crossing the street just now and got hit by a car and died, would you go to Heaven?"

Eddy paused. For a moment, no words could form as the unexpected question had taken him by surprise. He had never been to a church or knew anything about the Bible. His parents had a Bible on a shelf, but it was never read and covered with dust. It meant nothing to them other than it once belonged to his grandmother. She had passed away when he was eight or nine, but he recalled her being a religious person and telling him a story or two out of her Bible, including the story of Adam and Eve. Ron was an avid believer in evolution and occasionally, under the influence of some foreign substance, they'd discuss evolution over the creation of the earth. The theory of evolution sounded as reasonable as a monkey typing up their American History textbook by chance. The odds were about the same. It just didn't seem reasonable when Eddy really thought about it. Eddy didn't know anything about the Bible, but he believed that there had to be a God that created the earth because it was too perfect to be an accidental formulation of gases. There had to be a god, to believe in heaven, and he did believe his grandmother was there. At least that's what everyone always said, but how to get there, he did not know. He was a nice guy. He did what was right, well, occasionally at best. Didn't everyone go to heaven? That must not be because there are terrible people out there who don't deserve to go to heaven. Sadly, Eddy considered his own life and the guilt of hiding the truth about Karen's car came first and foremost to his mind, followed by stealing what wasn't his and the lies he told people. He felt a thickening of his wrongs over his rights and answered Pastor Dan honestly. "No," he said softly.

Pastor Dan frowned. "Why not?"

Eddy frowned as he shrugged shamefully. "I just wouldn't...I've done some things..."

"I've got some good news for you then, Eddy. The Bible says that all men fall short of the glory of God. We are all sinful and are condemned in our sins to die. But the good news is God sent his one and only son, Jesus Christ, to die for us on the cross so that we might believe in Him and be saved. If you will believe that Jesus died for your sins and accept Him as your Savior, He is willing and able to forgive your sins and become your Savior. That's all it takes to be saved and go to Heaven." Pastor Dan paused and then asked, "Would you like to accept Jesus as your Savior, Eddy?"

Eddy nodded thoughtfully. "I would."

"Repeat after me, Jesus, I recognize that I am a sinner. I ask you to forgive my sins and come into my heart and become my Lord and Savior. Save my soul, Lord Jesus, as I commit my life to you from this moment forward. In the name of Jesus, my Lord and Savior, Amen."

Eddy repeated the prayer. Immediately, from the crown of his head to the bottom of his feet, he felt like a wave of warm water had washed through him, cleaning out the guilt and the fears that had been plaguing him throughout the day. Eddy was all too quickly filled with a warmth and joy that he had never experienced before. He felt alive and brand new.

Pastor Dan spoke with a smile, "Welcome to God's family, Eddy. Do you know that the Bible says that a celebration is happening in Heaven right now because you just accepted Jesus as your Savior? It does. God loves you so much that He celebrates when one of His children comes home to Him. You have eternal life through Jesus Christ. You are going to Heaven."

"Cool!" Eddy said joyfully. "So now what?"

Pastor Dan chuckled and pulled his wallet out of his back pocket. He handed Eddy his business card and wrote Eddy's name and address down on another to keep for himself. "Come to church Sunday morning at eleven. I'm the Pastor at the Christian Church. My phone number is on the card if you need a ride or anything. There's a whole new world that you could learn about, but it takes some effort. Come to church and learn about your Lord. Do you have a Bible, Eddy?"

"No...well, we have my grandma's, but it's old."

Pastor Dan said, "I will get you a new Bible. I will have it for you Sunday morning at church. Until then, you can borrow one of mine, if you want to. So I'll see you at church?"

Eddy nodded. "I'll be there!"

Pastor Dan smiled. "Alright, have a great day, and it's great to meet you!"

"You too," Eddy said and began to walk away towards Ron's house.

Pastor Dan called his name, "Hey Eddy, after church, how about we buy a six-pack, watch some football and drink a few sodas down? It would be great just to sit down and visit."

Eddy walked at a new pace with a smile on his face. He stopped by O'Leary's Market, bought a soda, and then continued towards the river and sewer ponds to Ron's small trailer park. Eddy reached Ron's house just as he was stepping outside. "Hey, guess what I just did?" Eddy asked excitedly. He felt alive for the first time in his life.

Ron shrugged his shoulders uncaringly. "I don't know," he sounded bitter.

"I just accepted Jesus as my Savior! Man, you have to accept Jesus as your Savior too. This feels better than anything we've ever done before, man. I'm telling you; I feel awesome! My sins are forgiven and I'm going to Heaven! Now that's awesome!" His eyes sparkled with a life that they hadn't had before.

Ron wrinkled his nose distastefully. "Yeah, right. Come on, let's go in and steal a few of Jeff's beers. Let's get primed up for tomorrow night. I hear there's going to be like four kegs and around a hundred people or something. We're going to have some fun, huh? It's going to be the biggest Halloween par-tay! And I can't wait. What about you?"

Eddy shook his head. "No, I'm not going. I just accepted the Lord as my Savior, man. I'm changing my life to live for Him."

"Are you serious?" Ron asked skeptically. "We've been planning this for two weeks. Stop screwing around."

"Ron, I have given my life to the Lord. I'm not partying anymore. I can call Pastor Dan if you want to accept Jesus too. I feel brand new, and so could you. Let me ask you if you died, would you go to Heaven, Ron? Accept Jesus as your Savior and you will."

Ron laughed cynically and shook his head. "No thanks, Pastor Franklyn. You go tell it to someone else; I don't want to hear that stuff. Okay, Pastor Franklyn?" he asked sarcastically.

Eddy laughed. "Maybe someday I'll be a pastor, but…"

Ron interrupted him hastily. "Right, Eddy, you're a low-class loser like me to everyone around here. Do you really think you can become a pastor because you what? You accepted Jesus or something? You'll never be smart enough or good enough to be a preacher! Don't even kid yourself! No, you'll get over this religious thing in a day or two and come over here wanting to get high. Let me help you out with something, okay? There's no such thing as God. He doesn't exist, Eddy. Evolution has proven that time and time again! So get over this nonsense and let's go get high."

Eddy shook his head lightly. "I may be nothing, Ron, but Jesus has already proven Himself to me when I accepted Him as my Savior. I may never be a pastor, but I will always be saved. I cannot prove that He is real to you, but He's proven it to me. I can't explain it to you, but Jesus can prove himself to you if you give him a chance."

Ron shook his head with distaste. "Whatever, man. Last night you were all for scratching up Karen's car, and today you come here acting all holier-than-thou or something. Get a life, Dude! You might be interested to know that evolution's a scientific fact. There's no doubt about the facts!"

"Yeah, you're right about that," Eddy said. "The only fact about evolution is it's always evolving with every new fact, which disproves what facts there were the day before. That pretty much tells me evolution's not a fact at all. There are no facts in evolution, or they wouldn't change as often as they do. I just accepted Jesus as my Savior; I don't need any proof beyond that. It's too bad that you do because someday it might be too late when the only proof you get is when you die."

Ron waved a hand, not wanting to hear any more about it. "I don't think we're going to get along while you're going through this phase. Why don't you go home and tell your druggy family about Jesus? When you all get high tonight and back to normal, come over tomorrow and we'll go to Salem tomorrow night and get drunk." He waved Eddy away. "Go home, Pastor Franklyn."

"Fine, I'll leave, but it's not a phase. Jesus is real, Ron, and he loves you and me. It doesn't matter if we're losers, potheads, or scum to other people, Jesus still loves us. And he wants to save you. Jesus died to save us."

"Leave!" Ron ordered. "I told you, I don't believe in God and I don't believe in Jesus. If you want to believe in that, fine, but keep it to yourself! I don't want to hear it. By the way, Pastor Franklyn, you can't change your life any more than I can. I tried, remember? That tramp Karen still put me in my place, man. We're outsiders, rebels; any of those goody-two-shoes won't accept you. You will never fit in with those fake Christian people, or," he hesitated, "maybe you will after all. But you'll never be a pastor, Franklyn!"

Eddy frowned deeply. "I just have to do what's right, Ron. That's all I have to do."

"Yeah, you start doing that!" Ron snapped bitterly.

"I am, starting today. I'll see you later, Ron."

"Yeah, see ya, Pastor Franklyn."

he wants to save you, Jesus died to save us.

CHAPTER 24

THE DRIVE OUT VANDERVELD ROAD JUST OVER A MILE AND A
half to the Slater home seemed to take forever as Tina made
her way home. It was a drive she'd traveled for years
without ever feeling the anxiety that filled her. She
wondered if a news van might be parked across the road
with a reporter and cameraman ready to pounce on her
when she pulled into her driveway. The most recent days
had been unimaginable. She had never expected to see a
news van parked outside of her house, let alone being thrust
into the media limelight. As she neared their home, Tina
was relieved to see she wouldn't have to dodge any
reporters, but on the other hand, it scared her knowing she
was alone in a big house without anyone close by. The
nearest neighbor was over a half-mile in either direction.
With Rene unaccounted for, it was hard for her not to feel
some anxiety.

Tina pulled into her driveway beside the house. She held
the keys between her fingers as she entered the house. If
Rene were there, she'd only have one defense, and that was
a desperate swing of her right hand to jam the key into
Rene's throat or anywhere else it went. That moment would
give her just a few seconds to either run or grab another
weapon of some type. She knew she was no match for Rene,

but if he was in her house, he wasn't there to say hello. He would be there to hurt her. Tina wasn't overly strong or dangerous, but she'd rather die fighting to save her life than to submit in fear to him or anyone else that invaded their home. Greg had a pistol in the gun cabinet in their bedroom, and she considered going to get it as she unlocked the door but dismissed the thought as she wasn't so fond or experienced with it. Tina had hated guns ever since her father was killed by one. However, for the first time, there was a comfort in knowing that if she ever needed it, the pistol was there, and it could save her life.

Tina walked through the downstairs, checking the rooms before moving upstairs to check out the rooms up there. It was a little after two in the afternoon and she would be home alone until nearly six-thirty, or sometimes closer to seven, depending on the socializing of the kids and, of course, Greg. She had never thought too much about the size of their home or how silent it was when no one was home. Only since Tuesday had the house become too big and quiet for her to relax in; she was quickly beginning to hate being home alone.

Tina grabbed the dirty laundry basket out of the kid's bathroom and carried it downstairs through the kitchen into the small laundry room inside the back porch. She emptied Karen's dried clothes out of the dryer, moved the load from the washer to the dryer, and started it. She loaded the washer with a nearly full load of colored clothes, taking the time to use a spot remover. She turned on the washer and then picked up the basket of clean clothes and carried the basket out of the laundry room. Tina stepped towards the dining room just as Greg stepped into the kitchen. Terrified to see an unexpected man in front of her, Tina screamed and stepped backward quickly while dropping the clothes basket and grabbing her chest.

"Are you okay?" Greg asked through his laughter.

Tina took a deep breath and exhaled to calm her heart rate. She took another breath. Greg's humored grin angered her all the more. "It's not funny, Greg. You scared the hell out of me! What are you doing home?" she asked angrily. She had not expected him home for hours.

"I'm sorry, I didn't mean to scare you. Are you all right, hon?" he asked caringly. He stepped forward to give her a comforting hug. He wrapped his large arms around her softly. He still chuckled a little.

Tina's hands barely caressed his sides. She pulled away quickly. "What are you doing here?" she asked again. She had caught her breath and settled her heart rate down.

"Oh, Karen left her game shirt in the dryer. I'm getting it for her. Their bus is leaving at 3:30. I'll cut practice short so that we can drive over there by six." He bent over to pick up the clothes basket. He set it on the counter and quickly found the white game shirt.

Tina watched him, with frustration growing on her face. "Go where?"

"Neeld, it's their last volleyball game," Greg said as he folded the shirt and searched for Karen's other game sock.

Tina sighed. "Neeld is the worst team in the league. We're already the league champions and in the playoffs. Why do you want to go there watch them beat Neeld? It's an easy win," she said with irritation.

"It's her last regular-season game. After this season, we may never get to see her play again."

"I don't have an interest in watching them play against Neeld, again."

"What? It's Karen's last game, Tina. We won't ever go to Neeld to watch her play again after tonight."

"I've watched her play since fifth grade, Greg. Trust me; I won't miss anything if I miss the game tonight. She's playing all next weekend, so it's not like it's her last game. It's just Neeld," Tina said pointedly.

"The boys won't want to stay here, so you'll be alone," Greg said, trying to convince her to change her mind.

Tina shrugged. "I told you last night that I'm going to meet up with Abby and Dawn for a couple of drinks."

Greg took a deep breath as his frustration grew. "I thought you were kidding. What are you going to the bar for? You've never wanted to go out drinking before, but now you're perfectly willing to miss Karen's last game to go drinking with your friends?" he questioned.

Tina glared at Greg with defiance. "Yes, I am. I never get to do something fun for myself. I'm always running to this game or that one and when I'm not, I'm cleaning the house or cooking dinner. I'm going out with my friends tonight, whether you like it or not!"

"Fine, go. Where are you going, to sleazy Skeeter's Inn?" Greg asked sarcastically. Skeeter's Bar and Trailer Park was a local bar five miles outside of Ridgefield with a shady reputation for drugs, violence, and casual sleaziness.

"No," Tina replied sharply, "we're going to Tarlow's. It's ladies' night, as a matter of fact."

"Oh! Well, you can't miss that!" Greg said sarcastically through his growing irritation. "For crying out loud, do you even know what ladies' night is? It's where the men go to meet women. Do you think other guys won't approach you?"

"Are you jealous?" she asked mockingly.

Greg hesitated to answer. He calmly said, "No, but I am quite concerned that my wife wants to go to the bar all of a sudden after fifteen years of marriage."

"It's no big deal. I swear you try to control every part of my life! I just want to go out with my friends. You go golfing with yours. Why can't I go out with mine without you jumping down my throat about it? It's no big deal, Greg," she vented angrily and walked past him.

"No?" he questioned as he followed her. His tone grew hotter. "For the last month, month and a half, you've been acting like I'm a piece of trash, and I don't know why. Something's changed in your life; you act like you don't want to be here anymore, at least not around me. And now you're going to the bar? Why do you think I'd be concerned about that, Tina? Do you think there's a reason I might be concerned?" he asked in a raised voice.

"I'm just going for one night!" she hissed with her eyes burning into him.

"This week. But next Thursday night is ladies' night too..."

"Screw you, Greg!" Tina yelled. "This is exactly what I was talking about. You're making a big deal out of nothing. Maybe I should raise hell when you go golfing. It's the same thing!"

"No," Greg said slowly, thoughtfully. "We don't usually have sleazy girls trying to pick up on us along the fairway."

"Are you calling me sleazy now? Why am I not surprised by that?" She questioned Greg severely.

"I didn't call you sleazy. What I'm saying is there's a pretty big difference between a golf course and a bar! There's going to be guys there who will see you as a new piece of meat and swarm around you like flies," he explained.

Tina sighed. "Well, I'll be with Ray, so he'll keep me safe, I'm sure," she said with a sharp exclamation in her voice.

Greg frowned. "Who's Ray?"

"A lender. There's a bunch of us realtors and lenders meeting there," she explained quickly and turned to open the refrigerator. She bent over to find a soft drink. "Do you want a soda?" she asked as she pulled out one for her.

Greg shook his head. "No, I have to get back to work. So what time are you planning to come home?"

She sipped her soda. "We're all meeting there at seven, so I'm assuming nine at the latest."

"Fine, go meet your co-workers, but be careful. I love you, hon. I'm sorry for making a big deal out of it," he said and gave her a quick kiss. She turned her head and offered no response.

After Greg had left, she walked to the window to watch him drive back towards the school. She pulled her phone out of its case on her hip and pressed Ray's number on her touch screen. "Hey, you," she said, sounding rather joyful. "So I'll meet you at Tarlow's at seven. I hope you aren't upset about earlier today. I was just feeling a bit over-whelmed, but I feel better now." She grinned fondly as she listened to Ray's thoughtful response. "Nope, all is fine. Greg was kind of an ass about it, but what else would I expect. So, I'll be there at seven."

CHAPTER 25

MIDDLETON POLICE OFFICER STEVE TURLEY DROVE HIS
patrol car to the home of Eddy Franklyn. It was a small,
near dilapidated home with an unkempt yard and trash
piled on the front porch. It was a home that office Turley
had been to many times before for one reason or another.
He personally had no appreciation or respect for the
Franklyn family and just assumed to arrest them all, as to
keep enduring the same nonsense month after month. He
stepped out of his car and walked to the front door and
knocked.

The door opened, and Missus Franklyn stood in the
doorway with her bathrobe on and a cigarette in her hand.
The aroma of cat waste and cigarettes overwhelmed his
senses from the opened door. "Officer Turley, what a pleasure. What do you want now?" she spoke with no respect in
her voice. She was a bone-thin woman with a weathered
face beyond her years. Her graying brown hair was
unbrushed and matted from just waking up. Her dull blue
eyes watched him with contempt.

Steve curled his lips slightly with effort. "I'd like to speak
with your son, Eddy. I have a few questions for him."

"Regarding?"

"The vandalizing of a fellow student's automobile, the same as last night," Steve said without hiding his annoyance.

"He's already told you he doesn't know anything about it. I don't know why you guys keep harassing my son. He hasn't done anything," she said and remained in the doorway.

"Mom, it's okay," Eddy said from behind her and tentatively moved towards the door. He greeted Steve with a certain anxiousness that wasn't in his eyes the day before.

"No, it's not," his mother began to rant. "These hillbilly cops think that they can harass innocent..."

"Mom! It's okay," Eddy said, interrupting her. He stepped past his mother onto the porch to speak to Officer Turley. "Hi, Steve," he said softly.

His mother vented heatedly, "You don't have to tell him anything, Eddy! Don't let them scare you into saying something that's not true. These cops are dirtier than the sewer ponds!"

Steve spoke to Eddy's mother with irritation, "I'd like to talk to Eddy alone if I could."

"Forget it! He doesn't know anything about his rights; I do! I'll stay right here and protect my son if you don't mind."

"Go in the house, Mom. I can talk to Steve alone. Seriously," Eddy said calmly.

"You don't know about these kinds of..."

"Mom, I can handle it," he said more forcefully. He waited for his mother to step back into the house and close the door. He turned toward Steve and spoke nervously, "I lied to you last night. I was with Ron when he scratched up Karen's car."

Officer Turley was surprised by the confession. "Why don't you tell me what happened," Steve said and wrote in his notebook while Eddy told him what had happened the night before. Eddy told him all the details of Ron's actions and his own. When he had finished, Steve questioned him,

"So you didn't damage her car? You kept watch so Ron wouldn't get caught?"

"Right," Eddy said quietly. "I like Karen and her family. Mister Slater is a great teacher, and I wouldn't do anything to hurt them like that."

"But you did. You kept watch while Ron did it, and then you lied to me about it last night. Although you didn't commit the act of damaging Karen Slater's car, you did participate in it. Wouldn't you agree to that?"

Eddy's mother opened the door and stepped back out onto the porch quickly. "Don't you answer that, Eddy! He's trying to entrap you into confessing to the crime that you didn't do!"

Eddy spoke plainly, "I helped Ron by keeping a watch out for people. I knew what he was doing, but I couldn't talk him out of it. I did try, but he wouldn't listen."

Steve listened to Eddy with an awkward expression. He spoke slowly. "I could arrest you for your part in the property damage, but I won't. I appreciate your stepping up and being honest with me. That's what's saving you at this point. Um, I will be placing Ron under arrest, and you'll be expected to testify against him in court. Are you up to that?"

Eddy took a deep breath. The thought of testifying against his friend brought a wave of anxiety. It would've been so much simpler to have lied to Officer Turley, but if he really wanted to change his life and become a real man, an honest man, a man of genuine respect and integrity, then the lies had to stop. Eddy looked Steve in the eyes. "Yeah, I am."

Steve nodded appreciatively. "Okay. Thanks for your honesty, Eddy. Have a good night," he said and went to his patrol car.

His mother stared at Eddy with cold and hostile blue eyes. "What the hell do you think you're doing? Ron's your friend and you're snitching on him? I thought I raised you better than that? I didn't raise you to be a damn rat!"

Eddy frowned. "As I told you, I accepted Jesus as my Savior. I'm just doing what's right, Mom."

"Right for who? Ron?" she asked, raising her voice. "I'd say you've screwed him over by being a no-good, dirty snitch! Do you not know that could get you hurt, if not killed someday? Ron's supposed to be your friend, Eddy. You don't screw your friends! Who are you screwing next, me, your father? Once a snitch, always a snitch! I don't even want to look at you!" she said with disgust in her voice.

"I didn't screw over Ron. He chose to damage her car. I won't lie for him, you, or anyone else again. You know some parents would be proud of their son for being honest, but all you can say is I'm a snitch," he said quietly. He looked at his mother as she held a cigarette close to her face; she appeared to be upset and worried at the same time. He shook his head and went inside.

An hour later, Police Chief Harry Bishop and Officer Steve Turley pulled up outside the Myer's single wide mobile home in separate cars. They walked up to the front porch and knocked on the door.

Wendy Myers opened the door and was surprised to see the two officers again at her door. "Hi. How can I help you?" she asked, concerned.

"Missus Myers, we're here to see Ron if we could," Harry said simply.

She opened the door and stepped back out of their way of vision. "He's right here," she said and motioned to the small kitchen just inside the door. Ron stood by the counter, holding a beer can in his hand. He came to the door, holding the beer. "What's up?" he asked.

"Ron, I didn't realize you were twenty-one," Harry stated.

Ron shrugged. "I'm at home in my mother's house. She lets me drink," he said uncaringly and took a long drink to finish off his can of beer intentionally and then set it on the counter with a loud exhaled breath of satisfaction.

Wendy sputtered with irritation in her voice, "That's not exactly true. He doesn't listen to me. I can't control him anymore."

Harry answered her frankly, "You're his mother. You have legal authority over your son. Use it." He spoke to Ron, "Could you step outside with us, please."

Ron chuckled. "Sure, but I told you last night that I don't know anything about Karen's car, but we'll go through this again. So, what's up?" he asked as he stepped out onto the porch.

"We're placing you under arrest for Criminal Mischief in the First Degree for the intentional vandalism of Karen Slater's automobile. Steve, will you cuff him?" Harry said pointedly.

"What?" Ron asked in disbelief. "You can't arrest me without proof. You have no proof!" Steve took hold of Ron's wrist and cuffed one wrist before Ron resisted the other wrist momentarily.

"You can't arrest me!" he yelled.

"You're wrong," Steve said harshly as he forcefully pushed Ron against the porch rail to cuff his other wrist. "A little bird told us everything, and I mean everything. You're going to the county jail, Ron."

Wendy Myers covered her mouth with her hand and began to cry. "Oh, no! He didn't do it, Harry! Can't you hear what he said? He told you he didn't do it!" she spoke insistently and grabbed Harry's arm. "You have the wrong guy. My son wouldn't do that!"

"Ma'am," Harry spoke firmly, "let go of my arm!"

"Mom, you can't let them take me...Mom!" Ron cried out as Officer Turley led him towards his patrol car.

"He's my son," Wendy stated weakly to Harry through her heartbroken tears. Her boyfriend, Jeff, came up behind her and put his arm around her shoulders to comfort her.

She continued, "He's my son, Harry. He wouldn't do that!" she finished while wiping her eyes.

Chief Bishop spoke frankly, "Your son did do it and will be prosecuted for Criminal Mischief. It is a Class C Felony here in Oregon to deliberately cause over a thousand dollar's worth of damage to someone else's vehicle. Ron is facing up to a year in jail if he is found guilty. I am sorry."

"But, Harry, he said he didn't do it! I know when he is lying and he's not. He wouldn't do that!" she repeated desperately.

Harry watched her compassionately. "May I be frank with you?"

"Yes, of course."

"Your son's a liar, Missus Myers. You'd be doing him the biggest favor if you quit being his friend and became his parent. You have the authority not to allow him to drink in your home. If you allow him to drink, he'll think it's acceptable for him to drink anywhere, and it's not. Ron's accelerating down the wrong path, Missus Myers. If you love your son, the best thing you could do for him is draw some lines for him not to cross. Ron will have a tough road ahead of him if he doesn't realize he can't do everything he wants to do without facing the consequences of his actions. This is not the first issue we've had with Ron, as you well know. My suggestion is to quit coming to his rescue."

Wendy glared at Harry with hostility. "How dare you lecture me about raising my son? I'm a good mother, Harry. It's hard enough to raise him without his father, but I'll be damned if I will stand here and listen to you tell me how to raise my only child. I've done the best I can with what I have! Now when can I get him out of jail?" she said heatedly.

"His bail will be set tomorrow. You can contact the courthouse about that. Have a good night, Missus Myers," Harry said and walked off the porch.

Wendy slammed the door shut behind him.

CHAPTER 26

RENE DIBARI SAT IN HIS HOTEL ROOM, WATCHING THE NEWS for any new information released on his escape. He was still the top story and now getting national attention. They showed his latest prison photograph and quoted the local news with, "He is believed to be heading south to California or possibly Mexico. He is believed to be armed and dangerous." So far, the law agencies had discovered his every move up until the time he left the Eugene Mall. They had even discovered video of him buying shoes and leaving the hair salon having purchased a wig. They had video of him leaving the mall but had lost track of him after a certain point in the parking lot. They had not caught on to his hitching a ride back North. He was still ahead of the police by a single step so far.

He had remained in his hotel room exclusively, except for short walks to a local market and a fast-food establishment. All his outings were quick-paced and kept to short distances from his room. With his face on the evening news, it wouldn't be long until he was recognized, even with his long-haired wig and clean-shaven face. He feared he'd be recognized by any one of the cars that drove past him on the busy street. A simple cell phone call to the police at any given moment by a passing driver would quickly lead to his arrest on the Portland sidewalk. It would be a disappointing end to his only taste of freedom. He would go back to his prison cell for the rest of his life with nothing to show from his soon-to-be-legendary escape from prison.

What his old pal, Greg Slater, said on the news the night before was true. He had nowhere to go. He had no chance of mixing in with society and living a normal life. The world had changed, and the technology was far beyond anything he had ever imagined when he was younger. It was only a matter of time until he was caught. His time was short, so he needed to make the most of what little time he had. He would never live as a free man, as Greg so elegantly emphasized on the news, Rene had only one thing on his mind and that was to go back home. He wanted to collect the debt that Greg and Tina owed him. They would pay for ruining his life.

Rene lay on the bed and stared at the ceiling with a snarl on his face. In twenty-four hours, he'd be in Middleton. Greg had everything a man could want, including Rene's wife and daughter. Greg and Tina had something going on that New Year's Eve night. If Rene had not come home that night when he did, he might not have known about it until Tina gave birth to Greg's child, saying it was Rene's. That night he knew the moment he walked into the house that he had caught them in the middle of fornicating. It was evident from Tina being covered with her blanket with reddened cheeks and her classic frightened expression of being caught with her pants down. Greg was hiding in the bathroom, undoubtedly putting his clothes back on after hearing the car pull into the driveway. Rene wasn't a fool; he had caught them; unfaithfulness was written across both of their faces. When Greg left the house, Rene had ripped the blanket off of Tina, expecting to see her nude, but she wore sweatpants, which were easily slipped back on. The rage he felt couldn't be explained easily. He had caught his wife with her ex-boyfriend fornicating in Rene's own home. He had never been as wrathful as he felt at that moment. He could not remember how many times he hit her before he began to strangle the life out of her. She had cheated on him and he reacted. Greg came back inside and attacked him. Rene would never have grabbed the gun and used it if it wasn't for Greg. If he had wanted to kill Greg, he would've fired a killing shot into Greg's heart instead of running after Tina when she ran outside. He had chased Tina into her parents' yard to talk to her, but she was too hysterical to reason with. When her father came running outside with fury in his eyes, and as he claimed in court, he thought he saw a knife in Art Stewart's hand. He had no choice but to shoot his father-in-law in self-defense. It was a horrible misunderstanding and in the mayhem of Tina's screaming, Art was killed. If the media knew the whole story, it would have been proven that it was Tina and Greg's fault while Rene was the most innocent of them all. He never would've grabbed that pistol if Greg hadn't forced his way into his house the way he had.

The media criminalized Rene and made a hero out of Greg and his love for his high school sweetheart even before Rene and Tina were divorced. The media didn't care about her infidelity; all they cared about was Greg's heroic intervention while condemning Rene. No one mentioned that Tina was still married while the media drooled over the two young lovers cuddling together throughout the trial. Greg and Tina both testified to their best acting abilities to ensure he was put away for the rest of his life. And now, Rene had sixteen years of caged-up wrath to unload on Greg tomorrow night. He would have no mercy on either of them.

Rene would have his moment tomorrow night to savor his revenge. Then he would go into the local bar, covered in their blood, demand a drink or two, and wait for the police to arrest him. He wouldn't even try to run or resist. He might be sentenced to a second life sentence, or perhaps to death; it didn't matter which. He'd stay in prison for the next thirty or so years and die naturally, a happy man. Who could ask for more than that?

The only problem he did have was Middleton was fifty miles away and he had no way of getting there. He didn't want to hitchhike, and he couldn't take a bus. His options were slim but available. He'd just have to find another Jack Miller to offer his car to him. The only weapon he had was Gary Baugh's pocketknife, which had worked well with Jack Miller, but he wanted something bigger. He needed a larger knife that would intimidate anyone that he pulled it out on. The larger the knife blade, the more afraid people were, especially law-abiding citizens, who were less likely to fight back. Rene wasn't looking for a fight or someone who would cause a scene. He didn't want attention brought to him or any resistance at all. Rene was looking for someone who would cowardly remain silent and allow him to do whatever he wanted out of fear of being killed. The truth was he was going to kill them anyway. He could not afford for them to survive and go to the police.

Rene remembered seeing a large superstore when he first arrived in Portland that would sell hunting knives as a part of their outdoor sporting selection. It was about eight blocks away, but if he wanted a heavier knife, he'd have to go there to get it. It was after seven and dark outside, with a light rain falling that would reflect a glare of the lights off the street. It was still early enough that a passing patrol car shouldn't have cause to be suspicious of a man walking alone on the sidewalk, and there was still plenty of traffic to keep the drivers from noticing him. He reached for Gary Baugh's wallet and counted what money he had left over from Jack Miller's account; there was still over a hundred dollars in it. He put on his shoes before setting the wig on his head firmly and carefully studied himself in the mirror for any trace of obvious tells of it being a wig. When he was satisfied that it looked real, he got the room key and exited his room quietly.

Outside, it became evident that the local news weatherman had been right when he mentioned a cold front dropping down from the Gulf of Alaska. It was a very cold rain with temperatures in the low forties. Rene wished he had bought a heavier coat, as he was getting cold within a block of his motel room. He walked quickly but forced himself not to appear suspicious in any way. With the weather being as cold and wet as it was, few people were walking, and those who were moved hurriedly to get out of the weather. All eight blocks were filled with colorful store and restaurant signs, but he kept his face down and walked purposefully like everyone else on the street.

He ran the last block once the superstore was in sight. He stepped inside the two pairs of double sliding doors to get out of the weather and paused. He had entered the alcove where the shopping carts, public payphones, and two video games were placed between the exterior and interior sliding doors. There was also a large bulletin board for the public to place their ads along one wall. He moved to the bulletin board and pretended to look at the ads. He noticed the black dome lenses on the ceiling that recorded his every move. He knew that if he were recognized, the police would have the store surrounded within minutes and he'd have no choice but to run for his life. He forced himself to look interested in the babysitting and guitar lesson ads as his anxiety grew. He grew more anxious about being recognized the longer he stood there in a well-lit store with perhaps fifty people who had seen his face on TV by now. He could not get the courage to walk into the store and look at people face to face. It would only take one person in the store full of shoppers to recognize him for all hell to break loose. The longer he stood staring at the ads, the more desperate he was becoming. He tore a tab off an ad and turned around and left the store. About forty feet from the front door, he noticed two teenage boys about eighteen or so standing in the rain beside their car. They appeared to be up to no good as one of the boys nudged the other. "Ask him."

"Hey, sir," the second boy said awkwardly, "do you think you could buy us some beer if we gave you the money?" the boy who asked held the keys to his car. He was nervous about asking.

Rene hesitated and peered around the parking lot for any obvious people watching from their unmarked police car. "For you and your friend?" he asked.

"Yeah," the boy answered with a chill in his voice.

Rene looked the two boys over carefully without answering their original question as of yet. He watched their eyes and saw no sign of a setup but the simple youthful anxiety of asking a stranger to buy them beer. He remembered asking many strangers the same question in his youth. "If you give me a ride, I'll buy your beer for you. But not here; let's go somewhere else to buy it."

"Sure, man, that's no problem. Get in. My name's Jason, this is my friend, Tad," the driver said.

"I'm Johnny Gibson. It's nice to meet you," Rene said as he moved around to climb into the front passenger seat of Jason's older Dodge Neon.

"Do you play guitar by chance?" Tad asked as he climbed into the back seat.

Rene looked at him awkwardly as he paused at the door. "I do. Why would you ask that?" he sounded guarded.

Tad shrugged. "Because you look like a rocker, man."

Rene grinned. "Well, I am. I'm in between bands right now, but I was in a Seattle band for about ten years. We broke up about three months ago," Rene explained as he sat down on the seat.

"Were you guys any good?" Tad asked.

Rene laughed lightly. "Not good enough apparently, we never got a record deal. But we rocked. At least, I thought so."

"What store do you want to go to?" Jason asked as he backed out of the parking lot.

"There's one down the road about six blocks. Let's go there," Rene said, pointing towards his motel. "So what do you guys have planned for tomorrow night? Are you going to have a big Halloween party?"

"Yeah," Tad answered quickly from the back seat. "We have a friend who's having a party. We'll probably just hang out and get drunk. What about you, are you…is your band playing somewhere?"

"No, I'm not with a band right now. My nephew is playing in an important football game in a town called Middleton tomorrow night. I've never seen him play and I promised him I'd be there. It's their last game of the season, so I have to keep my promise to him. In fact, if you guys are willing, I'll make you two a heck of a deal," Rene said, turning towards them in his seat.

"What's that?" Tad asked.

"Well, to be honest, I need a ride to Middleton tomorrow night. I'll fill up your gas tank and buy you guys a case of beer if you drive me there. I'll buy you guys two cases of beer. It means that much to me."

"Hell yeah, we'll drive you," Tad said enthusiastically.

"I don't know," Jason said skeptically as he paid attention to the traffic. It was his car, after all, that Tad was committing to. "Where's that town at?"

"Middleton? It's about thirty-five to forty miles south of here. It's a small town. You'd be home before seven and have two cases of beer and a full tank of gas. I'll even give you whatever money I have leftover for your trouble if you want. I just want to be there for my nephew's game, man. Here, pull into this store and I'll get your beer," Rene said, pointing at a small privately-owned store.

Jason pulled into the market's parking lot. "So you'll get us two cases of beer and you'll pay for it?"

Rene nodded. "And I'll fill up your tank too."

"How are you getting back home? We don't have to wait there for you, do we?" Jason asked curiously.

"No, I'll just spend the weekend with my brother. I just

need a ride there. You guys can drop me off and come back here to your party. You'll be the men of the hour carrying in two cases of beer. Just think how appreciative the chicks will be, huh?" Rene said with a smile.

"Come on, Jason," Tad pressed his friend.

"Okay, we'll give you a ride."

"Excellent!" Rene said with excitement. "Give me your phone number and I'll give you a call. But you can't leave me hanging. I'm doing you guys a favor, and my nephew is counting on me being there."

Tad spoke from the back seat, "If you think we're going to bail out on two free cases of beer and a full tank of gas for an hour's trip, you're wrong! You just tell us where and when to pick you up; we'll be there!"

"Yeah," Jason agreed, "You've got a deal."

Rene chuckled with a wide grin. "Awesome, you guys are lifesavers. I'll go get your stuff, my treat."

CHAPTER 27

NEELD WAS TWENTY-SIX MILES WEST OF MIDDLETON AT THE edge of the coastal mountain range. It was a small town with a unique mix of farming and logging communities. Being further away from the county seat of Ridgefield and close to Brouwer and other small communities set into the mountainous terrain, Neeld was the center of local business. It had a good-sized grocery store with a pharmacy, an auto parts store, a doctor's office, and a dentist's office across the street. There was even a funeral home that served the residents of the Neeld, Brouwer, and their smaller surrounding communities.

Like Middleton's, the Neeld High School was small and close-knit, and the high school athletics was taken seriously by the community. The gymnasium was about the same size as Middleton's. The bleachers were full of Neeld supporters who disappointedly watched Middleton's Volleyball team win two straight games against the home team.

Karen had once again led her team to a victory with an impressive display of athleticism and leadership. She played with a determination that was paralleled by her anger that her mother refused to watch her play her last game. Greg had been taken by surprise when he entered the gymnasium door, and Karen ran up to him and handed him her cell phone with fury in her eyes. She snapped, "Mom's going to the bar!" Greg had no intention of telling his boys or Karen where their mother had gone, but Karen had text messaged Tina asking her to bring her something to drink. Tina texted back, saying she was going to the bar with friends and wouldn't be going to Neeld. Karen had text messaged her mother three more times, each text was angrier than the previous one, but it was apparent that Tina was not responding. Karen's feelings were hurt, and her anger was revealed on her face during her game performance.

The two boys, Robert, and Sam, then questioned Greg why their mother was at the bar. To some families, it may not seem so troubling or odd, but to Greg's family, it was as strange and unexpected as the escape of Rene Dibari had been. It was troubling, at least, especially after seeing Tina's attitude change over the past couple of months. She had changed and it was becoming increasingly clear that she was unhappy with her marriage in particular. Underneath the immediate concerns of Rene was the underlying fear that the foundation of their home was beginning to crack and weaken. The marriage of Greg and Tina wasn't as strong as they once were, and it was starting to show to their children. Greg felt his relationship dissolving. He just didn't understand why.

The game ended, and Greg stood up from his seat in the bleachers and stepped down to the gym floor. Across the gym, in one of the doorways, he could see his son, Robert talking to a couple of the Neeld wrestlers he knew. Samuel walked beside his father as Greg neared the middle of the gym floor where Karen was waiting. "Good job," he said as Karen approached him without a smile. "You played great!"

"Thanks, Dad," she said and took her cell phone from his hand. "Did Mom text me back? Nope," she said after checking. Animosity was in her voice.

Greg offered compassionately, "It's okay, Karen, Mom knew you girls would win, so she took the night off to go out with her co-workers for a bit."

Karen shrugged. "Oh well, it's her loss. Amanda said she'd drive me home from school, so I'll see you at home. I love you, Dad," she said and gave him a quick hug.

"I love you, too," he said and watched her walk away towards the locker room with her team. Though she celebrated with her teammates, her disappointment was still evident. Greg peered down at Samuel warmly. "Are you ready to go home?"

"I am."

"Go get your brother and let's get going. Your mother's going to be waiting for us." Samuel nodded and walked towards the corner of the gym to get his brother.

"Greg," Patti Moore said. She was the mother of Amanda and Bruce Moore. She was also one of Tina's best friends. "Where's Tina? Is she not feeling well tonight?"

Greg took a deep breath. "No, she's meeting with some co-workers."

"Oh," Patti said with hesitation. "Can I ask you something? I know Rene escaping must be a heavy burden on her, but is she okay? I tried to call her a couple of times, but she's...well, very distant, like she doesn't want to talk to me anymore. She hasn't for a while now. How come she doesn't come to church anymore?"

"I don't know what's wrong with her. Rene's escape doesn't help, but there's something else going on. I don't know what; she doesn't talk to me either."

Patti stepped closer to talk confidentially. "It's almost like she's having an affair. I hate even to mention that, but she's acting like it." There was nothing except concern in her voice. Patti wasn't the kind of person who gossiped about her friends.

"She says not," Greg replied with a quick shrug. He said softly, "She's meeting her friends at the bar tonight."

Patti's eyes widened. "Maybe you should go see who her friends are," she said pointedly.

Before she could say any more, the Neeld football coach, Russ VanCalcar, slapped Greg on the back and spoke loudly,

"How are you doing, Coach? Heck of a week you've had, huh?" he said as he shook Greg's hand. "Hopefully, it hasn't distracted your team much. You've got a tough game tomorrow night. I would wish you luck, but your loss would help put us in the playoffs," he laughed.

"That's funny, Russ."

"Yeah, you know I'm just kidding, kind of." He laughed and then said thoughtfully, "No, seriously, how are you and your family doing?"

Patti touched Greg's arm. "I'll see you later."

"Okay, Patti." He turned his attention to Russ VanCalcar. "We're taking it day by day. You know there's nothing else we can do. We can't stop living."

Russ nodded with sincere concern on his face. They weren't good friends, but mutual football coaches with a particular friendship and mutual respect on and off the field. "I hope all this news media hasn't distracted your team. Brouwer's a great team this year, we both know that, of course, but I was surprised by just how dominant their front line is. When we played you guys, our front lines were pretty even throughout the game, but Brouwer wore us down to nothing in the fourth quarter. They've got some strong kids. It's going to be a good game, I wish I could watch it, but we have our own game to play."

Greg nodded. "Unfortunately, we lost our left guard and nose guard, Bruce Moore. So that's going to leave us a bit weaker in those positions."

"Ouch!" Russ said. "Good luck to you anyway. I will see you later."

"You bet," Greg said as his boys walked towards him. "Are you guys ready to go home and see what Mom's doing?"

"It wasn't the same without Mom here," Samuel said as they left the Neeld High School to get into Greg's full-sized Ram truck. "She used to get excited about Karen's games, but not anymore. Remember last week when she just sat there bored and grumpy? She didn't even talk to Missus Moore hardly."

Greg tried to explain feebly, "Sometimes that happens when you become too busy with work and everything else. All of this Rene stuff has her on edge."

"Rene hadn't escaped yet last week, Dad," Samuel said simply.

Robert sputtered, "Yeah, Dad, Mom's been on the warpath for a couple of weeks now. What in the world did you do to piss her off anyway? Do you even know?"

"It's the economy, Robert. It's putting stress on everyone. Come on, guys, let's go home and see if she's in a better mood." They drove the twenty-six miles back to Middleton and pulled into their driveway to find Tina's car was not there.

"Mom's not home yet?" Robert asked curiously.

Greg answered as he climbed out of his truck. "She doesn't like being home alone right now. She's probably waiting for us to get home." He unlocked the front door and stepped into the empty house. It was a quarter after nine when he called Tina's phone. It went straight to voice mail, indicating that her cell phone was turned off.

"Where's Mom?" Samuel asked worriedly. "What if she came home and was taken by Rene?"

"Rene didn't take her. She's probably at Abby's or Dawn's. I'll give Abby a call. Mom's phone is turned off." Abby was one of the realtors at Tina's office. Greg didn't have Abby's number on his phone, but he knew it was written down on a list of office numbers on Tina's desk. He went into the office and quickly located Abby's cell phone number and dialed it on the desktop home phone. ", Abby, this is Greg Slater, Tina's husband. Hey, is Tina there?....No?....Oh? I thought you all were meeting for drinks tonight... No? What about Dawn?... Huh! So nobody from your office was going out for drinks tonight?... No. She said it was an office thing... Okay, well...thank you." He hung up the phone. For a moment, Greg sat behind the desk and stared at the top of her desk. His heart began to pound. Tina had lied to him.

Samuel stood in the office doorway, watching Greg curiously. "What'd Abby say, Dad?"

Greg took a breath to calm himself. "Um, I have to go pick her up. You stay here with Robert. I'll be back shortly." He stood up from the desk.

Robert began to laugh. "Mom's drunk?"

Greg shot a stern glance at him. "No, I'll be back," he said and walked out of the house. He got into his truck and left the house faster than he had in years. He was furious and determined to get to the bottom of Tina's deception tonight. It didn't matter if they had to park down at the river all night and yell and scream back and forth. He would no longer put up with her bad attitudes and sharp-cutting remarks while she's the one lying. He had wondered many times if he was the cause of their growing distance. He loved his wife and took every opportunity to tell her so. Even though he had tried to keep a conscious awareness to always listen to her, somewhere along the way, she began to withdraw, and now she was treating him spitefully a good portion of the time. Now she was lying about who she was having drinks with. He was going to find out who it was and put an end to the nonsense tonight!

CHAPTER 28

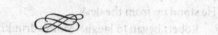

RAY TRISTAN PAID THE BARTENDER FOR A MIXED DRINK AND A glass of diet cola. With a large smile, he carried the drinks back over to his and Tina's table. He set the mixed drink down in front of Tina. "Here's another one," he said as he sat down beside her.

"I'm not even done with this one yet," Tina said loudly, clearly intoxicated. Her glossed-over eyes set on Ray affectionately as she said through a flirtatious smile, "I think you're trying to get me drunk. Are you?" she asked with the repeated raising of her eyebrows suggestively.

"No more than I am. Are you having fun?" Ray asked over the band's music. Tarlow's Bar was the only bar in town with live music every Thursday night for ladies' night. Being a college town, the students were a big part of Thursday night's success. As usual, Tarlow's was full of customers enjoying the libations and music.

She spoke loudly over the music, which suddenly stopped as she shouted, "I'm having a great time! Oh," she said quietly as the music stopped amidst her loud voice. She laughed. She gazed at Ray fondly with a gracious smile. "So, are you going to drive me home tonight? Because I think I am drunk. You're going to have to take me home," she said, raising her eyebrows repeatedly again. The band started playing their next song. "Oh! Come dance with me. I love this song. Come on, let's go rock this damn place!" she yelled suddenly and stood up quickly. She walked towards the dance floor and glanced back at Ray.

Ray remained in his chair, watching her. Tina was dressed in white slacks that showed the perfect amount of her curves and a pink blouse that was unbuttoned just enough to pique his interest. She appeared cuter than ever as she stood there waiting for him with a touch of her bangs covering her face. She had lost much of her inhibitions; every drink brought another side of her to the surface. The usual conservative Tina had become a loud and surprisingly foul-mouthed woman with no sense of danger. She started flirting with a young college student at the bar until the young man's girlfriend had enough and confronted her about it. Ray had to pull Tina away from her, as they were becoming overly hostile much too quickly. Tina seemed to enjoy the confrontation and her blue eyes flickered with mischief. She occasionally watched the young couple like a cunning eagle, waiting for the right moment to swoop down upon her prey. She wasn't interested in the young man but wanted to antagonize the young lady who had confronted her. Ray found it most entertaining and liked what he was seeing the more Tina drank. It was like Tina had saved every ounce of repressed energy throughout her life for this one moment where she was getting it all out. He had never heard her laugh so loudly or often. She was having a great time and she showed no indication of ending the night anytime soon. She was intoxicated, but one more mixed drink would be about all that was needed to take her back to his place for the night.

"Come on," she yelled as she stood waiting for him. She walked over and grabbed Ray by his hand to lead him to the dance floor that was partly full of ladies dancing together and one other couple fast dancing to the song's beat. Tina stared into Ray's eyes while she stepped towards him, put her arms around Ray's neck, and braced herself tightly against him. She swayed her body in a slow side-to-side rhythmic manner pressed against him intimately. Her warm breath caressed his neck.

Ray moved his hands up and down her back, slightly pressing her towards him invitingly. The realization that they were the only two intimately slow dancing to the 80's hard rock song made him somewhat uncomfortable. He never expected her to hold him the way she was, especially in the public venue of a bar in front of one of their fellow realtors they had run into there. Whatever the gossip would be, the fallout from that would be endured tomorrow, but tonight he had Tina in his arms. He moved his head back and maneuvered just enough to look into her eyes as they swayed slowly in each other's arms. He moved forward to kiss her, but she quickly let him go and stepped backward with multiple little steps as she leaned forward and challenged him to come after her by curling her index finger. Her hips swayed back and forth as she stepped backward flirtatiously. Her sensuous blue eyes never broke the connection with his as she dared him to follow her. The rebellious pout of her lips, dipping shoulders, and swaying hips to the rhythm of the pounding hard rock song drew Ray towards her like a moth to a flame.

Ray could not resist as he mimicked her moves and followed her across the dance floor. She broke from her erotic invitation and began to dance to the rhythm of the music by raising her hands over her head, revealing the soft white skin of her abdomen with closed eyes to feel the beat of the music. A moment later, her eyes opened and were back on him as Tina drew in close to him again. Placing her hands on her hips, she rubbed her pelvis against his groin in a grinding motion. Without warning, she turned around and bent over to begin massaging her buttocks up and down against him. Ray put his hands on her hips and pressed himself against her while she moved with her erotic motion. She stood up and turned towards him, then began to lean forward and take little steps backward again as she had before, but instead of inviting him to follow, she shook her index finger back in forth in a scolding fashion. Her seductive eyes once again stared into his while her lips sneered into a pout that was both adorable and irresistible to Ray. He stepped forward like a will-less sheep to the slaughter. Tina moved forward with the music to wrap her arms around Ray's neck to pull herself close to him again. She pressed her body against his and swayed slowly the way she had begun their dance, just as the music ended.

Ray exhaled a deep breath as she let him go. "You're an amazing dancer," he said, stunned by her suggestive dance moves. He wiped the beads of sweat from his forehead. He was pleasantly aroused and filled with great anticipation of taking her home. The stimulation he felt at the prospect of touching her after months of investing his time was nothing less than intoxicating. He was going to appreciate every taste and moment with her like a fine Pinot Noir wine.

Tina gave a flirtatious pout of her lips in response to his compliment. "I'm good at a lot of things," she said with erotic implications as she raised her eyebrows up and down at Ray. Her face was flushed with a touch of perspiration. "I need my drink," she said with a slight slur.

Ray put his arm around her mid-back to guide her while she comfortably nudged herself against him as they went back to their table. Tina quickly finished the last of her half empty mixed drink and took hold of the new one that Ray had bought her moments before they danced. Ray sipped his diet cola. "For being so confined most of the time, you can break out some moves! Wow, I wasn't expecting that."

Tina leaned towards him mischievously. "I know moves. My husband's the wrestling coach!" She began to laugh hysterically. "I could show you some moves. I could rock your world with my moves!" She laughed uncontrollably, induced by the alcohol.

Ray sat close beside her and rested his leg comfortably against hers under the table. Her leg had remained against his. He watched her laugh appreciatively. "I don't know about that," he said doubtfully, "I was the California back-seat state wrestling champion years ago," he said with a smile.

For a moment, Tina stared at him blankly and then burst out in a loud fit of laughter that bent her over on the table and brought tears to her eyes from laughing so hard. She glanced up at him and doubled over again in a hysterical laugh. "I have to pee," she said hysterically through a high-pitched voice and slowly stood up while trying to control her bladder. She walked to the restroom laughing as she went.

Ray watched her walk away with a fading smile. He was ready to take her home just as soon as they kissed. There was nothing more erotic than the first kiss. Tina was not like any other woman he had seduced before; she was the pinnacle of his greatest challenge, and she was one dance from surrendering to him. He had set his aim high with Tina, but he was about to receive his reward after months of playing his role. He would not be disappointed either, as the sexual tension between them was high. She was putty in his hands now he knew from her leg remaining comfortably against his for such an extended length of time. On their first lunch date, her leg jerked away immediately at the slightest touch against his. More recently, her leg would remain for a few seconds before moving away, and then in the past two weeks, it remained seconds longer until this week at the Rinaldi Café where it remained against his. He knew then that it was time to ask her out for a drink and what a fantastic week it was to do so. The stress of Rene's escape offered him the advantage of being her comforter on a cold and stormy night. She accepted his invitations like a lost sheep seeking its shepherd when the wolves began to howl. He had wrapped her with warmth and comfort just like a real friend would do, and then he bought her a drink.

One more mixed drink and Tina would be so intoxicated that she'd be willing to go home with a stranger and wonder what had happened in the morning. Ray watched drunk women go home with men nearly every weekend, and he knew some would most likely hate themselves in the morning. Every bar he had ever been to had regular customers who came in alone and went home with one woman one night and another woman the next night. It was a revolving door of who had who. Then one night, a young woman comes in who is new to the exciting bar scene and ends up drinking too much and going home with a man who has been around the bar-fly block before. The young lady has then exposed herself to any and all risks buried beneath the bar scene's attractive skin. The number of times a woman has woken up, wondering what had happened the night before after going to a bar, were countless. Tomorrow morning, Tina would wake up beside him and whether she regretted it or embraced him again didn't matter. He would have had his glory and would end it by tomorrow afternoon. Ray had another challenge in mind, younger, prettier, and far less drama. He was anxious to renew the hunt with her.

Ray watched Tina step out of the bathroom and start to walk towards him with a slight stumble. She caught herself on a chair and laughed. Ray watched with alarm as Carrie Walsh, a realtor in the community, stopped Tina and earnestly spoke to her. Tina waved her away, but Carrie seemed intent to lead Tina to her table. Ray approached them as the band finished another song.

"Hi, Carrie, how's it going?" he asked in his usual friendly manner. The fact was, Carrie wasn't a big fan of his. They had worked together once, and the deal went south. It was an error on his part and she hadn't worked with him since.

Tina wrapped her arms around him affectionately. "She wants to take me home, but I told her I'm not that kind," she said and laughed hysterically at her own joke.

Carrie glared irately at Ray. "She's drunk...and *married*! I'll take her home to her family now."

Ray was taken off guard. "I got her. We're just having a

few drinks." The band began to play a well-known love ballad. "Do you want to dance?" he asked Tina quickly.

Tina grinned as she snuggled up to his chest. "I do want to dance." She then grabbed his hand and started to lead the way to the dance floor.

Carrie stopped them by grabbing Tina's arm. "After the dance, I'm driving you home, do you understand me?" she asked Tina pointedly.

Ray turned on Carrie with a fury in his eyes that seemed far too elevated for friends having drinks. "Mind your business, Carrie! Do you think this is the first time we've been out? You have no idea what's going on between us. It's been going on for a while, okay? So stay out of it!" he exclaimed angrily. He had not come this far to have his trophy moment ruined by a concerned friend of Tina's.

Carrie's mouth dropped open. She was shocked that Tina would be unfaithful to her husband but also surprised by the venom in Ray's eyes. She watched Tina leading Ray towards the dance floor.

Tina wrapped her arms around Ray and drew close to him as her body swayed slowly with the music while the dance floor filled with couples slow dancing. He held her close and felt her warm breath on his neck as she nestled her face against him. As they danced, Tina spoke into his ear just loud enough to be heard over the music, "I want you to take me home with you. I love you, Ray."

He pulled away just far enough to look into her eyes, surprised. A devilish smile spread his lips. "Do you?"

She gazed at him fondly and nodded. "I do."

"Can I kiss you?" he asked.

She smiled and paused from dancing. "Yes."

Ray slowly placed his hands gently on her cheeks and held her face as he moved forward to press his lips to hers; he closed his eyes to kiss her. The moment he'd been striving for was at hand, the surrendering of her character to his will. The moment Ray expected to feel her soft, moist lips press against his was interrupted by a vice-like grip that yanked his right hand off Tina's cheek.

Suddenly, he was bent over due to a great deal of pain in his shoulder and spinning around backward in an armbar of some kind across the dance floor until his face slammed forcefully into the wall. He dropped to the floor and looked up as he began to stand. Greg Slater stood in front of him with a fury burning in his eyes. It was the kind of dangerous look that only a husband could have when he catches his wife with another man. Ray was quickly more afraid than he'd ever been.

"What the hell's going on?" Greg yelled at Tina. He turned back to Ray. "What are you doing with my wife?"

"N...nothing," Ray stuttered as the entire bar paused to watch with interest. The band quit playing, and the security guard stepped quickly through the crowd towards them. Some of the customers laughed, including the young woman Tina had nearly fought earlier in the night.

Tina glared spitefully at Greg without any shame or fear. She was angry that he interrupted her dance. "What are you doing here?"

Greg was stunned. "What am I doing here? Who is this, Tina?" He pointed at Ray

"That's my friend."

"Yeah, I'm sure! Get your stuff, let's go home," he said firmly. He turned back to Ray, tempted to drive a right fist through the man's bright white teeth to ruin the pretty-boy smile. "What are you doing with my wife?"

"Nothing! We're just dancing," he answered nervously.

The big but young security guard stepped in between Greg and Ray. He turned to Greg and spoke cautiously, "It's okay Coach. You need to take your wife and go, okay?" he asked. He recognized Greg from his high school years in Brouwer competing against Greg's teams. The respect he had for Greg was audible in his voice.

Greg recognized the young bouncer and patted his arm

understandingly. He turned towards Tina and reached for her arm, "Let's go."

Tina jerked her arm back. "You go! No one asked you to come here!"

"What?" he asked, horrified. "Never mind, we're going home. Now let's go. You're causing a scene," he tried to keep a reasonable tone. He tried to put his arm around Tina's shoulders gently, but she jerked away from him with a scowl.

"Don't touch me!" she yelled. "I'm not going anywhere with you. I'm going home with Ray! Tell him, Ray."

Greg turned fiercely towards Ray.

Ray held up his hands defensively and shook his head. "Nothing's happening here, man. Honest!"

The bouncer stood in front of Greg. "Coach, please, let's get your wife and leave."

Greg acknowledged the young bouncer and then pointed at Ray. "If I ever catch you talking to my wife again, I will hurt you! Do you understand me? I'm a Christian, and that's the only reason I didn't dislocate your shoulder tonight. But if you come around my wife again, I promise you won't be so lucky. Christian or not, a man has the right to protect his wife from snakes like you, and trust me, I will hurt you permanently!"

"Don't threaten him!" Tina yelled at Greg. She walked over to Ray. "I'm in love with him, Greg, and you won't touch him! Don't you have a football game or something to go watch? Why don't you leave us alone?" She tried to reach for Ray, but he sidestepped and moved away from her. " Don't be afraid of him!" she exclaimed bitterly, angry that Ray would move away from her. "Take me home with you, Ray."

"No! Don't come near me anymore," Ray shouted at Tina. Afraid of being hurt. He sputtered to Greg, "She's just drunk! There's nothing going on. I swear!"

Greg held his composure as her words had hit him with the force of a brick falling from a plane. He looked at Tina and tried to speak calmly, though his voice ached with emotion. "Tina let's go home. If you love him tomorrow, then you can spend the rest of your life with him, but not tonight. Now please, come on."

Tina got a hold of Ray's arm and begged him, "Take me home, Ray," she said and tried to embrace her arms around him. He quickly brushed her aside and stepped away. "No, you need to go home with him!" Ray yelled, pointing at Greg.

The bouncer rolled his eyes. "Coach, please take your wife outside."

Greg stepped forward and grabbed Tina's wrist. "Let's go."

Tina immediately tried to break his grasp but was unable to. She yelled out a flurry of curse words at him and slapped at his face with her other hand. Furious, Greg dropped down and swooped her up into a fireman's carry over the back of his shoulders and began to carry her out of the bar to the delight of the crowd. They applauded loudly and took pictures and video as Tina yelled for Ray to help her. The bouncer hurried through the crowd to open the door for Greg to carry her outside. The whole time she slapped, punched and tried to scratch his back with her only free hand. Greg ignored her attempts to fight him as he walked through the door.

The bouncer closed the door behind him and stopped the crowd from following them out. He pointed at Ray and yelled, "Get the hell out of here!"

Outside, Greg held her secured arm and leg with one hand while he unlocked the truck with his other. He opened the passenger door and set her inside of his truck before closing the door. He walked around to get in and paused to watch Ray step out of the bar. Ray noticing Greg watching him, scampered quickly towards a red Porsche. As soon as Greg opened his driver's door, Tina opened her door and fell out of the truck onto the pavement. She yelled out from the black top, "Ray, wait for me! I'm coming with you. Ray...I love you."

Greg hurried around the truck just in time to catch her from falling again as she tried to stand up. She cussed him out bitterly for stopping her from going to Ray. "He's gone!" Greg yelled angrily as Ray drove quickly out of the parking lot. "Now knock it off and get in!"

"I hate you!" she screamed and began slapping his face and arms as he put her in the truck and buckled her in. He closed the door, manually locking it, and took a deep breath. Greg fought to control the overwhelming realization that his wife had been having an affair. It literally took his breath away and it felt like his chest was tearing open as his heart shattered into pieces. He walked around his truck bed to meet the bouncer who carried Tina's coat and purse out to the truck.

"Thank you," Greg said.

"You're welcome. I didn't know she was your wife. I'm sorry, Coach Slater."

Greg took a deep breath and exhaled to try to calm his shaking hands and troubled heart. "Johnson, right?"

"Yeah, Scott Johnson."

Greg looked over at a group of people standing outside of the bar watching them. Greg shook his head. "She doesn't drink, Johnson. I don't know what's going on, but thanks. Have a good night."

CHAPTER 29

GREG WAS FURIOUS BY THE TIME HE DROVE THE TRUCK INTO the driveway and shut the motor off. He looked solemnly over at Tina and shook his head with disgust. She sat with her head slumped over and her hands on her lap. She hadn't said a word in a while as the alcohol was taking its adverse effects. He was thankful that she'd stopped yelling at him and screaming out the window while they drove through Ridgefield. He had never been more humiliated and thought he'd be pulled over for suspected kidnapping with the commotion she was making.

Greg watched her closed eyes as he spoke pointedly, "The kids are in the house. They're going to be surprised enough to see you like this. They don't need to hear how much you hate me or how loud you can scream." Her eyes opened slightly, but she kept her head down. "Okay?" Greg asked.

With an apparent effort, she lifted her head and looked at Greg blankly. "I'm not feeling so good," she said slowly.

"I bet not," Greg stated as he got out of his truck and came around to open her door. "Let's get you to bed."

Tina shoved him away meekly. "I'll sleep here. Just leave me alone!" she slurred her words with a touch of aggravation.

Greg sighed irritably while he reached in and helped her to stand. He put her arm around his shoulders and held her wrist with his left hand. His right hand was placed around her waist to guide her straight. "The kids don't need to know what happened tonight, Tina. But we're going to talk about this tomorrow. You can be assured of that!" he said as they neared the front porch. "Watch your step," he stated as he led her up the three wooden steps onto the front porch.

Tina tripped over the last step and fell forward; having control of her left arm by holding her wrist over his shoulder and his other arm around her waist, he swung her momentum around and into him. She stopped pressed up against him. She hesitated a moment and touched his cheek with her free hand. "I love you, Ray. Take me, no carry me to bed."

Greg's chest filled with an unexpected uprising of the severest pain he had ever experienced that throbbed with every beat of his heart. It was quickly compensated by a deep fury that rose like a coat of paint over the thick wall of pain from her betrayal. Despite wanting to lash out and unleash his wrath, he bit his lip to save his words. "You can walk," he said bitterly.

Samuel opened the door and asked worriedly, "What's wrong with Mom? Is she sick?"

"She's fine," Greg answered shortly while he led her inside.

Tina's breathing grew heavier and more rapid. "I don't... feel good."

"Are you sick to your stomach?" Greg asked.

Tina nodded wordlessly.

Robert stood up from the couch and began to laugh. "She's hammered! Oh my! Karen, Mom's wasted!" he yelled out and laughed loudly.

"Robert, please!" Greg scolded as he helped Tina towards the bathroom at the bottom of the stairs.

"Are you okay, Mom?" Samuel asked gently. He touched her arm caringly with a sincere expression on his face.

Greg winked at Samuel and said over Robert's laughter, "She'll be fine, son. You go get ready for bed."

Karen stood at the office door, staring angrily at her mother. "Wow, Mom," she spoke loudly, "thanks for missing my last game to go out and get drunk with your friends! It's a great example for me." Her tone was accusing with a disgusted roll of her eyes. She turned away and went back to the computer.

Robert stopped laughing and stepped over to his mother with a big smile. "Hey, Mom!" he said suddenly. When she turned her head to look at him, he quickly faked a head butt by stopping short of touching her.

The quick motion of his face coming towards her made her stomach churn. She bent over and covered her mouth as her stomach tightened. Greg quickly led her into the bathroom to the toilet, where she collapsed to her knees and vomited through her fingers onto the side of the toilet, projecting most of it onto the floor. The next heave of her stomach content went into the toilet, but her forearms and face lay heavily on the toilet rim. She vomited again and began a series of dry heaves where her stomach contracted violently without any more content coming up except blackish bile. Tears rolled down her face, running her makeup down her cheeks. The horrid scent of whiskey mixed with bile filled the bathroom.

Samuel stood in the doorway anxiously. "Dad, is Mom okay?"

Greg spoke to Samuel over Robert's hysterical laughing, "Yes, Sam, she'll be fine." Robert stepped over to the office to get Karen. Greg continued, "Sam, I really need you to get in bed. You have school tomorrow."

"What about Mom, though?"

"I'll take care of Mom," he said.

Karen peeked in through the door. "I'm not cleaning that up! It smells horrible," she said, shaking her head.

"I'll clean it up," Greg said, getting irritated. Tina's dry heaving had settled, and she now spit into the toilet. She laid her head on her forearms tiredly on the toilet rim.

Robert reappeared with their digital camera and moved Karen out of his way to get a good picture. "Hey, Mom!" he said enthusiastically and took a picture as she lifted her head slightly to look at him. When she did, her arm slipped off the toilet rim and she fell to the floor into the large pool of vomit beside the toilet. Robert took another picture while laughing hysterically.

"Put the camera away!" Greg yelled at Robert.

"Oh, come on, Dad, I won't put the pictures online or anything. I just want to show Mom how much fun she had tonight." He laughed.

"Trust me; she's going to be sorry enough without seeing your pictures." He bent down and pulled her out of the vomit. Her hair, face, and shirt were covered with vomit. Greg picked her up off the floor, cradled in his arms, and carried her out of the bathroom and up the stairs.

Robert had stopped laughing but continued to take pictures.

Upstairs, Greg set Tina down on their bed and called for Karen to come upstairs. He held Tina upright on the bed to avoid getting the rancid-smelling vomit onto their bedding.

"What?" Karen asked incensed at her mother. She stood in his bedroom doorway while Robert was taking another picture. Samuel was also standing by the door with the same concern that he had earlier.

"I need your help for a few minutes. Close the door behind you."

Karen stepped into the room and closed the door. "I don't want to get any of that crap on me. You should let her sleep in it. It was her choice to miss my game to get drunk. It would serve her right," she spoke bitterly. "What do you want me to do? I'm not touching any puke! You can forget that."

Greg spoke shortly, "Karen, I don't like this any more than you do, but we have to get her cleaned up. So lose the attitude and let's get this done. You can start by getting a wet wash rag for me and then we'll get her out of these clothes."

"Fine," Karen said reluctantly and went into the master bathroom to get a warm washcloth. Twenty minutes later, they had Tina cleaned up and sleeping in a dry T-shirt. Greg sat on the bed beside Tina, gently washing off the vomit that remained near her hairline on her forehead. The sadness was evident in his expression as he watched his wife sleeping. Though he was hurt and angry, there was no denying that fear was becoming his most noticeable emotion. The fear of losing his wife to another man, the fear of losing his family, and losing the life he knew and loved was all becoming a sense of desperation to know if their marriage was over. Greg wished he could wake her up and demand to know who Ray was and how long it had been going on and to what extent it had gone, and simply why.

Karen lay on the other side of the bed, watching Greg gently washing Tina's hair with the washrag. "Dad, how can you be so nice to her when she treats you like crap?"

Greg was surprised. "She doesn't treat me like crap."

Karen raised her eyebrows questionably. "Yeah, she does. It's been going on for a while, Dad. You don't have to pretend that everything's fine between you two. I'm almost eighteen; I'm not a child anymore. I can see with my own two eyes, Dad. Mom hasn't been the same lately. She doesn't smile anymore, and all she does is complain about everything."

Greg sighed as her words sliced like a sword across his stomach. He gazed down at Tina sadly and wiped her long bangs again. "Everything's fine, Karen. Every couple has moments, I suppose, of misunderstandings," he said, though internally, all he wanted to do was drop to his knees and sob.

"Yeah," Karen agreed, "But it's only getting worse. She's always in a bad mood. The only time she smiles is when she's on the phone or the computer. And, Dad," she had a soft touch of tears in her eyes, "I've never heard you two argue in my life. I know you always say parents shouldn't argue in front of their children, but you two are always arguing recently. You don't even hide it anymore."

"I don't argue."

"No, Mom does. That's what I'm talking about; Mom's always putting you down or has some condescending comment for you. She wants to argue with you. So how can you take such care for her when she treats you like that?"

Greg pressed his lips together emotionally and answered, "Because I love her."

"Does she love you, though?" Karen asked with a troubled expression.

Greg tried to be as reassuring as he could, "Of course. We've been in love since we were your age. Mom's just going through a hard time right now, and maybe it's partly my fault. I don't know, but I think tomorrow she'll realize what she's done, and we'll see what she has to say. But don't doubt that I love your mother or that she loves me. Love isn't always about smiles and feeling good. It's more about enduring the tough times because you care about the other person enough to do so. I promise you everyone who falls in love will face difficult times, and only love will survive them. Do you understand what I'm saying?"

Karen nodded. "So you aren't getting divorced?"

"No. At least not to my knowledge, as of yet. Why?"

Karen frowned. "Just because of what's been going on. Mom's..." she stopped as her eyes clouded with tears.

"Listen to me; the topic has never come up." He paused and then added lightly, "But let's see what happens tomorrow," he said with a touch of a sad smile, even though there was no light-heartedness within him. His eyes misted slightly as he glanced down at Tina and realized that his marriage might well be over after all. "You better get ready for bed."

"I'm not tired," she said. "So why did you and Mom

break up in High School again? Better yet, how did she ever fall in with Rene when she had you?"

Greg took a deep breath. "We broke up because we were going to different colleges. She and Rene were dating not long after I left, and the next thing I heard was she was pregnant and getting married. I didn't come back home too often after that."

"But you still loved her?"

"Of course, but she was married."

"And Rene was your friend?"

Greg nodded. "He was."

"What was he like? Was he always a scumbag?" she asked curiously.

Greg shook his head slowly. "No. He was a good guy. Back when I knew him, he liked to have fun and was always joking around. He had many of the same qualities that you do, a quick wit, great athlete, and outgoing personality. I would say Rene had your determination, but you get that from your mother," he said with a small smile. He continued, "Rene always had a temper, but it wasn't until he tried marijuana at the end of our junior year that he began to change. He became a pothead, which led to a new group of friends and other things like partying and experimenting with harder drugs. Rene wasn't a bad person, Karen. He just got caught up in the life of drugs and paid the consequences. I left soon after graduation, and I never saw him again until that New Year's Eve when your grandfather was killed. He wasn't the same guy I knew in high school, but that's what drugs will do to you."

"Were you still in love with Mom when you saw her again?" Karen asked.

Greg smiled slightly as a deep well of sadness opened in the pit of his stomach. Of all the emotions he had buried down and concealed from his children, his present devastation was the hardest. "You bet I did."

"Was she still in love with you?"

"She must've been. She married me." His bottom lip twitched as he forced a smile.

Karen frowned and asked, "Do you think Rene loved her?"

Greg took a deep breath and hesitated. "Maybe, but not to any real extent," he answered slowly. "I think Rene married your mother because she was pregnant with you. I don't think he loved her but felt he had to marry her. Marriage is tough, but it's tougher if you marry for the wrong reasons. It leads to bitterness and that leads to one form or another of abuse. Real love doesn't treat someone like he treated her. When someone hits you, sweetheart, it's not love. Get out of there while you can."

She appeared hesitant to ask but then asked quietly, "Did he love me?"

Greg answered honestly. "If there was anyone in this world Rene loved, it was you. You were his baby girl. Yes, he loved you."

"Hmm," Karen said, "well, you're my father, so you're stuck with me."

"I wouldn't have it any other way. I have to go downstairs and clean up the bathroom. Will you do me a favor and go out to the truck and get Mom's purse for me?"

"Sure."

Downstairs, Greg used a towel to wipe up the foul-smelling vomit off the floor and toilet. He was on his hands and knees spraying a disinfectant cleaner and washing the area as best that he could to leave no trace of the mess when Karen stepped into the doorway with tears in her eyes. Her expression was one of anger. "What's wrong?" he asked.

"I thought you said everything was fine. I knew something was going on. Here read this!" She handed him Tina's cell phone. Karen had opened the newest text message thread between Tina and Ray.

Greg took the phone and began to read the text messages. He would've fallen to his knees if he wasn't already on them. His mouth dropped open as he read.

Karen bit her bottom lip emotionally. "You caught them tonight, didn't you? Was she with him?" Her eyes were shielded with thick tears.

Greg was careful to display a confidant yet loving countenance. He nodded. "I did..."

"Why didn't you tell me that upstairs when I was talking about the way Mom's been acting? I knew something was going on! You can't tell me everything's fine, Dad because it's not!"

Greg stood up slowly. "Karen..."

"She's having an affair on you, on us! How can you just stand here and be so calm? How long have you known about this? You should've left her there and had her bags packed when she got home!" She shook her head in disbelief. "How can you clean the puke off her face and stick up for her, knowing she's cheating on you? You should've left her lying in her own puke! You caught them together, Dad! How can you still care enough to sit on the bed and clean the puke out of her hair?" Karen asked, exasperated.

Greg pressed his lips together emotionally as his bottom lip began to quiver. His eyes grew moist as he answered Karen's question, "Because I love her."

Karen rested against the door jamb, staring up at the ceiling. "Well, apparently, she doesn't love you. Did you know about this?"

"I didn't know until tonight," Greg said sadly. "I still don't know to what extent it's gone too."

"It's all right there!" she spoke loudly while pointing at the phone. "Well, I'm not going to forgive her and you're a fool if you do! I'll let you know right now that I'm living with you if you get divorced. I won't live with her!" She gazed at Greg with an anguished expression. "She's breaking our family up, Dad. She chose him over me," she said and began to tremble as her body crumbled into tears. She stepped forward to Greg's fatherly embrace. She hugged him tightly as she cried into his shoulder.

Greg held her in his arms while his eyes burned with

tears of his own. He struggled to fight them down and remain strong for his daughter. "It'll be okay," he said reassuringly, even though he wasn't so sure of that himself. "Let's just take this one day at a time."

After a few minutes, she let him go and wiped her eyes. "What else could go wrong this week? Rene escaped from prison, my car's vandalized and Mom's having an affair." She paused for a moment. "Are you divorcing Mom?"

Greg shrugged his shoulders. "I don't plan to at the moment. I think Mom deserves an opportunity to speak before we condemn her, don't you think so?"

Karen's eyes widened in outrage. "No, I don't! It's all right there on her phone. Maybe you should read it all and see what you say then."

"I will." He hesitated and then continued, "Karen, I know you're upset. I am too but promise me that you'll keep this between us. I don't want Mom to know that you know anything about it. Robert and especially Samuel don't need to know about this right now either. So I want you to act like nothing is going on. Give Mom and me some time to talk this through and find out what's going on. If we can work this out, there's no harm done, but if we can't, then we'll tell them. They don't need to know until then, though. That means your friends as well. I believe in keeping our relationship troubles between us without the community knowing."

"I'm not going to be nice! She's…"

Greg interrupted her. "I need to know if she's going, to be honest, or not, Karen! Just pretend like you don't know anything, please. Promise me you won't say anything to the boys or Mom."

"Fine, but I'm not going to be nice," she said defiantly.

"Let's not convict her just yet. Sometimes things aren't as black and white as they seem. It's the right thing to do," Greg offered.

"Fine," Karen quipped with a roll of her eyes.

"Alright, now you get in bed. I'm going for a drive. I'll be back pretty soon."

"Where are you going?" she asked. "Can I go?"

"No, I'll be back soon."

"Dad are you okay?" she asked, growing concerned.

"I'm fine," he lied. He grabbed his coat and keys, gave her a kiss goodnight, and stepped outside into the cold fall night.

CHAPTER 30

GREG DROVE INTO MIDDLETON AND PARKED BEHIND THE
football stadium. It was a full-sized covered stadium
centered between both thirty-yard lines. On the back of the
blue stadium lighted by security lights were the words
painted in black, "Home of the Middleton Giants. State
Champions." Under the heading were the five years
Middleton had won State Football Championship.

Like many small communities around the country,
Friday night football games were the highlight of the week
and there wasn't an empty seat in the stadium or a place
around the track that someone didn't occupy. Every Friday
night became a constant makeshift class reunion as many
school alumni came back to watch a game or two.

Every town hoped to build a powerful football team that
would consistently dominate their league and compete in
the state play-offs year after year. Middleton had such a
program once. It began when a big muscular physical
education teacher named Jake Wilson accepted a position at
Middleton High School and gradually transformed the
weakest team in the league into a competitive team. The
Middleton football team had begun a long reign as one of
the tougher football teams. Over his long career coach, Jake
Wilson had won multiple league championships and three

state championships. When he retired, he left some big shoes for the new head coach to try to fill. That coach was Greg.

Greg had played on two State Championship teams and played three seasons with the Boise State Broncos before coming home to teach at Middleton High. He was an assistant coach under Coach Wilson for nearly ten years when Coach Wilson retired. Everyone expected Greg to keep the Middleton football program on course and dominate the league without stumbling along the way, as so many coaches do that follow a local legend. Greg had taken the reins in his first year as head coach and won the league championship before losing in the state semifinal game. Now in his sixth season, he'd won two league championships and still had not made it to the State Championship game. The expectation that this season would be one of his best yet was deflated by the heartbreaking loss to the Neeld Lions during the season's first game. His team had pulled together and won seven straight games to tie Neeld for second place in the league rankings, but now they faced the powerful Brouwer Bulldogs. Brouwer was the defending league champion and placed second in last season's State Championship game. It was going to be a challenging game to win.

Greg walked into the stadium to the center of the faintly lit wooden bench seats and sat down near the top row overlooking the football field. He had played junior high, junior varsity, and varsity on the field. Now he coached the boys that played on it, including his two sons. Earlier that afternoon, he was consumed by the game against the Brouwer Bulldogs. Now he couldn't care less if they won or lost. All the time he had invested into this season boiled down to this one game, but it was just a football game. It didn't compare to the devastation that consumed him.

How had he been so blind not to see, let alone consider that Tina was seeing another man? Her actions over the past couple of months were as clear as glass now. How had he not suspected something like this was happening? He wasn't a fool. If it were happening to one of his friends, he'd suspect their wife was being unfaithful, but he never considered it with Tina. It wasn't in her character to get involved with another man, but her text messages made it clear that she had entered an intimate relationship with Ray.

Greg opened Tina's phone and reread the thread of messages between the two. There were many to read with the professional intermixed with the personal. She had opened up to Ray with the same trust she had given him for over fifteen years. Gradually she withdrew from him and opened herself up to another man. Throughout the thread, when she mentioned Greg's name, it was with growing animosity. Ray's replies took the liberty to reaffirm her discontent. Greg reread the thread word by word and noticed that Ray had picked and chosen his replies to carefully nurture the flames of her hostility towards Greg. If Tina's discontent was a smoldering flame, then Ray was the survivalist coddling the coals to build a fire. The spark of discontent had been intentionally nurtured into the flame of bitterness toward her marriage. It wasn't all Ray's doing, of course, but the man played his words well. He may have led Tina along unwittingly by exploiting her emotions, but Greg was a man who wasn't so easily fooled by another man's "innocent" motives with his wife. There was no doubt that they had an intimate relationship, but it was hard to say how far it had gone. A few texts from that afternoon were alarming and sounded ever more intimate, but no reference to the word "love" or having a physical relationship was evident.

Greg checked her call log and noticed the many calls to and from him. Some of the calls were later at night when she was supposedly working in her home office. It was easy to put it all together, like a puzzle with numbered pieces.

Greg had walked into Tarlow's Bar expecting to find Tina sitting with a group of female friends, but he was shocked to see her on the dance floor being held intimately by another man, who was about to kiss her. Fury might define the rage that filled him. But despite his immediate anger, he was shaken to his core by Tina's determination to go home with Ray. Maybe it was the alcohol, but Tina made it clear that she hated him and was in love with Ray. The humiliation came second to his aching heart that for a moment he swore could end in a heart attack and kill him then and there. There are times in a man's life when he wants to fall to his knees and bawl like a child stung by a wasp. To see his beloved wife reaching out and begging another man to take her home while hearing her say she loved another man nearly drove Greg to his knees.

Greg took a deep breath and watched the steam of his breath fade away in the cold night's air. Talking to Tina would not be easy. There was so much that had happened that he didn't know where to begin. There was so much to get out in the open, but it wouldn't happen anytime soon. He had classes to teach in the morning, a football game, and then the Halloween Dance to supervise whether he felt like it or not.

Life was changing. Greg doubted Tina would be interested in going anywhere once the media got hold of one of the videos caught by a cellphone at Tarlow's. He wondered if his marriage was about to end. Greg loved his wife, but after she's given herself to another man, it isn't the same anymore. He would never be able to trust her again and the thought of being married to someone you can't trust seemed pointless. After what he had witnessed at Tarlow's, Greg didn't know if he could trust her or not. Despite his usual ability to look for the brightness of even a dark situation, he could only feel the heaviness of a broken heart that could soon be a broken life. Divorce had never been a threatening word in his vocabulary, but it seemed like it could be a sudden and likely end to what he thought was a once happy and beautiful marriage. Tina said she was in love with Ray. No words could cut him deeper than those.

Greg sat with his elbows on his knees and rested his chin on his folded hands. He squeezed his lips together and closed his eyes as the warmth of his tears slipped down his cheek. "Lord, I don't know what's going on with Tina. I've spent my life loving her..." Greg said and nearly choked when he swallowed. "I tried to be a good husband, but apparently, I'm not. I don't know what's in Tina's heart or if our marriage can be saved, but I ask you to be in our midst. This is bigger than I can handle." He said and began to weep quietly as his emotions took control of him. He looked upwards with opened eyes. "Jesus, I surrender Tina and our marriage to you. This is too big and painful for me. I've never hurt so much! She's my life and it's being ripped apart. Lord, if she had sex with another man, will you please reveal it. I need to know what's going on, but don't let her get away with lying. I need to know the truth. And I don't know what to do or how to accept this. I just don't. Help me, Lord, to get through tomorrow because I don't have the strength to do it on my own. Whether you mend or end my marriage, I will trust you. Just please be with our kids, as this will tear their world apart too. May your will be done." Greg wiped his eyes and scanned over the football field. "And Lord, keep my players safe tomorrow night. In your mighty name, Amen."

CHAPTER 31

TINA OPENED HER EYES TO THE SUN SHINING BRIGHTLY through the closed blinds. She turned over to Greg's side of the bed; it was empty. It was then that she realized how still and silent the house was. She turned her head to look at her alarm clock, it was nearly eleven o'clock. For a quick moment, she panicked as she wondered if she was supposed to cover the office floor that morning. She sighed with relief as she remembered she wasn't scheduled to work until Monday morning.

She put her feet on the floor and stood up to walk into the bathroom. She sat heavily on the toilet seat and rested her head upon her hands tiredly. She wasn't feeling as good as she usually did in the mornings. She felt weak and her head seemed to weigh pounds heavier than usual. She closed her eyes and felt an overwhelming tiredness fall over her. A foul stench of vomit caught her attention. She flushed the toilet, opened the dirty clothes hamper, and pulled out the pink blouse she wore the night before. It was covered with vomit.

"Oh no," she said as her memory of the night before came back to her. A cold chill ran down her spine as she remembered Greg coming to Tarlow's and confronting Ray on the dance floor. She remembered Greg being very upset.

Greg didn't lose his temper very often, but she remembered that he had thrown Ray against the wall and begun to yell. Like a nightmare that haunted her, she recalled not wanting anything to do with Greg. She had wanted to go home with Ray and told Greg as much. She remembered screaming and calling Greg every foul word in a sailor's vocabulary like a mindless drunk. Her heart sank to her bowels, and a looming fear took its place as she remembered telling Greg that she was in love with Ray. Suddenly overcome by the memory, she walked to the foot of their bed and sat down. She tried to remember what else she had done or said to Greg. Like a horrible dream, blurred visions came to mind of her coming home. Samuel, she recalled vaguely, appeared concerned, Robert was laughing, and Karen appeared angry. The last thing she remembered was throwing up in the toilet. She didn't know how she got to bed or when she changed her clothes.

"Oh, no," she said and fell backward onto the bed and covered her face. Other memories flooded back, including her foul language. The alcohol had loosened her tongue to the lowest levels of her moral fiber. To her horror, she recalled seeing a few people who knew her there. Carrie Walsh, a realtor with a different agency, was there with her boyfriend, and a previous seller of Tina's by the name of Susan Reynolds was there with friends. They were both surprised to see her at the bar but were dumbfounded to see her there with Ray.

Tina closed her eyes in shame as she remembered the words spoken to her by Susan, "Dang, I thought you were one of those serious Christians. If I would've known you guys liked to party, I would've come to your church a long time ago!" It was in response to Tina's encouraging her to come to their church a year before. Susan was selling her home after getting a nasty divorce and going through a tough time. Ray had handed her another drink and led her away from Susan to their table so they could talk more privately. Tina recalled sitting at the table with him, talking with sexual overtones, and then dancing with him. She remembered straddling his leg and grinding her hips upon him and bending over to allow him to hold her waist and grind himself against her. She even remembered dancing so close when he asked to kiss her. She said "Yes" and closed her eyes, and then Greg pulled him away from her. Did Greg catch them kissing? She couldn't quite remember as it had happened so fast.

Tina covered her face with her hands as her heart began to pound. "Lord, what have I done?" she asked. She grabbed her blanket and wrapped it around her in a fetal position across her bed and began to sob. She cried heavily for a few moments and then laid there for another twenty minutes sniffling as she tried to recall what more she may have said or done. Her shame was becoming a heavy burden as every memory only added more shame. She couldn't imagine saying anything more painful to Greg than what she remembered saying, nor doing anything more degrading than acting like a whore on the dance floor unless it was kissing another man. She closed her eyes, silently praying that Greg didn't see them kissing. After a hot shower and dressing in gray sweatpants and a heavy sweatshirt over a T-shirt, she went downstairs to eat something to fill her upset stomach and take a couple of pain relievers for her growing headache. Tina found her phone lying on the table and noticed she had six voice messages. She sat at the table with a bowl of cereal and listened to her phone messages. The first three were from the night before; two were from Greg and the third from Samuel. The fourth was from a buyer who called earlier that morning wondering about the status of their offer on a home. The fifth was from her coworker and friend Abby.

"Tina, this is Abby. Hey, just so you know, Carrie told me what happened at the bar last night. Wow! Well, just so you know, Greg called me last night looking for you. He apparently thought you were with me. I told him you weren't, sorry. So, rumor has it you're having an affair with Ray. I just thought you'd like to know that. Call me, bye."

Tina closed her eyes with disgust. The world of realtors, like anything else in a local community, was a small universe of its own with its share of gossip and backstabbing. Some realtors had great sincerity and valued integrity, and then some seemed to thrive on other people's troubles. It wasn't quite noon and she and Ray were already the talk of the town. Like all gossip, it was being twisted as it was passed along. A tear slowly slipped down her cheek as she deleted Abby's message.

The last message was from another realtor named Linda Engle, who worked at another office across town, conveniently at Carrie Walsh's office. Tina reluctantly pushed the button to play the message.

"Hi, Tina, this is Linda Engle. Will you call me back when you get a chance? Talk to you soon. Bye."

After eating her cereal in silence, Tina picked up her phone and dialed Linda's number. "Hi Linda, this is Tina Slater," she said without her usual formal business tone. She was feeling sicker by the moment.

"Oh, hi, Tina, do you have a few minutes to talk privately?"

"I'm not going into the office today," Tina said hesitantly.

"Over the phones are fine. Can you talk privately on the phone?"

Tina took an anxious deep breath. "I'm home alone."

"Perfect. Tina, I heard that you were out with Ray Tristan last night. Is that right?"

Tina sighed irritably. "Linda, I don't want to talk about it. And I really don't appreciate you calling me to what? Get more details?"

"No. You don't understand," Linda said quickly. "You know I was divorced last year, right? I'm sure you heard about that."

"Hmm mm, yeah."

Linda asked pointedly, "Do you know why my husband divorced me?"

"No, I don't think I do. Why?" Tina asked impatiently.

Linda hesitated. "Because I had an affair with Ray Tristan. I never mentioned it to any of our mutual acquaintances because you know how they talk. Luckily, my ex-husband had enough integrity not to drag my name through the mud. But that's why."

"Ray's just a friend. I don't know what you've heard, but we're not having an affair," Tina said shortly.

"Tina, I'm not accusing you of having one. What I am trying to tell you is that Ray's not your friend. Let me guess, he's sending his clients to you exclusively and you're doing the same, right?" Linda asked.

"He's my preferred lender, yes," Tina answered defensively.

"Did he tell you he was referring his clients to you exclusively?" Linda asked pointedly.

"Yes, we do have that agreement. But that doesn't mean we're having an affair," Tina added pointedly.

"Of course not," Linda agreed. "Ray is lying to you. He's only saying that to build a relationship with you. He's referring clients to Michelle Landry too. He's moving on to her when he's done with you."

Tina grimaced. "What are you talking about, Linda? I don't understand what your point is," she said impatiently.

Linda hesitated and then spoke freely, "What I'm saying is Ray is a predator. He looks for a challenge, usually a married woman with whom he can seduce and get into bed. Once he does that a couple of times, he'll drop you like a rock and move on to some other woman. Certainly, you heard that he was a womanizer? How do you think he got that reputation? He seduced me, Tina. Look, I like you, so I'm telling you what he did to me. First, it was the premises of business lunches. I struck the same deal with him that you did, he was my preferred lender and Ray sent me his clients. I didn't think he was a womanizer. I thought he was my friend. He certainly pretended to care about me. He used to say I was the closest friend he had in a long time, supposedly. He'd tell me what a good friend I was, and I liked hearing that. I liked how he listened to me and my problems," she paused. "That's where the problem was really because he'd listen to me talk so much that I began to talk about my husband. He would draw it out of me, and Ray would point out what a lazy ass my husband was when I was out there trying to make a living. I listened to him put down my husband until I got resentful towards my own husband. I can't believe I was so foolish, but at the time, I was falling for every word that came out of Ray's mouth. Then came the nicknames. He made me feel young and alive again when he called me 'Missy' and gave me innocent hugs. Does any of that sound familiar, Tina?"

Tina was silent. "He called you, Missy?"

"Yes, he did. Tina, you're just another name on his belt. I don't know if you've slept with him or not, but he took me out to the bar too. He bought me blue Hawaiians and he drank soda all night. He got me drunk and I woke up in his bed. It basically ended then, but he played the game just long enough to get me in bed sober, and then he dropped me for a twenty-three-year-old college student in Salem." Linda paused and then said sincerely, "He used me, and then I lost my family because of it. That's the kind of friend Ray is. If I were you, I'd be thankful that your husband came to your rescue when he did. I wish mine would've come to my rescue. I might still be married to him if he had."

Tina frowned. "We've never slept together," she said quietly. She was still taking in all that Linda had said. Her breathing began to grow heavy as a wave of anger began to build up in the pit of her stomach the more she listened to Linda.

Linda continued, "I'm guessing you would've last night, right? Ray knows when you're hooked and uses alcohol to loosen any values you might have. He told me he was falling in love with me just a day or two before going out for drinks and I believed him. I was drawn to him like a moth to a fire and damn it. I got burned! I hope it's not too late for you because he'll burn you too."

"He said that to me too," Tina said softly. She was stunned. "I don't even know what to say."

"I understand that. If you're smart, though, you'll call Ray up and tell him to get lost and stay away from him. Save your marriage, Tina, that's all I wanted to tell you. You don't want to end up like me. I loved my husband too."

"I'll try," Tina said softly, "Thank you, Linda," she ended the call. Tina stared at the phone and shook her head with her mouth open. Her marriage was in jeopardy, and it was all her fault. Her attention had been given to another man willingly, who had been manipulating her emotions to satisfy his perverse game. All this time of gaining her trust was nothing more than a ruse to get her drunk and willing to give herself to him. She had confided in him as a friend and driven a wedge into her own marriage. Every now and again, Ray had a way of driving that wedge deeper into their marriage with his words. His timing was perfect. It was always at her weakest moments when she welcomed someone validating her momentary negative emotions. Now that she thought about it, he never once encouraged her to invest in her marriage. He never once asked about Greg unless it was to draw out the negative side of her. Ray had a way of making her feel at ease while she vented about her personal life, including her marital relationship. It was becoming clear that he couldn't care less if she lost her family if she had gone home with him. Ray would leave her in the wake of her folly and have no remorse for all the broken hearts that would pay for his good time. She knew Greg well enough to know he was hurting deeply at the moment, and their home was vulnerable to breaking because of her foolishness to listen to Ray talk about her husband. It quite frankly burned her to no end to learn that everything Tina knew about Ray was motivated to ruin her and her precious family. If her marriage was over and Greg asked for a divorce, it would be her fault alone. Tina refused to be a victim. She was committed to making Ray feel the wounds that he'd given others. Unlike Linda, Tina would let everyone know what kind of a man Ray was so that it wouldn't happen to anyone else. Tina was furious to be made a fool of and she would not let him get away with it.

CHAPTER 32

RAY TRISTAN HAD EATEN LUNCH AT HIS HOME BEFORE returning to his office to finish his day. He was not having a good day, necessarily. Rumors had not only begun but rapidly spread throughout the realty offices in town about what had happened the night before. He had seen Carrie Walsh from E.L. Cricket Reality at Tarlow's and knew she'd say something, but he never thought she could talk so much. Like any gossip, it starts with telling one or two people, and it spreads like a wildfire from there. He was aggravated because the stories were getting around and lunch wasn't even over yet. It wasn't simply that he had gone out with Tina that fueled the speed of the fire; it was the dramatic way it ended. Tina's ranting and fighting with her husband didn't help matters any either. Her defiant words to her husband that she wanted to go home with Ray were the pinnacle of the gossip. Now everyone knew something was going on between him and the respectfully married Tina Slater. Ray's own confirmation to Carrie that they were having an affair when she wanted to drive Tina home had driven the proverbial nail into the gossip coffin. It wasn't spoken as questionable gossip; it was being spread as news based upon facts.

In his profession, any negative to his reputation could

affect his business. There were a few realtors that would not work with him and referred their clients to other lenders. Of course, two of those realtors he'd had prior relations with, but they didn't spread any gossip as to why they refused to work with him. Both of those realtors were married at the time and refusing to work with a particular lender due to marital infidelity on their part wasn't likely to be talked about. A realtor's reputation was as crucial as the lender's; Ray's reputation had been virtually untouched to the broader market, as was the two realtors because it was kept quiet. This particular storm of controversy could blemish his professional and personal character a bit, but it would blow over in a week or two.

Ray liked courting married women that lived with a high moral fiber to challenge his predatory skills. He looked for women that were loyal to their spouses and family oriented. Tina was the perfect prey. She met every area of his criteria and appeared impenetrable to outside forces, such as him. She was a challenge that he resolved to conquer, and everything was going well. Little by little, he had maneuvered himself into her private life until he became her point of strength and encouragement rather than her husband. The escape of her ex-husband Rene Dibari was a godsend for him to lay out his plan. The added stress and fear to an already strained marriage was the perfect opportunity for him to turn up the heat and go for the kill. Under the stress of the week, she was willing to compromise her values and go out for a few drinks with him. What can one drink hurt? Well, it usually leads to two, then three or more. Everything was perfect. He was moments away from taking her home when her husband showed up and ruined everything. Not only did Greg ruin his night, but it was becoming now a burden with his plans for Michelle Landry.

He had to face the rumors, though, and play them down as no big deal. It was simply a pothole in the road, exaggerated tales by gossiping women. He stopped by the small, privately owned realty office where Michelle Landry worked on his way back to his office. Michelle was a young, extremely attractive new agent who'd been married for three years with another man's five-year-old son. Ray knew she was covering the floor from one to five and would be alone on a Friday afternoon. He carried a wrapped present into the office with a friendly smile. Michelle was sitting alone at one of three desks.

Michelle looked up from her computer screen, offering a friendly smile as he entered. She stood up and walked around her desk towards him. She was in her late twenties with shoulder-length straight blonde hair and bright blue eyes on a thin but elegant face. "Hi," she said with enthusiasm. "How are you doing on this beautiful day?"

Ray shook his head with a troubled smirk. "Well, even though the sun's out shining nice and bright, I'm not having such a good day. I went out with an agent to celebrate a difficult sale that finally closed last night, and her husband came barreling in like an out-of-control Freightliner and accused us of having an affair!" He shook his head and waved it off. "All we were doing was having a couple of drinks, nothing else. It was just an honest work-related, platonic celebration and it was blown out of proportion. I don't know what's being said, but apparently, some rumors are going around. The last thing I need is something like that affecting my reputation. So if you hear anything, ask me before you believe it. You know how gossip expands the further it goes."

"That's terrible," she said with concern. "Did he attack you or anything?"

"Yeah, but it was handled quickly. It wasn't a big deal, an uncomfortable one, most certainly, but nothing serious. Anyway, from what I heard; the rumors are out in force. I stopped by because I wanted to bring you an appreciation gift. It's nothing really, but I do appreciate you choosing me as your preferred lender. Here," he said, handing her the small, wrapped gift.

"Wow, thank you," she said, surprised by the gift. She

opened it with an awkward smile. Under the wrapping was a beautiful wooden pen box with matching silver pen and mechanical pencil set. "They're beautiful. Thank you, but I'm the one that should be thanking you. You're the one helping me."

Ray gave his handsome smile. "I know how hard you work to support your family. Real estate's not easy, and occasionally I can help someone out by referring my clients to a good agent. You're one of my agents. It's the least I can do."

"Thank you. I love the present," Michelle said with appreciation.

Ray nodded. "You're welcome. By the way, did your husband find a job yet? Did he try out my buddy Charlie's excavation company?"

Michelle shrugged. "I told him about it. I'm not sure if Dan called or not. He's been looking for more of a manufacturing position, but there's just not a whole lot of that around."

"No, there's not. I can call my buddy up and recommend Dan for the job, but I'm hesitant because it's my name and reputation on the line. Do you think Dan really wants to work? I mean, now that you're licensed and on your way to making good money, do you think Dan still wants to work so hard?" he asked sincerely.

Michelle frowned. She seemed hesitant to answer. "Dan's a hard worker. He hates sitting around the house, so yeah, he'll do it. At least until something better comes along."

"Okay then," Ray said, "I'll call my buddy up and do what I can. Tell Dan to give Charlie a call. Dan isn't the kind of guy who wants to sit around and play video games, is he? I know an agent whose husband just sits and plays video games all day while she's out supporting him. He's a great guy and all, so I'm not gossiping, but if Dan doesn't work hard, Charlie may not take my word seriously next time. You know what I mean?"

She gave a slight chuckle. "No, Dan doesn't play games. He's a hard worker."

"Awesome," Ray said. "You're my business partner, so when you succeed, I succeed. We both want to succeed, so let's get Dan back to work and we'll all succeed." He laughed. "Oh, one more thing," he added as he pulled a small red Porsche Carrera matchbox car out of his pocket. "This is for Justin."

"Oh, he'll love it, thank you," she said with a significant smile. Justin was her five-year-old son.

"Are you taking him trick or treating tonight?"

"Yeah, Dan and I are taking him. He's going to be dressed up in an adorable mouse costume. I love it! I can't wait to take him out tonight," she said with an excited grin.

Ray laughed lightly. "Take some pictures; I'd love to see them. Anyway, you guys have fun. Hey, are you free next Tuesday for lunch? I'd love to buy you lunch."

Michelle nodded. "I think that will work fine for me."

"All right, have a great weekend and be careful. There's going to be a lot of Halloween parties tonight. I'll call you next week." He left her office with a smile. The silver pen and pencil set was both platonic yet elegant, the perfect first gift. Every time her son played with that little red Porsche, she'd think of Ray, especially after he picked her up for lunch next week in his.

Ray drove across town to his office at the Sunnyside Financial Group. He said hello to the receptionist and continued to his small but private office. He sat behind his desk and checked his emails on the computer. He had work to do, but at the moment, he was in an awkward situation. He wanted to talk to Tina, but she understandably would not be having a good day. Last night's fight with her husband was undoubtedly just beginning. He had two choices: either wait for her to contact him first or go ahead and contact her.

Ray closed his glass-paned office door, returned to his desk to pick up his office phone, and dialed the Kathryn E.

Rupp Realty Office. His call was transferred to Tina's voice messaging. "Hi, Tina, it's Ray. Hey, give me a call when you can. I'm worried about you. I hope you're okay. What a terrible night, huh? I woke up this morning really hungover and thought, 'oh lord, what happened.' Wow, we got pretty screwed up, huh? Well, my apologies, Tina, I didn't intend to get you in any trouble. It's my fault; I shouldn't have bought so many drinks. I hope to hear from you soon. I hope there are no hard feelings, my friend. I'll see you soon, Missy," he said and hung up the phone.

When faced with a challenge, Ray wasn't one to throw in the towel. He had come close to taking her home, but it wasn't over by a long shot. If Greg and Tina separated, he'd be there to soften the blow and ease her landing. If they decided to work it out and found some strength left to continue forward, she would immediately withdraw from Ray and strive to prove herself to be a loyal and loving wife. With a new commitment and new direction, she would be hard to reach for a while, but Ray was patient. He would wait patiently like a spider, just waiting for her to return to his web. He would give her room and it could take months, but she would eventually come back to him. They had grown too close for her not to. She would end up in his arms and he would not quit playing her until she was.

A knock on the glass pane of his office door startled Ray. It was his office manager, Jeff Simmons, at the door. Ray waved him in. "Hey, Jeff, what's going on?" Ray asked without much interest. His attention went back to the computer screen.

Jeff stood in the doorway. "Do you have a minute?"

"Sure, come on in. What can I do for you?" Ray asked. He had a pretty good idea that it was either about the rumors or a possible error he'd made on a loan application the day before for a buddy of his. It wasn't a mistake; it was fudging the numbers to get the loan approved.

Jeff took a seat in one of the two chairs in front of Ray's

desk. "I heard you had an interesting night last night. What the heck happened?" Jeff asked with an interested smile.

Ray chuckled. "A terrible misunderstanding. I was out having a few drinks and Tina Slater's husband came bursting in and accused us of having an affair. He got a little rough, but it was no big deal."

Jeff watched Ray closely. "You need to watch that drinking, Ray. You're going to get arrested for driving under the influence and then you won't be able to drive that Porsche anymore. Besides, when you get drunk like that, clients see you make an ass out of yourself and that's not good either."

"I wasn't drinking. I had one mixed drink and then I switched to straight diet coke or whatever it was. Tina was drunk! She was quite obnoxious, actually. I don't drink hardly at all, Jeff, especially if I'm driving."

Jeff's eye's flickered with slight agitation. "I didn't think you did, but Tina's not much of a drinker either, I don't think. Do you know why she was there; did she go there with you?"

Ray furrowed his brow curiously. "No," he answered slowly, "We met up there. It was ladies' night and she wanted to go out with her friends, I guess. She said she wanted to blow off some steam after her ex-husband escaped this week."

Jeff nodded. "I'm sure Rene's escape has been tough on her and Greg." He took a deep breath and continued, "Somebody said you were buying Tina drinks. One person thought you might even be trying to get her drunk so that you could take her back to your place for the night. That doesn't sound very ethical to me, does it to you?"

Ray shook his head with disgust. "I know who you're talking about. Carrie Walsh was there. That's just woman's conjecture, Jeff, nothing more. Tina got drunk; there was nothing I could do about that. She is over twenty-one. Tina can do whatever she wants, I suppose." He shrugged his shoulders carelessly. "What's with all the questions? Didn't Carrie tell you everything?"

Jeff nodded. "Yeah, but it doesn't sound reasonable to me. I don't know Tina very well, but she just doesn't seem like the kind of person who would go out drinking with you out of the blue. There must be something more to it. Am I right? Come on," Jeff smiled. "She's awfully cute. Have you got something going on with her? I heard it was just you and her."

Ray chuckled slightly. "Okay, honestly, we're friends, but that's all."

"You two do a lot of working together, huh?"

"Yeah, we do. I'm her preferred lender."

"You do a lot of work through the same agents. Whatever happened to Linda Engle, she hasn't worked with you since her divorce last year." Jeff yawned and stretched his arms. "You were her preferred lender too for a while, weren't you? What happened with that?"

Ray shrugged his shoulders. "I don't know. She started working with Richard Morris over at Loren Financial."

Jeff stared at him. "She went to our competitor then. What about Edie Hutchinson? She was doing well with you until she just gave up real estate for some reason. I recall she got divorced too, I think."

"I don't know. She just quit one day. It was a surprise to me too," he said uneasily. He looked at Jeff, who peered at him harshly. "What?" Ray asked, growing uneasy under Jeff's awkward stare.

"I didn't talk to Carrie," Jeff said.

Ray laughed. "You probably don't need to; she's spreading rumors all over town."

"Tina called me," Jeff said pointedly.

"Tina?" Ray asked, surprised, "Why?"

"Linda Engle called her and then I called Linda, who told me about Edie. I called Edie, but she hasn't returned my call."

"I don't get the connection. Why would Linda call Tina? And what's Edie have to do with anything? What did Tina say?" Ray said innocently.

Jeff stood up and spoke firmly, "You're fired, Ray. You have ten minutes to gather your things and get out of this office. As far as I'm concerned, you're done in this county. You need to go back to Portland or L.A. or wherever you belong."

"Fired for what?" Ray snapped. "You can't fire me!"

"I certainly can. We pride ourselves on being an establishment based on trust and integrity. You have no idea what those concepts even mean. You have no business here in our community. You're using my office as a means to seducing married women, Ray. Our clientele? You have ten minutes and then I want you out!"

"Tina's a damn liar! She's just trying to save her marriage!" He exclaimed angrily.

Jeff spoke calmly, "We're a small community around here. You should know that by now. I'm from Middleton, Ray. I have known Greg and Tina all of my life. One thing I know is Tina's not a liar. Now get the hell out of my office!" Jeff demanded.

CHAPTER 33

TINA LAY ON THE COUCH COVERED WITH A BLANKET TO KEEP
warm as chills swept through her body. She felt sicker than
she had felt in a very long time. She had no energy and
didn't want to move, not even to use the bathroom. All she
wanted to do was sleep, but her headache so far wouldn't
quit hurting enough for her to do so. She knew she was
suffering from a hangover from the night before, but she
had no idea she'd feel so terrible. For being a lady that never
drank alcohol, it was a miserable reminder of why she
didn't.

The suffering of her hangover was severe, but it was
made infinitely worse by the knowledge of her actions the
night before. She was humiliated, but that was only a part of
it; shame, regret, and disgrace were all identified as she lay
there wishing she had never agreed to go to the bar. She
would never go to one again, nor ever take another drink.
Oddly, she remembered laughing a lot during the night,
thinking she was having a great time. It didn't seem so great
now. She had nearly gone home with another man, and as
guilty as she felt, it would've been debilitating if she
would've woken up in Ray's bed. No words could express
her thankfulness for Greg showing up when he did.

Tina had always lived by a personal rule never to place

work above her Lord or her family. Somewhere along the way, she had listened to Ray and compromised her own beliefs for the sake of real estate and making a sell. Ray had suggested it would be good to have an open house on a Sunday when most people had the day off. After two weeks of open houses and having some success, it had become a regularly scheduled event at her listings. Ray would be sure to stop by and bring her lunch to visit for a while. She enjoyed his company, little by little, even his derogatory remarks about Greg and her marriage sounded like honey to her ears. After missing church on that first Sunday, she didn't want to go back to church. At the time, she justified it by having to work, but now in hindsight, it was guilt. She was falling for another man, and it provided an opportunity to visit.

Tina had never believed she would ever contemplate having an affair on Greg; she wasn't that type of a woman. She was a loyal, committed, conservative Christian woman who loved her husband. For her to be tempted by the affections of another man was unimaginable. However, it happened so subtly that she was withdrawing from Greg and her regular group of friends before she knew it. It was easier to withdraw from her family and friends without going to church while spending some of that time with Ray. It was like being swept up in the rip tide along the Oregon Coast, she was being pulled towards him while losing her bearings along the way as she drifted freely with the current. She crossed lines that should never be crossed without even realizing it.

The vaguely subtle hand touching had become innocent hugs. Increasingly, the harmless hugs became a moment longer, and occasionally, during a hug, the temptation to kiss Ray had swept through her. She had never given in to that temptation, but there were times when she was tempted to. When Ray told her he was falling in love with her, she understood what he was saying because, at certain moments, she felt it too. She was married to Greg, though, and they had a life together. They had invested fifteen years into their family together. Loyalty to her marriage was only right, but she still felt like she belonged to Ray. Ray lavished his affection upon her like she hadn't felt in years, and she liked it. That moment in the car was a pivotal moment as she had to choose between loyalty and infidelity. All the time Tina had spent with Ray had reached the peak of its innocence and only a physical relationship could continue to meet their expanding emotional needs. She had never felt more confused or torn in her life. There was a choice to make, and she was not prepared to make it. Tina had a family and a loving husband, but at the same time, she felt strongly for Ray. She was overwhelmed with conflicting emotions that tore at the very fabric of who she was and left her spinning on an emotional roller coaster without a clear guide post to cling to as she fell.

Already embittered by Greg's devotion to Middleton High, she felt nothing except resentment when Greg stood in front of her in the kitchen questioning her about going to watch Karen's last season game in Neeld. She had no desire to watch the game or to listen to Greg's disappointment over her refusal to go. It was there in her kitchen with a flood of growing frustration that Tina decided to go to Tarlow's with Ray. It had been a growing temptation to go, but with another argument with her husband, she was giving in to it. There was a saying, 'nothing changes if it remains the same,' and her marriage had become unfulfilling and bitter. She and Greg argued more than talked and her resentment burned even deeper the more he tried to reach out and love her. Yesterday's little argument in the kitchen should have been nothing at all, but it turned into the proverbial straw that broke the camel's back. She called Ray to confirm that she'd meet him at Tarlow's. After Ray's heartfelt confession in his car, she knew meeting him might well lead to a physical relationship and making that phone call after Greg went back to work was like giving her permission for it to begin. In anger, she had made her decision. In folly, she had gone to meet him.

Thankfully, Greg had come looking for her. She didn't believe Linda when she called at first, but it all made sense now. She had been deceived from day one when Ray first approached her. It was another humiliating fact that she was trying to digest, but it was beyond her comprehension. How could anyone lie so sincerely for so long without her catching onto it? She never imagined that there were people out there who were capable of lying so well that even the sincerity of their heart was masked in a lie. She never imagined anyone could be so cold that they'd ruin another person's life for their own sexual gain. How could she fall for someone like that? How could she fall for anyone at all? She was married to a good man. She almost wanted to believe that Linda was lying and everything Ray had told her was true. She wanted to believe Ray was honest, but the evidence overwhelmingly proved he was playing her like he played Linda and an agent who had quit the business, named Edie.

Tina had called Linda back and they talked some more. Tina then called the new agent Michelle Landry, introduced herself, and welcomed her to the community. Through conversation, she discovered that what Linda had said was true. Michelle and Ray were working together. Tina resisted warning or disclosing her experience with Ray to Michelle. She had another plan of attack that she hoped would save the young agent from Ray. With much shame and anxiety, Tina called her and Greg's old classmate and friend, Jeff Simmons. In confidence and at length, Tina confided in Jeff and explained what had happened over the past months with Ray and its effects on her family. She took responsibility for her actions but explained the same thing had happened to Linda Engle and Edie. Tina warned Jeff about Ray's beginning the same process with Michelle Landry. With tears of shame, she confessed to her attraction to him and the near marital infidelity that God alone through Greg had stopped. The humiliation to speak freely was overbearing, but her only concern now was saving her marriage. It had all been a lie, and her family was paying the cost of her decisions. She felt like she had been seduced and it could ruin everything she loved.

She lay on the couch with her eyes closed as the bright sun of a beautiful fall day shone brightly through the closed blinds. Her eyes felt overly sensitive to the brightness, but she had no desire to get up and close the drapes. She was almost asleep when her phone rang. She opened her eyes and reached over to the coffee table beside the couch to see who was calling. It was Ray. She let it go to voice messaging. She listened to the voice message and was slightly surprised to hear the venom in his voice.

"You got me fired, you..." he went into a few unrepeatable words, "You believe Linda? You told Jeff that I seduced you? Who was all over me last night, huh? You were seducing me! Maybe I should tell your husband about our dances. Maybe he'd like to hear about that. I know Jeff would! Well, rest assured that I'm going to ruin your reputation too. I never lied to you once. I'm falling in love with you, and you got me fired to save your precious marriage? That's mighty Christian of you! We had a business partnership, Tina, me, and you. I can't believe you did this to me. I really can't. You're a piece of work! You stabbed me in the back. Wow! I hope your husband divorces your ass! Goodbye, Tina."

Tina listened to it again and texted him two words. "You lose." He texted back immediately, "Lose what, my job? Yeah, you screwed me there. You ruined my career; does that mean anything to you?"

Tina texted back, "I talked to Linda a lot. I also talked to Michelle. What you did to Linda and starting to do with Michelle is very familiar. I can see it now. It won't happen with Michelle, and it won't happen with me. You lose. Don't ever contact me again." Surprisingly, he didn't text back.

She glanced at the clock; it was 2:30. Greg would be

coming home in about forty minutes to get ready for the game. A cold fear began to grow inside of her. She would have to face him. There were too many words she wanted to say, but she didn't know where to begin. Nor did she know if he would be willing even to listen. Greg was very cautious not to raise his voice to her in the presence of their children, so she doubted that he'd come home yelling. He would come home, though, and the thought of facing him filled her with anxiety. She had nothing to offer him except humiliation and shame. It would still not excuse her actions from the night before or the months leading up to it. Greg deserved better than she had to offer when he came home.

She forced herself off the couch and went upstairs to grab her Bible. For the first time in over a month, she lay on the couch and opened her Bible. She hoped to look up passages about forgiveness to take comfort in asking God's forgiveness for her wandering away from the Lord and making a mess of her life, but those many verses she longed for seemed hard to find. She searched and found nothing except frustration building in her heart and a sense of abandonment filling her stomach. Perhaps she had messed up so bad that God was closing the door upon her to face the coldness of her consequences alone. And maybe the Lord would, as she knew she had made a colossal mistake, which could cost her everything, including her career, reputation, and family. Why would God want to help her when Tina had made a mockery of her faith to her ex-seller at the bar and committed emotional adultery on her husband? Even God seemed to be hiding his forgiveness from her. How could she possibly expect her husband to be any kinder? With a heavy sigh and a sense of loss and defeat growing within her, Tina closed her Bible. Seeing the purple yarn of the homemade bookmarker that Karen had made years before, Tina opened her Bible to where her book marker had been left when she initially laid her Bible down a month before. The book marker was placed in 1Corinthians chapter 4. A section of verse 5 was underlined. Her eyes were drawn to it and filled with heavy tears as she read, *"He will bring to light what is hidden in darkness and will expose the motives of men's hearts."*

A chill ran down her spine and a wave of emotion ascended from deep within as the words pierced her soul. She had longed for confirmation of the Lord's forgiveness, but what she found was God's protective hand upon her life despite her wanderings. Tina slid off the couch onto her knees and placed her elbows on the coffee table with the Bible still open in her hands. She bowed her head and prayed as hot tears streamed from her eyes.

"Lord…how can you be so good to me? How can you care so much to protect me when I've done nothing but shame you? I've messed up and I know I have, but I thank you for bringing Greg to the bar to save me. I thank you for never leaving me, even when I left you, and for showing me who Ray really is." She paused as a deep swell of emotion overtook her and she wept with her head bowed. "I've been a fool, an absolute fool and I am so sorry, Lord. I have stopped serving you to serve others, but I ask you to forgive me. I will serve you for the rest of my life, even if Greg leaves me, I will serve you. I recommit my life to you and ask you to forgive my sins. I've sinned, I've treated Greg like dirt and betrayed him in every way possible, except physically and even that's questionable as I would've if Greg had not shown up last night. Jesus, I have made a mess of my life and ask you to help me. I am so scared that Greg will leave me, but I pray he'll forgive me and give me another chance." She paused to take a deep breath. "I'm scared to face him. Lord Jesus, give me the strength to be honest and to leave our marriage up to you. Jesus, be my rock of protection because I am putting my hope into you. From this moment on, I give my life back to you. Jesus, I surrender everything to you. May your will be done and no longer mine. In your name, Lord Jesus, Amen."

Tina wiped her eyes and stood up. Despite being hungover and feeling like she had the flu, she went into the kitchen to start making dinner. It was the first thing she could do to help relieve an uncomfortable moment when Greg came home. Karen would have Volleyball practice, but the boys would come home with Greg. The uncertain outcome filled her with anxiety. The shame of knowing her children had heard and seen too much last night also troubled her. She wished she had gone to Neeld to watch Karen's last season game of her high school career.

WHEN THE WOLF COMES KNOCKING | 251

CHAPTER 34

GREG SLATER TOOK A SEAT ON THE GYMNASIUM BLEACHERS during his sixth-period free class. Typically, he stayed in his classroom to grade papers or planned the following week's lessons. However, today, he had no desire to do either. Greg had slept very little after finding Tina in the condition she was in and the circumstances of it. He was heavily burdened, and it allowed him no sleep as Tina laid unconscious beside him. All night, questions nagged at him that could not be answered. Despite his best efforts, sleep was out of the question. It was a long and restless night.

He had been short-tempered and quiet throughout the day, which was most unusual for his U.S. History and Government classes. He usually lectured a good part of the class time, but today he had each class read their textbook chapters and answer the questions at the end of the chapter. He didn't feel like talking or teaching, for that matter. His mind was on his wife. Every question he had still went unanswered like the most painful one he had to know, did another man touch his wife? The thought of it was torturous. It filled him with a pain-fueled rage that seemed to grow stronger with each exhausting hour.

Heartbroken didn't describe his agony. No word in his

vocabulary could summarize all the disillusionment, jealousy, confusion, anger, and heartache that he felt all in the same moment. Despite his desire to sulk in his own thoughts, there was an all-school pep assembly during seventh period in the gymnasium for the night's football game. He would have to get out in front of the student body and fellow teachers to enthusiastically speak about his team, players, and the game against the Brouwer Bulldogs. He would have to put on his smile and play along with the cheerleaders in whatever goofy game they'd have him, and the players take part in to bring some fun and laughs to the students. Normally, he was a willing participant ready to lavish praise upon his players, but at the moment, his heart just wasn't in it. A junior high boys PE class was getting ready to start a game of dodge ball while he sat on the bleachers, watching. It was a rare opportunity to raise their voices to be noticed by the junior high boys who wanted to impress the varsity football and wrestling coach with their athletic abilities.

Greg remembered acting the same way every time Coach Wilson walked through the gym during PE. He could remember the excitement of being young and dreaming of starting on Coach Wilson's football team. He understood exactly how the young boys felt because he had once been in the same position. Now Greg was the coach and he watched them play but had very little interest in them.

Throughout the day, Greg's thoughts were on Tina. They had fallen in love when they were going into their junior year at Middleton High School. There wasn't a hallway, classroom, bathroom, or hidden corner anywhere in the school that didn't hold a memory of his youth. He knew precisely where Tina would sit every day before school their junior year and where he'd find her at lunch their senior year. He knew what locker they shared and recalled the daily little kisses that happened there. He remembered being in his own classroom as a student and where he and

Tina always sat beside each other day after day. The school was full of memories. Everywhere he looked, there was a reminder of some moment with Tina.

However, nowhere was more sacred than where they had first kissed on that special night in early September after the first home football game, at the back-to-school dance. Although they'd both grown up in Middleton and knew each other well, it wasn't until a chance meeting in early August at a local swimming hole that he took an interest in her. Greg had gone there with Rene one Saturday to swim and perhaps meet a pretty girl from Ridgefield or somewhere. He had seen Tina and a few other girls from school lying on towels trying to tan and thought it would be fun to visit with them for a bit. Rene had other plans, as a group of girls from another school just down around a bend of the river's bank seemed to have more to offer than the clique of Middleton girls. Tina and her friends were academically talented but were not popular students by any means socially. Rene had no interest in flirting with them. He wanted to meet the girls dressed in two-piece bikinis and making a show of what they had to flaunt.

Greg had told Rene to go ahead of him; he wanted to say hi to his classmates and sat down beside Tina and the others. That afternoon had changed Greg's life. He found himself attracted to Tina in a way he never expected to be. He simply enjoyed her company. Even as Rene yelled for him to join him with those other girls, Greg never moved from Tina's side. For the rest of that summer, he chose to be with Tina whenever he could, not as a love interest but as a friend. The more he was with her, the more he wanted to be with her and the closer they became. They would talk on the phone or meet up to go for a walk around town, or sometimes they'd simply sit on a bench in the school's courtyard and talk for hours. They had become friends over the summer, and it only grew as school approached to begin their junior year. After the last night of summer football practice, they sat on the front steps outside the gym, holding hands and sitting close together. Greg had wanted to ask her to be his girlfriend, but the words wouldn't come out of his mouth. He was tempted to kiss her, but he couldn't find the courage to do so. It was on those steps that he realized for the first time that he loved the girl sitting beside him. It wasn't an emotional kind of love that swept a person off their feet in a flood of emotion, but a sincere and quiet love that had built a foundation day by day. Their relationship had taken a turn on those steps, and it moved to another level of intimacy.

Some places are sacred. The first Friday night football game was at Middleton and afterward was the "Back to School Dance." Greg had asked Tina to dance with him a few times, but none were more special than the last dance of the night. The gym floor was full of students, but Greg was only aware of the girl in his arms. He held her softly and his heart pounded as he casually swayed with her to the music. They were underneath the south basketball hoop when he gazed into her eyes and kissed her with a soft caress that meant so much more than a kiss. It was a kiss inspired by the love that he had inside of him. A kiss that marked the beginning of the rest of his life, despite his age, it was a love that was intended to last a lifetime. It was shared with equal devotion by her. It was a sacred moment that would never be equaled or surpassed. It was their first kiss.

Greg stared at the gym floor beneath the south basketball hoop and felt a surge of hopelessness fill him. He had spent his life since that night being committed to Tina. He had every intention of marrying her after high school, but it didn't happen the way he wanted. He was heartbroken when Tina broke up with him, but he was devastated a few months later when she married Rene. It wasn't reasonable because they were nothing alike. It devastated him like nothing ever had before. Three years later, when he saw them on the street outside of O'Leary's Market on New

Year's Eve, he could see the misery on Tina's face. He recognized the longing in her eyes, the shame as well. He also realized then and there that he was still in love with her.

He had promised his little sister that he wouldn't go to Rene's that night, but he did. Not only did he break a promise to his sister, but that night changed lives, many lives. He wondered what life would be like if he had never gone over there? Some questions just weren't worth asking, especially "what if" questions pertaining to that night. The facts were: Tina's father was killed, Rene was sentenced to prison, and he married the only woman he had ever loved because he had gone over there. Now fifteen, almost sixteen years later, he had no regrets about his decision. He loved Tina and would love her for the rest of his life. He thought they had a happy home for all these years, but apparently, it wasn't as happy as he thought. Tina had made it clear that she wasn't happy after all. The thought was devastating.

The junior high gym class went downstairs to the locker room to shower and prepare for seventh period. It left a noticeable silence as Greg was alone in the gym. He had no desire to glue a plastic smile to his face to appear enthusiastic for the students, while his marriage crumbled to his feet right in front of them. Greg had no desire to go home. He didn't want to face Tina because he had questions that would threaten the very foundation that their marriage and, to be honest, he was afraid to hear the answers.

Slowly students began to filter into the gym for the pep rally, slowly at first and then at the bell dismissing sixth period, a flood of students entered the gym using all four doors. Greg stepped off the bleachers and walked towards the main door to greet the students with a plastic smile that was far from sincere and said hello, to one student after another as they entered the gym. A hand tapped the back of his shoulder from behind him. He turned around to see Eddy Franklyn standing there expectantly.

"Can I talk to you outside real quick, Mister Slater?" he asked nervously.

Greg nodded. They stepped outside. It was the same stairs Tina and Greg had sat on many years ago. "What can I do for you?" Greg asked, looking up from the spot where he and Tina had sat. His attention was now fully on Eddy.

Eddy spoke awkwardly, "I did the right thing, Mister Slater. I told Officer Turley what happened with Karen's car. I'm sorry I lied to you yesterday."

"I heard. Chief Bishop called me last night. Thank you, Eddy. It's not always easy, to tell the truth, especially when it hurts a friend of yours. But you'll never go wrong if you do the right thing. That's what makes a man. Good job, Eddy." He put his hand out to shake Eddy's.

Eddy shook it. "Thank you, Mister Slater. You go to the Christian Church, right?"

Greg nodded curiously. "I do."

"I met Pastor Carter on the street yesterday, and I accepted Jesus as my Savior."

Greg smiled. "Really? Well, congratulations!" He shook Eddy's hand again. "That's a life-changing event, but you have to keep going forward. So, are you coming to church on Sunday?"

Eddy was hesitant. "I...don't know..."

Greg shook his head. "No, you have to. Come with my family and me. We'd love to have you join us. Okay?" The thought occurred to him that by Sunday, he may not have a family to take to church. He forced the thought away, resolving to take Eddy to church whether Tina was there or not.

Eddy agreed. "Okay."

"Great, we will meet you there. You can sit with us, okay? Let's get in there before they call my name," Greg said as the pep rally was beginning. He could hear Principal Bennet begin to address the students.

"Mister Slater," Eddy said quickly, "Ron's going to be waiting after school behind the stadium for me," he said nervously. "I'm afraid he and Jose are going to gang up on me for turning him in. Will you, kind of...I don't know..." he sounded hesitant to finish but was clearly afraid.

Greg's expression turned serious. "You bet. I'll be there."

"Thanks," Eddy said, relieved.

"Let's go enjoy this pep rally," Greg said without his usual enthusiasm and opened the door for Eddy.

CHAPTER 35

Ron Myers had parked his Datsun along the street behind the stadium. He knew Eddy always left the school out of the admissions gate behind the stadium to cross Fourth Street to walk home. Ron had a lot to say to his ex-friend; mainly, he wanted to say it with his fists. Ron had spent the night in the county jail and was released earlier that day. He had a court date in a few weeks, but for now, he wanted to know why his friend had betrayed him. Perhaps more than asking why, he wanted to let Eddy understand what he thought of him. Ron leaned against his car, watching for Eddy to come outside. He had a cigarette in his hand and a wry smile on his lips. "I texted him that we're waiting for him. I'll bet the coward doesn't even come out here, though. He knows I have to know that he ratted me out," he said to his friends, Jose Rodriguez and Derek Willis, who were both standing beside him.

Jose Rodriguez was a Middleton graduate from four years before. He was twenty-two years old and had a lean, muscular, athletic body reminiscent of his athletic past. His hair was cut short, and he had a goatee; both were always neatly groomed. Jose was a handsome young man, but there was a certain coldness in his eyes that left no doubt to the violence he was capable of. To those who knew him, he was a young man to be wary of, and his building reputation reinforced it. Jose still lived in his parents' home in Middleton and drove an Escalade with all of the flash and trim. He worked for a pavement sealing company during good weather but also dealt methamphetamines. Jose nodded towards the school. "Here he comes, just like you said he would. I can't believe he's that stupid. Remember, don't show any sign of being mad until we're out of town. We can beat the hell out of the snitch out in the country, not here, so keep your cool," he said to Ron pointedly.

Ron took a long pull on his cigarette. "Don't worry; he thinks we're going to Salem tonight. He'll come over here and say he's sorry for getting me busted and I'll play it off like no big deal. We'll smile and give each other a little hug and he'll get in the car." He looked at Jose seriously. "But I get first hit. I'm the one he screwed over, not you."

Jose's lips twisted cruelly. "Go for it. It doesn't matter to me, just as long as he learns his lesson. I hate snitches!"

Derek Willis was a high school dropout from the year before. He was eighteen years old and worked full-time for a local dairy. He was averaged sized with short brown hair under a John Deere baseball cap. His face was clean-shaven except for a thin mustache. Derek had text messaged Eddy to warn him about Ron and Jose's plans to beat him up. Derek asked Jose tentatively, "I thought you liked Eddy?"

"I did until I found out he was a snitch. I won't put up with snitches, Derek. It doesn't matter who it is." The look in Jose's eyes stated it was a warning to Derek himself.

Derek asked simply, "Well, what makes you think he won't snitch on us for beating him up? I mean, a snitch is a snitch."

Jose peered at him with his cold eyes. "By the time we're done, he'll know that there won't be a second warning."

Eddy came closer and slowed to a hesitant walk as he neared the open gate of the chain-link fence line. He was scared but found himself stepping forward anyway. He silently pleaded for the Lord to help him. "Hey, guys," he said as he stepped off the curb onto the gravel parking area beside the street.

Ron spoke through a forced smile, "Hey, bud, we've been waiting for you. Are you ready to go? We've got a keg to get to."

Jose offered a fake grin. "Ron's driving his piece of crap tonight, so we need to leave early to get there before the beer's gone and the pretty chicks are taken. Get in." He laughed slightly.

Eddy looked at Derek, who appeared very uncomfortable. A growing hesitation in the pit of his stomach urged him to flee from their company. "I'm not going tonight."

"What?" Ron stammered. "We've been planning this for two weeks. You have to go! Why wouldn't you want to? There are four kegs and girls dressed like zombies everywhere? It's a Halloween party, man. Come on, I brought you a sleeping bag and everything. I'm even paying the cover charge for you to go."

Eddy shook his head. "No, I told you yesterday that I wasn't going."

"Why not?" Jose asked pointedly. "Come on. We haven't partied together in a long time. We can get wasted and live it up. Come party with me, Ed. It'll be fun."

Eddy shook his head. "You guys go ahead. I'm a Christian now. I don't party anymore."

Jose laughed. "That's funny. That's what I love about you, Ed. You're always screwing around."

Eddy shook his head sincerely. "I'm not kidding. I accepted Jesus as my Savior and became a Christian. You should too. All of you should. If you guys were to die right now, would you go to heaven?" he asked them as a group.

Ron was immediately irritated. "I told you yesterday, I don't want to hear about that crap. Now get in the car and let's go!"

"Calm down, man," Jose said to Ron with a quick laugh. He turned to Eddy. "That's great, Ed. Why don't you tell me about it on the way to Salem? Let's head out, though."

Eddy refused. "Sorry guys, but I'm not going. I gave my life to the Lord, and I meant it."

Ron's patience was running out. "Eddy, stop messing around and get in the car! I told you that religious stuff doesn't mean anything. God's not real, dude. Evolution is a proven fact! Besides, why would you want to serve a god that sends people to hell anyway? He doesn't sound like a great god to me."

Jose shrugged. "He's got a point. That doesn't sound like a loving god to me either. So since we're all going to hell anyway, we might as well have some fun while we can. What do you say, Ed? Let's go get hammered!"

Eddy stared at the ground and moved a small rock around with his toe. He lifted his head to look them in the eyes as he said, "God doesn't send anyone to hell that didn't choose to go there by refusing to accept Jesus as their Savior. I don't know much about the Bible or what it says yet, but I will. What I do know is when I accepted Jesus, he changed me. He proved himself real to me, and that's all I can tell you. He'll change your life too. You don't have to go to hell if you accept Jesus as your Savior and get right with God."

Ron's eyes hardened with a growing rage. He stepped forward, spitting out his words like a sword slashing to maim. "Is that why you ratted me out to the cops? I spent the night in jail, Eddy! They charged me with a felony! I'm facing a year in jail because of you! Do you think that's funny? Why'd you tell the cops, huh?" Ron yelled, suddenly shoving Eddy backward.

Eddy began to tremble. He side-stepped to get around Ron to walk away, but Jose stepped deliberately into his path and pointed at the car. "Get in the car!" Jose ordered with a threatening glare. His cold brown eyes unnerved Eddy.

Eddy's breathing quickened. He was afraid to fight Ron but to have Jose threatening him to get into the car, petrified him. He knew by Derek's texts that they intended to hurt him. Fear or no fear, there was no way he would get into the car with them.

Ron pushed him again. "Why'd you do it, Eddy?"

Jose spoke quickly. "Are you going to push him or hit him? This is like watching fifth graders! Hit him if you're going to and let's get out of here. We can find the snitch another time."

"You're supposed to be my friend. Why'd you tell them?"

Eddy looked into Ron's eyes and answered honestly through a quivering voice, "Because it's the right thing to do. I'm not going to lie for you or anyone else anymore."

Ron suddenly swung a wide round house right-handed fist that caught Eddy on the cheek. Eddy stumbled back and nearly tripped over his own feet. He caught his balance, but another roundhouse right to his cheek caused Eddy to lower his head and step towards Ron with his arms flinging wildly. Ron stepped to the side, put his right arm over Eddy's head, and clenched his arm tight, putting Eddy in a headlock. Eddy tried to break the headlock but was unable. Eddy began to push and pull, trying to free himself, and fell to the gravel with Ron falling on top of him, still squeezing the headlock. "Let go of me!" Eddy yelled from the bottom.

"Oh, Come on!" Jose yelled with excitement over the trash-talking that Ron and Eddy were saying to each other in between their heavy breathing. Eddy was lying on his side with Ron lying horizontal to Eddy, squeezing his head. "Hold the snitch!" Jose said and stepped forward and kicked Eddy in the testicles. Eddy's pain-filled moan was muffled under Ron's tight grip.

Jose was about to kick him again when Greg Slater stepped through the admissions gate. "Don't you dare!" he warned Jose with an authoritative yell.

Jose looked up and stepped back to the car as Coach Slater stepped off the curb and walked over to the two fighting boys. Greg stood in place and watched for a moment while shaking his head with disgust. "Break it up, you two. Now!" he yelled. He reached down and pulled Ron off Eddy. "Get out of here!" he said to Ron with a slight push towards his car.

Eddy sat up and wiped the tears from his eyes. Ron stood above him and pointed his finger at him. "I thought you were my friend, man! Just remember I kicked your ass!" he yelled and walked over to his car. "We aren't through with this. We'll see you soon. Just wait, Eddy!" Ron warned before getting behind the wheel of his car.

Jose opened the front passenger door and got inside. He ordered Derek, "Get in, dude, let's go."

Derek was hesitant. "We're not going to Salem right now, are we?"

"No," Jose replied.

Reluctantly, Derek climbed into the backseat. Ron started his car and drove off quickly.

Greg extended his hand to help Eddy up.

"Thank you," Eddy said, standing. He rubbed his ear and bent over to regain his strength after being kicked in the testicles.

Greg spoke, "I couldn't help noticing that you weren't doing so well down there." He nodded towards the ground. "If you came out for my wrestling team, you'd never be put into that position again. In fact, after one season, I promise you, you'd beg Ron to put you in that head lock again."

"Think so?" he asked painfully.

Greg nodded. "I know so. Quit smoking and come out for wrestling. I'd love to have you on the team."

Eddy looked up at him from his hunched-over position. "I'm not so into sports, Mister Slater."

"Consider it a self-defense course then. Wrestlers are at home on the ground, Eddy. Anyone on my team would've had Ron crying like a baby within a minute of hitting the ground. So could you if you learned how. Come make some new friends on the wrestling mat. I'll teach you things you never thought you could do. And you'll have a lot of fun too."

"I don't think your guys would like me on your team, Mister Slater. They don't seem to like me very much."

Greg answered sincerely, "They don't know you, but if you give them a chance, they will begin to. You're starting your life over; I can already see it in you, so why not really change things and make some new friends? Try a new sport and learn how to defend yourself from guys like them?"

Eddy bent over to recover from the blow that still ached in his stomach. "I'd lose, and most of the guys on your team win. I'm afraid I'd embarrass you, Mister Slater."

Greg chuckled for the first time all day. "You won't embarrass me or yourself, my young friend. You will lose; everyone loses a match or two sometimes, but every day you will learn how to win, not just in wrestling but also in life. And that I can promise you."

CHAPTER 36

GREG DROVE HIS TRUCK TOWARDS HOME WITH A GROWING insecurity. He had no idea what to expect when he walked into his home. He didn't know if Tina would be there or if she had moved out. He had checked his phone for any missed calls or text messages from her, but she had not tried to contact him. Not knowing what to expect at home, he had left his son Robert in town to eat dinner with his friend's family. Samuel was staying the night with a friend of his and Karen had Volleyball practice. It all worked out well as he wanted to talk with Tina alone and find out what is going on with Ray. It wasn't too farfetched to say she may have left him for another man. It was best that he found out before the kids came home.

Greg pulled into the driveway and noticed Tina's Mountaineer was gone. It wasn't a surprise as they had left it at the bar the night before. Tina had been left without a car unless she drove Karen's Toyota that was vandalized and parked behind the house in front of the barn. With a deep breath and a silent prayer, he stepped inside to the sound of the TV on and the smell of Lasagna in the oven. Tina stood in the kitchen doorway by the dining table, looking at him.

"Where are the kids?" she asked. She was uncomfortable and appeared as nervous as she felt.

Greg set his briefcase down and looked at Tina with a restrained expression. "Karen's at practice, Robert's staying in town until the game, and Samuel's staying the night with Rick."

"Oh," she said, sounding concerned. "I wish I would've known that."

Greg leaned his elbows on the separation wall between the entry and the family room. "If you were here last night, you would've. How are you feeling today?" he asked, poorly masking the anger that boiled just under his skin.

Tina's facial expression revealed her shame. "Not good."

Greg nodded. "I bet not. So…what's going on, Tina?"

She shrugged her shoulders. "I'm making dinner," she said sweetly, though it was layered heavily with anxiety.

Greg walked into the family room with his eyes burning into her. He no longer restrained the volume of his voice as he shouted, "You know what I'm talking about. Who the hell is Ray and how long have you been seeing him? I called Abby and found out you lied to me, so I went to the bar and saw you about to kiss another man! How long have you been seeing him, Tina? Don't tell me you haven't screwed him because you sure wanted to last night!" He glared at her severely. "You said you were in love with him, so you better start talking!"

Tina's breathing was heavy as she wiped her eyes. She was taken off guard by his yelling and fierce glare despite knowing he would be angry when he came home. He had never spoken to her the way he now was. "I didn't sleep with him…" she said softly.

"Do you expect me to believe that? You've been seeing some guy for who knows how long, and you expect me to trust your word? Your word means nothing at the moment. I want to know how long it's been going on!" he shouted.

A tear fell down Tina's cheek. "I didn't sleep with him…" she spoke pointedly.

Greg's eyes grew larger with anger. He leaned towards

her and yelled sharply, "I didn't ask that did I? How long has it been going on?"

"We were just friends..."

"That's exactly what it looked like, Tina!" Greg shouted sarcastically.

"Are you going to let me talk?" she asked heatedly.

Greg raised his eyebrows expectantly. "Yeah, please do!"

Tina's hands fidgeted together at her waist and then crossed over her chest as she stood uneasily just inside of the dining room. "We were just friends. I swear to you that I never slept with him." She swallowed noticeably as tears flooded her eyes. "His name's Ray Tristan. He's a lender. We started working together and I don't know how it happened..."

"What happened?" Greg asked through a strained voice.

Tina looked into Greg's eyes sadly. "Our friendship got personal."

"How personal?"

"Very. I confided in him about everything. You, the kids," she spoke quietly, "Everything. I'm sorry, Greg."

Greg peered at her with a perplexed expression. "Sorry for what, exactly? I still don't know! You know I have friends too, but I haven't lied to you or gone out to the bar and make out with them on the damn dance floor!" he yelled. "And I sure as hell haven't wanted to go home with them!"

Tina stepped forward and sat down at the end of the dining room table. She placed her elbows on the table and hid her face in her hands. "I didn't want to go home with him," she said through her hands. Her shoulders shook slightly as she began to cry.

"Yeah, you did! You were screaming it to everyone in the whole damn bar! I had to carry you out of there while you were screaming that you wanted to go home with Ray!" He slammed his hand down on the table as he leaned over her and yelled, "I have never been more humiliated in my whole life than I was last night! So don't tell me you didn't want to go home with him because everyone in that whole damn bar knows you did! And they knew exactly who you were too, by the way! Now cut the bull crap and come out with it. Are you in love with him, Tina?" His eyes peered down at her unmercifully.

"No!" She uncovered her face and stood suddenly with a harsh glare. Tears streamed down her cheeks. "I'm not in love with him! I was drunk last night, alright? I didn't know what I was doing! And I thank God that you showed up, Greg!" She paused while looking into his eyes. She then turned away and wiped her eyes. "I'm sorry. I don't know how to say this, he became my friend, and I began to trust him. I believed everything he said about me, and about you. He'd say something bad about you and I found myself despising you and drawing closer to him." She looked at him with tears of shame filling her eyes again. She covered her mouth as she fought to keep her composure.

"And?" Greg waited for her to continue.

She sat down in defeat and spoke calmly. "And this whole time, Ray was playing me like he had other married women. I got a call from another realtor who had heard what happened last night. She said Ray had done the same thing to her, except her husband didn't come looking for her. Ray got her drunk and took her back to his place to seduce her. She woke up the next day hungover and naked in his bed. Ray had told her he loved her too, but he wanted nothing to do with her a few days later. Her husband kicked her out of their house and Ray didn't care. He got what he wanted and she ended up getting divorced. He's done it to other women too."

Greg stared at her with astonishment on his face. "He told you he loved you?" he asked loudly.

Tina nodded slowly. "Two days ago."

"Another guy tells you he loves you and that's okay? Did you tell him you loved him too, Tina?" He asked, outraged.

She shook her head slowly. "No, I told him I was married."

Greg's hand shook as ran his fingers through his hair. "That didn't seem to matter much, though, did it? You still went to the bar with your boyfriend!"

"He's not my boyfriend!" she yelled as she stood up.

His voice raised, "If he says he loves you, then it sounds like a boyfriend to me! Especially when you think it's okay to go out with him!" he shouted angrily.

"I wasn't going to go. I always said no! But I was mad at you!" She took a deep breath and added calmly, "I was mad at you, so I went."

"What were you mad at me for? What did I do that could possibly send you into the arms of another man?" Greg asked.

Tina stared at the floor with tears once again growing thick in her eyes.

"Come on, tell me!" he vented his frustration in his tone.

Her blue eyes met his. "You weren't protecting me from Rene," she said weakly.

"What?" he asked in disbelief.

"You didn't take us away when Rene escaped. I told you I was scared, and you kept us here. You didn't care. You even gave the news an interview." She flung her hands into the air. "The news showed our house on TV, Greg! They even showed Karen walking into our home. Now everyone knows we live in Middleton. If he saw the news, he'd come here, Greg! You didn't know him after high school. I did. He knows this house, remember, Lisa used to live here. If Rene saw the news, he'd know exactly where we are! Most people would've packed up and left for a few days, or until Rene was caught at least, but not you! You just kept us here like nothing was happening at all."

"And what did Ray say about that?" he asked sarcastically.

"He said if he were you, he'd take the kids and me to Disneyland for a week, or to the coast, anywhere safe. He said your football team was more important to you than me!" Her bottom lip began to tremble.

For the first time, Greg felt a touch of compassion for his wife. He sighed as his temper calmed slightly. "And you believed that?"

She nodded and turned her head into her hands as she began to sob on the table.

Greg watched her painfully. He spoke calmly, "I have never put football above you or the kids. If I felt like there was any danger, I would've taken you away, but all the evidence proves that Rene's fleeing for his freedom. He's running as fast as he can to Mexico to reach South America somewhere." He paused and then continued softly, "Is that what this is all about? Have you always felt that way because you've been critical of me long before Rene escaped?"

Tina wiped her eyes and sputtered through her crying, "No, it's just when someone points it out to you all of the time, you start to believe it. I don't know how he did it, but I started to hate you. It was all part of his manipulating me to go to bed with him." She closed her eyes pathetically. "I never thought anything like this could happen. We were work associates. He knew what to say to draw me in. That's the only way I can explain it. I allowed myself to listen to another man talk about my husband and I shouldn't have done that. I won't blame him for my actions, but I was misled, and I ask for your forgiveness. If it weren't for you coming after me, I'd hate myself much more than I am already. And I thank God for that anyway because I don't know how I'd be able to live with myself if you hadn't come after me."

"Be honest with me, Tina, because with all of the diseases out there, I deserve to know if you had sex with him? I deserve to know now instead of finding out later, so did you have an affair?" Greg asked softly.

"No, I never slept with him or even kissed him. I swear."

Greg calming down, sat down on a table chair not far from Tina. He rubbed his face tiredly. "If you'd been coming to church with your family, perhaps you wouldn't have been so easily misled."

Tina nodded. "You're right. I wouldn't have been," she said softly. She looked into his eyes sincerely. "I didn't cheat on you; I want you to know that. But," she spoke hesitantly, "I would be lying to you if I said I wasn't falling for his lies. Talking to Linda, the realtor I told you about, really opened my eyes. I was deceived and seduced every step of the way, right into the bar and almost into hell. He was drinking pop. Ray knew exactly what he was doing, and I fell into his trap, Greg. I don't know if you'll forgive me; I don't know if I'll forgive myself, but I do know that I made a fool of myself and have become the gossip of the reality offices. I don't know what kind of damage I caused with our kids or with you. I'm not just talking about last night; I mean since I began working with Ray." She reached over and grabbed his hand softly. "Greg, you don't have any reason to believe me, but I really am sorry."

Greg was about to speak, but Tina continued, "I ended the working relationship with Ray today. I also called Jeff Simmons and told him what Ray was doing to other women like me. Jeff fired him today. I don't have any excuses for allowing him to interfere with my marriage and family, but it will never happen again. I will never listen to anyone talk bad about you again, nor will I ever confide in another man about my personal life, except for you. I will never again get the lines of professional and personal friendship blurred without you being in the middle of it. Greg, I love you. You're the only love I've ever known or want to know. The thought of losing you to my own stupidity is unbearable. I know you're hurt and angry, but will you forgive me, please?"

Greg sat at the table and watched her quietly. He rubbed his eyes tiredly before answering, "Last night, I saw a stranger holding my wife on the dance floor two seconds away from kissing her. You can imagine how I felt as you held him just as close and already had your eyes closed, waiting to be kissed. And then to listen to you make a scene because you wanted to go home with him; it hurt. Drunk or not, to hear you say you loved another man is almost unforgivable. I didn't sleep any last night. I stayed up wondering if he had touched my wife..."

"No," she answered quickly.

"Or," he continued, "who had stolen her affection from me because I knew something was going on. You wouldn't talk to me or touch me anymore. Even the kids were wondering what was going on. Now I know, and I won't be able to get what I saw last night out of my mind for some time. I know you were drunk, but the emotions were still there."

"He was using me," she said softly.

"I know," Greg said softly with a hint of tears in his eyes, "but the problem is, you weren't using him."

"Greg..."

"Tina let's talk later tonight. I have to get back to the school and help get the field ready for the game. After the game, I have to chaperone the Halloween Dance. So, I'll see you late tonight."

"Okay," she said slowly. "Do you want to eat real fast? I made Lasagna? It's almost done."

Greg shook his head. "No, I have to get back. By the way, Samuel's staying the night at Rick's, Robert's staying the night at Jake's most likely and Karen's going out for dinner with her date after the dance."

"What date?" she asked with surprise.

"Chris Willis. Ross, Amanda, Chris, and Karen are going to eat somewhere in Ridgefield after the dance."

"I wasn't aware of that," Tina said.

Greg shrugged accusingly. "It looks like you have the house to yourself for the night. I'll be home late. I'll see you later." He walked to the front door and opened it.

"I love you," she said as she stood up and stepped towards him. She stopped when he looked back at her. The expression in his eyes took her by surprise. It wasn't the anger that had blazed in them earlier; it was a deep sadness that she had never seen in his eyes before.

He hesitated for just a moment. "Love you too. We need to get your car either late tonight or early in the morning. I'm afraid it'll get towed if we don't move it."

"I'll call them," she said as he closed the door behind him. She had been dreading the unavoidable conversation with Greg. With a sense of more stability in her relationship and soul, she picked up her phone and read a text message that had come in from her son, Robert. She opened it and read, "Look at the camera. Ha Ha!"

With the dread of more shame, she located the camera setting on the dining room table. She hadn't even noticed it being there all day. She turned it on and stared shamefully at the pictures of her lying unconscious in her vomit beside the toilet. Greg stood in the picture, looking down at her with a sorrowful expression on his face.

The following picture was a close-up of her face laying in the vomit. The next one showed Greg picking her up off the bathroom floor in his arms. The next one showed Greg carrying her up the stairs like a princess. It was all she could do to move the screen to the next photo. It was one showing Greg gently lowering her on their bed.

The shame that she had brought upon herself was unbearable. To see the love of her husband for her was heartbreaking. He truly loved her. And in return, she had hurt him deeply. Tears of shame and regret rolled down her cheeks slowly at first, and then abruptly as she lowered her head onto her arms and sobbed.

CHAPTER 37

THE DAY HAD BEEN BRIGHT AND SUNNY WITH A BEAUTIFUL blue sky. The bright orange, yellow and red leaves that still lingered on the few trees along 82nd Avenue were beautiful to look at, but it was a deceiving beauty, as the day was bitterly cold. As the afternoon wore on and the sun began to recede, it was replaced with heavy fog. Though it was just after five o'clock, the sun was setting fast, and the fog grew thicker. It was Halloween night and the weatherman warned of dropping temperatures and potentially freezing fog later that night. The temperature was going to fall into the low thirties or possibly even into the high twenties. Any trick-or-treaters were advised to dress warm, and the ones Rene had seen so far certainly were. He wished he had dressed warmer himself as he waited impatiently outside of the same store he had bought the two boys some beer at the night before. The two boys were supposed to meet him at five o'clock. It was now five-fifteen and they hadn't shown up yet. Traffic was heavy along 82nd, as a consistent line of cars moved slowly from one traffic light to another. It was certainly possible that they were stuck in the rush hour traffic.

Rene wore his long black-haired wig and Gary Baugh's black coat over his new sweatshirt, but he still felt the afternoon's bitter chill beginning to bite at his soul while he stood waiting. The growing fog helped conceal him from the passing cars that stopped for the red light, but he was concerned about the cars that pulled into the store's parking lot. More than one driver had eyed him curiously. He felt too noticeable and questioned if a couple of the drivers walking into the store had recognized him, but he reassured himself that they had not. He tried to hide his face as much as possible. He realized that to most people, he would look like a drug dealer waiting for a deal to take place, but it was also Halloween night and not everyone was who they appeared to be. However, he was growing more anxious the longer he waited. A Portland Police car drove past the store with the rest of the five o'clock traffic. He was unnoticed. With an increasing aggravation, Rene reached into his pocket and pulled out the cell phone number of the boy named Tad. He walked to the payphone connected to the store's exterior and dialed.

"Hello," Tad answered.

"Hey, man, this is Johnny Gibson. Are you fellas on your way? It's getting cold out here. I'm waiting for you guys."

"Oh, yeah, well… Jason's worried about the fog. He doesn't want to drive that far," Tad explained uneasily.

"What?" Rene asked, incensed by the sudden change of plans. He quickly collected his thoughts and kept his composure to keep a friendly tone with the teens. "Come on guys, you both promised me a ride, my nephew's counting on me being there. You can't let me down like this, especially this late in the day. I was counting on you guys."

Tad sighed heavily. "Hey, I'd love to, man, but Jason's the driver. I don't have my license, or I'd take you myself…"

"Who's that?" Jason asked in the background.

"Johnny Gibson, man. He still needs his ride, and we need some beer," Tad said to his friend.

"It's getting foggy out there," Jason said in the background.

"Let me talk to him," Rene said to Tad.

"Here," Tad said, handing the phone to his friend.

"Hello," Jason said, taking the phone.

"Hey, man, this is Johnny. I know it's foggy out, but you can handle some fog. All you have to do is follow the car lights in front of you and watch the white line. It's a rush to drive in fog. And you'll get two cases of beer, a full tank of gas, and some cash. I'll even toss in some more cash if that'll get you to take me to Middleton. Brother, I have to be there. If I had known you wouldn't keep your promise, I would've started walking hours ago. Come on, brother, a full tank of gas, two cases of beer, and another forty-fifty bucks for a one-hour drive, or if you want, all of the beer I can buy after filling your tank! You're getting a killer deal for an hour's drive. Look, you have me against the wall and I'm begging you to help me out. My nephew is counting on me being there, brother. What do you say?"

"It's a good deal," Jason said hesitantly, "But I don't know where that town is."

"It's just down the road forty miles or so. It's not that far. You'll be home before you know it. Even with Friday traffic, you'll be home by seven at the latest. Come on, man, you promised that you'd take me there if I bought you some beer, and I did my part. I'm even offering to buy you two cases of beer for a forty-mile trip. That's nothing compared to the party you guys will have later tonight when you get those pretty girls drunk and alone. You can thank me for it later, but I need a ride for that to happen, huh?" Rene chuckled. He listened to hear what Jason would say next. He had no intention of letting him off the phone without getting his ride.

"Well, okay, I'll drive you there, but remember your end of the deal," Jason said, becoming more determined.

"Excellent! I'll buy the beer right now. You guys just hurry up and get here. It's freezing out," Rene said with a friendly and pleasant tone to his voice.

"We should be there in about twenty minutes," Jason said.

Rene hung up the phone and spat out a mouthful of obscenities. He was furious that they were going to leave him waiting at the store expectedly. If Rene hadn't gotten Tad's phone number, he would've been stranded in Portland and would be forced to take a car to get to Middleton. He went into the store and bought two cases of beer and a cheap roll of duct tape. He carried them to a corner of the parking lot furthest from the video camera. Eventually, Jason's car pulled into the parking lot and parked in front of him.

Tad jumped out of the passenger side and helped Rene put the beer in the trunk. Rene then climbed into the back seat. "See, boys, I kept my end of the bargain. It's a good thing I got Tad's phone number, or I might not be so lucky to have a ride," he said with a touch of hostile sarcasm in his voice.

Jason didn't seem to notice. "So how do I get to what's it called again?"

"Middleton. South, take I-5 South."

Jason pulled out of the parking lot and worked through the heavy traffic to the Interstate on-ramp and merged into the traffic. Leaving Portland behind him, Rene said, "I've been waiting a very long time for this. You guys have no idea what you're doing for me."

Tad glanced back at him with a smile. "Glad we could help. Hey, did you buy duct tape in case we break down?" he laughed.

Rene had to think fast to explain such an odd item. "It's an inside joke for my nephew. You know, in case he breaks his helmet, we can tape it back together."

Jason frowned. "That's not very funny for a joke."

CHAPTER 38

SINCE KAREN HAD HER CAR TAKEN AWAY FROM HER FOR leaving school without permission two weeks before, she was forced to drive her dad's truck home after volleyball practice. However, she couldn't find him for the longest time after practice. She didn't have time to search every square inch of the school, just to find out he was where she'd already searched twenty minutes before. If he answered his cell phone, all her frustrations would be needless, but like he always did, he turned it off and put it in his office locker and left it there. Now she was running half an hour later than she needed to be, and she was furious. It was already six o'clock and she was stressed for time to shower, do her hair, makeup, and put together something to wear and be back at the football stadium by seven. She had planned on going to the store on Tuesday night to find a Halloween costume to wear to the dance tonight, but her parents wouldn't let her go due to Rene's escape. She had planned on driving to the store Wednesday night after Youth Group, but her car was vandalized. Now she was committed to dressing up as a pirate but had no time to buy a costume. She would have to make somehow due with her own clothing or not dress up at all. It aggravated her severely. She did not want to be the only one of her friends not dressing up for the Halloween Dance. She pulled into the driveway and ran to the front door. It was locked. Immediately she rang the bell and then unlocked the door with her dad's keys. Tina was midway to the door when Karen ran by her mother quickly. "Excuse me," she said and began to ascend the stairs.

"Hello," Tina said, "how was practice?"

"Fine," Karen said, continuing up the stairs without looking back. A moment later, the shower started.

Tina walked up the stairs and found Karen stepping into the shower. "So, your Dad says you have a date tonight?"

"We're just hanging out," Karen replied, uninterested in saying anything more to her mother.

"Who's we?"

"Amanda, Ross, Chris and me. It's no big deal. I'm sure Dad told you that," she said as she quickly rinsed off the sweat from practice.

Tina leaned against the door jamb and sighed heavily. "He did. I want to apologize for missing your game, Karen."

Karen didn't respond. She rinsed her hair and shut the shower off. "Will you hand me my towels, please?" she asked and held her hand out of the shower curtain.

"Sure," Tina replied and handed both towels to her.

Karen wrapped one around her hair and then the other one around her body before stepping out of the shower. "Thanks," she said as she walked past her mother without looking at her. Karen walked down the hall to her room and closed the door.

Tina hesitated for a moment and then followed and knocked on her door. "May I come in?" she asked gently.

"I'm getting dressed," Karen replied shortly. "Give me a few minutes."

"Okay, but I think we need to talk," Tina said sincerely through the door.

"I don't have time to talk. I have to get ready, and I don't know what to wear!" Karen opened the door irritably and explained to her mother, "I have to do my face, hair, and dress up as a pirate all within forty minutes, so I really don't have time to talk, okay? I was supposed to buy a costume on Tuesday night, but you wouldn't let me. Now I don't have anything to wear!"

"Karen, please," Tina sounded resigned. "I'll talk while you do your face."

"Fine, but I have to blow dry my hair, so I may not hear you. Talk all you want to, though." She turned away from Tina and walked to her antique vanity with an oval mirror. She sat down and turned on her blow dryer.

Tina watched her blow-drying her hair patiently until she was done. Karen looked up at her in the mirror. "Don't stare. It's unnerving," Karen said irritably.

Tina's lips pulled upwards just enough to offer a sad smile. "You're so beautiful."

Karen rolled her eyes in detest and went back to doing her hair wordlessly.

Tina continued, "I sometimes think that I haven't taken the time to just really look at how beautiful you are. I always think of you as a child, but you're not. You're growing up before my very eyes. A year from now, you'll be in college and living in a dorm. I won't be able to watch you do this anymore." Tina's eyes filled with thick tears. She sniffled. "I don't think I'm ready for you to grow up, sweetheart. I really don't."

Karen looked up into the mirror at Tina again with a callous expression and then began to curl her hair wordlessly.

Tina sniffled again and spoke with remorse, "I made a terrible mistake last night by missing your game. Will you forgive me, sweetheart? I promise I won't miss any of your games next weekend."

Karen's lips tightened slightly as she continued to do her hair wordlessly.

"I know you're mad about me missing your last game..."

"Mad about the game?" Karen snapped coldly. She turned on her stool to face her mother. "I'm not mad about you missing my game! So, who's Ray, Mom? I read your text messages and so did Dad. So, who is he, Mom?"

Tina sighed heavily. "Karen…"

"No, tell me! Are you and Dad getting divorced?"

"What?" Tina asked unexpectedly. "No, we're not getting divorced. What would make you think that?"

"You could've fooled me. Those were some pretty intimate text messages, Mother. I know that's who you were with last night! He must be pretty important to miss my last game. So excuse me if your emotional babble about me growing up doesn't affect me much. Are you sleeping with him? Are you having an affair on Dad, on us?" Karen accused loudly.

Tina's face fell with remorse. She spoke softly, "I didn't have an affair on your father. I made a mistake. I went out with a co-worker for a few drinks. I apologize for missing your game and for coming home drunk. I'm ashamed of myself and apologize if I embarrassed you."

"Who's Ray?" Karen asked pointedly. Her angry eyes stared at Tina, unmoved by her explanation.

Tina sighed and explained slowly, "He's a co-worker of mine. We've been working a lot together lately, but nothing was going on…"

Karen stood up with disgust. "There's nothing going on, Mom? A minute ago, you were saying you weren't ready for me to move on to college, but you chose to get drunk with him instead of watching my last volleyball game! I read your text messages. He can do no wrong! You seem happier with him than you've ever been with Dad. All you and Dad do is fight! I don't even know why, but maybe now I do. You can't be happy with Dad if Ray's the one you love, can you? So tell me, are you and Dad getting divorced? I deserve to know?" Her shoulders moved up and down with her heavy breathing and her eyes filled with fear-inspired tears as she waited for her mother's reply.

Tina shook her head with tears building of her own. She stepped forward and placed her hands on Karen's shoulders.

"I'm not in love with anyone except your father. We are not getting divorced, sweetheart. I can promise you that." She hugged her daughter close as Karen began to cry into her shoulder.

"I don't want you to get divorced," Karen said while weeping on Tina's shoulder.

A tear slipped down Tina's cheek. "We're not, baby. I promise you it's going to get better. I'm so sorry, Karen. I'm so sorry." Tina held her close and wept. Her actions had hurt her children as much as they had her husband.

After a few quiet moments of holding her mother, Karen pulled away and wiped her eyes. "I still have to get ready," she said.

Tina wiped her own eyes. "So, you mentioned dressing up as a pirate?"

"Yes, Chris and I are supposed to dress as Mister and Missus Pirates for the best costumes competition at the dance, but I didn't get to town to buy one. I don't know what to do."

Tina offered a comforting smile. "You finish your hair and make-up, and I'll find you a pirate costume. Between your clothes and mine, we should be able to come up with something. Oh, and I think Samuel has an eye patch somewhere in his room. You get to work. I'll be back."

"Mom," Karen said as Tina stepped towards the door.

Tina said, turning around to look at Karen.

"I love you."

Tina grinned emotionally. "I love you more."

CHAPTER 39

GREG SLATER STOOD ON THE TWENTY-YARD LINE UNDER THE lights that lit up the football field. A heavy fog covered the valley, reducing his vision down to a mere hundred yards at best. The fog might hinder some passing plays downfield, but he was much more concerned about the bitter cold that would surely numb fingers and hands by the game's end. It was thirty-four degrees at game time and the temperature was expected to drop a few degrees by the game's end. The threat of dropped balls and injuries was made higher by the biting cold. Dressed warmly, he watched his assistant coaches run drills with the team. Each one of his players should've been pumped up and ready to face their opponent, who was likewise warming up thirty yards away on the other end of the field. Greg watched each one of the players momentarily for any sign of horseplay or distraction. They would all need to be focused on their assignments throughout the game if they wanted to beat the Brouwer Bulldogs. There was much to distract his players, though, besides the weather. The stadium was full of spectators and so was the uncovered set of bleachers on the Brouwer side of the field. People were beginning to circle the track to socialize and prepare for the game. The Middleton High School Band practiced playing intermittently, and the cheerleaders from both schools rallied on the track in front of their prospective supporters. For the players warming up on the field, it was an exciting time. They were the center of the crowd's attention. For Greg, it was a time to keep his players focused on football and not the Brouwer cheerleaders or the dance later that night.

"Horton!" he yelled at one of his freshman linemen, "Eyes on Coach Peterson." The young man had been looking towards the stadium. He nodded at Greg and focused back on Coach Peterson. It was also Halloween night and many of the student body in the stadium wore their Halloween costumes, although most were covered with heavy coats or blankets. The excitement for the Halloween Dance was overly noticeable in the locker room and throughout the day. It was good to see students excited to partake in any school activity, but it could potentially take their focus off the game. Greg had given a pep talk before his team took to the field, reminding them to forget about the dance for the next sixty minutes and play football. He hoped he got his players focused. He'd know it soon enough.

The Brouwer Coach, Roy Sherwood, walked across the length of the field to talk to Greg. Roy was in his early sixties and had coached the Brouwer Bulldogs for over twenty years. He shook Greg's hand with a serious expression on his stern face. "I wanted to come over before the game begins and wish you luck. I also wanted to let you know that Clara and I have been praying for your family since we saw the news the other night. I know it must've been a tough week for your wife and you," he said sincerely.

"Thank you, Roy. I appreciate that. It has been a tough week; tougher than even the news can tell."

Roy frowned. "I can't even imagine. Well, again, we're praying for you and your family. Tough times you know, build tough players. Keep your eyes focused on God and you'll all get through this fine." He paused momentarily. He pointed a finger at Greg and spoke seriously, "You just keep remembering that the Lord is watching over you, no matter how tough it gets. Okay?"

Greg smiled. "I will. And thank you, Roy.".

Greg waited until there were two minutes left on the scoreboard as it counted down to game time. He stepped into the middle of the pre-game warm-ups and shouted, "Circle up and take a knee, helmets off. This is it, gentlemen. We have to win this game to make the playoffs. They're a good team, strong, powerful, and quick, but so are we. Focus on your assignments and play the game with integrity. That's all I can ask for. I want you all to know whether we win or lose, I have loved having each and every one of you on this team. Let's bow our heads." He removed his hat and dropped down to one knee and bowed his head as well. "Lord, I ask you to watch over this team and keep each and every one of these players safe tonight. In Jesus' name, amen."

"Alright, get your hands in here," he said as he stood up and stuck his right arm out. Twenty-four other arms soon covered it as the team circled him. He spoke earnestly, "Boys, we can beat these guys. Now let's do it! On three, one, two, three." In one loud, unison voice, the players yelled "Giants" and ran excitedly to the sideline in front of the stadium to the crowd's loud applause. Greg loved the excitement that filled the air just before a big game. He jogged behind his team with a deep appreciation for being in the position to coach football. He understood his players' excitement because, after all his years as a player and coach, he still felt the same excitement that the kids did.

As the Star-Spangled Banner played over a loudspeaker, the giants' football team held their helmets in their left hands and placed their right hands over their hearts. In a respectful single file line, they stared at the American Flag hung on a tall flagpole. Greg removed his hat and stood listening to the American Anthem with his team.

Across the field behind the visitor's small, uncovered bleachers, and beyond the tall chain-link fence, a small car pulled into the gravel parking lot and stopped just long enough for someone to climb out of the back seat. The car drove away, leaving the individual behind. The individual with long black hair and a black jacket neared the fence; he placed his fingers within the wire links and leaned on the fence. No one noticed that he was staring straight across the field at Greg Slater. No one recognized that Rene Dibari was back in town.

CHAPTER 40

RENE WATCHED GREG STAND ON THE FAR SIDELINE WITH A clipboard in his hand and occasionally yelling something to the players on the field. He moved between the two 30-yard lines with his team back and forth across the field with great emotion made evident by his body language ranging from excitement to disappointment. A clenched fist jerked downward indicated success, while a dropped head gestured to his disappointment. For a brief moment, Rene wished he could join his old friend with the coaching responsibilities. The nostalgia of having once been the star running back on a two-time state championship team stirred a long-forgotten pride of being a Middleton football alumni player. Being at a home game and hearing the crowd, the play by play calling over the loudspeaker, the cheerleader's cadence to entertain the fans, mixed in with the high school band playing, brought an unexpected excitement that he had long since forgotten. It was the atmosphere of a Middleton football game on a Friday night. But it was the sound of the pads hitting with force and the sound of the whistle after a tackle that thrilled him the most. The violence of a football game is what he'd always loved about playing. He remembered all too well trying to make a dollar bet with Greg before every game on who could hurt the most players from the opposing team. Greg was an outstanding linebacker, no doubt about that, but he lacked the desire to put another player out of the game, so he always refused to bet. Rene was also a great linebacker, but he hit with a ferocity to hurt the ball carrier. The viciousness of the Middleton defense backfield back then was well known and between Greg and himself, it was well deserved. They were both outstanding players, but Greg got the glory and the college scholarship. Rene received some interest, but his grades and SAT scores were well below average and reduced any chance at a college scholarship. Greg had it all back then, athletic talent, on the honor roll, a nice loving home with parents that loved each other, and a long-lasting and genuine loving relationship with Tina. Rene was never attracted to Tina until after Greg began dating her, and then he envied the relationship they had. Greg still had it all even now, including Tina and Rene's daughter, Karen.

Rene scanned the crowd in the stadium for any familiar faces, especially those of his ex-wife and daughter. He was too far away to see any faces clearly, but he knew they were there somewhere. Rene felt so close to being quote 'home,' but still miles away from ever knowing the only daughter he would ever have. Though he had grown up in Middleton and spent the best years of his life here in this town, it was fitting that he stood on the visitor's side of the field. He would never be welcomed home. The chain-link fence keeping him on the outside of the field of play reminded him of that. His only quote 'home' was the Oregon State Penitentiary.

Suddenly the Middleton fans roared as a receiver caught a twenty-yard pass and ran towards the end zone. The Middleton fan base thundered loudly as the receiver crossed the goal line giving them their first touchdown of the game. It was late in the first quarter, and the Brouwer Bulldogs were ahead 14-0 before the touchdown pass by Middleton. After a successful extra-point kick, the score was now 14-7. Rene looked back at Greg and was shocked to see Greg staring straight across the field at him. Rene knew he could stay where he was the whole game long and not worry about being recognized in the fog. However, he didn't come back to watch a football game. Despite the unexpected nostalgia that swept through him and the long-forgotten love for high school football, Rene focused his attention back on Greg. He was the reason Rene had lost his wife and his precious daughter. This moment was the closest Rene had been to his daughter in sixteen years. Fittingly, metaphorically speaking, Greg still stood between them as he stood on the field's sideline with the stadium and cheering crowd behind him. That was ending tonight.

Rene pointed his finger at Greg. "I'll see you soon," he said and stepped away from the fence. The first quarter was nearly over, and Rene had a long walk down Vanderveld Road to get to the old farmhouse that the Whites once owned. He had recognized the house immediately when it was shown on the news. Rene's old girlfriend Lisa White had lived there. Rene had been there many times and coincidently, it wouldn't be the first time he walked out Vanderveld Road on a cold night to break into that house late at night. However, this time he doubted Lisa had left the back door unlocked. He wouldn't be as welcomed tonight as he was back then. But then again, tonight wasn't about pleasure; it was about pain.

CHAPTER 41

DEREK WILLIS SAT IN RON'S LIVING ROOM UNCOMFORTABLY, waiting for Ron and Jose to return from driving to a neighboring town to buy some weed from one of Jose's friends. Eddy Franklyn was their usual guy to buy it from, but they weren't talking anymore after the recent events. Ron and Jose would've taken Derek with them, except Jose's friend was skeptical of strangers. Derek was left to wait with Ron's mother, who Derek had never spoken to before. He'd been waiting for nearly an hour and the awkward silence remained while Wendy sat in her recliner watching TV. Her boyfriend, Jeff, had gone to the football game, which left Derek alone with Wendy. He tried to start a conversation, but she seemed more interested in the TV than talking to him. Derek checked his watch; it was close to eight. "So are you going to the costume party at the bar tonight?" he asked, knowing she frequently went to the bar on the weekends. The local bar was having its annual Halloween Party.

Wendy nodded without any emotion on her face. "Yeah, Jeff and I will be going. It won't start until after the game is over, so I have time to get ready. If you want another beer, they're in the refrigerator," she said, waving her cigarette towards the kitchen before putting it to her lips.

"No, I'm fine," Derek said, holding an empty beer can. "What are you dressing up as tonight?"

She giggled lightly. "Jeff's going as a logger, big change there, huh?" she asked with a slight chuckle. "And I'm going as a hooker. Don't you dare say, 'big change there,' or I'll slap you senseless," she said with a short laugh.

"No, of course not," Derek answered uncomfortably.

"Well, if Jeff says it, he'll be out the door. What about you? Are you dressing up?"

Derek shook his head. "No."

After a moment's silence, Wendy asked, "Did you try calling them? They should be back any time, I'd think."

Derek shrugged. "I have, but Ron's not answering his phone and I don't know Jose's number."

Wendy sighed. "They're probably getting high or something. They wouldn't leave you here while they went to Salem, would they?"

Derek shrugged. It was becoming evident to him that he wasn't the only one who felt the awkwardness of his presence and was resolved to leave. "I don't know about those two anymore; they might've. But I should get going," he said and leaned forward to stand up from the couch. Wendy stopped him.

"Wait a minute, I usually try to stay out of Ron's business, but I have to ask. What the hell got into Eddy that he'd blame Ronny for damaging that girl's car? I know you're friends with Eddy too, but he sure screwed Ronny, and that isn't cool! You better be watching your back, or that scrawny little snake will stab you next!" she said bitterly with a hardness in her eyes.

Derek shrugged uneasily. "Um, I don't know," he said awkwardly, "I stay out of it."

"Ron's going to court over this, and he needs a good character witness, besides me. Maybe you'd like to help with that. All you'd have to do is say Ronny's a good kid. You know, a friend of yours."

"Yeah, I could do that," he said weakly.

Wendy leaned towards him in her recliner with interest. "You know, you could even testify that you were there and seen Eddy doing it. It would teach that worthless piece of trash a lesson about friendship. You don't stab your friends in the back, but once you do, you can expect to get stabbed every time you turn around from then on. That's my belief anyway. Would you be willing to go along with something like that?"

Derek shuffled into his seat uncomfortably. "I don't know about that. I wasn't there."

"Of course, you weren't, but suppose Eddy told you he did the damage to that car while Ronny watched. It's the truth, so why not say so? Of course, you'd have to testify in court, but I know Ron would appreciate it and so would I. Ronny's had a hard enough life without having to deal with this bull crap." She sneered. "Believe me, Eddy picked a fight with the wrong family!"

"Yeah," Derek said, standing. "I'm going to take off. I've been waiting over an hour. I might as well watch the rest of the game. Nice talking to you, Missus Myers."

"Wendy," she said, "I like all of Ronny's real friends to call me Wendy."

"All right, Wendy, I'll talk to you later."

"Think about what I said," Wendy stated. "Ronny could use some real friends right now."

"I will," Derek said as he stepped outside into the cold foggy night and closed the door. The fog was thick and cast eerie trails of light down from the few streetlamps along the gravel road of the trailer park, like a scene from a horror movie that he had recently seen. Being Halloween night and thoughts of the movie brought an unsettling touch of anxiety as he stood in near silence of the heavy fog. He zipped up his coat to block out the bitter cold before leaving Ron's driveway. He grabbed his phone and texted Eddy to see if he was at the game. A text came back that read simply "yes." Derek walked across town towards the high school at a fast pace. He passed an occasional Trick-or-Treater along the way, but not many as it was far too cold to be outside unless, of course, there was a football game. The town was still and quiet except for the echoes of the crowd, distant whistle, and loudspeaker of the football game. While he walked along Adams Street, the main street in town, he saw a man walking down Sixth Street towards Adams through the fog. The man wore a black coat and had long black hair and was clean-shaven. They met in the center of Sixth Street.

The man pointed down the sidewalk. "Looks like we're going the same way, mind if I join you?" he asked pleasantly.

"Ah…sure," Derek answered, slightly reluctant.

"My name's Johnny Gibson. I grew up in this town. What about you?" he asked while extending his hand out to shake Derek's.

"My name's Derek Willis," he said, shaking the man's hand as they walked side by side towards the school, which was only two blocks away.

Johnny asked quickly, "Did your parents grow up here? How old are you?"

"I'm eighteen. My dad's family lives around here. My mom is from California originally. My dad's name is Henry Willis."

"Hmm," Johnny thought back, "Yip, I know of him, I knew Chuck Willis, though; I went to school with him."

"He's my uncle," Derek replied, showing some interest in the conversation. "So you don't live around here anymore?"

"Why'd you ask me that?" His dark eyes burned into Derek curiously.

"You said you grew up here, and I've never seen you before," Derek stated with a shrug innocently enough. He didn't like the look in the stranger's eyes. They were ice cold and sent a chill down Derek's spine.

Johnny laughed slightly. "Oh, yeah, I forgot how small this town is. I left this place many years ago; I live in Seattle now. I'm a musician. I play guitar in a rock band. I just came back to see some old friends for the night. So do you go to school here?"

"No, I quit last year. I work for a dairy now. So what's your band's name? Are you famous?" Derek asked.

Rene chuckled. "I am famous," he admitted. "At least locally, I am. But you won't see me at the Grammys anytime soon." He said with a smirk. "So tell me, I heard on the news about Rene Dibari escaping from prison. I used to know him, Greg, and Tina. I went to school with them. What's Rene's daughter Karen like? Is she beautiful?"

Derek shrugged his shoulders. "Yeah, she is... So, you knew Rene?"

He nodded. "We'd party together. His wife was pretty hot before Greg stole her away from him. Is she still hot?"

Derek answered slowly, "I guess I haven't seen her in a long time. So you would've known my uncle Chuck. He went to school with them too."

"I already said so," Johnny said irritably. Once again, his cold eyes burned into Derek like a dagger and then returned to normal as he asked, "So what's Rene's daughter like? Is she smart like her mother, or athletic like her father, meaning Rene, not Greg?"

Derek shrugged. "Both, I guess. No one knew she wasn't Coach Slater's daughter until this week. It was quite a surprise. Nobody knew anything about it."

Johnny groaned from deep within. "She's my daughter! I mean, she could be. I had some good times with Tina while Rene was gone. Tina was quite easy back then; probably still is. Even after she married Slater, Tina and I would get together for a little rock and roll, if you know what I mean," he chuckled lightly. "She's a rocker. She'll rock your world. She sure as hell did mine," he said with a bitter tone in his voice. "Greg may have married her, but he stole her from me."

"I thought she was married to Rene? At least that's what they're saying on the news," Derek said questionably.

"After Rene. She was dating me after Rene." He answered impatiently.

"Oh," Derek said, a bit confused.

"So," Johnny continued, "tell me about Karen. What is she like?"

"I don't know her very well; she was never a friend of mine. But she is my cousin Chris' date tonight for the Halloween Dance. Chris is my uncle Chuck's son."

"Chuck's son is dating Karen?" Rene asked quietly.

"It's just a dance. She doesn't have a boyfriend."

"Is she popular?"

"Yeah, she's a very nice girl," Derek said as they crossed Fifth Street.

"How many other kids do Greg and Tina have now?"

Derek thought momentarily. "Two, I think, two boys."

"How old are they?" Johnny asked.

"Robert's a freshman this year. He's a cool kid actually. And his little brother is in junior high, I think. I don't know his name."

As they approached the high school, Rene wanted to ask more about his daughter, but the time with the young man was short. He needed to find out as much information as possible while he could. "So they're probably all at the game, huh?"

"Oh yeah, nobody misses a game here. You should know that; didn't you play football?"

Rene grinned. If there was anything he was good at, it was his years playing football and wrestling. "I did. We were two-time state champions, but we had a real coach back then. You guys will never win a state championship again with Greg as your coach. Hey, I saw a Middleton police car drive by earlier. How many cops are here now?" he asked.

Derek shrugged. "Well, not much has changed. Harry Bishop is the Police Chief and Steve Turley is the other full-time cop. He's a jerk sometimes, but they're usually the only two. Occasionally Martin and Joe will fill in."

Rene chuckled. "Old Harry is still here, huh? I thought Harry would've retired by now."

"Nope. Nothing ever changes here. You'll probably find him at the game with the best seat in the stadium. And Steve's probably there right beside him, or out giving tickets to trick or treaters." He turned to walk to the football field as they reached the corner in front of the high school. Johnny Gibson remained standing on the sidewalk. "Aren't you watching the game?"

Rene shook his head. "No, I've seen enough. I'm meeting up with some old friends tonight. Take care," Rene said and began to walk straight on Adams. He had another two blocks almost to walk before he could leave town on Vanderveld Road.

"Hey, I'll tell my uncle you said hello," Derek said as he received a text message on his phone. It was from Eddy, wondering where he was.

Rene chuckled slightly. "You do that."

Derek was pleased to find it was mid-way through half-time, so the admission was now free to get in. He walked towards the stadium where Eddy was waiting for him. He glanced at the scoreboard as he passed by. Brouwer was ahead by the score of 20-7. Derek met Eddy behind the stadium near the concession stand and immediately told him what Wendy Myers asked him to do.

Eddy held a cup of soda from the concession stand and shook his head. "I'm not surprised. It doesn't matter, though; the truth will still come out. You didn't go with them to Salem?"

"They never came back! I don't know where they are. They left me at Ron's house to get some weed from Jose's friend, and now I'm here. They might've left me. I don't know." Derek shrugged. "I guess they're not buying it from you anymore."

"I'm not selling it anymore, Derek. I don't smoke it anymore either, at least, I'm trying not to. I'm a Christian now; I'm changing my life around. I don't want to be like my dad going in and out of jail because of drugs. I don't want to be known as the town pothead anymore, either. I want to make a better life for myself, a clean life. I'm even joining the wrestling team."

Derek gasped. "You're going to get killed."

Eddy shrugged his thin shoulders. "At first, but I'll get better, and I'll be making new friends, jocks. Can you believe that? I accepted Jesus and God's already changing my life. I can't explain it, but I'm different in here." He padded his heart. "Jesus is real, man. He convinced me of that the moment I was saved. You can be saved too. Come to church with me on Sunday."

Derek hesitated uncomfortably. "I'll think about it." His phone vibrated, indicating a text message. "It's Ron. He wants to know where I am." He text messaged Ron. A moment later, his phone vibrated again. "Ron's coming to pick me up. He'll be here in a minute." He looked at Eddy. "I guess I'm going to Salem tonight after all."

Eddy took a deep breath. "Hang out with me tonight. It's way too cold to sleep in the back of Ron's car. I'll skip the dance and we'll go watch a movie at my house or something."

"No, you might've quit drinking, but I haven't. I'm going to go get hammered and have some fun."

"Remember that tomorrow when you're hungover and sick."

Derek laughed. "I will. Here they come," he said, nodding toward the orange 1972 Datsun 510 wagon coming towards the gate behind the stadium. Hard rock music pounded loudly through the speakers as Ron slowed to a stop on the street outside of the gate. He turned down his stereo and leaned out of his window to point at Eddy. "Hey, look everyone, it's Pastor Franklyn!" Ron laughed. "Pastor Franklyn, come on, buddy, hop in and come with us. We can be friends," Ron sounded drunk.

Jose was in the passenger seat and took a drink of his

opened beer. He was laughing lightly and waved his hand for Ron to go. "Let's go."

Ron continued to speak loudly out of the window. "Derek, get in, you too, Pastor Franklyn. Come here!" he shouted. It drew the attention of others that stood behind the stadium.

"I'll see you later," Derek told Eddy and walked towards the street. He stopped near the car; Ron's eyes were heavy, red, and glossy. He was definitely under the influence of alcohol, if not something else.

"Eddy," Ron yelled past Derek, "I'll see you later. It ain't over until it's over!" His glaring eyes turned from Eddy to Derek. "What are you waiting for? Get in!"

Derek shook his head as Eddy walked up behind him. "I changed my mind. I'll stay here."

"And do what, talk about Jesus? Get in and let's go!"

"No, you're already drunk. Maybe we should just go back to your place," Derek suggested. He didn't like the feeling he was getting at the prospect of driving with Ron to Salem in the fog as drunk and high as he appeared.

"We're not going back to my place! Are you coming or not? I promise you I'm not drunk. I've had a couple of beers, but I'm fine. Are you coming or not?"

Jose leaned over the driver's seat in front of Ron and pointed his finger at Eddy. "That snitch is going to call the police as soon as we leave. Let's get moving while we can." He nodded at Eddy and spoke purposely with an intense glare in his eyes, "Eddy, have you ever seen a panther stalk its prey?" Eddy shook his head no. Jose nodded slowly with his eyes penetrating Eddy dangerously. "You will."

Though Jose's words startled him. Eddy bent over to place his hands on his knees and spoke sincerely, "Go home, Ron. It's dangerous out tonight. Seriously, man."

Jose watched Eddy, with violence burning behind his eyes. It infuriated him that his threat went unnoticed. "Don't ignore me, snitch! I'll get out of this car and beat your scrawny snitch ass right now! Do you think I'm kidding? Your time's coming fast, Eddy. You're a dead man!" he warned severely in a loud voice and then noticed the county deputy sheriff walking towards the gate. "Let's go; a cop is coming!"

Ron grinned. "I guess you'll find out if your god's real or not pretty soon, huh, snitch?" he laughed and then drove quickly down Fourth Street.

Derek turned back toward the gate with Eddy. "I guess I'll hang out with you tonight after all. Ron's messed up on something, and I don't think it's just beer. They were sober when they left."

Eddy frowned. "Let's tell the police that he's drinking and driving. He's too messed up to be driving."

"Are you joking? You can't do that, he's your friend! Listen, they were going to beat you up earlier. If you rat them out again, they'll kill you. Maybe not Ron, but Jose will. You heard him, man. He's already got it in for you. If you tell the cops and he finds out, you're dead!" Derek said pointedly.

"And if he ends up killing someone tonight, he might wish we had told the police. You didn't go with him because he's too messed up on something to drive. He's not just drunk; he's high on more than just pot too. We have to do what's right, Derek. It could save a little kid out trick or treating's life, if not Ron's own. It's the right thing to do," he said and walked over to meet the approaching county deputy sheriff.

CHAPTER 42

Jose Rodriguez was turned in his seat, looking back to watch Eddy and Derek as Ron sped down to the stop sign at the corner. Suddenly Jose yelled, "Go! Eddy is talking to the cops! I can't believe this; I'm going to leave him lying face down in a ditch when I'm finished with him. Go, Ron, the snitch is ratting you out again!" he yelled.

Ron could barely make out the figure of his two friends talking to the county sheriff's deputy through the fog. Ron sneered and floored the gas pedal as he turned right onto Adams Street and shortly turned left on Vanderveld Road. He kept the fuel pedal floored as the road dropped down into a gully, crossed a narrow bridge, and back up the other side of the gully. He expected the sharp right turn at the top of the gully and made the turn with ease. Just as the road straightened, Jose yelled, "Watch out!"

A man wearing dark clothes and long dark hair was walking in the middle of their lane. Ron veered to the left just quickly enough to narrowly miss the man. If the man hadn't leaped to the right, he would've been run over. They flew past him and slid slightly on the thin layer of freezing fog. Ron controlled his car by releasing the accelerator but then pressed the gas pedal to the floor to distance him from town. The man they nearly hit was of no concern to him. It had happened in a split second, but they had not touched him.

"Wow!" Jose laughed. "What an idiot! That dude needs to stay off the road. Man, I can't believe you missed him! That was close."

Ron exhaled with relief. "I wouldn't have stopped, even if I had hit him. I'm not going back to jail for some stupid idiot walking in the middle of the road. I'd just keep going and hope he didn't damage my car too much. That was close!" He glanced down at his speedometer; he was going sixty miles per hour through the fog. "Hey, grab me another beer. That nearly scared my buzz away."

Jose turned around to grab two beers out of the half case in the back seat. He looked out the rear window. There was no trace of car lights, just a wall of blackness. He decided to bring the half case up to the front seat. "I don't see any car lights coming. I suspect the police will be looking for us." He opened a beer for Ron and handed it to him and then opened one for himself.

"Thanks," Ron said as he took a drink. "We'll take the back roads into Salem. I doubt they'll waste too many patrol cars looking for us, not with all of the other drunk drivers out there tonight."

Jose laughed heartedly. "Yeah, it's not like we're really as drunk as they are!" He took a long drink of his beer. "The cops need to work on a priority basis, like a fishing tournament, you know? Like arrest the most drunk and let us lesser drunks go. If we get pulled over, we can always claim we're not the drunkest fish. There's bound to be a drunken driver around somewhere on Halloween night. You know what I mean?" Jose laughed.

Ron quipped, "Yeah, they can always catch us later when we've had a few more beers," he said with a laugh. "You know, Karen's house is coming up; we should stop and break out the windows or something. They're all at the game, so no one's home. We might even make the news if we say we saw that Rene guy doing it and chased him away.

Then the police will be chasing that big fish and forget about us long enough for us to get to the keg. It sounds like a good idea to me. Are you up for that?" Ron asked.

"What?" Jose asked, not liking the idea. "Are you talking about Coach Slater's place? No way, man! You need to just leave them alone. Besides, you already passed their house, it's back there," Jose said, motioning behind them.

"We haven't passed it yet. It's up here."

"No, dude, you passed it."

"Dude, it's right up here! It's coming up..." He leaned forward to look through the fog to his left.

"You can't see anything out here. You've already done passed it. I'm telling you," Jose said and took a drink of his beer.

"No, we haven't! I've driven this road a million times. I know exactly where they live and it's coming up. Trust me, I know where they live." He took a drink of his beer and slowed down to about thirty-five miles per hour. "It's right in here, somewhere," he said slowly as he searched for the house through the fog.

Jose shook his head. "You passed it a mile back. I'm telling you it's way back there. You may want to speed up, remember the snitch ratted us out to the cops. I don't want to spend Halloween night sitting in jail for contributing alcohol to a minor."

"Ah, there it is, see! I told you we didn't pass it!" Ron spoke victoriously as he passed the two-story farmhouse that set alongside the road. Though there were no cars in the driveway, the downstairs lights were on. "I told you! Don't tell me I don't know where I am! I know this road like the back of my hand. Come on, tell me who was right!" Ron said as he pressed the accelerator to speed his car up. "Huh?" he chided.

Jose laughed. "Okay, you were right. I deserve it."

Ron laughed. "That's right. Now I say we rock!" he shouted and turned up the volume of his stereo system that played his favorite heavy metal band.

Jose watched as the fog rolled past them like a speeding train through a snowstorm. Visibility was low and occasionally, the fog thinned, revealing a further glimpse of the road before growing thick again. Jose knew Vanderveld Road had a seven-mile perfectly straight stretch across farmland, which was used for racing by generations of Middleton teens late at night before the road turned sharply to the left. The fog had disoriented Jose and he couldn't tell where they were precisely on the road. Ron was driving fast to gain some distance from any potential cops following them, but it was getting uncomfortable in the passenger seat. They could see the road in their headlights, but nothing beyond the fog they cut through. Without seeing any landmarks to locate their position on the road, Jose knew every minute at their higher speed was drawing them closer to the sharp left turn and the ancient old Oak Tree that greeted anyone who missed the turn. Jose reached over and turned down the loud music just enough to be heard. "Hey, man, that corner is coming up; you may want to slow down."

Ron finished the last of his beer, rolled down the window, and tossed the empty beer can outside. He rolled up the window in a hurry. "Damn, it is cold out there!"

"The corner, man," Jose mentioned again.

"It's way up there. We just passed the Slater's house a minute ago. Trust me; I know exactly where we are. I've driven this road a million times. Remember?" Ron tapped Jose's leg with his hand. "Beer me."

Jose finished his beer quickly and then opened another for Ron and one for himself. Jose watched the fog go by and listened to the metal rock pound his chest through the speakers. He took a drink of his beer. Jose knew the road, as well as Ron. He knew they had to be getting close to the corner. He remembered an old, abandoned house overgrown with briars within a hundred yards of the curve, but it was impossible to see it through the fog at the speed they were going. He turned the stereo down. "Dude, you better slow down; that corner is coming up."

Ron shook his head. "Man, It's not for a couple more miles yet. Relax. You are terrible at estimating distance. I told you, I know this road like the back of my hand. And quit turning down the stereo, this is my favorite song," Ron said, turning up his stereo and taking a drink of his beer.

Jose turned the stereo down just enough to speak with concern on his face. "Ron, it's coming up! Slow down, man," Jose said and immediately reached for his seatbelt to put it on.

Ron laughed. "Coward! What's the matter, you don't trust me? Check this out," he said and floored his accelerator. "See? There's nothing to worry about." He brought his beer to his lips to drink when a yellow warning sign of a sharp curve posting a 25 miles-per-hour flew by. Jose screamed as the fog thinned just enough to see the fast-approaching Oaktree.

Panic struck Ron with the force of a hammer. He lifted his right foot off the accelerator to hit the brake, but in a panic, slammed his foot back down on the accelerator. He looked down at the pedals in horror and then back up just as his car slammed head-on into the massive tree at seventy miles per hour.

Ten minutes later, a county sheriff's deputy looking for a possible drunk driver in a 1972 Orange Datsun 510 wagon neared the accident scene. He could see the orange car had hit the tree. He pulled over and turned on his strobe lights. He radioed immediately to notify that he had found an accident and called for an ambulance and assistance before stepping out of his patrol car. With his spotlight on and his flashlight, he stepped out into the heavy fog. The car had hit the tree with great force collapsing the entire front end into a mangled tight package of crumpled steel—the smell of steam, radiator fluid, and beer mixed in the absolute silence of the night. The driver was unbuckled and wrapped strangely around the steering wheel with his head and arms outside the window. He was deceased. The same could be said for the passenger. He was also unbuckled and had been thrown through the front window into the tree. His body laid lifelessly across the compressed metal of the car and bent unnaturally upward against the tree. A beer can was still grasped tightly in his hand.

CHAPTER 43

Tina had lain on the couch watching TV after Karen went back to the school. She was relieved to have been able to talk with Karen and apologize. It was good to get back to a new starting ground to fix the relationships that she had damaged. It had never occurred to her that the children might be afraid of their parents getting divorced. She was blinded by her selfishness, and her careless words and actions were the result. Sometimes it took some shame and humiliation to get one's priorities right again; certainly, it had hers. She once again thanked God for directing Greg to get her and bring her home. The thought both repulsed and scared her of where she'd be if he hadn't come after her.

Looking at the clock, she knew she still had time to watch the last part of the game. She had missed most of it, but if she hurried, she could be there at its end to show her support for her husband. More importantly, she wanted to be with him at the dance. She wanted to see her beautiful daughter and her date dressed as pirates. She wanted to watch Karen enjoy herself with her friends. It was Karen's senior year, and Tina knew she would never get the opportunity to relive this year again. Tina wanted to dance with her husband as well. She wanted to be held in his arms and be reassured that everything was going to be all right. She wanted to tell him she loved him, honestly and purely. With that in mind, she jumped off the couch and ran upstairs to shower quickly. She did her hair simply and put on just enough makeup to highlight her features. She dressed respectfully and was ready to go within half an hour. She was in a hurry and felt the pressure to get there before the game ended. She regretted waiting so long to decide to go. She grabbed her coat and purse, locked the house, and went out the back door to get into Karen's car, which was parked near the barn to hide it from the view of cars driving by. She started it up and went out of her driveway and onto Vanderveld Road. She didn't notice the man wearing dark clothing that darted off the road into the field as she pulled out of her driveway through the fog.

Rene watched the car pass by but was unable to distinguish who the driver was. He was only twenty feet from the driveway when the car pulled out. He crossed the road and stepped on their gravel driveway. There were no cars parked in the driveway and the house appeared to be dark and empty. There was no sign of a dog outside and when he peeked into an uncovered window, he saw no sign of a dog inside. He could see a nice-sized family room with a pair of lamps left on. He rang the doorbell and peeked through the window. There was no response. He tried to open the front door, but as he expected, it was locked. He moved around to the back door and tried it, but it was locked. As cold as it was outside, he knew there would not be any open windows. The only way into the house was to break in. However, he didn't want to kick the door in or break out any windows that the family might notice when they came home. He needed a less obvious entry point to give him the advantage when his ex-wife and Greg came home. Rene walked around the house shivering in the cold as he searched for the least noticeable entry point.

On the far side of the house, there was an upstairs bedroom window that once had belonged to his old girlfriend's little sister. It would be a good access point, but he had no way of getting up to it. He walked to the old barn and found a light switch. He found himself disturbing the sleep of three pigs, grunting curiously as they climbed to their feet, anxious for their dinner, and a lone cow in one stall waiting to be fed. In another stall, a horse waited as well. Rene ignored the hungry animals and searched for a ladder. He found a twenty-foot extension ladder, carried it to the side of the house, and set it up against the exterior wall to extend it to the bottom of the window. He returned to the barn to grab a crowbar and shut off the barn lights before anyone saw him. He climbed up to the window and pried the screen off, letting it drop to the ground below him. He then tried to force the crowbar under the wooden pane. With an effort, he pried and broke the lock. He pushed the window up to open it and climbed inside to the warmth of their home.

Rene grabbed the top blanket off the bed and wrapped himself up in it to warm himself before turning on the light and looking around the room. It was a small bedroom decorated with posters of the Seattle Seahawks. It was obviously a boy's bedroom by the decorations and personal items that set about.

He closed the window before turning off the light and leaving the room. He stepped out of the room and onto the hardwood deck wrapped around the grand stairway, leading downstairs. He remembered sneaking up those stairs and around the corner to reach Lisa's bedroom undetected. Her parents' master bedroom was at the top of the stairs on the right. He recalled the excitement he'd feel as he'd pass her parents' bedroom and those of her siblings.

Rene stepped into the master bedroom and flicked on the light switch, his breath was sucked away by the sight of Greg and Tina's bed. It was a high-setting king-sized bed with an ornamental headboard. It was left unmade. He walked into the room and felt the same rage begin to boil within him that he had felt at his sentencing hearing when he watched Greg comforting Rene's wife. He stared at the bed; it was where they held each other comfortably every single night that he'd been in prison. He pulled out his pocketknife, flung the blankets aside and stabbed the bed, and cut across its middle. He did it again and again, destroying the representation of their marriage with every cut.

Rene sat down on Tina's side of the bed and picked up her pillow. He sniffed it and smelled the fragrant scent of her, mixed with a vague scent of vomit. He tossed the pillow back on the bed and opened her bedside nightstand's drawer. He filtered through the items and slammed it shut. He noticed a wall-mounted jewelry box with family pictures on its door. He moved across the room to look at the photos. There was a picture of a beautiful young girl of about twelve years old. She was the perfect combination of Tina and himself. She was beautiful. The next photo was of Tina and Greg in a formal setting. There was a picture of their boys with Karen at the beach. Lastly, there was a family portrait. Seeing Greg with Karen in a family portrait infuriated Rene. He grabbed the jewelry box and ripped it off the wall and threw it to the floor.

He opened the walk-in closet and sifted through Tina's assortment of business suits, dresses, blouses, jeans, and T-shirts. He grew increasingly angrier as he noticed her many pairs of shoes. He left the closet and saw the gun cabinet that was beside the bedroom door. With a forceful kick, he shattered the clear glass of the double doors. He pulled out a wooden case with a flip-lock. Inside he found a 9-millimeter semi-automatic handgun. He checked the chamber and slipped in a clip containing fifteen bullets. He found the safety and injected a round into the chamber. He pressed the safety to on so he wouldn't shoot himself.

As he stood by the bedroom door admiring his new weapon, he took notice of a large professional glamour photograph of Tina hanging on the wall facing him. She was dressed in blue jeans and a white blouse in front of a white background, emphasizing her brown hair, soft skin, and beautiful blue eyes. Her red lipstick outlined her thin lips but emphasized her perfectly straight white teeth with a joy-filled smile. It was a beautiful portrait of her. For a brief moment, Rene felt an adoring warmth start to stir within him. He forced the nostalgia away and aimed the handgun at her picture. He flipped the safety off and pulled the trigger. The recoil of the 9-millimeter lifted his hand upwards unexpectedly. He almost dropped the weapon. He had never shot a 9-millimeter before and wasn't expecting its powerful recoil or the damage the hollow point bullet caused. The bullet had torn through Tina's face and penetrated the interior and exterior walls leaving a decent-sized hole in the house. The framed portrait had fallen to the floor and shattered the glass and frame.

He stood in their bedroom and looked at all the souvenirs and little knick-knacks that were put about here and there. Pictures of their family were framed and set on the dressers or hung on the walls. In every picture Greg and Tina were in, they were smiling and holding one another affectionately. It infuriated Rene to see them looking so happy. It fertilized his hatred all the more to see for himself how good they had it after setting him up to take the fall. It wasn't fair that they should live in abundance and carefree of trouble while he suffered. Just the things in Tina's bedroom were worth more than everything they owned when they were married. It didn't seem fair that she should have everything she ever dreamed of, while he was locked up in prison for the rest of his life, waiting to die. It was her fault that he was in there, to begin with. Before the night was through, he would even the score. He had nothing to lose, and he would take away all that they owed him. They would never smile again if they lived through the night.

Rene walked out of the bedroom and went downstairs to the living room. More pictures of their family hung on the wall. Again, he looked at the smiling faces of another family portrait. It was one fairly recently taken and he stared at the image of his daughter. She had grown up to be the most beautiful girl he'd ever seen. He stared at her image in awe. A slight mist began to gather in his eyes.

Suddenly, he froze when he heard sirens in the distance, and they were getting closer. It sounded like two police cars were coming his way. He didn't want to be trapped in the house if they covered all the exits. Quickly, Rene went through the kitchen to the back door and hurriedly unlocked it. The sirens were getting louder as he quickly opened the door and ran as fast as he could to the barn door. He went inside, closing the door behind him. He held the pistol in his hand while he waited for the police to pull into the driveway. Rene didn't think the car driver that had left the house had seen him run off the road, but they might have recognized him after all. Someone had to have called the police. Maybe someone heard the gunshot when he shot Tina's portrait, he thought. How could he have been so stupid?

The police were closing in and the sirens were growing much louder. Rene was ready to burst into a sprint at any second and escape through the horse stall to flee across the back pasture to the wooded creek at the property line, where he and Lisa used to picnic from time to time. He could follow the creek back to town if need be. The fog would help him escape quickly enough, but the coldness wouldn't make it comfortable or easy. He waited in the darkness of the barn for the police to pull into the driveway, and then he would burst into a run. He could see the blue strobe lights reflecting in the fog as the police cars neared the driveway. The sirens were loud and unnerving. Just when he expected to see the police car lights pull into the driveway, the two police cars sped past the Slater home without even slowing down. The sound of the sirens moved further away. Rene sighed with relief. He waited in the barn for his heart rate to drop back to normal and then he went back to the house. He went back upstairs but paused at the top of the stairs when he heard more sirens coming towards the house. Confident that they were going somewhere else, he searched the rooms upstairs until he found Karen's bedroom. Just so happened, it was the same bedroom that his old girlfriend, Lisa White, used to have. He turned on the light and stepped inside.

Karen's bedroom was painted a light shade of pink and was clean and organized. Her single bed on a white captain's frame with three drawers below the mattress set along the left sidewall. The covers were pulled back unmade and appeared as though she had just climbed out of bed, with a glass half-full of water was on a nightstand beside her bed. An antique green vanity with a large oval mirror in its center was straight across from the door and a matching padded stool. The vanity was covered with miscellaneous make-up and hair products. A standard dresser was beside the door and her closet was along the right sidewall. The walls were decorated with a poster of the U.S. National Softball Team. There was a poster of two horses running through the golden grass of the plains somewhere and she had a poster of some young actor that Rene had never seen before. Three matching small white shelves spread across her room held her knick-knacks and an occasional small, framed picture. There were also framed pictures of her friends and her that hung on her walls. It was a nice room that displayed her many interests and her tastes in decorations.

Rene walked to her vanity and picked up her hairbrush. He pulled out some of the hair and rubbed them between his thumb and forefinger. He tried to think back to the last time he touched her hair; it was when he had last held her in his arms the day he was arrested. A mist warmed his eyes as he set the brush down and moved over to her bed. He sat down and grabbed her pillow. He breathed in the scent of his daughter and could feel a long-forgotten adoration for his baby girl. He held the pillow close to his face, closed his eyes, and breathed it in. He opened his eyes slowly with an agonizing pressure compressing his heart. It was the yearning to break down and cry. Suddenly he felt like he had been kicked in the gut, as his heart fell through his chest like a rock plummeting to the floor.

On the nightstand in a 4x6 frame was a picture of Karen when she was just over two years old being held in her mother's arms. Karen was wearing a beautiful little green dress with white lace trimming and decorative breast. It was a dress he had picked out and bought for his baby girl himself. Tina also wore an attractive dress and appeared more beautiful than he ever remembered her being. The picture was taken in their old house on Sixth Street on their old second-hand floral couch. It was a picture that Rene had taken. He remembered it well. It was Easter Sunday. They had just come home from her parents' Easter dinner.

Rene laid the pillow down and picked up the picture. He held it in his hands and stared at Tina's face with deep emotion. She looked wonderful in the dress and her hair was done perfectly, but despite her slight smile, her unhappiness was clearly seen. He stared at his daughter in Tina's arms and tears began to burn his eyes. It was a picture of the life he had known when his daughter knew him as her "Daddy." She would hug him tightly then, the way only a daughter can. He sniffled, took a deep breath, and wiped the thin tears from his eyes. He lay back on the bed and smelt the scent of his daughter now and stared at the picture. He missed her. A tear slid down out of his eye.

CHAPTER 44

GREG SLATER WATCHED THE GAME CLOCK COUNT DOWN TO zero. The buzzer rang, ending the game. The Brouwer Bull-dogs had won the game by the score of 27-7. Greg walked disappointedly to the middle of the field to shake hands with the Brouwer head coach, Roy Sherwood. After a few moments of shaking hands with the players from Brouwer, he finally met Coach Sherwood in the middle of the field. They were surrounded by people supporting both schools in a large circle of fans, parents, and players. The handshake they shared was both firm and friendly. "Good game, Coach. I expect to see you guys in the state finals," Greg said with a smile, despite his disappointment.

"Thanks, Greg. Your boys played a good game. It was a closer game than the score reveals." He nodded behind Greg. "I see Channel 9 News is here, but I'll bet they're not here to talk to me."

Greg turned around to see a young female reporter walking towards him with a cameraman. She was a very attractive blonde-haired lady wrapped warmly in a heavy coat with Channel 9 News embroidered on it. Greg said to Coach Sherwood, "I'm sure they're not here to talk about the game at all."

Roy shook his head. "Well, listen, Greg, we'll keep

praying for you. We'll get together soon," he said and turned away from Greg to talk to a sports reporter from the local county newspaper.

Greg shook hands with a few more people before the reporter got to him through the crowd. He saw her approaching and waited. He didn't look at all pleased to see the news coming to interview him again.

"Hello, Coach Slater, my name's Nadia Kirkpatrick and I'd like to get a quick interview if I could?" She didn't seem interested in his response as she directed her cameraman to get into position.

Greg hesitated as he watched her. He was surrounded by people from both towns and felt out of place as they quieted down to watch the TV news do an interview. "Make it quick. I need to go in with the team."

Nadia took her position beside Greg and waited for the cameraman to get situated. She spoke into her microphone on cue by introducing Greg then surprisingly emphasized the importance of the night's game to Greg's team. She then turned to Greg. "Coach Slater, your team needed to win tonight to make the playoffs. Some of the fans I've talked to have indicated that losing by twenty points might show a lack of concentration on your part. How has the escape of Rene affected your family and your team this week?"

"Our team has been focused on this game all week. The Brouwer Bulldogs and Coach Sherwood simply outplayed us. That's all there is to it," Greg answered plainly.

"Are you saying the escape of Rene Dibari hasn't affected your personal life? We have a source that indicated that it has drastically affected your personal life. In particular, an incident that happened last night in a Ridgefield bar?"

Greg stared at her, wishing he had never agreed to speak with her. As attractive as the young lady was, he now knew she was as slippery as an eel. His eyes flickered with indignation as he nodded shortly. "I think your source has an agenda to harm my family. So I won't respond to that. I don't appreciate being blindsided by questions that have nothing to do with football or Rene. But I will answer your question; of course, Rene's escape has affected our family, but not as much as the media has. Every aspect of our life has been put on TV for everyone to see, where we work, where we live, even our house! If Rene didn't know where we lived, he does now just from watching the news! That's the threat that's looming over us. Thank you for that," he said heatedly and stepped away from her.

Nadia asked quickly, stepping to his side, determined to keep the interview going. "Is it true that you caught your wife having an affair with a Mister Torres? Isn't it true that you physically assaulted him last night in a bar that you caught him and your wife in?"

Greg stopped and looked at her in disbelief. He could not believe that she had the audacity to ask such questions in public, let alone expected him to answer such a personal question for Channel 9 News. He was dumbfounded and didn't know how to respond. The crowd of players, parents, strangers and old alumni were all quietly waiting with interest for his answer. He felt his heart rate quicken and his anger beginning to get the better of him. He felt like the field was starting to spin as he looked into the camera light. He longed to run to the locker room and get away from the attractive reporter with no conscience. He looked longingly towards the locker room door. Near the goalpost, he saw Tina standing by herself waiting for him. She was dressed in blue jeans and wore a black turtleneck under a black wool coat. Her hair was in a ponytail covered by a gray wool knit cap, with her long bangs moved off to the side of her face. She was looking at him with a small empathetic smile. She was beautiful. Her presence was comforting. Like a compass, his spinning world found its true north and he regained his strength and composer.

Greg shook his head and offered a small laugh. "If I had caught my wife having an affair, she wouldn't be right over there." He pointed at her with a smile. He looked back at Nadia. "I think I understand what's happening here, my wife reported some unethical practices to your source's supervisor today and he was terminated. I believe he's trying to get even through you. It won't work. Maybe you should investigate your source a little deeper; it would make a good story. I have to go," he said and quickly stepped away from the attractive reporter. She faced the camera and signed off.

People patted his shoulders and shook his hand, and some even commented on next year's season as he strolled towards Tina. When he was free from the crowd of people, he neared his wife. She waited for him with a nervous smile. He stopped in front of her and looked at her with a deep sadness in his eyes. She noticed it and her eyes began to cloud. She shrugged her shoulders guiltily. "I'm sorry," she said softly.

He took a deep breath. "I wasn't expecting you to be here." His mouth tightened with emotion and his eyes began to mist. "I didn't think you were here."

She wiped a tear from the corner of her eyes.. "I've never missed a home game. I didn't want to start now."

A Middleton player ran past Greg towards the locker room, hollering, "We have a dance to get to, Coach! Hurry up!"

Greg smiled. "I have to go. The boys are excited about the dance. I'll see you later..." he paused uncomfortably. "It sounds like Ray called the news and told them about last night."

She shrugged sadly. "I deserve it," she said softly.

Greg shook his head. "No, you don't. I'll be home late."

"Aren't you going to ask me?" she asked quickly.

"Ask you?" he questioned.

"To the dance?"

"You don't have to come to the dance."

"Greg, just ask me."

He looked at her awkwardly and then slowly asked, "Tina, will you go to the dance with me tonight?"

"I'd love to. I don't want to miss another game or dance

ever again," she said with tears in her blue eyes. "Even away games, no matter how far away they are. I want to be there, Greg, to support you and our kids. I don't know what I was thinking, but I hope you have it in you to forgive me."

His smile was warm and tender as he watched her beautiful blue eyes fill with water. "Come here," he said, and she stepped forward into his arms. He held her close in a loving embrace and looked into her eyes. He kissed her, but as soon as his lips touched hers, he heard, "Coach!" Chris Willis yelled from near the locker room. "Come on! We're waiting for you!"

Greg chuckled and shook his head. "The timing of these kids is ridiculous. I have to go."

Tina smiled good-naturedly. "Go inside, Coach. We'll finish this later," she said softly.

WHEN THE WOLF COMES KNOCKING LATE

CHAPTER 45

EDDY FRANKLYN STOOD ON THE FOOTBALL FIELD WITH DEREK Willis, watching Coach Slater talking to the TV news reporter, Nadia Kirkpatrick from Channel 9 News. Even though Nadia was the best-looking news anchor on TV, Eddy's eyes kept going over to where Karen Slater stood talking with a group of her friends with her little brother, Samuel, and one of his friends on the track. Karen was dressed in black loose-fitting cotton pants, black boots, and a white loose-fitting long-sleeved dress shirt, with a broad red sash tied around her waist. She had a black handker-chief covering her hair, with one side of her hair pulled beautifully down over her face and a black eye patch covering her right eye. She looked adorable and more beau-tiful than he'd ever noticed her being before. Karen was the most beautiful girl he'd ever seen and quite literally, she took his breath away. Deep inside, where his heart converged with his soul, he could feel the longing to be someone special in her life. She was always so kind to everyone she spoke to. Even when her friends shunned him, she would at least look him in the eyes and respond respect-fully. Karen wasn't just beautiful; she was also a wonderful human being. In his opinion, she was as close to perfection as a girl could be. At the very least, she was a rare jewel, like the Hope Diamond that he longed to have in his life. If she would ever give him a chance, he would honor her as a true friend. Simply, he would treasure her like the treasure she was.

Derek, however, stared at Nadia. "Man, she's even prettier in person than on the TV. I'm going to ask her to be my friend on…"

"Derek," Eddy said, "you can already follow everything she says on social media."

"I'm going to. Don't you think Nadia is good looking? I mean, she's beautiful!"

"She's not as good-looking as her," Eddy said, watching Karen put her heavy coat back on over her costume.

"Who?" Derek asked.

"Karen. I've never realized how beautiful she really is."

Derek laughed. "Man, she's out of your league. She won't have anything to do with you."

Eddy peered at Derek skeptically. "And you have a chance with Nadia Kirkpatrick?"

Derek laughed. "No, but it's nice to dream. And I'll have some sweet dreams tonight."

"Hmm, yeah, me too. I wonder if she'd dance with me if I went."

"Nadia?" Derek asked.

"No, Karen."

Derek turned his attention over to Karen. She was huddling in her coat, trying to stay warm after revealing her costume to her friends. He shook his head and spoke louder than he wanted to, "No way, Nadia's better looking!"

Eddy had not taken his eyes off Karen; it was noticed by her best friend, Amanda, who commented on it to her group of friends. Karen turned her head to look at Eddy. He turned away after becoming the focus of their attention. A junior high boy who was friends with Samuel called, "Stare hard, you greasy loser!" he was quickly hushed from his laughter by Karen's soft rebuke.

Eddy's face turned red from the humiliation of being

pointed out and being made fun of. It tore into his gut. Who was he kidding? He would never be more than he already was to her. He turned his back to them and watched Coach Slater walk away from the attractive reporter. Eddy was unimpressed by reporter Nadia Kirkpatrick; she was pretty for sure, but she was a far cry from Karen.

Derek shook his head with a compassionate smile. "I told you, man, Karen is way out of your league."

Eddy shrugged. "Oh, it doesn't matter. I just don't want to be labeled anymore," he said, humiliated by the kid's comment.

"Hey, Eddy…" came the voice of Karen Slater. He turned around to see her approaching him. Her expression seemed very sincere. "I wanted to apologize for my little brother's friend's rude comment. He's an immature kid with no common sense. I suppose that makes him an idiot," she said with a coy smile. "Also, I wanted to thank you for telling the police it was Ron that did that to my car. I don't know why he treats me the way he does but thank you."

Eddy frowned. "The dance last year. The one where you slapped him, he's never forgiven you for it. You embarrassed him," he said softly. "That's why he doesn't like you."

Her mouth dropped open. Speechless, she looked quizzically at Eddy. "Well, maybe he should learn how to treat a girl before he asks them to dance, huh?" she asked, raising her eyebrows questioningly.

Eddy grinned, humored by her expression. "He should indeed. Some girls need to be treated like the lady they are."

"At least some guys think so…"

Amanda called impatiently from the group of girls, "Come on, Karen, let's go inside."

Karen turned back at Eddy. "Well, I have to go; thanks again." She put out her hand to shake his. Eddy shook her soft hand stumbling for something to say. "Thanks," he said awkwardly and watched as she stepped away.

"Hey, Karen," he called while his heart began to pound.

She turned around. "You look absolutely beautiful tonight," he said sincerely. He didn't know how she would respond, but sometimes the truth needed to be spoken. He doubted there was a woman in the world more beautiful than Karen tonight.

Karen gazed at him appreciatively. "Thank you. Are you coming to the dance?" she asked.

Eddy shook his head. "No, I don't think so."

"That's too bad. You should reconsider. Have a good night, and thank you, again."

Eddy added quickly, "I don't have a costume."

Karen shrugged her shoulder carelessly. "Good, that means you can come as you. I hope to see you there, Eddy." She continued to join her friends.

"I'm going to ask her," Eddy said determinedly.

"Ask her what?" Derek asked.

"To dance with me."

Derek frowned. "She's going to the dance with my cousin, Chris. He'll kick your butt if you ask her to dance. He's liked her forever. Besides, I thought you were going to hang out with me?"

"You can come to the dance."

"No, I can't. I'm not a student."

Eddy stared at Karen as she and her friends walked towards the school. "I'm going to marry her."

"Who?" Derek asked.

"Karen."

Derek laughed. "There's no way! She just said hi to you, and now you want to marry her?"

Eddy answered Derek confidently, "I will."

Derek watched his uncle Chuck Willis approaching them on his way to his truck. "Hello, Uncle Chuck, how's it going?" Derek asked with one eye going over to Nadia as she finished a short conversation with one of the spectators. She seemed anxious to get off the field and uninterested in talking to anyone else.

"It's a tough loss tonight, but other than that, it's going

great. Are you staying out of trouble?" Chuck Willis asked his nephew.

"So far. I met one of your old classmates tonight. He said to tell you 'hi,'" Derek said.

"Who's that?"

"Johnny Gibson. He's in a rock band in Seattle now. He's here for the weekend."

"Johnny Gibson?" Chuck said skeptically. "Johnny Gibson...I don't remember anyone by that name."

Derek shrugged. "He remembered you."

"Huh! Well, you be careful driving. I just heard there's a bad accident outside of town. It's gotten real foggy out, be careful," he said and walked away.

"The fog's not so bad when we're walking, huh? Hey, here's my chance, watch this," Derek said and walked over to meet Nadia and her cameraman as they crossed the field to leave. "Hi," Derek said as they crossed paths. The cameraman said, "Hello." Nadia Kirkpatrick walked past him without saying a word or even a glance.

Eddy laughed. "I hate to say it, my friend, but at least Karen talked to me."

Derek was disappointed. He pointed at Coach Slater hugging his wife by the goal post. "Speaking of your future wife, I met this guy tonight named Johnny Gibson; he went to school with my uncle Chuck, Coach Slater, and his wife. Guess what he said about the Coach's wife? You won't ever look at her the same way again."

CHAPTER 46

WENDY MYERS STARED INTENTLY INTO THE BATHROOM mirror as she carefully applied fake eyelashes to enhance her costume. It was one of the final touches before she was ready to go to Middleton's Union House Bar for the annual Halloween party. She was excited to have some fun. It had been a long week at work, and she was ready to cap it off with a night of fun, laughter, and getting drunk. She had held off from having any drinks until shortly before Jeff came home from the game. She was now drinking her second beer and looked at her reflection with a near juvenile glee. Wendy couldn't wait to walk into the Union House and let all the other patrons see her. She would turn some heads tonight. The annual Halloween Party was her absolute favorite of all the events and holiday parties that the Union House put on. She loved to see the many ghoulish decorations around the bar and the atmosphere of the party. She loved the creativity of the costumes as everyone strived to win the best costume award and the fifty bucks that came with it. She had never won the best costume yet, but she could tonight. She finished her fake lashes and looked at herself in the mirror. She struck a provocative pose while giving her best seductive heavy eyes. She slowly placed her cigarette to her lips and practiced seductively breathing in the smoke slowly. Satisfied with her provocative pose heavy with sexual overtones that would win the contest, she left the bathroom. She once again struck her enticing pose and breathed in the smoke while eyeing Jeff seductively. She lowered the tone of her voice and spoke intentionally, "What do you think, big boy?"

Jeff sat on his favorite end of the couch, holding a can of beer. "Nice," he said simply. She wore a tight leopard skin mini skirt over a dark pair of fishnet stockings with a pair of high heels. She wore a see-through black blouse over her black bra and an imitation short-cut white fur coat. Her hair was pinned up into an attractive bun exposing her long slender neck. Her face was heavily covered with makeup, but not enough to be absurd. Her fake eyelashes added depth to her eyes, and the cherry red lipstick was carefully shaped onto her seductive lips. Jeff nodded at her approvingly. She had wanted to appear demure yet radiant with sensuality. Wendy would turn the men's head tonight. "How much would you be willing to pay for me?" she asked playfully.

Jeff rolled his eyes. "A fortune every month."

The sarcasm of his words was not hidden from her. "You're an ass," she said, disheartened. "I'm sorry, we have to use some of your money to pay the bills, okay?"

"I don't mind paying my part, but I don't think I need to help pay for Ron's auto insurance. He has a job; he should pay that himself."

"He'll pay you back, or I will. You'll get your money back either way. Now let's drop it before we get into a fight and ruin the night," she stressed with irritation clearly on her face. She added, "You're not going dressed like that, are you?"

Jeff nodded. "Hmm, mm." He was wearing blue jeans with a green flannel shirt over a white under-shirt.

"I thought you were going to dress up as a logger? We won't be the best-dressed couple if you don't dress up," she pressed and breathed in her cigarette.

Jeff held up his hands while looking at his clothes. "What do you think loggers wear? I am dressed like a logger. If anyone asks, just say I'm a logger."

She was annoyed. "I at least thought you'd put on a hard hat and suspenders. A little effort to be imaginative would've been nice. It's Halloween, for crying out loud! You could try to have fun occasionally. I swear you're the most boring guy I've ever known!"

Jeff frowned. "How old are you?" he asked. "I'm in my forties, sweetheart. There comes a time when you look around and see how ridiculous people our age look on Halloween."

"Are you saying I look ridiculous?" she asked sharply.

"No, but I would! Don't you ever think that maybe there's something else besides going to the bar that we could do?"

Wendy narrowed her eyes questionably. "Now you don't want to go to the bar? Now that I'm dressed up, you don't want to go? I've been planning this all week and now you tell me you don't want to go? Maybe you're too old to go have fun, but I'm not!"

Jeff shook his head. "I didn't say I wasn't going. I said I was getting tired of going to the bar all of the time. I don't want to be like ol' Herb and have nowhere else to go, except to the bar when I'm old," he explained.

She opened a can of beer. "Then don't be like Herb. Tonight, we're going, though. So get up and let's go! Where's my purse?" she asked. She walked back towards the bedroom.

Jeff stood up and spoke loudly enough to be heard in the bedroom. "I don't think you get what I'm saying. I'm forty-five years old and on disability from a broken back. My whole life consists of sitting around or going to the bar. That's it. My life is empty, that's all I can say. I just feel empty."

"Drink a beer!" Wendy yelled from the bedroom.

Jeff shook his head. "It doesn't help," he said quietly.

A knock on the door startled him slightly. It was just after ten at night. He stepped over to the door expecting to see one of Ron's druggy friends. He opened the door and saw Chief Bishop and Officer Turley from the Police Department. "Hi," he said questionably.

Chief Bishop spoke quietly, "May we step inside, please?"

"Who's that?" Wendy called from the bedroom. "Tell those kids the porch lights off for a reason. We don' have any candy."

Jeff knew immediately that something was wrong. "Yeah, come in." He called to Wendy, "It's Chief Bishop and Officer Turley."

"Can you tell them Ron's not home?" she said, sounding embittered. She quickly came walking from the bedroom, carrying her purse. She spoke hurriedly to Harry, "You know Ron didn't damage that car; Eddy did! Come to find out, that Derek kid was with them and is willing to testify that Eddy did the damage to it, not my son. You're just lucky we're not going to sue you for false arrest. So what are you here for tonight?" she asked disrespectfully.

The momentary silence of the two officers and the expressions on both of their faces sent a chill down Wendy's spine. She asked with a sudden hint of fear in her voice, "What's wrong?" She automatically stepped closer to Jeff.

Chief Bishop spoke softly with nothing except empathy in his voice, "Missus Myers, Ron was drinking and driving with Jose Rodriguez. They had an accident..."

Wendy cussed in frustration. "Is he in jail again?"

Harry shook his head slowly. He took a deep breath. "There's no easy way to say this; Ron was killed in the accident. I am sorry."

"What?" she asked with her eyes glaring into Harry.

"Ron is dead, Missus Myers. I am sorry to have to tell you that."

"No...No!" She shook her head as her body stiffened and her voice cracked with terror, "He can't be!" Jeff wrapped his arms around her and closed his eyes. Wendy stared at

Harry with her eyes filling with a lake's amount of water. "Please, tell me you're lying, please..." she pleaded desperately. "Harry...please!" Her breathing grew rapid.

Harry shook his head sadly. "I'm sorry."

Her arms came up to her chest. "He can't be dead. He can't be! He's my only son. Please, Harry, tell me it's a mistake." The desperation in her eyes begged Harry to tell her Ron was okay.

Harry's eyes misted. "Ron and Jose were both killed. I am very sorry, Wendy, but it was Ron."

"Oh my god!" she screamed emotionally as the news struck her with the force of a comet falling unexpectedly from the sky. She crumbled into Jeff's arms and began to wail loudly and inconsolably from deep within. She would have fallen to the floor if Jeff hadn't held her up and walked her over to the couch, where he sat down with her. She leaned on Jeff's chest and sobbed heavily with loud wails of grief.

Harry asked softly, "Is there anyone we can notify for you?"

Jeff shook his head. He held Wendy as she continued to wail from the very depths of her broken soul...

Harry and Officer Turley stepped out onto the porch and closed the door before walking to their patrol cars. Harry paused after a moment and said to his young officer, "After all of these years of being a police officer, there are a few things you never get used to and this is one of them. I can't think of a worse part of the job." He paused to look at Steve Turley. "Now we get to go tell Jose's parents," he said as Wendy's cries could be heard through the thick fog.

CHAPTER 47

KAREN WAS STUNNING IN HER HOMEMADE PIRATE COSTUME. She had taken the Pirate costume to a level way above that of her pirate date. Chris Willis' costume was store-bought and appeared juvenile compared to the outfit Karen and Tina had put together. Nonetheless, Chris and Karen made an excellent pair of Pirates and if there were a best couple's costume nomination, they certainly would've won. As it was, Karen took runner-up in the best costume competition. She had lost to a sophomore named Grant Penchow, who'd spent some thought and time creating a Rubik's cube that was built in three separate layers and each layer was quarter-turned rows of matching color. It was suspended over his shoulders and covered all of his upper body. The general consensus of the boys was that Karen got robbed, but the judges were two parents and Principal Bennet. They were apparently more interested in creativity rather than beauty.

Karen had danced with her girlfriends and also with her date Chris Willis. The fun of a dance wasn't just dancing. It was being able to sit down and socialize with friends in a darkened and music-filled environment celebrating a special moment. The gym was decorated with paper jack-o-lanterns, skeletons, spiders, ghosts, and pumpkins hanging on the walls. The tables spread out across half of the gym floor were covered with black or orange tablecloths with small plastic bowls of candy. The music was hosted and played by a DJ that more or less ran the tempo of the dance. It was the last Halloween Dance that Karen and her fellow seniors would ever have at Middleton High School. She had every intention of enjoying the night and making the most of it. The plans to go to Ridgefield for a late dinner with her friends had been canceled by their parents. It was not safe for them to be driving in the fog and near-freezing temperature. Their night would end after the dance.

Karen sat at a table with her friends and watched with annoyance as her little brother Robert went from table to table to flirt with the prettiest girl at each table. It didn't matter to him if the girl had a date or not. Robert had even invited himself to Karen's table to flirt with Amanda like he always did, even in front of her boyfriend, Ross Greenfield. He had embarrassed Karen immensely by telling her she had a booger hanging out of her nose in front of Chris. There wasn't anything there, but Robert had gotten a good laugh while she checked. She had every intention to beat him up the following day when he came home from his friend's house, but for the moment, she remained serene. It surprised her that not one other person in the gym wanted to kick his butt yet. She kind of hoped someone would. Robert had danced with many different girls, but he hadn't danced with the one girl he liked. Her name was Cindy Thomson, and Robert had been avoiding her for most of the night.

She watched Robert sitting four tables away and heard him telling a group of juniors about his rotten trick on his sister. A round of laughter followed it. Having endured enough, Karen stood up and walked across the gym to the table where Cindy Thomson sat with her group of friends. Karen tapped her shoulder. "Hi Cindy, my brother would like to dance with you, but he's too shy to ask. Will you dance with him?"

Cindy was surprised. "How sweet."

"Yeah, he's real sweet. Come on," Karen said and led her to where Robert was busy talking. She tapped his shoulder. He glanced up, surprised to see Cindy with Karen. "Okay, I asked her to dance for you, so now you're on," Karen said simply.

"Hi Robert," Cindy said with an expectant smile.

Robert stood up awkwardly. "Hi Cindy, well, let's dance," he said slowly.

Karen placed her hand on Robert's chest to stop him and Cindy before they left. "Cindy, Robert really likes you. He has your name written on a little heart on his bedroom wall that says, 'I heart Cindy.' I think it's his immature way of saying he's in love with you; at least he acts like it." She smiled sarcastically at her brother. "Have fun," she said with a smile and walked back to her table. She grinned all the more while watching Robert's face turn red while trying to play off her words. The coy smile on Cindy's lips revealed her interest in him as well.

"What's so funny?" Chris asked with a smile. He knew she must've done something to her brother to earn such a mischievous grin.

She shook her head. "Oh, nothing, really. It looks like they're actually enjoying themselves, doesn't it?" she asked, watching her brother and Cindy dancing together. It was a fast dance, but they were talking far more than dancing on the dance floor. She was expecting to see Robert at his uncomfortable best, but he seemed to be enjoying the conversation with Cindy.

Amanda Moore nudged Karen's elbow to get her attention. "That loser is staring at you again. Someone should tell him it's not polite to stare," she said distastefully. She was talking about Eddy Franklyn. He was standing across the gym near the bleachers, staring at Karen. When Karen looked over and met his eyes, he quickly turned away.

Chris Willis stared at Eddy with a scowl. He turned to Ross Greenfield. "That stoner doesn't learn! I think we need to have a talk with him and tell him to quit staring at Karen. She's creeped out enough without having him stalking her."

Ross shrugged. "I'll back you up."

Chris started to stand. "I don't need backup for that pencil neck! Let's go tell the scumbag to stare at Gina or some other pothead. He needs to stick with his kind."

Karen spoke with a touch of anger in her eyes, "Sit down! He isn't doing anything to you. You guys are acting so immature."

"He's staring at you like a demented stalker! He needs to knock it off," Chris said as he slowly sat down.

Karen frowned. "He's not doing anything that you haven't done."

"No, I look, he's staring."

"It doesn't matter, Chris. Let him stare." She had caught Eddy looking at her often enough. Eddy's sincere comment after the game had flattered her. She did look beautiful thanks to her mother's sense of style and creativity for her outfit and hair suggestions to make it all come together and work out as wonderfully as it had. To be hurried, the thrown-together costume was far beyond her expectations. She had been the object of many eyes that evening; Eddy certainly wasn't the only one who had been caught staring at her. However, he was the only one staring that her friends seemed to notice and despise.

"Oh, no," Amanda said, turning her head towards Karen, "Here the creepo comes."

Karen looked up to see Eddy Franklyn walking towards her as a slow dance song started. He wasn't dressed in a costume or nicely. He was wearing the same dingy blue jeans, black T-shirt under a lightweight cotton flannel. His long stringy brown hair fell straight over his flannel shirt. He looked nervous as he approached their table under Chris's disapproving glare.

Eddy stopped at the table and looked at Karen. "Um, would you dance with me?" he asked nervously.

"What?" Chris asked, raising his voice. "Get out of here! She isn't going to dance with a scumbag like you!"

Eddy was surprised by the sudden hostility of Chris' immediate response. He looked at Karen desperately. He was humiliated and felt the sinking emotion of being rejected coming over him. He was grateful when she stood up quickly.

"Argh, a jig it is, Matie!" Karen growled with her best pirate's impression. "Let's go dance," she said with a smile and led him out to the dance floor. Chris stood up in protest, but he said nothing as he watched Karen lead Eddy to the dancefloor.

Eddy placed his left hand in hers and put his right hand respectfully on her upper back as they danced slowly to the music. His heart pounded with anxiety now that she was in his arms for the first time. He longed to say something, but he felt his throat tightening. He swallowed nervously. "You look beautiful tonight. I mean, you always do, but...you do," he choked out softly.

She could see the honest discomfort in his expression. "Thank you. So what are you dressed up as tonight?" she couldn't think of anything else to say.

Eddy frowned. "Just me, I guess," he said with an uncomfortable shrug.

"It's a nice costume, don't change it."

Eddy smiled shyly. "Thanks." He couldn't think of anything else to add.

They danced.

Tina Slater stood along a wall, watching Karen and Eddy dance slowly. Tina furrowed her brow disapproving of her daughter dancing with one of the town's known teenage thieves and drug dealers. Eddy held Karen at a respectful distance, but it put a sour taste in Tina's mouth just the same. She recalled all too well how easily Rene had changed her life after she had graduated from high school. Tina would not permit Karen to get involved with a boy of Eddy's reputation because she knew exactly how fast a friend could ruin a young lady's life. Any threat to Karen's future was one Tina would not tolerate, no matter how "nice" the boy appeared. Though it was merely a dance, she cringed at the sight of Karen dancing with him.

Greg stepped back into the gym after checking the boy's restroom. He stood beside Tina and noticed her disapproving expression. "What are you scowling at?" He searched for some public display of affection or anything inappropriate taking place on the dance floor.

She drew near to him to speak without raising her voice above the music. "I don't like our daughter dancing with him."

His surprise to see Karen dancing with Eddy was evident in his voice, "That's Eddy Franklyn. Huh, he's okay, but Chris doesn't look too happy, does he?" he chuckled. "Would you like to dance?"

Tina nodded with a sly smile and was led by the hand out onto the dance floor underneath the south basketball hoop and taken into her husband's arms. Tina peered over at her daughter. "I really don't like her dancing with him," she said.

Greg shook his head unconcerned. "Trust me, she's fine. Now, how about we just enjoy the dance." She smiled slightly and then rested her head upon his chest as they held each other closely and danced slowly together.

Tina lifted her head and looked at Greg sincerely. "I'm sorry, Greg, for everything I've done to you. I've never wanted anyone to forgive me as much as I want you to." Her beautiful blue eyes misted over slightly with a silent pleading within them.

Greg took a deep breath and then asked, "Do you remember what we were doing back when we first kissed?"

"Dancing," she answered.

"Where?"

"Here in the gym."

Greg looked up. "We were right here under the basketball net. I sat in the bleachers today staring at this spot on the floor, wishing I could go back in time to that moment and do it all over again. I love you, Tina. I have since the night I first kissed you right where we are standing."

She began to speak, but he stopped her. "After the football game, when that reporter was asking me questions that I wasn't prepared for, I felt like I was sinking. It's hard to explain, but I was beginning to panic, and the world was beginning to spin until I saw you. When I saw you standing there looking at me, I knew everything was going to be okay. You are my compass, my strength when I don't have any left. You are the reason I love my life. You, my dear lady, are my life and I don't want to ever be without you, Tina. Of course, I forgive you."

Tina pressed her lips together to fight the emotions that welled up within her. Her tears grew thick in her eyes while she looked into his eyes. "I love you," she said honestly. She tried to kiss him, but he turned his head.

"Do you remember the song we danced to?" he asked suddenly with an expectant smile. She looked at him awkwardly and then listened to the music. Her eyes slowly filled with reminiscence while a warm glowing smile lifted her lips as it dawned on her that it was the same song from their first kiss. "This one."

"I asked the DJ to play it. Let's start this week over by recommitting to our marriage by going back in time, well, as close to it as we can get." He looked at her lovingly. "Tina, may I kiss you?"

"Please do," she whispered. He kissed her. Almost immediately, the students who saw it began to whistle, shout and draw attention to Mister and Missus Slater kissing on the dance floor. The short moment had caused the whole gym full of students to stop dancing and raise a playful ruckus to embarrass the coach.

Greg laughed. "Oh, can you believe this?" he said, and

then spoke loudly in defense, "We're married!" He looked at Tina with a smile.

She laughed with embarrassment and said, "It's okay, we'll finish this later."

Karen stood on the dance floor not far away, shaking her head. "Mom, Dad, really? Oh, you guys are embarrassing!" Though she acted humiliated, there was a great deal of joy in her eyes to see her parents being affectionate with one another. She was standing beside Eddy as the interruption had prematurely ended their dance. Eddy stood awkwardly, wondering if they should continue to dance or not, as the music still played.

"Karen, bring Eddy over here," Greg called out as the music neared its end. Eddy followed a step behind her under the gaze of her parents.

"Eddy," Greg said before the next song started, "I would like for you to meet my wife. This is my wife, Tina. This is Eddy Franklyn. Eddy just accepted the Lord as his Savior yesterday. He'll be coming to church with us on Sunday, huh, Eddy?"

Karen gasped with surprise. "You did?"

Eddy nodded to Karen's question while he reached a hand out to shake Tina's. "Yeah, I did. It's nice to meet you, Missus Slater."

Tina shook his hand. "I'll look forward to seeing you on Sunday then. It's nice to meet you," she said with less enthusiasm than Greg expected.

Greg added with enthusiasm, "Eddy's also coming out for the wrestling team, huh?"

Karen was shocked. "You are?"

Eddy nodded. "I am."

"Good," Greg was pleased to hear it. "We'll start practicing next week. Talk to me on Sunday about getting you some shoes. Maybe we can run into Ridgefield after church and get you some, okay?" He knew Eddy's family most likely couldn't afford a new pair of wrestling shoes, but he was more than willing to buy them himself if it meant a fresh start for Eddy. It wouldn't be the first time he had bought cleats or shoes for a student that wanted to join a team but couldn't afford the necessary footwear. "And don't worry about anything, Eddy. You'll do just fine."

"Um, thanks, but…" he glanced at Karen, embarrassed to continue, "I don't know if my mom will buy…"

Greg interrupted him quickly, "Don't worry about it. I'm just glad to have you on the team. But more importantly, I'm excited that you're coming to church with us. I look forward to it."

"Thanks," Eddy said with a smile. "Missus Slater, it was nice to meet you," he said and then paused as Principal Bennet got everyone's attention as he spoke into the DJ's microphone.

Principal Bennet said, "Um, this is a reminder for the students, parents, and *faculty*," he emphasized, "that there is to be no public displays of affection tolerated at a high school dance. Thank you for listening, Coach Slater," he said with a laugh. There was a sudden loud applause of laughter and whistles.

Greg waved the cheering off and yelled out defensively, "We're married!"

Principal Bennet, still on the stage with the DJ, waved his finger at Greg and shook his head, which caused more laughter.

Eddy laughed as he watched Mister Slater say through a laugh, "Well, Babe, it's been a long time since we've gotten in trouble at school, huh?"

Tina was embarrassed and red-faced. She was about to say something when she glanced over at the main gym entrance and saw Harry Bishop and Steve Turley standing in the doorway looking for someone. They motioned for Tina to get Principal Bennet's attention. "Greg…" she said warily, nodding towards the officers.

"I wonder what they want," Eddy asked no one in particular. He looked at Greg and said with a sense of anxiety, "I haven't done anything wrong."

"Excuse me," Greg said with a humored smile as he also made his way across the gym to meet the two officers. He and Principal Bennet arrived at the same time.

Harry spoke, "Can I talk to you gentlemen outside for a moment?" All four men left the gym. A few "Oh's" and "Busted" echoed from the students as they stepped outside. The DJ played the next song.

Eddy looked at Tina sincerely. He spoke loudly over the music. "Misses Slater, I have made some bad choices and I can't change those, but I am trying to start a new life by doing what is right. And I apologize for my part in what happened to Karen's car. I didn't do it, but I was there. I just wanted you to know that Missus Slater because I am sorry."

Tina smiled slightly as she looked at the sincerity in his eyes. She knew he was speaking from a deep desire to be forgiven. She knew that desire all too well herself. "I appreciate your honesty. I understand it wasn't your doing and that you're doing the right thing now, so you're forgiven."

Karen spoke to Eddy, "You didn't tell me you had accepted Jesus as your Savior!"

Eddy shrugged uncomfortably. "I did yesterday after school. I ran into Pastor Dan on the sidewalk, and he told me about Jesus. I accepted him there."

Karen was excited for him. "You need to come to the youth group. We have a great youth group on Wednesday nights and every June, we take a white-water rafting trip. You'll love it. It will be good to have you with us."

Eddy looked surprised and too uncomfortable to say what he was thinking.

"What?" Karen asked quickly.

He spoke with a mild shrug. "I just never expected to be invited anywhere...especially by you."

Karen frowned. "Well, unlike some other kids, my parents taught me that if someone is good enough for Jesus, then they are good enough for me. Isn't that right, Mom?"

Tina smiled softly as her eyes misted. She was slightly convicted for her callous heart for judging Eddy but stood in wonder at the beautiful nature of her daughter. She was overwhelmed by how proud she was of her daughter. "It is indeed. We'll expect you to join us for church, Eddy."

"I'll be there."

"Great! Hey, let's finish our dance. The last one was interrupted by my parents!" Karen said with a scolding glance at her mother.

"Ah, it's a fast dance," Eddy replied reluctantly.

Karen shrugged her shoulders. "Well, dance fast then. But let's go." She took him by the hand to lead him out onto the dance floor. Eddy glanced at Tina, who was laughing slightly at her daughter's response.

A few moments later, Greg came back into the gym alone and searched the gym for someone. Spotting who he was searching for, he walked over to a table where a group of younger students sat laughing. He tapped a young lady named Evita Rodriguez on the shoulder. She was Jose Rodriguez's younger sister. "Evita, you're needed at home, sweetheart. Principal Bennet is going to drive you home."

"What's wrong?" she asked anxiously as she grabbed her things.

Greg refused to tell her. "I don't know, but let's go meet Mister Bennet."

She gazed at him with a mist of fear growing in her eyes. "Mister Slater, I know you know. What's wrong?"

Greg hesitated as he looked into her youthful eyes. "You need to go home," he said softly. He led her to the main door, where Principal Bennet waited for her with his coat on. Outside, Chief Bishop had the unfortunate duty to tell her that her brother was killed in an automobile accident. Principal Bennet drove her home to her grieving family. Greg wiped his eyes and walked back to the gym door. The news of the accident had left him feeling sick to his stomach. It was just that afternoon that he had pulled Ron and Jose off Eddy by the stadium. He was overwhelmed by the tragedy. However, standing with Evita while Chief Bishop told her the terrible news had broken his heart and brought tears of compassion to his eyes. To hear Evita begin to grieve was something he never wanted to relive again.

He took a deep breath and entered the gym. Tina met him at the door with a concerned expression. "What's going on?" she could see his reddened eyes and sorrow-filled face.

Greg shook his head as tears filled his eyes. They were tears for the two young, troubled men whose lives ended way too soon, and tears for their grieving families, especially young Evita, who no longer would have an older brother. Small towns were close-knit communities, and any tragic loss was felt by all.

Greg stepped past Tina with a forced smile and walked to the DJ's table. He looked at the dance floor and saw the many students dancing or sitting at the tables enjoying themselves. Ron Myers should've been at the dance, but he would never be seen again. With a heavy heart, Greg interrupted the DJ and stopped the music.

He spoke in the PA's microphone. "Um, can I have your attention, please?" He hesitated while the noise quieted down. Some of the students called out light-hearted jokes, but Greg ignored them. "I have some terrible news..." He felt the muscles in his jaw tighten with emotion. "Ron Myers and Jose Rodriguez were killed tonight in a car accident." He paused as a gasp and shocked replies went through the gym. Gina Wickering began to wail loudly. Greg continued, "They were drinking and driving. We hear it all of the time, don't drink and drive, don't we? Well, this is why. I hope this burns it into your brains, kids, don't drink, period, but if you do, please don't drive." He sniffled as some more crying came from a few of the students around Gina. "With respect for their families and their memory, we're going to end the dance at this time. You can stick around and talk for a while, but no more music will be played. Thank you." He handed the microphone back to the DJ, who was now done for the night.

Eddy stood on the dance floor in disbelief. The news sucked the wind out of him and left him in a void of emotional paralysis before the cries of Gina Wickering brought to reality the words he'd just heard. The sinking sensation of dread began to fill him as his heart quickened with the shock of hearing that his friend was dead. He could not believe it and suddenly, his whole being seemed to float in a strange dreamlike numbness of his surroundings. It was impossible that Ron was gone; he had just seen him and Jose not two hours before. In shock, he stood stiffly and stared at the stage with his mouth open. He could feel his heart pound in his ears and felt as though a part of him had been torn away suddenly with no chance of ever finding it again. Numb and in disbelief, he was drawn toward his friends who were comforting Gina Wickering near the bleachers. She was Ron's ex-girlfriend on and off over the past year since she moved to Middleton. Eddy naturally stepped towards his group of friends. In the back of his mind was the intent of getting high to soften the blow that had taken his breath away and left him desperately seeking his friends. He did not want to be alone.

Suddenly a hand touched his shoulder from behind him. He turned around to see Karen looking at him with empathetic caring in her beautiful brown eyes. "Are you all right?" she asked.

Eddy nodded silently. He blinked rapidly to fight back the tears that filled his eyes. He simply couldn't digest that his best friend was dead. He had never experienced someone dying so young in life. It was hard to believe.

"Are you really? I know Ron was your friend. I'm sorry, Eddy," she said with tears forming in her eyes.

Eddy fought the tears in his own eyes. "He's...my friend," he said with a shaken voice and wiped his eyes that refused to contain his heavy tears. "I'm sorry, boys aren't supposed to cry. He liked you, Karen. You were the girl of his dreams, but he knew you wouldn't have anything to do with him."

Karen frowned. "Well, he had an odd way of showing it. And just so you know, only boys think it's manly never to cry. Real men aren't afraid to be human, and humans cry. Do you want to go outside and talk for a bit?"

Eddy nodded his head silently.

Amanda Moore approached them, followed by Chris Willis and Ross Greenfield. "Hey, why don't you come join us at the table, Karen? Chris is your date after all," Amanda laughed slightly as a polite but blatant attempt to separate her from Eddy.

"Yeah," Chris added pointedly to Eddy, "your dance with Karen ended a while ago. Besides, it looks like your stoner friends need you." He nodded at Gina and the others in a small group near the bleachers. Gina happened to be looking over at Eddy before they started walking towards the gym door.

Ross looked at Eddy and frowned. "I'm sorry about Ron, Eddy. I really am."

Eddy nodded uncomfortably. "Thanks." He looked over to watch Gina and his friends leaving.

"Me too," Amanda added, suddenly sympathetic.

Chris shrugged. "Personally, I think it's just two less scumbags we have to deal with."

Eddy looked at Chris with a mixed expression of horror and anger converging in his eyes. The words had left Eddy speechless and unable to digest what he had just heard. "I'll see you later," he said to Karen and followed his friends.

"Eddy, wait up," Karen called. She turned to Chris. "You are a callous jerk!" she spat out and started following Eddy.

"Wait!" Amanda called, "I thought you were hanging out with us. I mean, Chris is your date after all, not him."

Karen ignored her.

Chris spoke with astonishment, "He's a loser, Karen!"

Karen turned around suddenly and stepped towards Chris with an indignant expression. She jabbed a finger into his chest. "He's a human being, Chris! That's what he is! When are you ever going to see people for who they are instead of what labels them? He can change his label and he's trying to. The question is, can you? What you said to him is so incomprehensible! How could you be so heartless to say something like that about anyone? Especially to someone who has never done anything to you? He's a human being! And so were Ron and Jose, and their families still are. How would you like little Evita to hear about what you said about her brother? Words hurt, Chris! And sometimes they are not forgotten, no matter how much you regret saying them. Eddy just became a Christian yesterday, he's trying to change his life and you just shot him down because of what, Chris? You need to grow up!" she said with disgust and then ran after Eddy before he disappeared.

Chris stood in silence with reddening cheeks watching her run towards the door.

Ross spoke quietly. "That wasn't cool, man. Ron may have been an ass, but he was still a person."

"So I hear!" he said quickly in defense. "I can't believe she left me for him." He was stunned.

Eddy had just stepped outside onto the top of the stairs and peered through the fog to locate his group of friends. He shivered in the cold and strode down the first three steps. When the door opened behind him, he heard Karen call his name. He turned around to see her standing on the deck of the entry.

"What are you doing out here?" he asked curiously, surprised to see her coming after him.

"I came to see you. We were talking, weren't we? It's rude to walk away in the middle of a conversation, just so you know," she said light-heartedly.

"I thought you might want to go sit with your friends."

Karen shook her head with disappointment. "My friends can be very shallow and jerks. I have a new friend, though, who might need me a little more than they do right now. Correct me if I'm wrong."

Eddy frowned and glanced in the direction his friends had gone. He asked pointedly, "Why are you doing this? I mean, why do you want to talk to me? You've never wanted to talk to me before, especially when your friends and your date are inside waiting for you. So, why now?" He was upset by Chris' words.

Karen shivered. "Because I care, Eddy. I know we haven't ever been friends, but that doesn't mean we can't be."

"What about your date?" he asked spitefully.

"Chris is a jerk! And I told him what I thought of him after you left. I do apologize. It was inexcusable."

Eddy's tears formed as his lips tightened. "I should've been in that car with them. If I hadn't accepted the Lord yesterday, I would've been. They were going to a keg in Salem; we'd been looking forward to it for a couple of weeks. I was going until yesterday," he said softly. "And now they're dead." A tear slipped down his cheek. He turned his head and wiped his eyes with a sniffle.

Karen's body shivered in the cold. It was apparent in her voice as she spoke, "It sounds like God saved you in more ways than one."

"I guess so. I don't know why, though. All of my life, all I have been is a failure. Even when I tried to do the right thing, as your Dad says, and told the truth to Officer Turley, I was called a 'snitch' by my mother. And by Ron just before he beat me up. I can't win for losing no matter how hard I try. I will never be anything more than a loser to everyone around here. Can you imagine what Chris would say if I were killed too? There'd be three dead losers, drug dealers, and or whatever else he said about my friends. That's my reputation, and no matter what I do, that won't change. I just don't fit in anywhere. So I do not know why God would bother to save me. I have done nothing to deserve it."

Karen hopped lightly in the cold to warm herself. Her teeth began to chatter, but she refused to go inside and leave Eddy alone. "None of us deserve God's goodness, Eddy. God saved you because he has a plan for you. And your reputation can be changed easily enough. It's only been one day, and you already have a new friend," she said with a quick shrug through a shaking voice. "Start coming to youth group with us and you will make new friends to hang out with. You're not a loser, Eddy, not by a mile."

"You're cold. Would you like to go back inside?" he asked. He was pretty cold himself.

"No," she sounded unconvincing. "We're talking."

"You're freezing."

"I'll be okay...I am cold, though. If we did go in, my friends would interrupt us, and those who didn't would gossip. You know how small towns are," she said with a smile. "Unless, of course, you don't want to talk to me?"

He shook his head. "I enjoy..." he paused as the door opened. Greg and Tina stepped outside of the door. Greg spoke, "Here you two are. Mom's ready to go home, so why don't you ride home with her. We're going to be sending everyone home anyway."

Tina handed Karen her coat. "Put this on, you're freezing." She looked at Eddy. "It was nice to meet you, Eddy."

"Nice to meet you, Missus Slater," Eddy said awkwardly.

Karen put on her heavy coat. "It was nice talking to you, Eddy."

"Yeah, you, too."

Tina gave Greg a loving hug and kissed him. "I love you. I will see you at home."

"I love you, good-looking. Drive safely."

"I will. Come on, sweetheart, let's get going," she said, putting her arm around Karen to lead her down the steps towards the car.

Karen paused. "Dad, can I borrow your pen?" She took it from his shirt pocket and then grabbed Eddy's wrist and began to write on it. "Here is my cell number. Call me tomorrow and let's talk some more. Before I go, promise me that you will call me and that you will come to church on Sunday."

Eddy looked at her fondly. "I promise."

"Then you'll call me tomorrow?" she asked.

"Karen, let's go," Tina called from the sidewalk.

"Okay, Mom. Have a good night, Eddy. See you at home, Dad," she said and quickly walked down the stairs. She turned back to look at Eddy. "Remember you promised, and I will hold you to it!"

Eddy covered his mouth with his hand to yawn. "I'll call you tomorrow."

"Perfect. I will see you later."

Eddy explained quickly to Greg, "We're just friends."

"You'll make a lot more, Eddy. Do you want to help me close up?" he asked. He sounded exhausted and worn down.

"Sure. You look tired, Mister Slater."

"I am exhausted. It's been a long day. So how are you doing, young man? Come inside and let's talk about it."

CHAPTER 48

RENE HAD SEARCHED KAREN'S ROOM AND FOUND A DRAWER of handwritten notes to and from her friends and her journal in the bedside nightstand. He read through the notes quickly but sat on her bed under the light of the lamp to read her diary. He started at page one and read with interest and an occasional smile.

Her handwriting showed an intelligent vocabulary and elegant penmanship. She was undoubtedly an honor roll student and on track to further her academic career at a state college. He could tell that she was highly competitive in her athletics. A sense of pride swelled in Rene as he read about her daily routines and adventures. He chuckled when she wrote about her frustration with her brothers, day after day. He laughed heartedly for the first time in years as he read about her pouring pickle juice into Robert's soda and his reaction. She wrote similar practical jokes that she'd pulled on her family members, like spreading cream cheese on her mother's deodorant stick. The final results didn't turn out quite as humorous as Karen had hoped, but Rene got a hearty laugh from it. For just a few moments, he felt closer to Karen and experienced a sense of joy and pride in having a daughter. For just a moment, he had forgotten that the words "Dad, Daddy, and Father" were all references to Greg. She mentioned him often and loved him like he was her real father. If someone were to read her journal, they would have no way of knowing Greg wasn't her real father. Every time he read the words referring to Greg as her father, it sent a spear into his heart.

As the journal entered October, the vibrant life of her writing took an ominous tone concerning Tina. It was almost unnoticeable at first, but Karen's references about her mother became cynical as the days moved forward. She wrote detailed descriptions of Tina's attitude changing and becoming more impatient, angry, and bitter towards Greg. It was interesting to Rene that Karen's loving relationship with her mother, which made him smile earlier, was growing more strained by the day. It also interested him to see the handwriting change in the journal as more entries were written in frustration to vent her anger at her mother. It was becoming clear that Tina and Greg were not getting along and it worried Karen. Despite his daughter's fears, Rene felt an exhilaration run through him at the prospect of their perfect home being torn apart by a divorce.

He read Monday night's entry which again mentioned her parent's arguing. He turned the page to Tuesday's entry. The day he escaped from prison. Nothing on this earth could have prepared him for what she had written about him. After reading through two months of entries, he felt like he knew her, but all of the pride and warmth that Rene had felt crashed as he read, *"Rene Dibari is not my Father!! All he is to me is the man that murdered my grandfather and wanted to kill my mother. That's the man that the news calls my father? No!! I refuse to be known as Rene Dibari's daughter. I'm my dad's daughter and have always been! Oh, yeah, he was shot by Rene too. I think I will knock the block off of anyone who mentions Rene's name to me tomorrow at school."*

Rene turned the page and read about the "horror" of becoming the object of ridicule at school. She mentioned being teased by her classmates and the fight between Ron Myers and Bruce Moore. He read about the news crews and the plague of having them sit outside their home like vultures waiting for their moment to feed. He read about the hostility she felt from being referred to as his daughter and the humiliation of the media broadcasting it for everyone to know. Rene no longer felt the warmth of his daughter but the ice of her wrath. She hated him. He continued to read and discovered her day was made worse by heavy damage being done to her car. Unmentionable words were carved into nearly every panel and door. Thursday was filled with Karen's fury that her mother had missed her last game and came home drunk from the bar. Three pages were devoted to Karen's repulsion of finding her mother's text messages to Ray on her phone. Karen's final thoughts questioned if her parents would be getting divorced. *"If they do,"* she had written, *"I'm living with my dad. I've got the greatest Dad in the world; I just wish Mom could see that."*

Rene closed the journal and laid it on top of the bed. The journal had mentioned pictures on the camera of Tina being sick. Rene went downstairs and found the camera on the table. It took him a little time to figure out how to use it, but soon he was sifting through the pictures and saw Tina lying beside the toilet in her vomit. He finished with the photos of that night and sifted through older pictures of their family. He paused at one in particular of Tina holding a baby at a birthday party. Tina was looking into the baby's face playing with a large grin. It reminded him of watching Tina hold Karen many years ago. He stared at the picture and felt a twinge of sweet reminiscence of the days when she belonged to him. Rene recalled watching her playing with Karen in that same way. He had loved Tina then.

His moment of reminiscence was short-lived. Lights shone in through the front window as the truck pulled into the driveway. Rene set the camera down and ran back upstairs; he darted into the first bedroom to the left of the stairs, straight across from the master bedroom. It was the oldest boy, Robert's room. He closed the door leaving a small gap to look out through while he stood in the darkness, waiting. He realized he had made a foolish choice because now he stood trapped in the room. If the boy came upstairs, Rene had no other option than to finish him with his knife quietly if he could. Rene could not risk getting into a fist fight and alerting the others of his presence. He pulled out the pocketknife and held it in his hand. He had come to confront his cheating wife and slippery old friend; they would pay for ruining his life. He had every intention of destroying theirs, starting with the first person who walked through the bedroom door.

The sound of the front door unlocking echoed through the silent house, and then he heard Karen's voice for the first time since she was a baby. She sounded like an angel as she laughed. "Mother, it was just a dance, nothing more. I do not have a crush on Eddy, and if he has one on me, too bad. You're worrying about nothing."

"I don't know about that. I saw the way you danced with him," Tina teased. She closed the door and locked it. "I think maybe you do like him. Isn't that the reason you gave him your phone number and invited him to church?"

"No!" she laughed lightly. "Dad invited him to church. I don't know what difference it would make even if I did; inviting someone to church isn't a date."

"Oh, now you're talking about a date," Tina joked. "Is that why you gave him your phone number to ask you out for a date?"

Karen laughed lightly. "Mom, you're being ridiculous. He needed a friend, and I think as a Christian, we need to encourage him, don't you?" she asked sincerely.

Tina smiled at her daughter. "Yes, I do. And I am very proud of the young lady you are becoming," she said seriously with a sense of pride in her voice. "Now, do you want to watch a movie? We can start it when your Dad gets home. It would be nice for just us three to spend a little time together."

Karen hesitated. "Sure, but I get to pick out the movie. And you have to make some nachos and popcorn; I'm starving."

"I made Lasagna for dinner; I'll warm that up," Tina offered.

"No, I want nachos first and then some popcorn. I'm going to take a shower and get into my pajamas. I'll expect some nachos when I come back down."

Tina frowned. "You took a shower before the game."

"Mom, I rinsed off before the game. I didn't have time to actually shower," she explained. She ran up to the top of the stairs, walked past Robert's door to her room. She turned on her light and paused. She picked up her journal off her bed and walked to the stairs and leaned over the banister. She yelled, "Mom, were you reading my journal?" she accused more than asked.

"No. Why?" Tina's voice came from downstairs.

"Because it was on my bed. Someone was reading it. It was probably Robert. I'm going to break his model airplanes if he did!" She turned around and put the journal back into her drawer. She grabbed her pajamas and went into the bathroom, locking the door behind her.

Rene had listened to their conversation and longed to have his position as husband and father back. If he could be granted one wish, it would be to have his wife and daughter still. His heart pounded with the painful regret and unrealized dream that he could have been the husband and father they loved and honored. He could've had it all rather than the stranger hiding in a dark room. He had watched Karen come upstairs, and his heart nearly melted by the beauty of his daughter. Tears had filled his eyes as a longing to hold Karen in his arms one more time consumed him. For a brief moment, the thought occurred to him that if he could just hold his daughter one last time, he could go back to prison, satisfied that he had gained a once-in-a-lifetime opportunity from his escape. He pushed that thought away and focused on his rage at Tina and Greg. They had no right to keep her away from him for all these years. He had missed his daughter's life, and they were to blame for that. He forced the yearning to love his daughter away and focused on his mission. He had one chance for the rest of his life to make them pay for their crimes against him. He refused to compromise all those years of rage for a hug. He wanted blood!

Tina came up the stairs and turned to her bedroom and reached over to turn on the light. She stopped in place and stared at the destroyed room. The bed was sliced up, the gun cabinet doors were shattered, her jewelry box had been torn off the wall and thrown across the room, and her glamour portrait was broken on the floor with a hole in the wall where it once hung.

She was horrified. Then with sudden alarm, she remembered that Karen's journal was left out. She started to turn around, but before she could, she was grabbed from behind. A left hand covered her mouth, and a right hand held a gun to her head. She froze in terror.

"Shut up!" Rene growled quietly. "Aren't you going to welcome me home, sweetheart!"

Tina began to tremble uncontrollably, recognizing the low growl of pent-up rage from many years before. Rene always sounded like that before he'd beat her up. "Where's Greg?" he asked urgently and lifted his hand from her mouth just enough for her to answer.

Tina could barely speak through her choking sobs, "He's coming home," she barely got out.

Rene covered her mouth again and led her backward to the stairs. "We're going downstairs, don't try anything," he growled and turned her towards the stairs while shifting to her side and descended the stairs with his left hand over her mouth. At the bottom, he took her to the dining room table, where he placed the duct tape he bought. Rene roughly bent her face down over the side of the table. "Don't do anything stupid!" he warned. Removing his hand from her mouth and setting the gun on the table, Rene picked up the roll of duct tape and taped her wrists together behind her back.

She spoke desperately, "Please don't hurt her, Rene, please." Tears rolled down her cheeks in a continuous flow.

Rene stood her up and spun her around to glare into her terror-filled eyes for the first time. "My daughter? Do you think I'm going to hurt my own baby girl? Shut the hell up, Tina! You and Greg might be a different story, but I won't hurt my baby girl."

"Rene, please..." she pleaded.

The snarl on his lips left no doubt of his intentions. He threw a hard right open-handed slap across the cheek. Tina fell to the floor with a scream, followed by loud, terrified wailing. Rene yanked her to her feet and covered her mouth with his hand. "I told you to shut up!" he snarled. He ripped another piece of tape off and covered her mouth. He forced her to the couch and set her down before grabbing her feet and wrapping tape around her ankles. "Stay put!" he ordered. "I'll bring our daughter down here, and then we'll wait for Greg and your boys. I don't think you'll be as lucky as you were the last time we were together. You're wondering what I'm going to do? I'll put it to you this way. We had a beautiful little life until you and Greg robbed me of it. Now you and Greg have a beautiful life and I'm going to rob you of it. Just like you two did to me. Oh, don't worry, Tina, you'll be fine. But I'm going to rob you of your boys the way you robbed me of my daughter. Don't forget I lost you as well. I'm going to rob you of Greg too. At the end of the night, you'll know what it feels like to lose everyone you love just like I did!" he snarled with great intensity.

Tina's eyes were wide and streaming with tears that saturated her face. She was trying to yell through the tape, but she couldn't be understood. Rene put a finger to his lips to indicate for her to speak quietly. He lifted one side of the tape from her mouth. She pleaded desperately, "Don't hurt my children to get to Greg and me! Please, Rene, they're just kids. They have nothing to do with this. They're just children." She wept. "Please, Lord, please don't let him hurt us..."

He covered her mouth back up with the tape. "Maybe you have forgotten that you were my wife. You had no right to even have those kids!" Rene said with a bitter taste in his mouth.

From upstairs, Karen yelled down, "I'll be down in a minute. Those nachos better be ready."

Rene leaned over Tina with a sad slight hint of a smile. "We would still be together if you weren't such a whore." He pushed her forehead back with a hostile shove. He walked over to the bathroom at the bottom of the stairs and stepped out of view.

A moment later, Karen came running joyfully down the stairs in her matching pajama pants and long sleeve shirt. She jumped off the last step and turned to go into the living room. Karen stopped suddenly, shocked, perplexed to see her mother taped and gagged on the couch. "Mom!" she exclaimed. Tina's eyes widened in horror as they stared at Rene behind Karen. She nodded her head towards Rene and tried to yell "run" through the tape. Karen turned around just in time to see a flash of a man wrapping his arms around her. Instantly, panic surged through her and the self-defense lessons through her church ladies retreat sprang into action. Her right knee came up hard into his groin, which loosened his grip. She then stomped as hard as she could with her heel down on top of Rene's foot. He moved his foot back and released his hold on her to bend over just a bit, cursing in unexpected pain. He lifted his head, surprised by the two unexpected blows. Karen head-butted his face with enough force to drop him to the ground, where he held his nose painfully. Blood seeped out between his fingers. Karen ran to Tina and pulled the tape off her mouth.

"Run!" Tina yelled, "Run, Karen, Go!"

Karen paused, hesitant to leave her mother. She turned around and sprinted towards the front door. She leaped over Rene to get past him while he tried to stand, but he reached out and grabbed her ankle causing her to fall face-first to the floor. Rene held onto her ankle and tried to reposition himself to get control of her. His eyes burned with anger while he warned her to be still. Terrified, Karen used her free leg to mule kick his face as hard as she could. Stunned by yet another hard blow to his injured nose, Rene let her ankle go and covered his face with his hand again.

"Go, Karen!" Tina yelled as Karen climbed to her feet and reached the door; she tried to pull it open, but it was locked. She reached for the deadbolt, but her attention went to Rene, who was quickly coming for her with the cruelest expression she'd ever seen. Panic-filled, she pulled on the door, but she had not unlocked the deadbolt. Rene wrapped his muscular arms around her from behind, trapping her arms to her side, picked her up, and turned her away from the door. Karen screamed and tried to head-butt him with the back of her head, but he expected that and kept his face buried close to her shoulder. As he carried her into the living room, she tried to break his grasp by pressing downward on his locked hands around her abdomen. She hooked her right foot behind his right calf to stop him from picking her up any higher or throwing her down. She continued to push down at his hands desperately.

Rene chuckled slightly humored at her foot locked on his leg. "So he taught you how to wrestle? That's good." He kicked his right leg straight back, overpowering her feeble attempt to block him from moving her. "I wrestled too!" he exclaimed. He was about to slam her down to the floor, but before he could, Karen threw her head back wildly and connected a solid blow to Rene's chin. He dropped her immediately and cursed.

Karen ran to the front door and turned the deadbolt to unlock the door. She barely got the door open when Rene slammed it shut from behind her. Karen spun around with an elbow that connected with his ear. With the same spinning motion, she had cleared a space to escape from him and began to run past him to the back door. He grabbed her by the hair and yanked her back, slamming her against the door. Before she could strike him with another knee to the groin, he threw a hard right-handed fist into her abdomen that forced the wind and fighting spirit out of her. Karen dropped straight down to the floor, unable to catch her breath. Rene stood over her and wiped the blood from under his nose.

Tina could do very little to help Karen except for screaming vehemently through her helpless sobs, "Get away from her! I swear I'll kill you if you touch her again. Don't you hurt her, Rene! She's my daughter!" Tina strained to pull her wrists free from the tape and jerked her body around forcefully to do so. She rolled off the couch and landed on her stomach on the floor beside the table in front of the sofa. Tina glared at Rene with hatred in her eyes. "Leave her alone!"

Rene pulled Karen to her feet and forced her arm behind her back, putting pressure on her shoulder until she cried out in pain; then, he knew he had control of her. He held her arm with his left hand and grabbed her hair with his right hand to guide her to the dining room table where his roll of duct tape was. She wasn't done fighting him. She attempted to stomp on the top of his foot again and then throw a backward mule kick to no avail. He yanked her head back towards his face by her hair, adding pressure on her shoulder. He shouted, "Settle down! I'm not going to hurt you unless you force me to, okay? I'm your father, damn it! Now settle down."

Tina sobbed helplessly while watching Rene bind Karen's wrists behind her back. Karen began to wail loudly, knowing she was now captive. Rene then picked up Karen's feet, forcing her to lie on the table, and bound her ankles together. He scooped her up, carried her to the matching love seat parallel to the couch, and set her down.

"What do you want?" Karen yelled angrily through her frightened tears. "Why are you doing this?"

Rene ignored her and stepped over to Tina and set her back onto the couch. He hovered over her while smearing the blood under his nose across his cheek with a quick wipe of his hand. He exhaled as he stared at his ex-wife. "One thing is for sure, she sure as hell didn't inherit her fighting spirit from you." He covered Tina's mouth with a piece of tape without waiting for a response.

"What do you want?" Karen yelled louder than she did before. "You have no business being here!" Her eyes reflected her father's fierceness.

Rene gazed at his daughter for a moment before answering. "Do you know who I am?"

Karen answered with a scowl, "Rene."

Rene's countenance grew softer. He asked in a softer tone, "Do you remember me?"

Karen grimaced. "No, I don't remember you! I've never seen you in my life."

Rene's eyes hardened. "I'm your father! The same father you denied having in your journal. Without me, you wouldn't even exist. Have you ever thought about that? I was there when you were born. I'm the one that named you, Karen! So yes, I think I do have some business being here. I am the one that took that picture of your mother and you, that's sitting by your bed. I took that picture. You were my baby!" He flung his arm towards Tina. "Your mother's the one to blame for taking you away from me. I never would have left you!" He sighed and added gently, "You've grown up, and I've missed it all," he said with a soft shrug. He turned his head to look at Tina as a dangerously cruel grimace took over his appearance. "And you're going to pay for it!"

Tina's eyes widened with fear, and she whimpered through the tape.

Karen answered coldly, "So I should praise you for getting my mom pregnant because that's all you did for me."

Rene pointed at her irritably. "You have no idea what I did for you! All you know is what your mother has told you. Did she tell you I was at the hospital when you were born? I was the first person to hold you; I remember it like yesterday." His voice softened, "You stared into my eyes and I into yours, for what seemed like a long time. I loved you immediately more than anyone in the world. You were my baby girl." He pointed his finger towards Tina. "And she took you away from me. I married her because of you, and you were my world for the first two years of your life. You were my girl, and I was your father, Karen."

Karen defiantly shrugged her shoulders. "Not anymore."

Rene's face went cold and blank. He sat down in a recliner facing her as if all the energy had left him. "Yeah," he said slowly, "That's what I read in your journal. You made that clear."

"I'm glad you read it." Karen's lip sneered, reminiscent of Rene's.

Knowing Rene much better than Karen, Tina began speaking through the tape, covering her mouth, and shaking her head while pleading with Karen with her eyes to be quiet.

Rene turned his head to glance back at Tina with a hardened glare. He sighed loudly. "See what you've done?" he asked in a threatening tone. "You've turned her away from me. She was my baby girl once. My daughter and you and Greg turned her away from me." His upper lip twitched before shouting, "You let him take over my life!"

Tina shook her head quickly, trying to talk. Rene stood up and ripped the tape from her mouth. "What?" he growled.

"Please, Rene, you've seen Karen. Please just go. This is my family. Please don't hurt anyone, I beg you. You don't have to do this..." she begged him to leave softly. "You can take my car and bank card and get away."

Rene kneeled to one knee to look evenly into Tina's eyes. He offered a cold smirk of a smile. "Where would I go, Tina?" His expression turned to stone. "Where are your boys? Are they with Greg? I imagine they'll be home soon, right? Take a good look at them when they come in because that's the last time you'll ever see them walking through the door. You should never have taken my daughter away from me."

Tina's eyes filled with thick horrified tears of gratefulness. "They're staying the night with friends," she squeaked out emotionally. No matter what happened within their home tonight, she knew Robert and Samuel would be safe, and wholeheartedly thanked God from the deepest part of her soul for her boys not coming home tonight.

Rene grimaced. The boys would have given him the leverage and two disposable hostages to use to reap his vengeance. He didn't care about their innocence or their ages. He cared about ruining the lives of the two people that had destroyed his. He was going back to prison, but at least he could go back satisfied that he had brought complete destruction to those who hurt him. Greg was the only person left to subdue, and then he would have them at his mercy. "Lucky for them," Rene replied, displeased.

"You were going to hurt my brothers?" Karen asked in disbelief. "Why, because Mom divorced you after you tried to kill her?"

"Karen, please…" Tina stressed urgently.

Car lights pulled into the driveway and Tina screamed, "Greg!"

Rene quickly covered her mouth with the same piece of tape and moved quickly to rip some tape off the roll and cover Karen's mouth; she was yelling for her dad to call the police. After a short moment of screaming, Rene had the two women silenced and bound. He grabbed the gun. Rene didn't know which door Greg would enter through, but the car pulled around to the backside of the house. Rene went through the dark kitchen into the laundry room, where the back door was. He peeked out through the window blind and saw Greg enter the barn. Greg turned on the barn light and stepped further inside, leaving the barn door open behind him.

Rene opened the back door and slipped outside into the cold and foggy night.

CHAPTER 49

GREG WAS EXHAUSTED BY THE TIME HE GOT HOME FROM driving a freshman named James Mosier home. James' parents were apparently at the bar celebrating Halloween and he had no ride home. According to James, his parents expected him to get a ride home with someone else, walk the eight miles to their home, or wait in their car for the bar to close. Sometimes, the irresponsibility of some parents who put their own entertainment above their children's welfare was sickening. The drive out to James' place, which was in the foothills north of town, was eerier than Greg expected due to the thick fog. He was relieved to pull into his driveway and see that Tina and Karen had made it home safely. He pulled Karen's car around to the back of the house and waited for a song to end on the radio. He got out of Karen's car and stood in the silence of uncommonly cold fog and looked around. It was a peculiar night that made him feel uneasy. Perhaps the tragic news of Ron's accident still affected him or the lack of sleep and exhaustion that took its toll. Nonetheless, he was ready for bed.

He entered the barn and flipped on the light. Immediately three pigs climbed to their feet, grunting hungrily. Likewise, Karen's horse noticed Greg's late entry and let him know she didn't appreciate having such a late dinner either. Their year-old steer waited in its stall for some hay. Greg leaned over the wooden plank panel that made up the pigpen and scratched one pig's back. "Oh, you ladies, quiet down. I'm just a little late for dinner," he said with a slight smile.

He removed the sheet of plywood that covered an old bathtub set against the wall that contained the pig feed. He grabbed the shovel used for feeding and scooped out three shovel fulls into the feed trough. The pigs ate hungrily. Greg held the shovel as he reached over the panel and patted one of the pigs. Their water trough was half full and could wait until morning. The steer bellowed loudly, getting his attention. Greg looked at the steer tiredly. "Moo," he copied the steer in a deep voice. "I know, you're hungry too." A low, sinister chuckle spooked Greg and he turned around and stopped cold when he saw Rene Dibari standing inside the barn. Rene was staring at him with cold dark eyes and dried blood smeared across his face. His lips were twisted in a wicked sneer. Rene's left hand hung free at his side, but his right hand was behind his back. Greg stood motionless, unable to speak as a thousand thoughts filled his mind; most clearly, Tina was right.

Rene spoke with a touch of bitter sarcasm, "You're a regular farmer John now, aren't you? Pigs, cow, horse, my wife!"

"Rene?" Greg asked in disbelief. He could barely speak as he came to terms with the absolute shock of seeing Rene in front of him. The momentary shock had stunned him, but fears were beginning to take root. "Where's Tina?"

Rene exaggerated a naive shrug and gave his best impression of a friendly farmer, "Why, partner, I gist don't know, but by-golly Joe, I came yonder over to see ya anyways!" His face contorted into a dangerous scowl while he whipped the 9-millimeter handgun around from his back and aimed it at Greg. He spoke harshly, "Just like I told you, I woulda long time ago! Now put the shovel down!"

Greg's breathing quickened. He released the shovel and

held up the palms of his hands. He repeated softly, nervously, "Where's Tina?" His fear was evident in his voice.

Rene pointed the pistol at the floor near Greg's feet and pulled the trigger. The loud and powerful percussion echoed through the heavy fog. The wooden plank floor splintered beside Greg.

He jumped to the side and pointed his palms out towards Rene like a shield. Greg yelled, "Don't shoot! We can discuss this like old friends."

"Friends!" Rene exclaimed suddenly. "Friends, Greg? You and me? You're the guy that stole my family from me, remember that? I do!"

"I didn't steal them away."

Rene's head tilted to the right. "I'm not the one that lives with them, am I?" Rene questioned with a restrained voice. He aimed the pistol at Greg and quickly moved it to the right of Greg and pulled the trigger.

"Stop it!" Greg yelled. He heard the bullet pass by him far too closely. "Killing me is not going to change anything!"

"Put your hands in your front pockets."

"Why?" Greg asked heatedly. "If you're going to kill me, then do it! But I won't humor you in doing so."

"If you want Tina to survive this night, then you better put your hands in your pockets. I won't ask you again!"

Greg stared at Rene for a moment and then hesitantly put his hands into the front pockets of his pants. "Where are the girls? What did you do with them?"

"If your hands come out of your pockets, I will shoot you. Keep them in your pockets," Rene said and stepped forward and kicked Greg between his legs with the full force of a fifty-yard field goal attempt. "Keep your hands in your pockets!" Rene yelled quickly as Greg dropped to his knees and fell forward in agony. His forehead landed on the wooden planks with a painful grimace.

Rene began to curse and kicked Greg in the stomach, ribs, and face while reminding Greg to keep his hands in his pockets. When Greg's face was bloodied, Rene stopped and stood over him, breathing hard. Greg's hands were clenched into fists inside of his pockets to keep them from coming out of his pockets as he laid face down on the barn floor. Rene gave him one more solid kick to the face and then walked over to where some orange baling twine hung from a nail on the wall. He grabbed a piece of twine and went back over to Greg. He placed the 9-millimeter within easy reach, grabbed Greg's arms one at a time, and pulled them behind his back. Rene tied them together at the wrist as tightly as he could.

"Get up, Greg. Now we'll have some fun," Rene said and pulled Greg up to his feet. His mouth and nose were bleeding. Rene put the gun to Greg's back. "Start walking," Rene said and pushed Greg out of the barn towards the backdoor of the house. Tina and Karen were both sobbing through their taped mouths when they entered. They both feared Greg was dead and began to panic when they heard the back door open. Rene pushed Greg through the house and into the family room, where the two girls remained. Rene quickly pushed Greg to the floor.

Rene's attention went to Tina and Karen as they had both moved off of their matching couches and sat back-to-back on the floor. Tina had nearly unwrapped the duct tape from around Karen's wrists. She was close to having it fully unwrapped and Karen's arms free. If Rene had lingered any longer in the barn, Karen's hands would have been freed and she would've shortly un-taped her feet and escaped. The threat of it infuriated Rene. He grabbed Tina by the hair and mercilessly dragged her across the floor to the couch and tossed her back upon it by her hair. She screamed in pain through her taped mouth.

Greg got to his feet. "Leave her alone! Untie my hands and let's see who wins. If you came here to get even, at least be a man about it! There's no honor in beating someone who's tied up. Is that how you fight nowadays? The least amount of resistance makes you tougher? Untie my hands and come get your revenge," Greg yelled with his eyes burning into Rene.

Rene ignored Greg momentarily while he re-taped the tape undone by Tina and then picked up Karen and set her on the love seat forcefully. He then put his eyes on Greg. He walked around the glass table and with a vicious right fist, he hit Greg in the face. Greg fell to the floor. Rene quickly taped Greg's ankles together. Both of the girls began to scream through their taped mouths fearful for Greg. Rene then stomped on Greg's head before turning to glare at Tina. "There!" he yelled, pointing down at Greg. "There is the reason you left me! You left me because of him?" he asked strenuously and kicked Greg in the ribs. "You took my daughter," he emphasized, "and married him!" He again kicked Greg in the face. "You testified against me! You lied and got me sent to prison for my entire damn life! All while you let my daughter call him Dad!" he screamed, outraged. He then kicked Greg in the ribs repeatedly. He turned back to Tina. His eyes burned with anger as he breathed heavily through his wicked sneer. "He came into my house, and you screwed him on our couch! We were married, Tina! That was sixteen years ago, and I've never seen a picture of my daughter until tonight!" he screamed. He then kicked Greg in the face again. "I will never forgive you for what you've done! I'm going to make you hurt, the way I've hurt. You don't deserve to live a good life; you're the one that caused all of the pain I live with! You're the slut that couldn't keep your legs closed when good old Greg came over, aren't you? You robbed me of my life!" he yelled. He added pointedly, "Now...I'm going to rob you of yours."

Tina shook her head rapidly with tears flowing down her cheeks. Her eyes pleaded with Rene desperately. She tried to speak through the tape. Rene yanked the tape off her mouth. "What?" he yelled.

"I never cheated on you! Nothing happened that night when you came home. You just assumed something did..."

"Don't lie to me! You were hiding under your blanket,

and he was getting dressed in the bathroom! I know you, Tina. You can't tell me that you didn't do anything because I saw the fear in your eyes!"

"Why do you think that is?" she asked pointedly. "You beat on me all of the time. I told you I was leaving you, and you threatened to kill me that night before Greg even came over! Or did you forget about that? You lost me long before Greg ever got there. You're here hurting my family for something that is your own fault!"

"What's my fault? That you screwed your old boyfriend on my couch? You're the one that slept with my friends, not the other way around. Manny told me about you and Jessie when I wasn't home, remember? You were a whore and you're trying to blame me? You're the only one to blame for this. You and this piece of..." he growled savagely and turned to kick Greg in the ribs. Greg grimaced in pain.

Tina spoke angrily, "If you think Jessie and I had anything going on, then you're an idiot! Manny told you he was kidding right then and there. I never cheated on you once during our marriage, but you wouldn't believe it then, and you won't believe it now."

"No, I won't believe it! How can I? You're still whoring around on your husband. I read Karen's diary, so who's Ray, Tina?" he asked with a disgusted glare. "Sixteen years later, Greg finally figures out what kind of a woman you are! Maybe I should get her diary and read what Karen wrote about you. I think she has a pretty good grip on who you are, an adulterous slut! That's what she called you, among other things. I could read it to you if you'd like?" Tina shook her head slowly as her eyes downturned with shame. Rene continued through a scowl, "Don't blame me for your being a slut. I didn't do anything to deserve what you guys did to me."

Tina's eyes narrowed with venom. "You killed my father!"

"It was self-defense! He was coming at me; what other choice did I have? You're the one that pushed me over the edge. If you would've been faithful, none of this ever would've happened. It's your damn fault for running over there anyway!"

"You tried to kill me. Where else was I supposed to go? I was running for my life! You took my father away from me and you would've taken me away from Karen. You pulled the trigger. No one made you do a damn thing except you. You're still trying to justify your actions by blaming other people; me, Greg, your dad. When are you going to realize that you made your choices and it's nobody's fault but your own? You take no responsibility for my father, do you? Well, now Karen can see that and know exactly what kind of a man you are!"

"And what kind of a man is that?" he asked dangerously.

Tina's scornful eyes watched Rene with pure resentment. "You're what you've always been, a damn coward!" she spat out vehemently.

CHAPTER 50

AFTER THE FOOTBALL GAME, CHUCK WILLIS HAD TOLD HIS son Chris that he wasn't comfortable with Chris driving his friends into Ridgefield after the dance due to the freezing fog and potential drunk drivers leaving multiple Halloween parties. Chris was disappointed, but Chuck was firm with his decision. Chuck had driven home after the game, disappointed by the loss and the end of this year's football season. There was nothing as exciting as the high school football playoffs, but Middleton wouldn't make it there this year. He had always hoped that his son would get the opportunity to feel the same exhilaration that he had felt when he and his teammates won their first state championship game. Chris would never know that phenomenal sensation of winning the state championship. His team didn't even make the playoffs his senior year. It was disappointing.

Chuck had lived his whole life in Middleton and now had taken over his family's construction business. He knew nearly everyone in town and had a good memory of his glory days at Middleton High School, but for the life of him, he couldn't remember anyone by the name of Johnny Gibson. Chuck had pulled out his old yearbooks from seventh grade through his senior year and casually looked through them while watching a movie. The movie was one Chuck was enjoying, but yearbook after yearbook revealed no one by that name. He went through every name of every class to no avail. The name was slightly familiar, but he couldn't place where he knew the name Johnny Gibson from. He searched the class pictures, the athletic teams, social clubs, even the choir, and band but shrugged it off as a lost cause. He laid his yearbooks down beside his recliner and finished the movie.

After midnight, Chris came home and told his father what had happened to Ron Myers and Jose Rodriguez. Even though Chris didn't like either one of them, he was troubled by the news of their deaths. Chris didn't expect to be as troubled as he was, especially after saying what he had to Eddy. He had hoped to ask Karen to be his girl-friend after the dance, but she had suddenly seemed to care more about Eddy Franklyn than him. It put a sour taste in Chris' mouth, and he had spat out the resentment to Eddy. True, Eddy had never done anything to him personally, but the stoner was with Ron when Karen's car was vandalized. He was a druggy and a thief. And most of all, he interfered with his plans of asking Karen to be his girlfriend. He didn't honestly mean what he said about Ron and Jose dying, and in the safety of his home, he was filled with regret. Karen was right, he had no reason to say what he did to Eddy, and the guilt weighed heavily upon him. He needed to apologize and hope that it could be forgiven. He also knew by his father's reaction that he would be greatly disappointed if he heard what Chris had said.

When Chuck heard about the two boys being killed, he was relieved by his decision not to let Chris take his friends to town after the dance. Chuck didn't know Ron, but he knew his mother's boyfriend, Jeff, reasonably well. Only one teenage kid drove a bright Orange Datsun wagon around town, listening to death metal music as loud as it could go. For being such a young kid, he already had a reputation as a troublemaker even without Jeff's complaints about him.

Chuck did know Jose, though. Jose's father had worked for their company for over fifteen years and was a valued supervisor and friend. Chuck had watched Jose grow up and knew his parents had to be devastated. They had a wonderful family, and Jose's path had caused his parents' much concern over the past couple of years. Chuck's eyes watered at the news. He considered getting dressed and going to the Rodriguez home to offer his condolences in their time of devastating grief. The news of Jose's death made him sick to his stomach. He spoke to his son, "Chris, do me a favor and don't drink and drive. You hear it all of the time, but it's all fun and games until someone is killed. It's not worth the risk," Chuck said to his son as Chris took a seat.

"I don't drink, Dad."

"Well, if you ever find yourself doing so, for whatever the reason, promise me you won't drive or get into a car with someone who has been drinking. It's better to call me to come get you than for me to get the police knocking on the door. I promise no matter where you are. I will come pick you up. I don't want you to be afraid to call me, Chris."

"Honestly, Dad, I don't drink."

"Promise me that you'll call me if you ever do," Chuck said, standing up from his recliner. "I love you too much not to have an open agreement about that."

"I promise, Dad. If I ever drink, I will call you to pick me up."

"Alright, well, I'm going to bed. Hey, pray for those boys' families tonight. Don't ever put me in that situation, Chris. I would much rather go pick you up. I love you, son. Goodnight," he said.

"Goodnight, Dad," Chris said solemnly. Again, the thoughts of the grieving families passed through his thoughts. With a heavy heart, he grabbed the remote for the TV.

Chuck climbed into bed beside his wife. He considered waking her up as his thoughts were heavy about the Rodriguez family but decided to wait until the morning. She had not been feeling well and needed to rest. Gradually after praying, he began to drift towards sleep. Suddenly his eyes opened. He got out of bed and walked quickly into the dark living room, where Chris lay on the couch watching a movie in the dark. Chuck sat down in his recliner and promptly turned on the lamp beside his chair. He reached down to select his senior yearbook.

"What's up?" Chris asked curiously.

Chuck opened the yearbook and flipped it to the back inside cover. "Oh my Lord," he said with alarm.

Chris sat up, intrigued. "What?"

"Chris, go find Derek's phone number for me, quick," he said, staring at the book.

"Why?" Chris asked, remaining where he was.

"Just do it!" Chuck ordered.

"Fine," Chris answered and checked his phone's contact list.

Chuck stared at the handwriting on the back cover of his yearbook written almost twenty years before. It read,

> *"Chuck, it's been fun, but not real fun! Good luck in the future and keep your ear open for me on the radio: your friend, Rene.*
> *AKA Johnny Gibson!"*

"Give me your phone!" Chuck grabbed his cell phone and dialed the number. "Derek, it's Uncle Chuck. Hey, that Johnny Gibson, what did he say? Did he mention the Slaters at all?... He did?... Karen, huh?... Okay... thanks," he said and hung up suddenly.

"Dad, what's going on?" Chris asked with more urgency.

Chuck held up a finger to indicate one minute and pressed in another series of numbers to call.

"Dang it, Harry," he said impatiently and called it again. He had called his friend Harry's cell phone. Finally, Harry answered the phone tiredly.

"Harry, it's Chuck. You need to get out to the Slater's place right now! Rene is back in town," he said urgently.

CHAPTER 51

RENE GRABBED TINA BY HER BLACK TURTLENECK AND PULLED
her up from the couch to her feet. He held her with his left
hand and slapped her fiercely with his right. His eyes
glowed with hostility. "I've never been a coward in my
life!" he sneered. "You made sure of that by getting me
sentenced to prison!" He hit her with a hard right-handed
fist into her face that drove her back down on the couch.
He jumped on top of her and began choking her with both
of his hands wrapped around her throat. She tried to fight,
but all she could do was twist her body slightly under his
weight. "I'm going to kill you!" he hissed as he strangled
her heartlessly.

Greg lay on the floor with a bloody face and his hands
and ankles bound. He strained to break the twine that was
wrapped around his wrists with no success. He had a fury in
his eyes that matched Rene's own, but all he could do was
yell, "Get off her, you son of a bitch! Let her go! Lord, help
me," he prayed desperately.

Karen screamed through her taped mouth and forced
herself to stand up on her taped feet. She hopped once and
then dove forward, hitting Rene's back with her shoulder.
The force of her momentum propelled her off Rene to the
floor, but it broke his death grip. Tina sucked in a deep

breath of air and began to cough while gasping to catch her breath.

Greg got to his knees. "Leave her alone! She's not the one you came here to kill. I am. So come do it while you can."

Rene cast a cold glance at Greg before kneeing Tina in the ribs. She bent over sideways in pain. "This isn't over," he said to her and stood up. He stepped over Karen and approached Greg just as he got to his feet.

Greg shook his head. "Prove you're not a coward and untie me. Earn your victory like a man if you can."

Rene smiled slightly. "Really, Greg?" he asked. He threw a hard right-handed fist into Greg's face. It dropped Greg to the floor with force. "Earn my victory?" Rene asked questionably. "Do you think this is about winning a fight like in high school? Let me tell you a secret, in prison, you fight for survival. You fight to kill. Earn my victory? It's not about victory. It's about making you hurt before I kill you."

Karen had climbed back up to her feet with hatred burning in her eyes. She was trying to say something through the tape on her mouth.

Rene walked over to her and bent down to pick her up over his shoulder. She screamed through the tape and flailed her legs as best she could, but he efficiently carried her across the living room towards the bathroom at the bottom of the stairs.

Tina tried to stand. She yelled, "Leave my daughter alone! Don't you dare hurt her, Rene!"

Greg rolled back to a sitting position watching him carrying her. "Don't you touch her, you piece of..."

Rene opened the bathroom door and set Karen inside on the floor. He closed the door behind him as he entered the living room. He stood in place and glared at Tina. "She's my daughter too, remember? I don't want her to see what I'm going to do to you two."

Tina babbled through a quivering voice, "She'll never forgive you."

Rene extended his arms to his side uncaringly. "She won't anyway, thanks to you."

Greg got to his knees. "You won't get away with this!"

Rene looked at the clock and leaned over Greg to speak plainly. "I have no intention of getting away with it. I have nowhere to go, remember? What I am going to do is show you what it's like to watch someone else touch your wife, as you did to me. And then I'm going to put a bullet in your head, and go sit in the bar, order a beer and wait for the cops." He chuckled lightly. "What are they going to do, sentence me to life?" He pushed Greg to his back and stepped towards Tina. "It's time for you to pay back your debt, sweetheart."

Tina couldn't control herself and curled up on the couch, wailing in terror. She was helpless to defend herself and feared the worst. Her nightmare was just beginning as she knew firsthand the brutality that Rene could inflict. He wasn't there to reconcile their past, he was there to inflict pain and he would. She could see it in his eyes. "Lord, please help me…" she cried into the couch cushion. "Jesus…" she screamed as he grabbed her legs and turned her to face him on the couch.

Rene peered back at Greg with a wicked grin. "Paybacks are a bitch, huh, Greg? You should've thought about that when you made your move on my wife!" He began to un-tape her ankles. Tina did her best to fight him from doing so.

Greg was infuriated and desperately strained to break the twine. He pulled with all his might and could feel the twine burning into his flesh. He watched Rene un-tape her ankles and force himself between her legs.

"Get off of me!" Tina screamed angrily. She was fully dressed but having him near her and threatening to hurt her and her family, drove her fear away while a wave of deep-seated anger rose to the surface.

Rene was pleased to see her squirm. Her hands were taped behind her back, leaving her exposed and helpless as he gently moved her bangs out of her eyes and rubbed her cheek. "Just like old times, huh?" he asked with his foul breath caressing her skin. Tina pulled her head back into the couch cushion while he moved forward to kiss her with a sadistic grin. In desperation, Tina head-butted him as hard as she could. The top of her forehead connected favorably with the bridge of his nose.

Rene rolled off the couch painfully and screamed with rage. Blood flowed from his nose. On his hands and knees, he raised his head and peered at her dangerously. "You're dead!" he yelled and then quickly jumped on top of her with his hands going around her throat again. Tina kicked her legs to no avail.

Greg grimaced and pulled his hands as hard as he could to break the twine. He screamed out in agony as the twine cut into his wrists, but the twine broke. He quickly untaped his ankles and stood. He hooked the crook of his left arm around Rene's neck and jerked him off Tina and threw him backward. Rene tripped and fell over the glass table. Tina once again began to gasp for air.

Rene rolled across the floor and came up quickly, alarmed to see the gun resting on top of the dining room table behind Greg. Greg's eyes burned into Rene's own with a fury that Rene had not seen since that night many years before. Rene spoke to keep Greg's attention on him and not noticing the gun. "Here we are, man against man. Like I said, in prison, you learn to play for real. Life and death, so do you think you can go that far, Greg?" he asked, staring intently into Greg's eyes. "I can see it right there," he pointed at Greg's eyes. "Yeah, I can see it in your eyes; you have it, you're willing to go that far. The question is, are you good enough?" Rene asked and raised his hands to fight. He stepped back to invite Greg to step around the glass table and further away from the gun. Greg followed, oblivious to the weapon behind him.

From the bathroom came the sound of Karen kicking the bathroom door to get out. Tina, hearing the sound forced herself to her feet and, having her ankles freed, ran past Greg to the bathroom. She turned around to open the bathroom door with her hands taped behind her back.

Rene circled as Greg stepped near. "How's it going to feel for the big tough coach to be humiliated in his own home, huh?"

Greg shook his head slightly. "If you can do it, I'll let you know."

Rene chuckled lightly before throwing a hard right hand towards Greg's face. Greg ducked down and shot forward with a double leg and picked Rene up and pivoting to the side, slammed Rene down face-first into the carpet. Greg positioned his hips to use his weight to keep Rene's hips flat against the floor. Greg placed his right arm under Rene's armpit and grabbed Rene's right wrist to hold his arm tight against his body. Rene turned his head and bit the top of Greg's hand. Greg released the wrist and pulled his hand back from under Rene's armpit. Greg slammed his right forearm down across the back of Rene's neck to keep Rene's head down.

Rene, now with both of his hands free, tried to push himself up to his hands and knees strenuously, but just as he rose his hips up, Greg quickly slipped his left leg between Rene's legs and hooked his ankle around Rene's. The leg ride stopped Rene from being able to stand any further. Greg then leaned over Rene's back, reached down, and grabbed Rene's right wrist and jerked it back and upwards and over Greg's head, and then fell backward, bringing Rene's arm with him. Rene cried out in pain as his body was twisted and stretched into what was known as the "grapevine" in wrestling. Rene was being stretched with his back flat against the floor while his hips pointed to the left. Greg hooked his left arm around Rene's head and pulled it fiercely to the right to increase the pain level. Rene cried out with a painful grimace and tried to fight, but he was helpless to do anything except curse liberally with his tongue, which he did.

In the meantime, Tina had opened the bathroom door and found Karen lying on the floor where she could kick the door. Tina told Karen to stand up, but Karen could not immediately do so from her position with her hands taped behind her back and feet taped. Tina carefully bent her knees and fell beside her daughter. They lay back-to-back. "Un-tape my hands," Tina said urgently. Through her falling tears, Karen tried to find the end of the tape on Tina's wrist.

Upon hearing Tina say that to Karen, Rene gave everything he had to break free from the grapevine. He couldn't. He reached with his free left arm into his pants pocket and uncomfortably pulled out Gary Baugh's pocketknife. Rene fumbled to open the knife blade and then slammed it down into Greg's arm that held his head. Greg yelled from the stab and quickly released Rene's head. Seeing the knife in Rene's hand and his own abdomen exposed, Greg quickly released Rene's arm that was around Greg's head, and automatically Rene turned once again to his hands and knees with Greg on top of him. His left leg was still hooked inside of Rene's, which was an easy target. Rene plunged the knife into Greg's leg. He pulled out the knife and plunged it in again. Greg cried out with the stabs but grabbed Rene's left arm to take control of the knife.

Now having Greg's attention on the knife and his weight off to one side, Rene quickly kicked his left leg out straight and turned his hips away from Greg. It freed him of Greg's leg ride. Both men stood up, fighting over the knife. Greg held Rene's left wrist with both of his hands. Rene clenched his right fist and drove his forearm powerfully into Greg's face. Greg released his grip on Rene and stumbled back before falling into a sitting position dazed behind the two recliners in the pathway to the dining room.

Rene focused his attention on the gun. He moved quickly to get around Greg; however, Greg rolled backward and stood up, blocking the path with his hands open, ready to continue the fight. Rene cursed under his breath. "Get out of my way!" he exclaimed and tried to jab the knife in short quick jabs towards Greg's abdomen.

Greg moved his hands protectively with every jab. Anticipating another quick jab he tried to grab Rene's wrist but missed. In quick response, Greg swung a hard right fist into Rene's face. It glanced off Rene's cheek, but it was enough of a distraction for Greg to grab Rene's wrist that held the knife. Greg stepped forward and hammered Rene across the mouth with his right elbow. Rene dropped the knife, stumbled back a couple of steps into the living room, and fell to his back. Stunned, his eyes widened with a touch of alarm as he felt his front teeth missing from his torn gums. Greg was coming towards him with a quick limp. Rene tried to stand, but Greg dove to tackle Rene back down. Rene adapted to Greg's diving tackle by quickly grabbing his elbow and using Greg's momentum to turn Greg to his back as they landed. Rene landed on top of Greg and immediately began to elbow the side of Greg's head repeatedly.

In the bathroom, Karen had un-taped Tina's hands. Tina pulled the tape off Karen's mouth. "Why's he doing this, Mom?" Karen cried, filled with terror.

Tina slipped behind Karen to un-tape her hands. "When I get you free, I want you to run outside and keep running until you get to Wilmot's place and call the police, okay? And no matter what, do not come back here until we come to get you. Do you understand me?" she asked firmly. She moved around her daughter and looked into Karen's terrified eyes. "You run and don't come back!" She undid the tape around Karen's ankles. She stood Karen up and hugged her. "I love you, sweetheart, now run!"

"Mom..." Karen was afraid to leave the bathroom. Her body shook.

Tina glanced fiercely at her daughter. "I'll go out first, but you run and do not stop!"

Karen nodded quickly.

Tina opened the bathroom door and stepped out. She

saw Rene lying across Greg's chest, elbowing his head. Tina froze when Rene looked up at her with crazed fury in his eyes. He stood up and stomped down hard into Greg's gut. Greg curled up in pain. Tina momentarily froze as Rene stepped towards her. She screamed, "Run Karen, Go!"

Immediately Karen sprang for the door. Rene darted forward to catch her, but Tina stepped in his way and tried to grab hold of him. She grabbed his shirt and then his hair to slow him down. Karen opened the unlocked door and ran outside barefoot. Rene cursed and focused on Tina. He hit her in the stomach to break her grip on his hair, and then he hit her face with his fist. She fell. Rene turned around and went towards the dining room quickly to grab the gun. He picked up the 9-millimeter handgun and turned towards the living room to see Tina coming at him with her arms swinging and blood dripping from her fragile nose. Her eyes were ferocious. Behind her, Greg was also standing tiredly up onto his feet.

"Put it down! Put the gun down!" Harry Bishop yelled as he entered the house through the opened front door with his pistol drawn and pointed at Rene.

Rene, with ease, reached out and spun Tina around and pulled her towards him. He pointed the gun at Tina's head. "You put yours down!" he shouted at Harry. "I'll kill her, Harry. You know I will. I haven't got a damn thing to lose. Put your gun down. Toss it towards the stairs!"

Harry carefully surrendered to Rene and slowly lowered his handgun slightly. It was against practical police training to lower his weapon in any circumstance where the suspect held a weapon, including a hostage situation. However, he did not doubt Rene would kill Tina without any second thoughts if he didn't comply. He also knew Steve Turley was going around the back of the house and Harry could save Tina's life if he kept Rene's attention on him.

"Come on, Rene, let her go. She's the mother of your daughter; you don't want to take her from Karen, do you?"

Tina stood paralyzed in fear as the gun was pressed

against her head. She stared at Greg with large glossy eyes helplessly.

Greg stood helpless as well.

Rene shook his head with a smirk. "It doesn't matter to me anymore. Now toss your gun!"

Harry reluctantly tossed it to the floor and remained shielded slightly by the four-foot separating wall between the entry and the living room. He raised his hands. "No one needs to get hurt tonight," Harry said softly. "How about you letting Tina go?"

"Nope, I'm taking her with me. You never should've come here, Harry."

Steve Turley ordered loudly from behind Rene, "Put the gun down, or I'll blow your head off!" He had not expected the back door to be unlocked, but being so, it gave him the opportunity to come inside unnoticed. He had his revolver pointed at Rene's back.

Rene quickly spun Tina towards Steve and yelled, "Get your man out here, Harry! You know I'll kill her. I'm not repeating it!"

"Steve, put your gun down and come out here!" Harry yelled, observing Rene carefully. He had no reason not to believe that he would kill Tina. He had to do everything in his power to try to save her life, even if it put his and Steve's lives in danger. He hoped he could reason with the man he had watched grow up in their community. "Put it down, Steve, and come out here. Rene, don't you dare shoot my officer. We're going to do everything we can to meet your demands, but you have to promise me that you won't hurt Tina, okay?"

Rene watched Steve grudgingly lay his pistol down and walk towards the living room with his hands raised. Steve's expression showed his resentment of being disarmed. Rene backed up into the living room with his eyes quickly scanning all three of the men. He turned his back towards the wall, holding Tina between him and the three others, while Steve walked slowly across the living room towards Harry.

He glanced at the bloody face of Greg and then around the house to gather any mental information he could of what had happened.

Rene asked Greg, "Where's your car keys?"

Greg's eyes widened. " Let her go and I'll give them to you." His voice shook with desperation for the first time.

Rene pressed the barrel of the pistol harder into the side of her head until she cried out. Rene shouted, "If you want to see her again, you'll give me the keys!"

"Rene don't do this. Please, we have a family," Greg spoke softly.

Rene yelled loudly as the sirens in the distance became audible. "I did too, Greg, remember? I don't care about your family!" He grimaced angrily and spoke into Tina's ear, "Say goodbye to your husband because he's about to die!" Her body began to shake in response as her face distorted into sobs of terror. Rene shouted into her ear, "Tell him goodbye!" He quickly moved the pistol away from Tina's head and rested his upper arm on her shoulder to aim the gun at Greg.

Harry stepped forward urgently. "Rene, don't! You can take the car, and we'll call off the other officers. We'll let you go if you'll let Tina and Greg go. Rene, think of your daughter. You have a chance to get away if you leave. But you have to decide fast because they're almost here."

Rene's eyes went to Harry as his jaw clenched tightly. "You'll let me go?"

"You have my word. And you know me, my word is my bond. Just say the word and I'll call it in as a false report," Harry said with growing anticipation. "Say the word and hand over the gun. And you can drive away a free man."

Rene sniffed Tina's hair thoughtfully as she cringed. "A free man," Rene repeated. "I'll never be a free man because of you!" he shouted to Greg. With a growing snarl on his lips, he hissed into Tina's ear, "Say goodbye to your perfect life!"

Tina, in a wave of desperation, yelled, "No!" She lifted

her shoulder to raise the level of the gun's barrel what little she could while throwing her right arm back around Rene's extended arm quickly in a desperate attempt to drive her thumbnail into his eye. The thumbnail penetrated Rene's skin, just missing the corner of his eye. At the same time, she pushed him back against the wall. The pistol fired, missing Greg by mere inches. Tina tried to pin Rene against the wall as she jabbed her thumbnail into his face again. Rene struck her across the head with the gun, knocking her to the floor.

Rene tried to aim at Greg, but Greg was too close and grabbed Rene's right wrist with a firm grasp with both hands and twisted Rene's arm upwards while shifting his hips in front of Rene, while at the same time yanking Rene's arm in front of Greg's chest and leaped into the air, forcefully twisted his body as it fell with all the force he could. Rene quickly flew over the top of Greg and landed abruptly flat on his back from the spinning arm throw. The unexpected force of Rene's landing had knocked the wind out of him, and he lost his grip on the handgun. It fell to the floor close to Rene. Greg immediately took advantage of the air leaving Rene's lungs and moved to sit across Rene's chest, pinning Rene's arms under his knees. Rene immediately arched his back to force Greg off him, but Greg slipped his feet under Rene's raised hips to hold him still and unable to protect himself. Greg grabbed Rene's hair with his left hand and glared mercilessly into his eyes.

Immediately, Officer Turley kicked the weapon away from the two men and dropped down onto Rene to help restrain him.

Greg turned fiercely to Officer Turley and yelled, "Get away from me!"

Harry spoke loudly to his deputy, "Let him be, Steve! This is between the coach and Rene."

Officer Turley was taken back by yet another order that went against all police procedures. "Harry, Greg could kill him," he stated taking the wrath and power of Greg and the helpless condition of Rene into consideration.

Harry shrugged his shoulders before answering, "Rene broke into their home intending to harm Greg's family. I call it self-defense if Greg does, but we won't let it go that far. Get up, Steve. This is personal between two old friends."

Steve loved Harry and his sense of old-fashioned small-town justice. Officer Turley released his grip on Rene.

Greg leaned over Rene and yelled ferociously, "You broke into my house and threatened my family!" With a heavy right hand, he began to hit Rene's face repeatedly with a flurry of hard solid blows.

Harry watched for a moment and then knelt by Rene's head to watch Greg as he hit Rene again and again. After a moment longer, Greg ceased the hitting and looked at Harry, exhausted.

"Are you through?" Harry asked.

Greg took a deep breath. He raised one finger covered with Rene's blood and then looked back down at the now barely conscious Rene. "Can you hear me, Rene? You lose, again!" With an outraged snarl, Greg raised his fist and hit Rene one last time as hard as possible.

Harry helped Greg to stand. Tina came to him immediately and wrapped her arms around Greg, weeping. He held her close and closed his eyes. Steve Turley assisted Harry with rolling Rene to his stomach, placing Rene's hands behind his back, and cuffed his hands together. Sitting Rene against the wall momentarily, Steve walked past Greg and Tina to the front door and whistled. "You can come back in," he hollered over the sirens that were quickly approaching in the dense fog. Momentarily, Karen ran into the house. She went immediately to her parents' arms crying uncontrollably.

"It's all right," Greg said to his two ladies comfortingly. "Thank you, Jesus," he said. Greg didn't say another word; he just held them close and fought the tears that wanted to fall.

CHAPTER 52

WITHIN MINUTES, THREE COUNTY SHERIFF DEPUTIES WERE AT the house and an ambulance and the Middleton Volunteer Fire Department were on their way. Harry still had Rene sitting on the floor against the wall momentarily while updating the sheriff deputies on what had happened since his arrival.

Rene lifted his head from his sitting position. His nose was broken and set sideways, and he was missing two front teeth under a deeply split lip. His face was covered with blood as he looked at Tina through his swelling eyes. He spoke with defeat in his voice, "I just wanted to see my daughter."

Harry looked down at him and then at the Slater family. "Steve, let's get him out to the car." He and Steve both went to grab him by his upper arms and lifted him. "We'll take him outside to wait," he explained.

"Wait..." Rene said, pleading. "I loved her, Tina; you had no right to keep her from me."

"Let's go," Harry said and began to lead him across the living room.

"Wait a minute, Harry," Tina said and then spoke coldly to Rene, "The only person you've ever loved is yourself. You're a coward, Rene! You say you loved your daughter, but when you had the opportunity to see her, all you cared about was getting even with me by wanting to hurt my boys. Since you love her so much, why don't you tell her? She's right here, tell her how much you love her!"

Rene glared at Tina for a moment with a hostile narrowing of his swollen eyes. He slowly moved his attention to Karen and spoke with a certain softness to his voice but couldn't mask his indignation towards Tina, "I don't know what your mom's told you, but I loved you, no matter what she's said. You were my life. We were close, Karen until she cheated and lied and got me sent to prison. I love you, though."

Karen's eyes burned into him mercilessly. "You've shown me just exactly how much you love me by breaking into our house, taking me as a hostage, and trying to kill my parents! If you loved me even a little bit, you'd thank my dad for raising and providing for me the way that he does. You'd be thankful that my parents are teaching me to be a good person and giving me a loving home where I am safe. That's what love is, seeking the best for others, not wanting to hurt them! If that's love to you, then I don't want any part of it!"

Rene shook his head. His eyes were swelling quickly to nearly closed. "They've filled your head with lies about me!" he said, raising his voice in anger. "I came here to get the truth out of them while I had the chance. I'm not the man they say I am, Karen."

Karen stepped closer to Rene. She spoke pointedly, "Well, you're right about that. Just for your information, I asked my dad about you just last night. He told me that it was unfortunate that you got into drugs because you were a good guy, a good man, he said. He also said you loved me a lot. So, don't assume you know what my parents tell me because you don't!" she spat out angrily.

Rene's countenance fell silent as his mouth opened. A perplexed expression took over the rage that moments before had filled his eyes. He glanced over at Greg, momentarily dumbfounded. His attention was drawn back to Karen.

Karen continued, "Unfortunately, after meeting you tonight, I don't believe a word he said! You are a horrible man, and I don't ever want to see you again."

A flash of a camera took her attention from Rene to the front door. A man named Dave Simpson, who had been listening to his police scanner at his home in Middleton, stood just inside the door and took a picture of Karen yelling at Rene.

"Dave, get out of here!" Harry yelled forcefully, "Wait outside. And no pictures of Karen, do you understand me?" he shouted as two of the other officers ushered Dave outside just as the Middleton Medic First Response truck pulled up to the house with its siren in full alarm.

Karen looked at Harry with disgust. "Get him out of here."

"Karen...wait!" Rene pleaded. "Wait... Harry, she's my daughter! I just want to hold my daughter. Please!" Rene cried desperately while Harry and Steve led him forcefully towards the door. He peered back towards Karen as they led him outside. "Let me just hug my daughter, please!" he pleaded desperately. His face was distorting into desperate wailing to hold his little girl one last time. Rene disappeared out the door to the flash of Dave's camera.

"No," Karen said, repulsed. She turned to her mother and asked sharply, "How'd you ever get hooked up with him?"

Tina's lips twitched emotionally as she smiled proudly and put her arms around her daughter in a tight hug. A tear fell from her eyes. "If it weren't for him, I wouldn't have you."

"Yeah, you would, but I'd be Dad's daughter."

Tina moved her hands to Karen's cheeks to look into her eyes. "Sweetheart, you already are. I see so much more of Greg in you than Rene. You amazed me tonight, Karen. You didn't get that fighting spirit from Rene or me, that is all from your dad. So is your compassion for helping others, like a certain young man that no one else cares about in his time in need. I heard what your friends were saying," she explained. "All of that comes from your father, sweetheart. And I'm not talking about Rene. I'm talking about him." She turned Karen to look at Greg, who was sitting on the couch. A medic cleaned the blood off Greg's hands and face, the other medic checked the puncture wounds from the knife. They had cut his pant leg off and his shirt sleeve to see the wounds clearly. Tina continued, "You already are his daughter. And I couldn't be more proud of you."

Greg had been listening. He brushed the medics away and stood up despite the medic's advice to remain still. He stepped painfully to his ladies and hugged them both in his arms. "Have I ever told you both how much I love you," he said and pulled them both closer to him with a big hug. After a moment, he looked at Karen and put both of his hands on her shoulders to look into her eyes. "Karen, I couldn't love you any more than I already do. You are my daughter, sweetheart; you've always been and will always be. Don't ever doubt it. I love you so much."

She hugged him tightly despite the blood on his shirt. "I love you, Dad," she said in a quivering voice, "I was so scared."

"I know," Greg said softly while holding her. Tina bit her bottom lip with thick tears bubbling heavily in her blue eyes. Greg lifted his left arm invitingly and Tina joined them in an embrace. She held Karen tightly as she said, "It's okay, sweetheart, everything is going to be okay. Isn't it?" she asked Greg.

"It is. It really is."

Tina kissed him gently on his swollen lip. "I love you," she said softly, "with all my heart."

WHEN THE WOLF COMES KNOCKING | 389

CHAPTER 53

SUNDAY MORNING, THE PICTURE OF RENE BEING BROUGHT out of the Slater's home by Chief Bishop and Officer Turley was on the front page of nearly every paper in Oregon and beyond. Rene's face was covered with blood from a broken nose and split lip that appeared to need stitches where his top front teeth had been knocked out. His eyes were swollen nearly shut, distorting his appearance from the tough-looking prison photographs that had been released to the public. Blood had dripped onto his shirt, leaving a telltale sign that he had been thoroughly beaten, but perhaps the most obvious of details in the photograph was Rene bawling like a child that had just been spanked. The headlines varied, but the story ended the same as it had fifteen years before. The media had frenzied around the Slater home early Saturday morning, starting with a helicopter that landed in the field across the road in a race to be the first to break the latest news. The media once again penetrated the town of Middleton to cover the story. Even the young attractive reporter, Nadia Kirkpatrick, who had questioned Greg about rumors of Tina's apparent affair, was much more interested with the latest events rather than the gossip and discovered video of Tina's drunken exit out of Tarlow's bar.

Greg had spent most of Saturday lying in his hospital bed watching the news. The media interviewed many locals that Greg knew and was occasionally humored by their comments. However, he refused to submit to another interview himself. He found it tragic that the media was more interested in talking to him about Rene than the loss of two young men that died in a needless car accident the night before, only a few miles from where they stood to report Rene's capture. Two reporters mentioned losing a football game, but not one reporter said a single word about the two young lives lost due to drinking and driving. If he were to give an interview, it would be to condemn his family's overemphasized back story during this week and the lack of emphasis on a story that might persuade other teens from drinking and driving.

Greg sat in a pew of the Middleton Christian Church with his arm around Tina. Their three children, Eddy Franklyn and Derek Willis sat with them in the pew. Pastor Dan had bought a new Bible for Eddy and had his name printed on the front cover. He presented it to Eddy in front of the congregation when he told how Eddy had accepted Jesus as his Savior on the sidewalk. Eddy seemed uncomfortable, but the congregation needed to hear the story to accept him into their flock as a new creation in Christ. Pastor Dan feared that if he did not make it publicly known, some in the church might judge him on his past reputation rather than who he was now.

Greg adjusted his weight in the pew and cuddled up with Tina just a bit more as Pastor Dan neared the end of his sermon. He smiled affectionately at Tina and peered past her to Eddy Franklyn, who sat next to Karen. Eddy had his new Bible opened and was listening to Pastor Dan with great interest.

Pastor Dan stood behind a podium and looked down at the Bible that lay open before him. "To finish up today's sermon on having confidence in the Lord; in Isaiah 41, God is speaking to the nation of Israel, but the promises are also for us, His children. Verses 10 thru 13 say:

"*So do not fear, for I am with you; do not be dismayed, for I am your God. I will strengthen you and help you; I will uphold you with my righteous right hand. All who rage against you will surely be ashamed and disgraced; those who oppose you will be as nothing and perish. Though you search for your enemies, you will not find them. Those who war against you will be as nothing at all. For I am the Lord, your God, who takes hold of your right hand and says to you, Do not fear; I will help you.*"

Pastor Dan looked up from his reading to his congregation. "If you've been a Christian for some time, then you should know the comfort in the Lord's words; 'do not fear, be not afraid,' and 'fear not,' those phrases are layered throughout the Bible from Genesis through Revelation. They are consistent, like the white dashed lines in the center of a passing lane as you're driving down a long stretch of straight highway. They're dotted throughout the Bible, but they are always there to remind us not to fear. I've not counted them myself, but I am told that there are 365 times the Bible refers to not being afraid. Why is that do you think? I think it simply means what it says, 'do not fear.' Throughout the Bible, the Lord is referred to as our Shepherd, and we are the sheep. Jesus said He is the good shepherd.

"There is a reason God compares us to sheep. Sheep like to wander. A sheep will graze and graze until it is eventually lost. Sheep are stubborn; the same sheep will get tangled in the same spot in a fence multiple times before it learns it can't get through the fence...right there. Sheep will not drink from a moving creek; the water has to be still for them to drink. However, if that same creek is flooded and the water's raging by with a torrent, that sheep will jump into it to get to the other side. Sheep are rather stupid at times. They are also easily afraid. Sheep are quick to panic. Sheep are the only animal that requires a shepherd to watch over them twenty-four hours a day, which goes clear back to Creation almost as Abel was a shepherd of sheep. It is essential to their survival that they have a shepherd to watch over them. Sheep have no means of defending themselves; in the wild, they are helpless. The only defense sheep have is to run, usually right into trouble.

"It's the same with us, isn't it? We try to go through doors that are not opened; we get tangled up in the same sins over and over again. We prefer not to drink from troubled waters but will jump into a flood of trouble without thinking about it. We are easily panicked, and our lives are lived in fear of this or that. Anxiety is everywhere in today's world just look around. However, if you know the Lord Jesus Christ and are one of his sheep, you have no reason to be afraid today, tomorrow, or any other day. Jesus is the Good Shepherd; he watches over his flock and no thief or predator can touch one of his lambs without him knowing it. It doesn't mean everything will be great, but it does mean God *is* in control. We must learn to trust our Shepherd in times of calm waters, and especially in times of troubled waters. We have one defense as well, we run from trouble. Sometimes, we run away from God because we are angry over our circumstances. Sometimes, we run away from God out of fear, sometimes we just don't believe he's really there and think we can handle it better on our own. I cannot emphasize enough the importance of running *to* our Shepherd in times of trouble rather than away from him. If you're afraid, run to Jesus. He is the only source of peace there is. He cares about you. He loves you; He will give you peace if you will seek him and trust him. Jesus promises to give you peace if you seek him and his Kingdom first above all else. Fear is the opposite of faith. Christians should not be living in fear, they should be living in faith. How does one learn faith? By reading your Bible. If you read your Bible every day and pray often, you will start living a life of faith and fear no more. It is that simple."

Pastor Dan continued, "Before we leave today, coincidently, there's a little evidence of God's faithfulness to what I've been talking about in today's message. Psalm 3: verses 7 and 8.

'Arise, O Lord! Deliver me, O my God! For you have struck all my enemies on the jaw; you have broken the teeth of the wicked. From the Lord comes deliverance. May your Blessings be on your people.'"

Pastor Dan held up the front page of the Sunday paper showing the large photograph of Rene Dibari being taken out of the Slater home. "Greg and Tina, without offering any details, did the Lord help you during this time?"

Greg stood with tightened lips as his eyes filled with water. He had much to be thankful for. Though he had caught Tina on the dance floor with another man, he was blessed to have arrived in time to save her from further shame. That same action had saved the lives of their two sons, ultimately, as Greg had encouraged his sons to stay the night with their friends on Halloween night, so he could talk to Tina alone before the game. If they had been at the house, Rene surely would've harmed them, if not killed them. Greg knew he would've been killed if Harry had not already been at the house when Rene grabbed the gun off the table. The Lord had kept his family safe and maneuvered in other ways to bring help at the perfect moment. Even in the action of one teen's vandalism, the Lord had shown His glory by the Salvation of another stemming from that pointless crime. The Lord had protected his family like a shepherd protects his sheep from a wolf. Greg squeezed his lips together tightly and nodded. He struggled to remain composed as he thought about how blessed they were to have made it through the week intact and still together. A tear slipped out of his eyes and rolled down his cheek. His voice cracked with emotion, "Don't ever think that the Lord doesn't watch over his children. The Lord protected our family in more ways than any of you know. All I can say is, thank you, Lord." He waved off any more of an explanation and sat down covering his mouth with his hand and blinking away the moisture that filled his eyes. He was overwhelmed with gratitude.

Pastor Dan nodded empathetically. "Indeed. Lord, may your blessings be on your people, Amen."

CHAPTER 54

AFTER CHURCH, GREG HAD NOTICED KAREN INTRODUCING Eddy and Derek to the youth minister, Cory Higgins, while Amanda and Bruce Moore stood nearby wanting to talk to Karen. Derek seemed to be in a hurry to leave the church while Eddy spoke with Cory. Amanda had gotten Karen's attention, and when some parents wanted to talk to Cory, Eddy was left momentarily alone. Greg watched him say goodbye to Karen and walk to the door, where he paused awkwardly, waiting to talk to Greg. However, many other people were also interested in talking to Greg and Tina, as much of the congregation circled them to have the chance to offer their love and support. Greg shook one man's hand while watching Tina hug a couple of older ladies, welcoming her back to church. He noticed the glow in Tina's expression. His eyes misted just a touch as he realized again just how beautiful she was. The warmth of his love must have touched her arm as she gazed at him with an affectionate smile. For a moment, they stared at each other with the same adoration. It was a moment unlike many others; it was a moment of profound contentment. It was a moment of realizing that they had it all in one other and the thankfulness to God for keeping them together. No words could describe the joy that met between their eyes. It was the indescribable fullness of being in love.

The moment of gazing into her eyes and feeling like a newlywed was quickly over, as another lady got Tina's attention with a tap of her shoulder. Greg was approached to shake another hand. Greg glanced towards the door and saw Eddy departing the church with a slight wave. Greg ended his conversation abruptly and followed Eddy as fast as his leg would let him.

"Eddy," he called, stepping outside into the beautiful bright sunshine of an early November day. Though it was a clear blue sky, it was still quite cold. " I didn't get a chance to talk to you much before church, but I'm glad to see you. So, how are you?"

"I'm okay," Eddy said questionably with a shrug.

"How did you like the service?"

Eddy shrugged uncomfortably. "I didn't really like being called up in front of everyone too much, but it was good."

"Pastor Dan just wanted to introduce you to everyone. That's a nice Bible, by the way. For a new believer just starting to read the Bible, you know you should start in the Gospel of John. That's a study Bible, so it'll help explain everything to you. You'll find that Pastor Dan's biggest emphasis is on reading the Bible for yourself. He'll tell you himself that you can come to church every week and listen to every sermon he's ever done, but you won't grow spiritually until you open up your Bible and read it."

"Oh, I'll read it," Eddy said with a hint of hesitancy. "Mister Slater, can I ask you a question?"

"Absolutely."

"Why would God let someone so young die? I mean, like Ron. It just doesn't seem fair."

Greg frowned. "Are you thirsty? How about we walk to O'Leary's Market, and I buy you a pop? We can talk on the way."

"What about your leg? I heard you got stabbed?"

Greg chuckled lightly. "Oh, I've been hurt worse. We'll

walk slow. Let me get my coat and talk to Tina real quick and we'll go. I'll be right back," he said and limped back into the church. A moment later, he came back outside wearing his coat. "So," he asked as they began to walk, "how are you really?" He stepped slowly and with a limp. O'Leary's Market was three blocks away from the church

"I can't believe Ron's gone," Eddy said, hesitating to continue. "He's too young to die. It doesn't seem right. I mean, look," he opened his new Bible's front cover to read the handwritten note and verse written by Pastor Dan.

It was Jeremiah 29; 11. *"For I know the plans I have for you," declares the Lord, "plans to prosper you and not to harm you, plans to give you hope and a future."* "See?" Eddy asked, "What about Ron's future?"

Greg took in a deep breath. "Open your Bible and continue to read verses 12 and 13 of Jeremiah 29 and you'll find that we are supposed to seek the Lord with all of our hearts. God does have a plan for every person, Eddy. However, we have to submit to them. We have to walk near the Lord to stay on his course. If someone makes choices that are not part of God's plan, is it the Lord's fault? No, it's not. The Lord didn't buy beer for Ron, nor did He cause the accident. We make choices and we pay the consequences for those choices. Sometimes, it hurts us and others. Ron knew not to drink and drive, yet he decided to do so in dangerous driving conditions for anyone. It's tragic, but it's not the Lord's fault. The Lord had plans for Ron's life *if* he would've submitted to them. But that's true of everyone. Do you understand?"

Eddy nodded. "He didn't believe in God, Mister Slater. I told him about Jesus, but he just laughed at me. Ron didn't want to hear about it anymore."

Greg spoke softly, "Unfortunately, a lot of people don't want to hear about it. Trust me, Eddy, it won't be the last time someone laughs at you or resents you because of your faith in Jesus. Look around; there is a hatred for real Christianity growing among the population. They're okay with anything else, but they don't like those who are genuinely dedicated to Jesus, real Bible-believing, born-again Christians, which shouldn't surprise us any. Jesus said two thousand years ago that people would hate us for following him. And I think as time goes on, they'll hate us all the more."

"Mister Slater," Eddy asked tentatively, "what do you think Heaven's like?"

Greg answered after a short pause. "I'm not the one to ask about that if you want details, but I have a straightforward answer which works for me. I believe God created this earth in six days. I am constantly amazed at how beautiful this world really is and yet, it's an evil world despite its beauty. There is none of that wickedness in the presence of God. And there will not be any of it in Heaven. So my answer is very simple, we will be welcomed eternally into the presence of God. There won't be any evil people, harm, sadness, or tears. I think heaven will be the most beautiful, peaceful, and loving place beyond anything we can imagine. Whether it's on a newly created earth or in a different dimension, it doesn't matter to me. I cannot imagine a greater picture of Heaven than simply being in the presence of Jesus. I am quite content with just knowing that the Lord loves, blesses, and makes life so much better here on earth, that it's hard to imagine how great it will be when we are in heaven with him. Whether the streets are made of gold or not doesn't really matter to me."

"Do you think Ron's in Heaven?" Eddy asked quietly.

Greg stopped at the corner across the street from the City Park. "Did you tell him about Jesus?" Greg asked.

"Well, yeah, but he just got mad. He believed in evolution. He said there was no God."

"Eddy, one time I told a friend about Jesus, and he rejected the Lord. He didn't want to hear about Jesus either. A few days later, a drunk driver ran into him on his way home from work and he was killed. I wondered about that. I wondered if I could've said more, done more, or pressed harder for him to understand how great Jesus is. But you know, the fact is, he heard the Gospel. I did all that I could do, I shared the Gospel. He refused it. That was his choice, his decision to make, not mine. However, our God is a God of hope, and who knows, maybe my words sank into his heart, and he did accept Jesus as his Savior somewhere along the line of those few days. I hope so. Maybe your words sank into Ron's heart. Jesus died on the cross to save us, just so we could be with Him, so it couldn't be any easier to be saved from condemnation in hell. But because of people's disbelief, they choose it rather than the gift of salvation through Jesus." Greg paused purposefully. "You did your part and that is all we can do." He paused to watch the sadness on Eddy's expression. "People make up their own minds, Eddy. It's our job to tell them, pray for them and be a witness with our lives, but beyond that, everyone has to make that choice on their own. We can hope though." Greg grimaced as he stepped off the curb onto the street to cross over to the park. O'Leary's Market was at the far corner directly across the park.

Eddy said empathetically, "Mister Slater, you don't have to buy me a pop. You can go back to the church."

"No, come on. I'd like a pop myself."

"Okay," Eddy said with a shrug. He then offered with a quiet voice, "Ron called me Pastor Franklyn. It's one of the last things Ron said to me."

Greg raised his eyebrows as they walked through the dry leaves that littered the grass beneath a tall Oaktree. "That has a nice ring to it, actually. Who knows, maybe someday I'll be calling you Pastor Franklyn too."

"I could never be a pastor. I'm not any good at public speaking. I freeze up when I have to read out loud in class. I could barely stand up in front of those people in church today without passing out."

Greg chuckled. " Remember, if you seek God first, he has a plan for you. A good one, maybe even one that you could never imagine yourself doing like speaking in front of people."

Eddy slowed to a stop as they approached the curb to cross the street to the store. "Do you think so, Mister Slater? I mean, really? I'm just a stupid guy who can barely pass English class. I can't even spell."

Greg answered, "You used to be a stupid kid who could barely pass English class. Thursday afternoon, you became a child of the living God. There are no red lights anymore, Eddy. God can do anything. You have a new life; don't limit it to your past. When you accept Jesus as your Savior, the past is gone. It's like starting over again with a brand-new hope for the future. And what a future it can be if you are serious about serving the God that has a plan for you, It's the promise in Jeremiah 29, which Pastor Dan wrote down for you. That's called hope, my friend. It really is. Now let's get a pop."

As they stepped outside of the store with a soda in their hands onto the sidewalk, Eddy paused and spoke sincerely, "Mister Slater, I don't have a good reputation. I'm not liked so well around here. No one's going to believe I changed or trying to change anyway." Behind Greg, Eddy could see Tina pull her car over beside the curb halfway up the block behind a line of cars. She got out of the driver's seat and walked on the sidewalk towards them.

Greg hadn't noticed Tina, as he kept eye contact with his young friend. "Eddy, remember when I said, 'do what's right'?"

He nodded. "Yes."

"Then here's what you do about your reputation. You simply *do* what is right from this point on. Your integrity will speak louder than your past if you walk in your own integrity every single day. That is what will be seen and that is what matters. The past is past, right? Then let it go and pick up your mat and walk. If you do what's right, you will prove everyone else as a liar if they talk bad about you. It's a new day, my friend."

Eddy nodded with a slight grin. "I will…" he said and noticed Tina stopped walking about six feet behind Greg and waiting with a somber expression on her face. Feeling like she was displeased about his walking with his injured leg, Eddy felt the need to end the conversation and leave quickly to avoid hearing an argument. He listened to his parents argue so much that he hated to hear arguing and didn't want to be around to listen to another one. Worse, he didn't want to be the cause of one. "I gotta go, Coach. Thank you for everything. I'll see you tomorrow at school," he said and stepped towards the street.

"Well, wait, I'll walk with you," Greg said.

"No, take care, Mister Slater," he said hurriedly and ran across the street as a car approached.

Greg turned around and saw Tina standing under the branches of a tall barren Maple tree. He took notice of her somber expression. "What's wrong?" he asked with concern.

She shook her head. "This is exactly where I was standing all those years ago when I ran into you on New Year's Eve. I was just coming to get you, but you were talking to Eddy. It looked important, so I stopped. And déjà vu, this is exactly where I was standing. This is where it all started when I saw you that day. I realized right then that I was still in love with you." She squeezed her lips together tightly. "This is where it all started."

"Yeah, this is the spot, under the Maple tree in front of O'Leary's. Who could forget the greatest day of my life?"

She shook her head. "It wasn't a great day for me."

He stepped closer and put his arms around her softly. "It wasn't a good day, but if I hadn't met you at this very spot, I wouldn't be married to you today. I can't imagine not spending my life with you, Tina. When I saw you with Rene that day, the same thought occurred to me. I love you."

"Déjà vu, I'm still in love with you," she whispered.

Greg went to kiss her, but just as his lips touched hers, a car drove by and Ross Greenfield yelled out the window of his parents' car, "Get a room, Coach!" he laughed loudly as they passed.

Karen honked the horn of her mom's Mountaineer and yelled out of the passenger window, "You guys are so embarrassing!"

Tina laughed lightly while still in his embrace. She gazed into Greg's eyes and saw his wry smile.

He shook his head in disbelief. "There's just no privacy in a small town, you know., And we're right in front of the gossip center too. Shall we finish this later?" He asked with a wink.

Tina smiled slowly. "No. It will always be a small town; let them say whatever they will," she said and kissed him. It was a long embrace, filled with the longing of their youthful desire and a forgotten passion that was long overdue. The kiss was long, passionate, and gentle. It was the definition of love.

A LOOK AT: A BRANDON HALL MYSTERY BOXED SET

BY JOHN THEO, JR.

Pulled straight from today's headlines!

Brandon Hall is drawn back into his previous life as a private investigator with an explosive first case!

Murder at Cluster Springs Raceway -

Virginia Senator Gregory Schilling's son died in a fiery crash on a racetrack. But was it an accident? Or murder?

Only Brandon Hall can figure this one out. But he's still recovering from the death of his 2 year old son at the hands of a drunk driver. Will he learn to rely on God to get him through his grief while trying to find justice for a young race car driver?

The Dismal Swamp –

This mystery is pulled straight from today's headlines!

When the daughter of a close friend goes missing, Brandon Hall will stop at nothing to find her before the clock runs out.

But when the trail the leads him into the depths of Virginia's Great Dismal Swamp, as well as that of the larger one in Washington DC, Brandon's going to need the help of someone larger than life. Will he turn to the only One who can help defeat a devil?

Beneath DC –

When Brandon's working a freelance gig in DC, he comes across something that puts him in the crosshairs of one of the deadliest foes he's ever come up against.

This time, Brandon's going to team up with a government agent. But when they find something even more treacherous than the swamp known as Washington DC, Brandon's going to wish he'd never heard of the secret globalist organization known as Gehenna.

Adrenochrome –

The adrenaline gets ratcheted up to full volume on this one.

When the supposed prison suicide of a billionaire recently arrested on sex trafficking charges makes front page, Brandon is sucked in again.

This time he's contracted to retrieve and protect the only witness left. As he and Gabrielle Maxine Walters are tracked across the world, even more treasonous government agents will be unmasked. But that is if Brandon can bring his charge in – alive.

Looking for an adrenaline filled read with a variety of cast and locations? Then pick up your copy of the Brandon Hall Mystery Boxed Set today!

AVAILABLE JANUARY 2022

ABOUT THE AUTHOR

Ken Pratt and his wife, Cathy, have been married for 22 years and are blessed with five children and six grandchildren. They live on the Oregon Coast where they are raising the youngest of their children. Ken Pratt grew up in the small farming community of Dayton, Oregon. Ken worked to make a living, but his passion has always been writing. Having a busy family, the only "free" time he had to write was late at night getting no more than five hours of sleep a night. He has penned several novels that are being published along with several children stories as well.

CPSIA information can be obtained
at www.ICGtesting.com
Printed in the USA
LVHW040714230222
711784LV00004B/203